KENTUCKY DREAMING

KENTUCKY DREAMING

A Historical Novel

Clint McCullough

Clindale Press,
A Division of The Falcon's Focus, Inc.

First Edition

To my sister-in-law, Paula McCullough,
whose assistance has been invaluable

A special thanks to Nick Nicholson, who took the time while I was researching this book to give advice and show me around Bluegrass farms. He later read the rough manuscript, made key corrections and offered encouragement. Without his help and enthusiasm for the project, *Kentucky Dreaming* may have never seen the light of day.

Contents

To achieve the possible, we must attempt the impossible,

To be as much as we can be, we must dream of being more

Anonymous

PART I

1937-1945

Today will be historic to Kentucky annals,
as the first 'Derby Day' of what promises to
be a long series of annual turf festivities
which we confidently expect our grandchildren
100 years hence to celebrate in glorious
continued rejoicings...

Louisville *Courier-Journal*, the morning of the
first Kentucky Derby, Monday, May 17, 1875.

1

They sat close together on the steep hillside, bare toes digging abstract patterns in the moist earth, the girl's hair glowing like a red flame amidst the riot of springtime colors. She glanced at her companion. "You're extra quiet today, Cawood." She pronounced his name "Cay-wood". There were other Cawoods scattered around the area, named for a nearby Kentucky community a few miles from the Virginia border.

"Not as quiet as them down there." The boy pointed at the little cemetery that clung to one side of the narrow valley.

"Maybe they're the smart ones."

"Maybe." Cawood reached inside his bib overalls and pulled out a cigarette.

"Let me try one."

Cawood slapped her hand away. "You're too young, Maripat. Besides, it don't look right, a girl smokin'."

She twisted around, green eyes blazing. "You somebody special 'cause you got that thing between your legs?" A toss of waist-length red hair. "Fourteen ain't too young."

"Thirteen."

"Fourteen next month."

"Still too young." Cawood lit up with a kitchen match.

Maripat hugged her knees to her chest. "Nobody stays young around here very long."

Cawood stared down at the small family cemetery. A sister and a brother lay there, both dead before they were ten—victims of childhood diseases that rarely kept city kids bedridden for more than a few days. Their mother was buried beside them. She had died four years ago giving birth to a baby girl.

"I hate this place!"Maripat cried. She pounded her knees. "I hope everybody kills each other!"

Cawood Tanner studied the ground at his feet. A mountain boy of seventeen in Harlan County knew little about giving comfort. He was more familiar with violence and death. Born in 1920, he had spent much of his life listening to the sound of gunfire and explosions in these dark brooding hills—wondering if a kin or friend might be wounded or dying at that very moment. When he was twelve, a coal mine owner's thugs dragged his father from their shack and left him badly beaten in a ditch. Jake Tanner had walked with a limp ever since.

Maripat said, "I'm gettin' out of here someday."

"You and most everybody else."

She jumped up, young breasts stretching the faded pattern of the flour-sack garment that hung loosely around her tiny waist and clung to her hips. "Look at this!" she cried, yanking at the flimsy material. "I've never had a store-bought dress in my whole life! Never had a China doll with eyes that shut when you laid it down! Think I'll do any better if I stay here?"

Cawood drew on his cigarette and blew out a cloud of smoke. It seemed every time they got together their talk ended up like this. "You know how I feel, but sayin's a lot easier than doin'."

Maripat plopped down beside him. "Pa grabbed me last night."

Cawood sat up straight, face white with anger. "That's three times this week!" He looked away. "What did he do?"

"Tried to run his hand up under my dress. I started to yell, and he slapped me. I bit his fingers. Should have heard *him* holler! It happened out back by the outhouse."

"Jesus, Maripat!"

"I ran back in the house. He didn't say nothin' this mornin'. Wouldn't dare with Mabel around. If she knew he was sniffin' around me, she'd cut his balls off!" Widowed last year by a mine explosion, Mabel Crutcher had moved in with her three young children six months ago. A lazy slovenly woman, she had increased Maripat's chores to the point that the girl had to sneak away from the house to get some rest.

Cawood threw a clump of grass down the hillside. "I'm goin' to take a pick handle to that bastard someday!"

"If I don't do it first," Maripat muttered. "He ain't been right in the head since those goons beat him up, but that don't give him no excuse to paw me. Next time he touches me, I'm goin' to claw his eyes!"

"Best you put that out of your mind, Maripat. It'll only make things worse."

"I can take care of myself."

"He out-weighs you by eighty pounds!"

"I've got sharper teeth," Maripat grinned. Grabbing the cigarette from his mouth, she took a puff. Smoke went up her nose and sent her into a coughing fit.

"Real tough!" Cawood laughed. "Can't even smoke a cigarette!" Removing the stub from her slack lips, he crushed it in the dirt.

Maripat pounced on her brother, knocking him on his back and straddling his waist. Gazing through burning eyes, she waved a fist in his face. "How'd you like a fat lip?"

Cawood enclosed the fist in a big hand. When he was six and his older sister died during a measles outbreak, he took little Maripat under his wing. Because she had a fiery temper and wouldn't back down to anyone, he was constantly defending her honor. She always joined in. Over the years, they became a formidable team. Boys, however, were paying a different kind of attention to her lately. The last six months, she had blossomed like a beautiful springtime flower. Many girls in the eastern Kentucky hills married at thirteen. Men had been noticing her, too—including their father.

Cawood made the decision he'd been putting off since the winter snows melted. "I'm takin' you out of here, Maripat."

"When?" she asked eagerly.

"The next week or two. Wish I could talk Tom into goin' with us. Weren't for him helpin' his pa organize the miners, he'd probably do it."

Maripat bounced on Cawood's stomach. "Where we goin'?"

"Cincinnati sounds like the best place to find work."

Green eyes huge in her heart-shaped face, Maripat said, "How much money you got?"

"Six dollars and fifty-six cents. Get off my stomach; you're sittin' on my backbone. I'm so hungry I could eat the south end of a north-bound skunk."

"I've got seventy-three cents." Freckles stood out on Maripat's nose as she bent closer. "You mean it? We're goin'?"

"I said so, didn't I?" Cawood lifted Maripat's small body to one side and sat up. "Time to git. It's almost noon. They'll be ringin' the dinner bell any minute."

They moved down the steep hill, picking their way around flowering dogwood and blossoming sarvis and redbud trees. Wild geraniums tickled their bare ankles as they neared the creek bed that also served as a road.

High above, a deer watched the young couple until they disappeared. Taking delicate steps, the doe led her fawn across the ridge. Birds chirped, and the raw beauty of the land seemed to deny the rivers of blood and tears that had flowed across the eastern Kentucky coal country for nearly two decades.

2

The road leading to their home was rutted with wagon tracks. The Tanners didn't own a car, few mountain folk did. Some didn't even have a horse or a mule. If they wanted to go to town, they hitched a ride or walked.

A cleared area revealed a weathered plank shack and two men sitting under a tree. Behind the barn, children played a noisy game of hide and seek. A baby crawled in the dust, testing clumps of dirt for edible content. Chickens scratched and clucked. A huge black and white Poland China sow unearthed a rock with her nose. Grunting with satisfaction, she chewed on the tender roots that grew underneath.

"'Bout time you came home," Ezra called from the stump where he sat whittling on a stick. Married to Mabel's sister, Bessie, he had moved in last month with his wife and their year-old girl. They had been evicted from their company house when Ezra joined the striking miners.

"Don't look like we missed much," Cawood said.

Ezra grinned at Maripat. "You got green stuff on the seat of your dress. Want me to brush it off?"

"You touch me, and I'll feed your hand to that sow"

Cawood shot Ezra a hooded look. He considered Bessie's hus-band a lazy no-account and didn't like his suggestive remarks about Maripat. Just because she moved like a burlap sack full of kittens didn't mean she was a bad girl.

His father stood and spat a stream of tobacco juice in the dust. Jake Tanner was a lean wolf of a man with whipcord muscles and piercing brown eyes. Cawood had often wondered if he would look like that when he got older. They had the same build, eyes and wavy dark brown hair. At six feet, Cawood was an inch shorter, but he figured he wasn't fully growed yet.

"Mabel's been lookin' for you, Maripat," Jake said. "Her and Bessie had to do all the cookin'."

"Ain't that too bad!" Maripat said. "I cooked breakfast and cleaned the downstairs while they sat around and gossiped!"

"Watch your mouth, girl."

Maripat was preparing a reply when Bessie came out on the porch and rang the metal triangle. After dipping water from the big wooden bucket and washing with homemade yellow lye soap, they trooped into the house.

That night, Maripat sat with Cawood and Tom Perkins on a

hill above the house. Twenty years old and living within "shoutin'" distance of the Tanner property, Tom was Cawood's best friend. Down below, Jake and Mabel sat on the porch in rocking chairs. Ezra and Bessie had gone into Harlan to see a ten-cent picture show.

Tom's father was on the United Mine Workers of America organizing committee. He had sneaked into town to a secret meeting that morning. It was against the law for more than two to gather at a time, even for a brief chat on a Harlan sidewalk.

Tom passed a jug of moonshine to Cawood. "Bennett Squires and his boys beat up JoJo Walker last night. He's laid up at Ma Snyder's. Doc says he won't be up and about for weeks."

Mariipat shuddered. The whole nation knew of this mountain region as "Bloody Harlan." The sheriff recruited many of his "deputies" from state penitentiaries. The hardened criminals relished carrying out the mine owners' orders.

Wearing tied-down revolvers, the hired thugs roamed the hills in bullet-proof cars and dragged striking miners out of their homes in the middle of the night. Some were never seen alive again. The lucky ones got off with broken bones.

Tom retrieved the jug and took a swig. "We sent two men up to Washington to meet with John L. Lewis and some congressmen. Word gets out, the mine owners ain't goin' to like it one bit."

Cawood said, "Maripat and me ain't waitin' to see what happens. We're takin' off for Cincinnati the next week or so."

"That's mighty sudden."

"We been talkin' about it for a long time," Maripat said.

Cawood nodded toward the house. "Too many people livin' down there."

Tom glanced at Maripat. He, too, had noticed the dramatic changes in her looks. Having observed Ezra's open admiration, he figured that was behind the surprising announcement.

"It may not be any better in Cincinnati," Tom cautioned. "People are goin' without all across the country. They're pourin' into cities lookin' for work."

"We'll make do," Cawood said determinedly. "At least they ain't shootin' each other."

"You left grade school to work in the mines," Tom said. "Lack of schoolin's goin' to keep you from gettin' the better jobs. City folks will treat you like you're some kind of freak."

Maripat wondered what it was outside of Harlan County. An occasional picture show provided glimpses of glittering cities, big flashy cars and endless prairies filled with cowboys and Indians. Despite the danger, she couldn't wait to leave.

3

Three nights later, Cawood was awakened by the sharp crack of rifle fire and the heavy boom of shotguns. It came from the direction of Harlan, two miles to the south. Pulling on his overalls, he ran barefoot down the stairs.

His father was standing on the porch, cinching his belt. "Powerful lot of shootin'."

Ezra joined them. "I heard they were having a meetin' in town tonight." A small thin-faced man, he tugged nervously at his ragged suspenders.

Maripat appeared and Cawood joined her at the other end of the porch. The gunfire died to a few sporadic shots, then nothing. "Didn't Tom go to that meetin'?" Maripat whispered.

A nod. "It should have been over an hour ago."

The others went back to bed. Ten minutes passed. Maripat gripped Cawood's arm. "Somethin's out by the barn!"

They ran across the yard just as Tom slid off the back of a big black mule. Clutching the reins, he collapsed on his face.

"Tom!" Cawood cried. He fell on his knees beside his friend and rolled him over. Blood plastered the jacket to Tom's stocky frame, and he shivered violently.

Maripat unbuttoned the bloody shirt and stared at the ragged hole in Tom's chest. Ripping the bottom off her dress, she pressed the rough fabric against the frightening wound. She had lived through many horrors and tended gunshot victims and helped prepare bodies for burial since she was ten.

"What happened, Tom?" Cawood asked.

"Bennett Squires...jumped us in Smith's livery." A ragged cough. "Shot Pa...Caleb Short...Bob White. Ed Macy killed one. They'll be comin'."

"Let's get you into the barn," Cawood said.

"No...first places...look."

"We'll patch you up," Cawood said desperately. He glanced at Maripat. She made a helpless gesture with her hands.

"Put...on mule. Can't find...here."

Cawood was torn between helping his friend and protecting his own. Two brothers and a sister were asleep in the house.

A gagging sound. Tom shuddered, then stared blankly at the moonlit sky.

"He's gone," Maripat said. "Best we get him on that mule and out of here."

They draped Tom's body over the mule's bare back. The big animal snorted and rolled its eyes to the rear. While Maripat held the reins, Cawood got a rope from the barn. After tying Tom's arms and legs together under the mule's belly, they led it a short way up the hill. Aiming the mule in the direction of Tom's home, Cawood slapped it on the rump. It bucked, then trotted off.

2:12 AM. Cawood lay awake in the dark attic beside his sleeping brothers on the corn shuck and feather mattress. An owl hooted, then the whine of car engines broke the stillness.

Gears shifted for the steep grade up the hollow. Cawood dashed to the window just as three cars burst into the yard, rifle and shotgun barrels bristling from windows. Two cars skidded to a halt in the front yard while a third roared around the rear. Men spilled out and ran swiftly toward the house.

Cawood's brothers sat up, eyes round with fright. "Stay put, you hear?" Cawood ordered, shoving one leg in his overalls just as the men kicked in the front door. It was a favorite tactic—flushing the prey out the back door to be gunned down by those lying in wait.

Bennett Squires' deep gravelly voice thundered over the crash of breaking furniture. "Where's that goddamn Russian-red-son-of-a-bitch!"

A heavy slap. "Answer me, you little cunt!"

Cawood took the steep stairs two at a time. A man held Maripat's arms from behind while Squires raised his hand for another blow. *Leave it to her to jump right in the middle of a ruckus!* Charging across the crowded room, Cawood leaped on Squires' back.

"Get the whelp off me!" Squires shouted as Cawood dug at his eyes and pulled his hair. A rifle butt crashed into Cawood's head over the right ear, another into the back of his neck. He fell to the floor, blood flowing from the torn flesh.

Squires stood over Cawood, a barrel-chested man with a taunt belly overflowing a wide leather belt. Drawing one of his two forty-fives, he roared, "I ought to blow your head off, you little prick! You're Tom Perkins' friend. Where you got him hid?"

"Don't know nothin'," Cawood mumbled.

"Take him outside and beat it out of him!" Squires ordered. Two men dragged Cawood away.

Maripat was still kicking and trying to bite her captors. Crawling on the floor in his long underwear, Jake Tanner howled as men kicked his ribs and beat on his back with rifle butts. Ezra crouched in a corner, arms protectively over his head.

The rough porch surface scraped Cawood's back. His captors kicked him down the steps.

"Lookie here!" One of the men picked up a heavy whip. He gave it an expert snap, then brought it down on Cawood's back. The boy moaned and clawed the dirt.

"Give me a chance after you get in a few licks," the other man said eagerly.

The pain was excruciating, and despite his efforts to keep silent, Cawood cried out. The men traded off, once, twice. The screams from the house faded, and the whip seemed to fall on someone else's back. Then everything went black.

4

Cawood floated in a world of blurred images and unintelligible words spoken from a great distance. Lying on a narrow cot just off the kitchen, he was vaguely aware of the door opening and children peeking in. He tried to question Maripat when she spoon-fed him and doctored his back, but he couldn't get the words past his lips.

Pans rattled in the kitchen. A narrow band of light shone under the door. Cawood held his hand up. Five fingers, not seven or eight. Satisfied, he went back to sleep.

When he awoke again, the sun was shining through the muslin curtains and Maripat stood beside the bed holding a steaming bowl of soup. She set the bowl on a chair and bent to help Cawood up.

"I can do it," he croaked.

Dropping to her knees, she grabbed his hand. "You thinkin' straight again, Cawood?"

"I see one of everything. Beats seeing two of you."

Maripat slapped his hand and jumped up. "You're back to normal, all right."

Cawood winced as his lacerated back touched the wall. "How long I been here?"

"Four days." Maripat lifted the bowl and sat on the edge of the cot. "You got it the worst. Pa has a black eye and some stove-in ribs. Ezra's moanin' around, but that's mostly show. Bessie's been cluckin' over him day and night."

"What about Tom's pa?"

"Dead in the livery. That damn mule took Tom clean over to Newt Sweeny's place. Me and Tom's mother washed 'em up and laid 'em out for viewin' two days ago. They were buried yesterday." A concerned look. "You look like somethin' the cat drug in."

"Feel like it, too."

Maripat's green eyes softened. "Don't seem right without Tom around."

"He was all fired up about bein' a union leader someday. We

probably never would have seen him again after we left."

Maripat leaned closer. "We still goin'?"

"Now more than ever."

She dipped the spoon in the bowl. "Eat your fill, then go back to sleep. The more rest you get, the quicker we can leave."

The following morning, Cawood tried to stand, took a step, stumbled and fell over a chair. The door opened. Hands on hips, Maripat said, "What you tryin' to prove?"

Grinning sheepishly, Cawood rolled on his side. "Nothin' much. Thought I'd walk around a spell."

"Bein' as you got that far, you can get back in bed by yourself." The door shut firmly. Cawood crawled across the cold wooden floor. A few hours rest and he'd try again.

Maripat sat beside the cot. On second try yesterday, Cawood had taken several steps. At noon today, he'd made it into the kitchen and had eaten dinner at the crowded table.

"The nerve of Pa," Maripat fumed, "blaming you for him gettin' beat up because Tom was your friend! At least he's hurtin' too much to bother me."

"Too bad they didn't break his leg," Cawood muttered. He had once worshipped his father. The last fragments of respect had been ripped away when Jake Tanner had begun to make sexual advances toward Maripat.

"Somebody's goin' to get Bennett Squires one of these days," Maripat said. "Only reason he's lasted this long is he's got an army to back him up. If the union wins, he'd better cut and run mighty fast—and not stop until he's plumb out of Kentucky!"

"I'm not waitin' that long."

Maripat's big eyes grew bigger. "What you goin' to do?"

Lowering his voice, Cawood told her.

"I'll start gettin' stuff together!" she enthused.

"It's goin' to be dangerous," Cawood warned.

"It'll be worth it if we can get that scum."

They discussed alternative plans for another hour, then daily over the next two weeks. As April drew to a close, they were ready to go.

5

Streaks of pale moonlight illuminated the inside of the barn. Working swiftly, Cawood and Maripat filled a burlap sack with items they had been storing under the stone foundation. Cawood threw the sack over his shoulder. Maripat picked up a bedroll and a paper sack. They moved quietly past the house and down the dry wash. Neither looked back.

They stopped to rest at the base of a steep hill. Cicadas buzzed and fireflies danced in the air. Cawood sat on a rock beside Maripat and touched the red mane that hung to her waist.

"Got to do something about that."

"I'll stick it under your cap."

Maripat would change later into bib overalls and wear Cawood's leather-billed cloth cap. With plans to hop the Louisville & Nashville freight, she had to look like a boy. Even in Harlan, they had heard terrible stories about what happened to girls riding the rails.

"You'll need a stovepipe hat to get that all in," Cawood said. He gathered her hair behind her neck and flapped the rest up and down. "Hmmmm."

Maripat stiffened, and her eyes grew enormous. "Don't you even think it!" Pulling her hair over her shoulder, she hugged it protectively.

"Just the last foot or so," Cawood said.

Measuring off a thick rope of hair, she said miserably, "Does it have to be that much?"

"I won't cut off any more than I have to."

She didn't look convinced.

Crouched in the dense underbrush, they watched the activity below. "Looks like they're havin' a party," Maripat said.

Cawood nodded. "Could go on all night."

A dozen cars were parked in front of Bennett Squires' house. It was nestled in a lonely wooded area two miles east of Harlan. Men lounged around the yard, laughing and passing jugs of moonshine. A man emerged from the outhouse, tightening his gun-belt as he swaggered toward the group.

"Must be at least twenty," Maripat said. "No tellin' how many in the house."

A man stepped out on the porch. He wore two guns, low-slung holsters tied with leather thongs around massive thighs. "Squires!" Cawood hissed.

They watched the big man strut down the steps and lift a jug to his lips. A cheer went up as he tilted his head back and took several long swallows. He wiped his mouth on his sleeve and tossed the jug to a man sporting a handlebar mustache. The man duplicated Squires' feat to another round of applause.

Cawood felt the burlap sack."Maybe I can sneak down while they're out front."

"Cawood, you can't! They'll see as sure as shootin'. Get caught with that dynamite and they'll blow your head off. *After* they bust every bone in your body."

A reluctant nod. The last thing he had expected was a party. They'd have to come back tomorrow night.

He backed out from under the prickly bush. "We'll stay in Zeb Jones' barn; he won't be back 'til next week."

6

Early morning sunlight illuminated the inside of the loft. Rising from their straw mattress, they made ham sandwiches and ate molasses cake Maripat had sneaked out of the house. She wore bib overalls that had belonged to Mabel's ten-year-old son. The theft had undoubtedly been discovered by now—along with their disappearance. Had they been able to conclude their business with Bennett Squires last night, they would have jumped the freight that passed through Harlan a few hours before midnight.

Cawood pulled his Arkansas Bowie knife from the leather

sheath strapped inside his overalls. The wicked-looking eight-inch blade had a buckhorn handle and was honed to razor sharpness.

"Sit here," he said, pointing at an empty nail keg.

"You can't use that on my hair!" Maripat yelped.

"Got a pair of scissors in your hip pocket?"

"Let me braid it first," she pleaded. "Maybe it'll all fit inside the cap."

"I'll just cut off a little," Cawood said. "You'll never get it all in the way it is."

Maripat sat down, forearms tucked inside her overalls. "You ruin my hair, I'll cut you where it *really* hurts!"

Seizing a hunk of hair, Cawood sawed away. "Like trimmin' a mule's tail." He tossed the red tresses on the floor.

"That's too much!" Maripat cried, reaching back to check the damage.

"Look out or you'll lose some fingers, too." He grabbed another hunk of hair.

The protests turned to tears, but Cawood stubbornly hacked away until Maripat's hair reached to just below her shoulders.

She crawled about, gathering the silky strands and sniffing while she worked. "I can sell this when we get to Cincinnati. It'll look real pretty on one of them china dolls."

They waited above Bennett Squires' darkened house. It was just past ten, six hours before the early morning freight passed through Harlan. "Now's as good a time as any," Cawood said. He picked up the burlap sack. "Whistle if you see anybody comin'."

"Be careful," Maripat called softly. Sitting back on her heels, she followed his progress as he started down the slope. In overalls and with her braided hair pushed up under the cap, she looked like a handsome young boy.

Cawood was crawling toward the outhouse when a low whistle came from the top of the hill. He backed into the trees.

Three cars pulled into the front yard, and a dozen men got out. Two dragged a limp figure from the back seat of Bennett Squires' shiny new Packard. Rifles slung over shoulders, some carrying clubs, they trooped into the house.

Minutes passed, and Cawood crept closer. Shouts and the sounds of heavy blows came from the house. A voice bellowed with pain. The blows continued, and the voice grew weaker. Cawood shivered. Some lived through these interrogations, others didn't. Bodies had been recovered with few bones intact.

Knowing this might be his only chance, Cawood crawled toward the outhouse. It was slow going, dragging the burlap sack.

A scream, accompanied by laughter, came from the house as Cawood reached the rough siding of the outhouse.

He emptied the contents of the sack on the ground. The dynamite, blasting caps, crimper-pliers and wire belonged to his father, along with the generator-type blasting machine left on the hill with Maripat. Jake Tanner had purchased the dynamite from the coal company before the strikes began. After blasting loose and loading sometimes as much as ten tons of coal a day, he was issued script worth fifteen cents a ton. The script was redeemable only at the company store.

Four sticks of dynamite were tied together. Removing a rock from the outhouse foundation, Cawood crimped blasting caps to the fuse ends and joined them to the detonating wires. Setting the dynamite inside the footing, he replaced the rock.

On his retreat from the outhouse, he had to cover twenty yards of open space, burying the wires as he went. The ground must look undisturbed. Should no opportunity arise tonight, he would have to wait another twenty-four hours, perhaps longer. The area had to withstand scrutiny in the daylight.

Digging a shallow three-foot-long trench with a sharp rock, he pressed the wires into the dirt, then scattered leaves and bark over the refilled area.

The back door of the house opened. Two men walked down the steps and headed his way.

Cawood scooted backwards. Attached to the dynamite, the exposed wires couldn't be moved. Reaching the trees, he pressed down into a thick bed of decaying leaves.

One of the men was already loosening his belt. "Best you stay outside, Bob," he said. "I'm goin' to set a spell. Feel like my insides are 'bout to pop like a gas drum on a hot day."

"Don't worry about me," Bob laughed. "I just got to piss."

Unbuttoning his fly, Bob splashed a copious yellow stream against a rock. Inside the outhouse, his companion loudly proclaimed the success of his efforts. "Better watch out or you'll blow the place up!" Bob yelled.

Cawood winced. Exactly what he had in mind, only with a different occupant.

Bob lit a cigarette. Flicking the match behind the outhouse, he leaned against a tree.

The burning match fell into a pile of dry brush. Horrified, Cawood watched the brush begin to smoke. If the men left quickly, he could smother the smoldering embers.

A tiny flame appeared, was swallowed up in smoke, then appeared again. Any second and the brush would begin to burn and light the whole area.

A muffled curse tore Cawood's eyes away from the flickering flame. Bob trotted toward the now burning pile of brush. Still cursing, he stamped on the fire. As he kicked dirt on the flames, the wires caught on the heel of his boot. He continued to kick, tearing the strands out of the trench.

Hands on hips, he searched the ground. If he turned, he couldn't miss the foot-high loops of tangled wires.

The outhouse door opened. "You still there, Bob?"

"Yeah, just moseyin' around." Bob walked away, dragging the wires. They caught on a twig and broke free as he rounded the corner of the outhouse. The men's voices faded in the distance.

Sweat running down his back, Cawood crawled out of his hiding place, replanted the wire and buried the fifteen feet that remained to the trees.

Working faster, he started up the hill. He didn't dig a trench, just laid rocks on the wires and covered them with leaves.

Maripat helped him complete the last fifty feet. "I 'bout died when those men went to the outhouse," she whispered while they worked. "What was that guy doin'?"

"Damn fool tossed a match and started a fire. Kicked the wire all around puttin' it out."

Maripat pressed her hand over her left breast. "Oh, lordy, I ain't cut out for this kind of stuff."

"Quit the actin' and get back to work."

A sidelong glance accompanied by a wide grin. "Maybe I ought to be in the movies."

"Yeah, and I'm goin' to be president of the U-Nited States."

They reached the hilltop. While Cawood attached the wires to the blasting generator, Maripat watched the house. "Did you see who that poor man was?"

"His head was hangin' down when they took him in. Maybe they're done—haven't heard anything for a while."

They sat against the tree, worldly belongings in the open bedroll at their feet. Cawood had put one of the two wool blankets over their shoulders. He touched the stem-wind watch in his pocket. If they weren't on their way to meet the train in two hours, they would have to stay another day.

Cawood jerked upright, drawing a mumbled protest from Maripat who dozed against his shoulder. Down below, men came out of the house and got into two of the cars. Doors slammed and engines revved.

"They're leavin'," Cawood whispered into Maripat's ear.

She sat up. "They got that man with 'em?"

"Put him in first. Took four men to carry him out."

The cars left. Bennett Squires stood besides his Packard a few moments, then went back into the house.

"Keep your eyes peeled," Cawood said. He pulled the blanket over his head and the watch from his pocket, then struck a match. "Almost one," he said as his head emerged.

"Don't leave us much time."

"Little more than an hour."

Minutes passed. "He's comin' out!" Maripat hissed.

Cawood watched Bennett Squires go down the back steps. If he just needed to piss, he could do that anywhere.

"He's headin' right for it!" Maripat whispered excitedly.

Rising to his feet, Cawood gripped the wooden handle that protruded up out of the box-like generator. As Squires neared the outhouse, Cawood bent to his knees and prepared to push.

"Go in! Go in!" Maripat urged, leaning forward and digging fingernails into upraised knees.

Squires went inside. Cawood gave him a few moments to get comfortable, then shoved down with all his strength. A clap of thunder rolled up the hill, and the outhouse disappeared in a dense cloud of smoke and debris.

Maripat was already on her feet. "Let's get while the gettin's good!" Cawood yelled. He tore the blasting generator wires loose while Maripat re-tied the bedroll. They hurried across the ridge, Maripat carrying the bedroll, Cawood the generator. He would bury it on the way.

7

The engine's whistle echoed mournfully over the hills. Still sweating from the three-mile trek, they waited beside the tracks. "Right on time," Cawood said. The westbound freight was leaving Harlan after refilling at the water tower.

Maripat hopped up and down. "We're really goin', Cawood!"

"Better be. We ain't exactly welcome around here anymore."

"I don't care," Maripat said. "You couldn't drag me back with a team of mules!" She stood on one of the steel rails. "It's gettin' close. I can feel it in my feet!"

The rails began to sing as the train picked up speed down a nearby hill. Grabbing Maripat, Cawood pulled her into the trees. The engine's powerful light would appear any moment.

Black smoke billowing from its single funnel, the huge engine careened around the bend, gathering speed as it neared the hill they stood on. "Watch for bulls,' Cawood said. "Sometimes they ride in cars lookin' for a chance to beat up 'bos."

The train began to slow, sending up great puffs of smoke as the giant pistons labored to turn the six-foot iron wheels. Boxcars passed where Cawood and Maripat stood. "Wait," he said, holding an arm in front of the anxious girl. "It's pullin' a lot of cars—be crawlin' in another minute."

Boxcars rattled past, some with doors sealed, many open on both sides, so they could see right through. "Let's try that one," Cawood said, pointing at the car with the big L&N in a circle on the side. He handed the bedroll to Maripat. "I'll jump in and check to see if it's empty. If it ain't, I'll get out. When I signal it's clear, toss me the bedroll, and I'll help you in."

Trotting alongside the boxcar, Cawood gripped an iron bar and leaped aboard. Finding it empty, he sat down, legs hanging over the side, arms outstretched. Maripat threw the bedroll, then reached for his hands. He pulled hard, and she jumped at the same time. The result was a collision that sent them tumbling into the center of the car.

They rolled over several times with Maripat ending up on top. She pushed off Cawood's chest, the cap hanging down over her eyes and the braid wrapped around her neck. "We made it!" she cried. Pulling the cap back on her head, she jumped up, lost her balance and sat down hard in a pile of trash.

Laughing, Cawood tackled her. The rolled around, then got to their fee and danced a jig.

"Cincinnati here we come!" Maripat sang.

"So long, Harlan!" Cawood shouted.

The train gathered speed as it started down. They stared as the dark forest flashed by. Smoke drifted into the car and stung their eyes. They didn't care. They were on their way.

8

The freight arrived in the Middlesboro switching yards early in the morning. Located on the Tennessee border and at the north end of the Cumberland Gap, Middlesboro was the biggest town in south-eastern Kentucky. While eating a free meal at the Salvation Army station, Cawood and Maripat got a lot of advice from the men who sat near them at the long table.

"If you catch the northbound freight that leaves around eight tonight, it'll take you right into Livingston," a bearded old man said from across the table. "You'll have to change there for Lexington and Cincinnati." He dipped a piece of bread in his soup. "Been travelin' long?"

Cawood said, "We hopped a freight outside of Harlan."

The old man's rheumy eyes flicked back and forth between the young couple. "I've been doing this for nigh onto forty years. Gets in your blood, goin' from one place to the next."

"Forty years," Maripat said in an awed voice.

"We're gonna find Baltimore Billy layin' dead by a water tower someday," a baldheaded man said on Cawood's right.

"Baltimore Billy—that your name?" Cawood asked.

"Us old timer's usually pick up a nickname after a while on the road. You'll hear a few more before you make Cincinnati." He sank yellow broken teeth into a dripping chunk of bread.

"Be glad you're not headin' west," a small weasel-faced man said. "Lots of tough towns between here and there. They got a bum blockade along the California border. At least Jeff Carr's dead, so we don't have to watch out for him."

"Who was Jeff Carr?" Cawood asked.

Weasel-face laughed harshly. "Jeff Carr worked out of Cheyenne. He was the meanest deek that ever lived. Had a long, black curled-up mustache and tied-down six-shooters. Rode his white horse beside the trains and shot 'bos. Sometimes, he'd grab 'em by the collar and yank 'em under the rails. If a 'bo lived through that, Carr would bust him up in jail. Got his in a fight with some 'bos—they bashed his head in with a coupling pin."

"God, he was really somethin'," another man said.

While Cawood and Maripat finished their meal, they were showered with advice. "Don't sit in a car and hang your legs over the side. Trains hit a bend and the door shuts, it'll slice your legs off clean as a whistle… You want to travel fast, catch a cannonball express. Fast freights have red tags or yellow manifests showin' they're carryin' meat…Keep away from the firemen. They'll throw coals and hot ash at you, know a guy who lost an eye from a burnin' cinder…You can tell how fast a drag is by listenin' to the puff. Jump a train that's goin' too fast, you'll get your arms yanked out of their sockets."

When Cawood and Maripat arrived at the rail yard that evening, they joined dozens of shadowy figures waiting for the northbound freight to roll. Getting on too soon risked discovery by the detectives and brakemen who roamed the area.

"Hope we can get a car to ourselves," Maripat said.

Cawood looked around. "Must be at least fifty waitin'."

A shout came from near the engine, and a lantern waved. Steam hissed, and smoke puffed into the dark sky. As the locomotive began to roll, couplings snapped tight, creating a domino-effect that rattled the length of the train.

Shadowy figures bounded across tracks and followed thrown bundles into open-cars and flat-beds. Cawood said, "We'll have a better chance of bein' by ourselves if we catch a car further down the line."

"If it ain't goin' too fast by then," Maripat fretted.

Cawood grinned as she gazed at the passing cars, the cap accentuating her big eyes. "Sometimes you're worse than a bear with a sore tooth."

"Better than draggin' my butt like some people I know." She waved at the accelerating train. "We goin' or not?"

"Last one on is buzzard bait!" Cawood darted over the tracks, Maripat right behind. "Watch when you jump in the car," he called over his shoulder. "You'll hit pretty hard."

"Save your breath for somethin' useful. I can take care of myself good as you any day!" Racing past Cawood toward an empty boxcar, she landed sprawling on the rough wooden floor. "Beat you!" she cried as Cawood rolled beside her.

The dramatic events of the past twenty-four hours finally took their toll. Snuggling under the blankets, they went to sleep.

9

The hobo jungle stretched for a quarter-mile, scattered campfires giving it the appearance of an army camp. Maripat pressed close to Cawood as a group of men broke out of the brush and ran toward their slowly moving boxcar.

A bundle landed on the floor, followed by a big man who swung inside with the ease of long practice. "Come on, you old fart!" he shouted, reaching down and yanking another man into the car. Standing in the open doorway, they yelled encouragement to the half-dozen others who ran along the tracks, tossing in bundles and jumping aboard. The train picked up speed, and the town lights faded in the distance. Hoping to remain unnoticed until the next stop, Cawood and Maripat huddled together in a far corner. They would have been further up the line if they hadn't gotten off another train in Corbin to avoid a disreputable-looking bunch like this. These weren't honest men down on their luck; they would be riding the rails even if times were good.

The big man pulled a wine bottle from his bedroll and took a long swallow. Wiping his mouth with the back of his hand he belched loudly. "Anybody for a game of cards?"

"What are we bettin'—matchsticks?"

"How about your pretty pink ass?"

The men roared with laughter.

"Gimmie that lantern," a man said.

As the lantern exchanged hands, Cawood whispered into Maripat's ear, " Get behind and scoot under that cardboard."

A match flared. Lowering the glass over the flame, the man set the lantern next to the big man. "There you go, Harv."

With expert flicks of the wrist, Harv dealt cards to the seven men. They frowned and haggled, tossed out cards and asked for more. One man reached for a card and looked straight at Cawood. "Hey, look what we got!" he exclaimed, lifting the lantern and peering across the car.

"Got us a young rooster," another man said. "Come here, boy.

Sit beside me and bring me luck!"

"I saw him first! You're my lucky piece, boy."

"That piece ain't for gamblin'!" a voice cackled lewdly.

Harv got to his feet. He was over six feet tall and broad as a barn. Well muscled and not emaciated like many transients. "Forget the others," he said to Cawood. "I can take care of you better'n any of these bums."

When the man who had spotted Cawood protested, Harv slapped him viciously across the face. Cawood retreated on his knees, feeling Maripat's body against his back as she squirmed further under the pile of cardboard.

He had no illusions about Harv's intentions. It was common practice for older 'bos to take boys under their wings. Labeled "punks," the boys were taught to provide sexual services and beg for their masters.

Harv walked toward Cawood, swaying easily with the motion of the car. His companions rose behind him, the flickering lantern casting eerie shadows on their unshaven faces.

Cawood stood and glanced quickly downward to make sure Maripat was hidden. The big man stopped ten feet away, legs spread, hands on hips.

"Leave me alone," Cawood said in a quiet steady voice.

"Ain't he a feisty one!" Harv said. He signaled to the men. "Split up and block the doors. Jim, get on his right."

Jim wasn't as big as Harv, but he had a lean feral look that reminded Cawood of an angry badger. With little room left in which to maneuver, Cawood reached inside his overalls and pulled out the long Arkansas Bowie knife.

"Bastard's got a pig-sticker!" Jim yelled, almost tripping as he jumped out of the way.

"He ain't the only one," Harv said, producing a knife that was three inches shorter than Cawood's but double-edged and honed to gleaming sharpness. Harv kicked a crushed box out of the way. "Nobody pulls a knife on me and gets away with it."

Cawood nudged the cardboard with his foot. "Get up and stay behind me."

"Two of 'em!" Harv shouted gleefully as Maripat got to her

feet. "A young tender lamb! This is the one we want, boys. We'll get rid of the rooster, then have some fun!"

Snatching up the bedroll, Maripat rose on her toes and peered defiantly over Cawood's shoulder.

Knife moving back and forth in wide sweeps, Cawood whispered over his shoulder. "We've got to make the door and jump. It's our only chance. Move with me."

A small chin nodded against his back.

Cawood took a step to the left. "Get ready, Jim," Harv said. "The rest of you look sharp!" The men spread out.

Jim opened a pocket knife and edged closer. Cawood took another step, Maripat pressed against his back.

"Now, Jim!" Harv yelled, leaping forward and stabbing viciously at Cawood's chest.

Spinning, Cawood slashed Harv's arm from elbow to wrist. The big man howled and dropped his knife. Intent on Harv, Cawood lost sight of Jim. Screaming, Maripat shoved the bedroll between Jim's knife and Cawood's ribs. The hobo was pulling his knife out of the bedroll when Cawood cut him across the chest.

Blood soaked Jim's shirt and dripped on his legs. He sat down spread-legged and pressed his hands against his chest in an attempt to staunch the flow.

"Cawood!" Maripat screamed. "Behind you!"

Cawood turned just in time to receive Harv's knife in his stomach. They stood locked together for a moment, then Cawood whipped the Bowie across Harv's throat. The big man staggered about, blood spurting from severed arteries.

Weakening fast from his own terrible wound, Cawood shoved Maripat toward the open doorway. The men guarding it shrank back, wanting no part of that bloody knife.

"Jesus, it's a girl!" a hoarse voice exclaimed.

Cawood glanced at Maripat. Her hat had fallen off, and the heavy braid hung behind her neck.

It was pitch dark, and nothing was visible except the graveled roadbed sloping into the black abyss. "Go!" Cawood shouted.

Maripat leaped into the night. The bedroll cushioned her violent collision with the ground. She rolled down a hill. Breathing hard but intact, she looked up just as Cawood tumbled out of the boxcar.

A fallen tree blocked the way to where Cawood fell. She scrambled back up the steep bank, reaching the tracks just as the caboose rattled past. A short trot between the rails brought her to where Cawood had landed. A voice called, "That you, Maripat?"

"Cawood!" she cried happily. Rocks and dirt tumbled in her wake as she slid down.

He was sitting against a tree, arms wrapped around his middle. Blood was everywhere. "Bastard cut me real good," he said as Maripat knelt at his side. He moaned as she started to unfasten the top of his bib overalls. "Leave me be."

"I've got to look," Maripat insisted as she undid the hooks.

"No use," Cawood said. "My insides are comin' out."

A whimper escaped Maripat's lips, but she continued to pull the blood-soaked bib down. Cawood groaned as she moved his arms.

Streaks of moonlight revealed what Maripat already knew. Cawood had lost too much blood, and the damage was beyond repair.

"I'm cold," Cawood murmured.

"I'll build a fire," Maripat said through her tears. She gathered scraps of bark and broken limbs and struck a match taken from the bedroll. Flames leaped as she sat close to her brother.

"Money's in...watch pocket," Cawood said.

"We'll talk about that later."

"Can't...not much time."

"Don't say that!"

Cawood looked up at his little sister. "Stay off trains. Hitch rides...walk. Forget Cincinnati. Try get job in Lexington."

Tears poured from Maripat's eyes. "I need you, Cawood!"

"Since when...you needed anyone?"

"I'm just a big bluff! You know that!"

Cawood looked at the nearby trees. "Leave me...here. Reminds me...home."

"Cawood, I can't!"

"Got to...least one body in boxcar. Cops...come lookin'."

The talk sapped the last of Cawood's strength. Huge sobs racked Maripat's body as she hugged him tightly. She kissed his lips. He died moments later.

10

Maripat stood on the corner of Main and Upper Streets and gazed up at the Fayette National Bank building. Fifteen stories high, it was the tallest structure in Lexington. Passersby smiled at the young girl in bib overalls gawking at the buildings and busy traffic. Unlike most of the hundreds of transients who rode trains in and out of Lexington every day, this small redhead belonged. Those she spoke to instantly recognized her distinctive eastern hill-country accent.

Walking west on Main, Maripat felt the paper money and coins in her pocket. After spending thirty-seven cents that morning buying bread, bologna and milk at an A&P grocery, she was down to two dollars and six cents. The ride on the bus from Richmond had cost fifty cents, and a dollar-eighty had gone for food during the four days it had taken to reach Lexington.

She had buried Cawood in a shallow gully. After washing his face and hands with water from a nearby creek, she wrapped him in a blanket, laid him in a shallow gully and piled rocks on his body. Using a stick to loosen the moist earth, she spread soil over the rocks and tamped it down with her feet. As she trudged off in the darkness beside the tracks, she turned and noted the small hill a hundred yards to the east. A lightning-blasted tree stood beside the grave.

Because she was still close to the scene of the fight, she avoided a nearby town and the farms that dotted the rolling countryside. By the time the sun began to set in the west, she figured she had walked at least ten miles. Building a shelter with some fallen branches, she cried herself to sleep.

The next morning, she caught a ride with a farmer returning from selling hogs at an auction. He dropped her off north of Berea. After spending the night in an abandoned barn, she purchased food at a grocery store. That kept her through the long day as she hitched rides and walked to Richmond, She slept in a park, then took a bus to Lexington.

As she walked the streets of Lexington, Maripat marveled at the tall buildings and wondered what it was like up there. She had watched people getting on the elevators in the Fayette National Bank building. One part of her wanted to take a ride, the other was too scared to try.

A few blocks north on Broadway, she stared at the impressive buildings on the Transylvania University campus. Having completed the eighth grade, she was better educated than most in Harlan County. The idea of continuing after *high school* made her dizzy.

She watched a pickup baseball game in Woodland Park and read a discarded *Lexington Leader* newspaper. This was horse country, and racing news made the front page, especially this week. Tomorrow was Saturday, and the Kentucky Derby was being run in Louisville. It was the biggest event of the year in Kentucky, and the excitement wasn't confined to the Bluegrass State. The whole nation turned its attention toward the Churchill Downs racetrack in early May.

Later, Maripat left Maxwell Street and cut across the University of Kentucky campus. She decided to take a chance and sleep under a tree near a dorm. Compared to camping in the hobo jungle south of Virginia Street, the risk was minimal.

11

By Tuesday, Maripat was getting desperate. She had knocked on dozens of doors in a futile search for work. Her physical appearance didn't help. After sleeping outdoors for over a week with no opportunity to bathe, she didn't look like anyone a woman would want to invite into her home. Having only a faded flour-sack dress in her bedroll, she continued to wear the pilfered bib overalls. There were shelters where she could clean up and get a meal, but she feared they might turn her over to the authorities.

Despite selling the hair Cawood had cut off to a doll shop for forty-five cents yesterday, she was down to a dollar and twenty-one cents. That was a cold hard fact. She had counted the coins several times that morning to make sure.

She was walking along High Street late that afternoon when she passed a vacant lot where several teenage boys were playing football.

One yelled, "Hey look what they let out of a cage!"

Shrill whistles were followed by catcalls and laughter. One boy ran behind Maripat and grabbed at her bedroll. She whirled and struck him in the face.

Eyes watering with pain, he felt his nose. "I'm *bleeding!*"

"Let's get her!" a voice shouted.

The boys surrounded Maripat, yanking at her bedroll and pulling her hair. She kicked one beside the knee, and he fell to the ground, moaning with pain.

"All right, break it up!"

The boys fell silent and backed away.

Maripat looked up into the face of a tall policeman. He said, "Where you from, girl?"

"Harlan."

The boys hooted with laughter.

"Shut up and get out of here!" the policeman snapped.

The boys left, slapping each other on the back and looking over their shoulders to make faces at Maripat. The one she had kicked hopped on his good leg to keep up.

"Where are your parents?" the policeman asked.

"Dead." That was true about her mother and as far as she was concerned her father, too.

"Better come with me. You need lookin' after."

"No—please!" Maripat cried as the man took her arm. "I just need a job."

A Model A Ford pickup loaded with sacks of feed slid to a stop at the curb, and a tall lanky gray-haired woman got out. She wore a denim shirt, baggy pants and knee-high rubber boots. "What's going on, Henry?" she demanded.

"Not much, Mrs. MacKay. Some boys were pesterin' this girl."

"I saw it. I was turning around when you came along. What are you doing with her?"

"She's all alone and got no kin. I thought I'd see if some shelter might take her in."

"Fat chance of that!" The woman looked down at Maripat. "Is that what you want, child?"

"I just want to be left alone," Maripat answered hotly. She started to add that she wasn't a child but decided it would only get her in more trouble.

"What's your name?"

"Maripat Tanner."

A smile wiped the stern look from the woman's face. "That's a pretty name. Mine's Elizabeth. My friends call me Libby." She looked at the policeman, then back at Maripat. "Would you like to come home with me? I have a farm out near Midway."

Maripat nodded vigorously. She had no idea where Midway was, but anyplace had to be better than a police station!

"That's sure nice of you, Mrs. MacKay," the policeman said.

Libby winked at Maripat. "Us women have to stick together. Toss your bedroll in the back."

"We just crossed into Woodford County," Libby said as she drove northeast on Old Frankfurt Pike. "Some call it the 'Asparagus Bed' of the Bluegrass."

"Why's that?" Maripat asked, eyes rounding and head twisting as she tried to take in everything at once.

"The richness of the earth and the variety of trees—black walnut, ash, hard maple, oak, hickory, elm and many others. I've lived in Woodford County for thirty-five years and couldn't imagine living anywhere else."

Maripat understood what Libby meant as they passed huge homes surrounded by acres of lawn and manicured fields criss-crossed by miles of white fences. Slave-built mortarless stone walls lined portions of the narrow rolling road, and tree branches laden with the fresh leaves of spring formed occasional tunnels.

Adding to the tranquil scene were hundreds of beautiful horses roaming about as if this marvel of nature had been created exclusively for them. Some lifted their heads to watch the pickup pass while others nipped the lush grass, unwilling to take time out for mere mortals. Playful foals, unaware of their illustrious destinies, ran circles around their mothers.

"Here we are," Libby said as she drove between two stone pillars with "Elkhorn Farm" etched into bronze plaques. On a distant knoll and partially obscured by a stand of stately trees, a white-columned mansion gleamed under the waning afternoon sunshine.

Maripat had never seen anything so beautiful. "You live in that big house?"

"Every day. A lot is closed up…too big for one person."

"You're all alone?"

"My husband died six years ago. We had a large staff once and three times as many horses. Then Ralph lost a small fortune when the stock market crashed. We had to sell our racing stable and cut the breeding program back. Ralph never recovered from the shock of losing all that money."

Maripat wondered what a "staff" was and how a stock market crashed. Farm animals were called "stock." Was the "crash" about a bunch of horses butting heads like goats? Did they kill each other and lose lots of money for Mrs. MacKay's husband?

Three yearlings raced beside the bordering white paddock fence. On the opposite side of the lane, a dark brown horse shoved its head over the top rail and watched them with interested eyes.

Libby drove behind the white house and backed inside the largest of four barns.

"Wow!" Maripat said as she got out and looked at the long double row of stalls. "I've never lived in a *house* this nice!"

Libby laughed and lowered the tailgate. "Grab one end of this sack, Maripat. I'll give you your first lesson how to be a horse farmer."

They were returning for another sack of feed when a small black-haired man entered. "Who's your helper?" he asked.

"Shawn , meet Maripat," Libby said. "Some boys were pushing her around downtown. She gave one a bloody nose and kicked another one real good on the leg."

"Doesn't sound like she needed to be rescued." He grinned and stuck out a hand. "Welcome to Elkhorn Farm, Maripat."

She shook his hand, liking him instantly. "Nice to meet you, Mr. Shawn."

"Just Shawn," he smiled. "Last name's Phelps, but I don't use it much."

"Maripat's from Harlan," Libby said.

"No kidding! I was born below the Smoky Mountains near Bryson City, North Carolina. My mother was a full-blooded Cherokee. Pa was a white tobacco farmer. He died when I was eleven. When Ma moved back to the reservation with the rest of the kids, I took off—been working with horses ever since. I wanted to be a jockey. I'm still short enough, but I was too heavy by the time I turned sixteen—that's when I came to work here. I never got past being an exercise rider anyway." Dark eyes twinkled as he threw a sack over his shoulder. "I learned a lot about Thoroughbreds. That's what counts."

12

Maripat awoke before dawn and padded barefoot to the window that overlooked the moonlit paddocks. Several horses grazed beside a huge bur oak. Another drank at the round concrete trough. She had awakened several times during the night wondering if this was all just a dream that would end any moment. But the beautiful bed was real. Also the wonderful clean sheets. And the soft nightgown that Libby had said once belonged to her daughter.

That came up after Maripat had her first bath in a real bathtub. It was big and white and she almost jumped out of her skin when Libby turned two handles and water poured out of the spout. *Hot* water! The water back home had to be carried from a well in buckets and heated on the cast-iron wood stove. Then you bathed in a metal washtub. Once a week if you were lucky.

After scrubbing until her skin was pink, Maripat put on one of Libby's robes. It dragged the floor and tangled her feet as she walked down the hall.

"Aren't you a sight!" Libby said as Maripat entered the kitchen. Libby had exchanged the rubber boots for slippers, but she still wore the baggy pants.

"It's a little big." Maripat said. If she let her arms hang down, her hands would disappear.

Libby studied Maripat for a long moment. "Come with me," she said. "I want to show you something."

Maripat followed Libby up a winding staircase. Hanging from the thirty-foot ceiling, a crystal chandelier sparkled above the wide foyer at the base of the stairs.

Opening a door facing the second-story landing, Libby turned on a light and stepped inside. Mouth agape, Maripat stared at the fairy tale room. Dainty lace curtains covered the windows, and a huge four-poster bed stood against one wall. Beneath the silk canopy, a trio of dolls rested against a set of pillows.

"This was my daughter's room," Libby said. "Everything's just like it was when she died."

Maripat's hands emerged from the oversize sleeves, and she laced her fingers together. "When did she die?" It was impossible not to see the pain in Libby's eyes.

"Seventeen years ago last month. It was during the great influenza outbreak that killed so many all over the world. She was twelve. Her name was Tess. That's her picture on the chest of drawers. I have others all over the house."

Maripat walked across the plush carpet and looked at the face of a young girl with laughing eyes and a mop of curly hair. "You must have loved her a lot."

"Oh, yes! I had so many plans for her. We had a son eight years before Tess was born, but he only lived a week." Libby opened a door. "These were her clothes."

Maripat gasped at the sight of two rows of colorful dresses and coats in the walk-in closet. Shoes and dainty leather boots lined the floor. Libby took a beautiful blue robe off a hanger and held it out. "This should fit you."

Tears filled Maripat's eyes. "I can't do that!"

"Why not?"

"Cause these things belonged to your daughter, and you've kept them all these years. You've been so nice to me. I don't want to make you sad."

Eyes bright with her own tears, Libby gripped Maripat's shoulder. "That's just it—you'll make me *happy!* This room shouldn't be a memorial. It should be filled with laughter. Just like it was when Tess was alive!"

"Why me?" Maripat whispered. "Why did you pick me?"

"Because when I saw you fighting with those boys, you reminded me of when I was your age. I grew up on a horse farm and could outride and out-fight boys for miles around. I had three older brothers who encouraged my independence. My mother wanted me to marry into a genteel family and hold society teas. Poor mother! Outside of my wedding, she seldom saw me in a dress. Put this robe on. You look ridiculous in mine."

Maripat slipped into the soft robe and tied the silk belt around her waist. "It fits perfectly!" Libby said. She walked to the bed and removed the dolls. "Get a good night's sleep, Maripat; you were yawning all through dinner." She took a pale blue nightgown out of a drawer and laid it on the satin spread. "We'll have lots of time to talk tomorrow."

13

When Libby went out early the next morning to help Shawn check the horses, Maripat insisted on going along. Anticipating this, Libby had washed Maripat's overalls. Wearing clean underwear, one of Libby's flannel shirts and her own Sears, Roebuck shoes, Maripat helped clean stalls and carry hay to the horses kept in one of the barns.

Shawn had spent the early morning hours assisting in the delivery of a foal, and he let Maripat lead the mare to a clean stall across the aisle. Still wobbly on its slender legs, the little filly stayed close to its mother's side all the way.

Maripat was surprised to learn that there were no other workers on the farm. "We had a dozen farmhands," Libby explained as she pushed a wheelbarrow full of straw and manure out of a barn. "More horses, too. Breeding farms were hit hard by the depression. We sold two-thirds of our stock. When my husband died, I sold all the stallions but two and kept thirty broodmares. Shawn does the work of two men anyway. He's been around so long, it seems like he's older than thirty-three."

Later, Libby drove Maripat around the farm. It covered eight hundred acres, bordered on the south by Old Frankfurt Pike and the north by Elkhorn Creek. "My husband received a large inheritance when he was in his mid-thirties," Libby said as they sat on a rock beside the private road that circled the property. "Ralph was a city boy who dreamed about raising Thoroughbreds." A merry laugh. "But he didn't know anything about horses except betting on them at the track. That's where I came in."

"You?" Maripat asked. She couldn't get enough of Libby's wonderful stories.

"All I *knew* were horses! My oldest brother, Steve, worked with Ralph in Ralph's father's bank in Charlottesville, Virginia. Our farm was forty miles away near Fredericksburg. When Ralph's father died, Steve brought Ralph home for a visit. I'm not sure whether Ralph fell in love with me or my knowledge of horses, but we had a wonderful marriage. We bought this farm right after the wedding. That was thirty-seven years ago. I was twenty-six."

Maripat waved an arm. "How..." She clamped her mouth shut.

"I'm sixty-three," Libby laughed. "That must seem awfully old to you." Libby had already learned Maripat's fourteenth birthday was two weeks away.

Maripat said, "We had a neighbor lady who was sixty or thereabouts. She looked *lots* older than you!"

"Why, thank you Maripat. That's the nicest compliment I've had in a long time."

On the way back to the house, Libby parked beside a knoll that overlooked Elkhorn Creek. A white picket fence enclosed an area at the top, and the trees inside had obviously been planted years before. Libby led Maripat up a gravel path and opened the gate. A rainbow of flowers surrounded three marble headstones.

Libby pointed at the headstone on the left. "That's Ralph's grave," she said quietly. "Our son, Lawrence, is in between. Tess is next to him."

"You must come here a lot," Maripat said, noting the carefully tended, clipped grass and varnished wooden bench.

"Once or twice a week," Libby said. "It's so peaceful. It wouldn't be the same if they were in some impersonal public cemetery. The ones you love should be close, even after death."

Tears appeared in Maripat's eyes, and she brushed them away with the back of her hand. More came until they flooded over her cheeks. A deep sob racked her body, and she turned away.

Alarmed, Libby asked, "Maripat, what's the matter?"

Chest heaving and continuing to wipe her eyes, Maripat could only shake her head.

Libby pulled Maripat into her arms. "Cry it all out, Dear. It's the best medicine in the world." Minutes passed. Libby led Maripat to the bench, sat her down and handed her a big red bandanna. Neither said anything for a while.

"It's my brother, Cawood," Maripat said. "I left him all alone with nobody to take care of his grave." A fresh round of tears followed as she told Libby about her abusive father, the love she and Cawood shared, their flight from Harlan County and how Cawood died protecting her.

While Maripat sobbed against her breast, Libby looked down at the shiny red hair and knew her judgement had been correct. Despite her impoverished background and lack of education, this girl was one in a million. *And to think how close I came yesterday to sending Shawn into town instead of going myself!*

"Let's go see Shawn," Libby said, lifting Maripat's head and kissing her wet cheeks.

Shawn knelt on one knee on the barn floor while Libby repeated Maripat's story. Sitting beside Libby on a bale of hay, Maripat listened quietly. When Libby finished, Shawn stood and dusted off the seat of his pants. "Guess we're thinking the same thing," he said briskly. He looked at Maripat. "It happened last Monday?"

"Yes."

He thought a moment. "Nine days."

"It will raise questions if I buy a coffin," Libby said.

"I'm a fair carpenter," Shawn said. "I can pick up some pine this afternoon and have it ready tomorrow. It won't be pretty, but it'll do."

Eyes big as saucers, Maripat perched on the edge of the hay bale. "What are you sayin'?"

Libby smiled and squeezed her hand. "We're going to get your brother and bury him here."

Tears filled Maripat's eyes. "You'd do that for me?"

"For both of you," Libby said.

Maripat kissed Libby, then jumped up and hugged Shawn.

14

The pickup bounced over rough terrain. "It's railroad property along the tracks," Shawn said as he steered around a fallen tree. "We won't be messing around on some farmer's land."

Sitting between Shawn and Libby, Maripat peered through the windshield. They had left early that morning and passed through McKee an hour ago. A mile back, Maripat had directed Shawn to leave the highway and drive alongside the railroad tracks.

"There's the hill!" she cried, pointing. "And the tree!"

Shawn drove down a steep grade, then across a gully. "Good it hasn't rained for a while or we'd never make it through," he said as they approached the lightning-blasted tree. He parked in a thick stand of elms. "Nobody'll see us here."

Putting on gloves, Libby said, "Show us the place and we'll take care of everything, Maripat. You can wait in the truck."

"I'm helpin'," Maripat said stubbornly.

"You sure? It won't be pleasant."

Maripat's head bobbed up and down.

Libby sighed and handed a bandanna to Shawn. He soaked it in gasoline from a can, wrung it out and returned it to Libby. She gave it to Maripat. "Tie that around your nose."

Shawn prepared a bandanna for Libby, then one for himself. He pulled an oiled canvas off the pine coffin and followed Maripat to the shallow grave. When they returned for the coffin, she insisted on carrying one end.

They worked silently and swiftly, knowing the damp spring soil had hastened decomposition. When the body was exposed, they wrapped it in the canvas and laid it gently in the coffin. Shawn nailed the lid tight and sealed the joints with pitch. After placing the coffin in the back of the pickup and covering it with another canvas, they drove back toward the highway.

They reached the farm an hour before sunset and lowered the coffin into the spot prepared the day before. Libby read a prayer while Maripat knelt beside her brother's grave. When the last shovel of earth was tamped down, she felt a great burden lift from her heart. Smiling through her tears, she laid fresh flowers on the grave, knowing that Cawood's soul was at rest.

15

One evening two months later, Maripat sat with Libby and Shawn on the front porch of Shawn's home. Shawn lived in one of the four tenant houses. The others were vacant.

"Exactly how tall are you, Maripat?" Shawn asked.

"Five-two," she said, sticking her legs straight out and admiring her shiny new black shoes.

"Five-two, my eye. More like five-foot. I think you were taller last week. You must be shrinking in the heat."

Maripat's feet landed with a thud. "I'm five-two and I ain't shrinkin'! Sorry, Libby, I shouldn't have said 'ain't.'" Libby had been tutoring Maripat in preparation for entering high school next month.

Shawn said: "Can I borrow your yardstick, Libby? I'd like to measure this young lady and get it settled once and for all. She changes her height and weight as often as I change my socks."

Maripat wrinkled her nose. "Which *isn't* often."

Libby smiled. "Why don't you two compromise a little?"

Shawn looked at Maripat. "Five-foot?"

"Five-one."

"Five-foot, one-half inch?"

"Maybe."

"Eighty-nine pounds?"

"Ninety-five."

"Ninety-one?"

"Ninety-three."

Shawn grinned at Libby. "Know something? I think we finally got it right."

"I'm still growing," Maripat said.

"So I've noticed," Shawn said, leaning forward and leering at the perfect little body encased so neatly in a green and white checked gingham dress.

Maripat's face turned as red as her hair, and Libby chided, "Shawn, leave the poor girl alone. She's having enough trouble growing up as it is."

Summer turned into fall and as winter approached, Maripat was no longer recognizable as the bedraggled waif who fled Harlan County. Brilliant hair falling softly on her shoulders and looking lovely in her pretty new dresses, she radiated a confidence beyond her years. If the Lexington boys who had tormented her saw her now, they would follow her with admiring eyes. If one were able to draw her into a conversation, he would hear a soft southern accent that was rapidly replacing harsh hill-country vowels.

Living with Libby and attending Woodford County High had unveiled a world Maripat never dreamed existed. Driven by an insatiable desire to learn and continuing to study with Libby at home, she made the honor roll her first semester.

What especially delighted Libby was Maripat's natural affinity with horses. They sensed her fearless affection and returned it in kind. And she rode as if born in the saddle. "The way she rides and with that hair, she's more like a red Indian than me," Shawn said admiringly one day as he sat on a fence rail beside Libby and watched Maripat send her horse over a three-foot jump.

A longtime member of the Iroquois Hunt Club, Libby loved chasing foxes near Boone Creek south of Lexington. It was a dangerous sport. Riding full tilt over one of the largest stands of uninterrupted hunt country in the United States, falls were frequent. A member once described the sound of breaking collar bones as "cracking like popcorn."

For Christmas, Libby presented Maripat with a 16.2 hand gray Thoroughbred gelding named "Iron Man." Seven years old and the winner of several timber races in Virginia, he loved the hunt as much as his new owner. They soon became a familiar sight— Maripat dressed in red jacket, white pants, knee-high black boots and black derby hat dodging underbrush and flying over fallen trees and ditches on the huge gray horse.

16

Libby taught Maripat the history of Thoroughbred racing and famous bloodlines and shared hands-on training with Shawn.

No longer a racing stable, Elkhorn Farm was still a well-known nursery with two stallions and thirty-three broodmares. With Maripat in school during the busiest months of the year, Libby and Shawn were taxed to the limit.

The breeding season began in mid-February and extended into June. March brought the beginning of a twenty-four hour foal watch. This perpetual grind of breeding and foaling continued through April and May. Added to that was the care of the mares and the new foals, preparing yearlings for the summer sales and the general tasks and upkeep that was necessary around the farm.

"Sometimes you wonder if it's worth it," Shawn said to Maripat one night as they knelt beside a newborn foal. "A year from now, what will this little guy be worth? Three-four hundred? Ten years ago, he would have brought at least fifteen. Demand's shot to hell. Kentucky sold more horses thirty years ago than it does now! That was before all the tracks shut down."

Maripat pondered Shawn's words while he treated the foal's broken navel cord with iodine to help it close and prevent infection. Libby had shown her old newspaper and magazine accounts of the over expansion and criminal infiltration that had brought about anti-betting legislation and the closing of hundreds of racetracks around the turn of the century.

As a bulwark against this flood of corruption, the Jockey Club was formed in 1894. Its ultimate purpose was for individual clubs to relinquish racing management and authority, the setting of meeting dates and the licensing of jockeys and trainers to the Jockey Club's authority. The Jockey Club would also serve as a final court of appeals.

That prestigious organization, however, was unable to save Thoroughbred racing in its present state of self-destruction. In 1897, there were three hundred-fourteen racetracks in twenty-nine states. By the end of 1908, that number had dropped to twenty-four in eight states, including Kentucky.

Tracks across Canada and in Juarez and Tijuana, Mexico benefited from the closings. While racing continued in Kentucky, the nations' breeding industry suffered. Thoroughbreds were shipped by the thousands from America to other countries, as owners and trainers moved their racing strings to Canada and Europe.

Gradually, the Jockey Club nursed the nation's tracks back to health. Racing returned to New York's Belmont Park in 1913 on a non-betting basis. In 1920, a new plant replaced the one destroyed by fire three years earlier. That was also the last year of clockwise racing during which Man o' War won the Belmont Stakes by twenty lengths. Betting remained illegal in New York until 1934.

Miami's Hialeah—Florida's first racecourse—opened in 1925, the same year Chicago reopened Washington Park and held Lincoln Fields' inaugural meet.

As the Depression deepened, other states recognized the benefit of revenues from pari-mutuel betting and voted racing back into business. In 1933, California, Michigan, New Mexico, North Carolina, New Hampshire, Ohio, Oregon, Washington and West Virginia legislated the reopening of tracks that had been closed for decades. Texas, also, but pari-mutuel racing was later repealed in that state.

The Kentucky Association track closed in Lexington, not for financial or illicit reasons but because the century-old plant was deteriorating and unable to expand in its downtown location. A group of men headed by Hal Price Headley and Major Louis A. Beard, formed the Keeneland Association and purchased one hundred forty-seven acres on Versailles Pike two miles west of Calumet Farm. Surrounded by horse farms, the beautiful new track opened October 15, 1936 to a slogan that would become world famous—"Racing as it was meant to be."

17

Though one of the more popular girls at Woodford County High, Maripat had little time for school activities. Her life revolved around horses. Every spare moment was spent feeding, grooming, helping with breeding and foaling and riding with the hunt club. Libby commented once to Shawn that Maripat was crazier about horses than she was at the same age. A remarkable statement, considering Libby's own single-minded devotion.

Boys pursued Maripat to no avail. For one thing, she didn't have time. For another, she resented their immature advances. Her best friend, however, turned out to be a boy her age. His name was John Calhoun Kershaw. The son of Stanton Kershaw, a widower who owned White Oak Stud on nearby Craigs Mill Road, John wanted to be a lawyer.

"I don't understand you," Maripat said one day as they sat on the bench in the Elkhorn Farm cemetery. They had just finished tending the graves. She had given special care to Cawood's that was now marked with a marble headstone. She missed her brother and often wondered about the rest of her family. A query by Libby had revealed that the Tanners had moved away shortly after Maripat and Cawood had left Harlan County. Maripat felt Bennett Squires' death was probably a deciding factor. Having been beaten twice by Squires' goons, Jake Tanner would have been a prime suspect.

"Don't understand what?" John Kershaw said.

"You wanting to be a lawyer," Maripat said. "Why sit in a stuffy old office and argue in court when you can work with *horses*? It doesn't make sense!"

John offered a big toothy grin and tugged at a lock of red hair. "Not everybody's got a screw loose like you, Maripat. Believe it or not, there are other occupations in the world beside shoveling horse shit."

"Watch our language or a I'll stick a bar of soap in that big mouth! And get your paws off my hair!"

"Yes, Ma'am. I do apologize for being disrespectful."

Maripat bit her lip, but she couldn't help smiling at the tall, loose-jointed boy. Already over six foot, John was the classroom character who was always pulling something behind the teacher's back. Since entering high school, he had evolved from frogs in girls' restrooms and pigtails in inkwells to more ingenious pranks. Beneath that mischievous grin, long bony face, big ears and shock of sandy hair hanging over his forehead, was a very sharp mind. It made Maripat angry that she had to study twice as hard to achieve the same top grades as John.

He pointed at the twelve hundred acres that bordered Elkhorn farm on the west. "Old man Albright was wandering around yesterday. First time I've seen him since Bob left for Harvard."

"Mr. Albright stopped by our place. He's awfully nice."

"Not according to my Uncle, Jim. Albright's bank foreclosed on his tobacco farm back in Thirty-One."

"Lots of farms have gone under since the Depression started," Maripat said. "Even Mr. Albright's bank got hurt. Central Kentucky Trust used to have three branches. All they've got now is the main branch in Lexington."

John looked at the adjacent rolling acres. "Too bad the way he let the farm go. My grandfather remembered when Albright Stud was right up there with Woodburn and Elmendorf."

Maripat had met Bob Albright last summer. In his last year at Harvard, he planned to work in his father's bank after graduation. Libby called Bob a "miracle baby." His father, Travis, was fifty-three and mother, Helen, forty-one when he was born.

Shortly after inheriting the famous farm in 1903, Travis Albright dispersed the breeding stock and racing stable. Never interested in raising horses and foreseeing the closure of racetracks that would sweep the nation, he used the proceeds to open a bank in Lexington. After Bob was born, Albright closed the big Georgian-style family home and moved into town.

Travis Albright wasn't the only Kentucky horseman to shut down his operation before and during the Great Depression. While Travis wasn't interested in carrying on a family tradition, most were forced to do so for economic reasons. Many, like Libby, cut back and waited for better times to come along.

It took a lot of hard work and doing without, but Libby's tenacity paid off. As tracks began to reopen, the increased demand for yearlings brought higher prices. She used the extra money to hire a half-dozen farm workers, buy more broodmares and restore Elkhorn Farm to its previous glory.

The white-columned mansion, barns and miles of fencing sparkled under new coats of white paint. Most exciting for Maripat was the restoration of the quarter-mile oval track behind the barns.

While the track's perimeter fence was repaired and painted, the ground was scraped and re-surfaced.

Five colts and three fillies had already been selected for training. Shawn would begin conditioning those yearlings in September. After being broken to the bridle and saddle, they would be walked, jogged, galloped, then "breezed" (pacing a horse as if in a race) over a period of months. If everything went as planned, the Elkhorn racing stable would be back in business.

18

Activity was at a fever pitch on Bluegrass farms and at railroad sidings as horses were shipped to Saratoga Springs for the races and summer yearling sale. The annual trek to upstate New York for a month of "August Madness" had been a ritual for Kentucky horsemen since the end of the Civil War.

"We'll have so much fun," Libby said to Maripat as they finished packing.

"I can't wait to see the races!" Maripat said. "Especially when Devil's Fire runs."

"I'll be overjoyed if he comes in second or third. He'll be running against the best two-year-olds in the country."

"He'll win—wait and see," Maripat said confidently.

Devil's Fire was a homebred—sired by Elkhorn Farm's prize

stallion, Black Satan, and out of a mare named Red Lady. A flashy chestnut colt, Devil's Fire had won his first race (breaking his maiden) at Churchill Downs in May and setting a track record at 5½ furlongs. His real trial would come in the Saratoga Special. If he made a good showing, he'd be entered in the Hopeful. It was the biggest early test for a two-year-old and one of the last scheduled races at the meet.

Like many August visitors to Saratoga Springs, Libby had leased a house for the month. She and Maripat arrived by train on July 27. After checking with Shawn who had preceded them with the racing string and sale yearlings, they toured the town.

"You think there are a lot of people here now," Libby said as they worked their way through the throngs on the elm-shaded sidewalk, "wait until the rest arrive. It'll be like the Fourth of July everyday!"

Standing in the big city park, Libby pointed at the casino. "My father watched a poker game there once that Harry Payne Whitney and his brother, Payne, were in. When some of the players ran out of cash, they bet their racing stock. They'd call a bet with a colt and raise it with a filly!"

"That's awful!" Maripat burst out. Gambling with money was one thing, but risking a horse was unthinkable!

A voice boomed behind them, "That was nothing compared to the stakes they played for in the private rooms upstairs!"

Startled, Maripat and Libby looked over their shoulders at a portly white-haired man. "Hello Libby—Maripat," he said. "You know my son, Bob."

Libby smiled at the tall slender blond young man. "Is your father telling you about his wasted past?"

Bob Albright laughed. "So far, all I've heard is what *other* people did."

Travis Albright nodded toward the casino. "Like what they did in those private gambling rooms. The smallest chips cost a hundred dollars, the largest a hundred thousand."

Maripat stared at the elegant mid-Victorian building. "If a man lost ten times in a row, he'd lose a million dollars!"

"Right! This town's seen some of the biggest spenders of all time. They used to compete to see who could wear the biggest diamond and the fanciest duds, shipped so many clothes they had to use special hogsheads called Saratoga trunks.

"The real characters are gone. I saw them all—Diamond Jim Brady, Coal Oil Johnny and 'Bet a Million' Gates. Johnny turned up one August with a Negro band following him playing 'Coal Oil Johnny Was His Name.'"

Maripat looked at Bob, who rolled his eyes toward his father and grinned. Fingers over her mouth, she stifled a giggle.

Travis waggled an eyebrow at Libby, then said to Bob, "Why don't you show Maripat around town? Libby and I will rest on that bench and wait for your mother. Let's meet at the Grand Union Hotel at noon for lunch."

19

Dawn was breaking as Maripat and Shawn leaned on the grandstand rail and watched the mob of horses walking, trotting and galloping around the track. "The Devil's going into the turn," Shawn said. Thumbs poised over their stopwatches, they clicked them on as the big colt reached the 3/8 pole.

The exercise rider sat down and leaned over the horse's neck. Head pumping up and down, the big chestnut streaked past the 5/16 pole. "Got him at eleven and four on that first furlong," Shawn said as Devil's Fire left the quarter pole and entered the final turn. "A little fast, but Joe's getting him under control."

Maripat checked her watch as the red colt reached the eighth pole. Eleven and eight. The ideal would be even fractions of twelve seconds for each of the three eighth-mile furlongs.

"Not bad, not bad at all," Shawn said as the colt swept past the grandstand and approached the finish line.

"Thirty-five and change," Maripat cried, clapping her hands as Devil's Fire streaked under the finish wire and the exercise rider stood in the irons, slowing the colt down.

Shawn grinned and squeezed her arm. "Pretty good looking horse we've got there."

Maripat sighed as Devil's Fire galloped around the clubhouse turn. "Hope he still looks this good next week."

The big day came, and the crowd was going wild, but it wasn't for Devil's Fire. The eastern favorite, Jim Robby, had just taken the lead in the Saratoga Special.

As the horses neared the far turn, Maripat hopped up and down for a better look. Frustrated, she stood on a chair, one hand on top of her wide green hat, the other on Bob Albright's shoulder.

Binoculars pressed to his eyes, Shawn said to Libby, "He's trapped; Billy's taking him wide."

Entering the homestretch, Jim Robby led by a length on the rail with Devil's Fire in sixth place on the outside. Bob let out a rebel yell. "There he goes!"

Thundering down the stretch, the big chestnut ate up the ground, passing horse after horse. The noise from the grandstand was deafening as the race turned into a two-horse duel. Maripat pounded Bob's shoulder as she urged Devil's Fire on.

Passing the 16th pole and heading for the finish wire, Jim Robby and Devil's Fire were neck and neck. Then Jim Robby edged ahead, only a few inches but enough to win by a nose.

"Drat!" Libby exploded.

"Nothing to get upset about," Shawn said. "He almost beat the best of the juvenile crop."

Maripat added, "The Devil will show Jim Robby what-for in the Hopeful!"

Bob grinned up at Maripat who was still standing on the chair. "Remind me to stay away from you next time. My shoulder's going to be black and blue by morning."

20

Although racing purses had shrunk drastically at Saratoga during the depression years, the wealthy still arrived each August to participate in the festivities, bet on horses and purchase some of the nation's finest yearlings.

The Saratoga and Belmont Park racetracks had been supported and built by financiers like William Collins Whitney, August Belmont, John Sanford, William R. Travers, Leonard Jerome, James R. Keene and Pierre Lorillard, who once said that "only men of wealth" should be allowed to gamble at tracks and then they should race "for each other's money." The public was "welcome to attend but only to watch."

Time, however, proved that without the income from pari-mutuel betting by the "common man," no racing program could be successful.

But maintaining a racing stable required huge outlays of cash. In this respect, Thoroughbred racing remained the "Sport of Kings."

For Libby to have a two-year-old in the Hopeful was not a matter of riches but a miracle of breeding. Devil's Fire's sire, Black Satan, had come to the breeding shed with a splendid pedigree but no track record. The financial losses at Elkhorn Farm had ended any racing hopes for the promising colt—unless Libby sold him, which she refused to do.

Because he had been sired by Sir Galahad III, Black Satan's offspring brought better than average prices, but none proved to be superior runners—until a homebred filly, Red Lady, was mated to the dark brown stallion. Devil's Fire was special.

By the time the parade to the post for the Hopeful began, Maripat thought she would burst. While last-minute bets were placed with bookmakers perched atop their three-foot-high stools, excitement built in the packed grandstand. The race might provide a look at next year's Kentucky Derby winner.

As the twelve-horse field approached the gate on the backside of the track, Maripat got on a chair between Bob and his father and peered through her binoculars. "Jim Robby's feeling his oats."

Adjusting his binoculars, Bob watched the bay horse dance sideways and pull at the reins held by the pony rider. Jim Robby was the favorite, going off at eight to five.

A cheer went up as the track announcer called, "The horses are at the gate."

Devil's Fire was in the fifth slot, Jim Robby, third, and Camera-man, Hollywood talent agent Myron Selznick's entry and the number two betting favorite, sixth. Cameraman was the only Western entry in the 6½ furlong race.

Wearing the red and white checked silks of Elkhorn Farm, Billy Thomas, Devil's Fire's jockey, settled in the saddle.

Moments after the last horse was loaded, the bell rang and the doors flew open. In a flurry of color and flying dirt, the horses burst out on the track.

Irish Eyes broke fast and took the lead, Make Believe a half-length back with Cameraman third on the rail. Passing the 5 furlong pole, Jim Robby was fourth, Devil's Fire fifth.

"He's dropping back!" Maripat screamed as the horses reached the middle of the backstretch.

"Don't get in a tizzy," Shawn said, eyes glued to his binoculars. "Billy knows what he's doing."

Bourbon Delight briefly held the lead at the half-mile pole, then relinquished it to Irish Eyes. Devil's Fire was the trailer, ten lengths off the pace.

Like he'd done in the Saratoga Special, Jim Robby took the lead on the far turn. The field began to close up, with Speedy Bob gaining on the leader.

"He's moving up!" Shawn pointed gleefully at the red and white colors of Elkhorn Farm weaving through the packed field.

"Go! Go!" Libby yelled. As if in answer, the big red colt passed Irish eyes, then Speedy Bob.

"He's lookin' and cookin' now!" Shawn whooped.

Lookathimgo fought with Jim Robby for the lead as they approached the final turn. The giant crowd was on its feet, urging the horses on as they reached the top of the stretch.

"Come on, come on!" Maripat called as Devil's Fire gained on the two leaders. "You can do it!"

The roar from the grandstand crashed down on the three horses as they passed the eighth pole. Jim Robby was still first, but only by a half-length.

Helen Albright jumped up and down and waved her hat as the horses thundered down the homestretch.

Devil's Fire put on a burst of speed, passing Watch Him Go and Jim Robby and taking the lead. Maripat knocked her big hat askew and almost fell off the chair

Lunging toward the finish line, Devil's Fire opened his lead to one length, then two. Jim Robby's jockey was whipping his colt right and left but to no avail. Devil's Fire was going away as he flashed under the wire, the winner by three lengths.

Maripat hugged Libby, then Shawn. "What about me?" Bob said.

She hugged him, too.

"Let's get a move on," Shawn said. "The Devil will get to the winner's circle before we do."

The next morning, Maripat and Libby visited Devil's Fire on the backside. Just returned from a walk, he was washed and groomed and very interested in Maripat's straw hat.

"Hey, cut that out!" she cried as the big chestnut nipped at the green bow on the crown. Offering an equine version of a smirk, Devil's Fire stretched his neck and seized the wide brim in his teeth. As Maripat jumped back, he lifted the hat high, then bobbed his head up and down, fanning her flushed face.

"You—you *crook*!" she sputtered, grabbing at the hat.

Turning his head to one side, Devil's Fire rolled a big blue-black eye downward and studied the diminutive redhead. Nodding as if reaching a decision, he dropped the hat at her feet, laid his chin on her shoulder and blew wetly into her ear.

"He's happy to see you," Libby said.

"I wish he'd find another way of showing it," Maripat grimaced, rubbing the heel of her hand over her damp ear and hair. She rubbed the colt's velvety nose. "I was just kidding."

Libby picked the hat up and fingered the teeth marks on the brim. "Looks like you'll need a new one."

Maripat patted the colt's thick neck. "Guess the Devil thinks with all the money he earned, he can mess it up."

"He's got a point," Libby laughed. "Nineteen thousand will buy a lot of hats."

21

Just days after Devil's Fire won the Hopeful at Saratoga and established himself as the best two-year-old colt in America, Europe erupted in flames. Following Neville Chamberlain's declaration of war on Germany on September 3, 1939, the British Bloodstock Agency shipped nearly six hundred Thoroughbreds out of Great Britain. The United States received the largest number, with India close behind. Australia, South Africa, the Malay States and South America also benefited from the mass exodus.

Deeply concerned over what the future might hold and anxious to conclude something she had been planning for months, Libby contacted a Louisville detective agency. Five weeks later, they submitted a report. She talked to Maripat that night. They had finished dinner and were sitting in the drawing room in front of a crackling fire.

"Next Thursday will be exactly two and a half years since you came here, Maripat," Libby said.

Eyes shining, Maripat squeezed Libby's hand. "I know. That's one day I'll never forget!"

"You were such a little ragamuffin!" Libby smiled. "And the way you hit that boy in the nose! I just loved it!"

"I was so scared when that cop grabbed my arm and started to drag me away! I was getting ready to kick him and take off when you drove up."

"I'm glad you waited."

"Me, too. It's been so wonderful being with you, Libby. I can never thank you enough for all you've done."

"Having you here is the best thanks you can give." A pause. "We need to talk about something. It's your father."

Maripat's eyes grew large, and she straightened on the couch beside Libby. "What about him?"

"I had a detective agency try to find him. They called me today. Your father was killed when a wagon rolled in a ditch. It happened last March."

Maripat blinked and clasped her hands. "I know I should feel sad, but I don't. I've often thought that if he hadn't done those things to me, Cawood wouldn't have taken me away when he did. If we'd gone later, we wouldn't have run into those hoboes, and he'd be alive today. What about my brothers and sister?"

"Your father married that woman—"

"Mabel?"

"Right. They were living near Lebanon, Tennessee, when he was killed. She moved away last summer. I asked the detective to keep looking." Libby touched Maripat's arm. "There was a reason why I was searching for your father."

"Oh?"

"I wanted to ask him—pay him if necessary—to let me adopt you. You're already like a daughter to me. I want to make it legal. If that's what you want, of course."

Maripat sat very still, repeating Libby's words over and over in her head. *I want to make it legal.* Smiling through happy tears, she threw herself into Libby's arms. "Yes! Oh, yes!"

Two months later, the papers were completed and filed with the court. Maripat Tanner was now Maripat McKay.

22

In February, Devil's Fire ran his first race as a three-year-old, winning the Fountain of Youth by four lengths. When he won the Florida Derby by another impressive margin, he was clearly the early favorite for the Kentucky Derby on May 4. Then disaster struck in early April. Entering the far turn and gaining on the leaders in the Flamingo Stakes, the chestnut colt suddenly broke stride, nearly unseating his jockey. By the time the last horse had passed and the rider had dismounted, Devil's Fire was limping badly. He was taken off the track in an ambulance and diagnosed with a badly torn digital tendon in the front right leg. The prognosis was announced two days later. He would never race again.

The Thoroughbred's bones are fine, legs as fragile as glass, the demand prodigious. Running full out, gravity increases the animal's weight to almost a ton, crashing every tenth of a second down on one foot. Injuries are common, forcing runners to miss races, a season, a promising career. For some, the worst possible scenario—humane destruction.

"In time he'll walk and run around like nothing happened," Shawn said to Maripat and Libby as they watched Devil's Fire limp around his stall. "He just can't take the stress of training and running on a hard track."

"He looked so good for the Derby," Maripat mourned.

"He's already looking good for the breeding shed," Libby said. "I got three calls today from breeders wanting to reserve matings. We could keep them mostly to ourselves like Sam Riddle's doing with Man o' War. No telling what Man o' War could produce if he covered a wider selection."

Spring came to the Bluegrass and wanting to introduce her new daughter and celebrate Derby week with friends, Libby planned a party in early May.

Partially closed for years, the huge house was cleaned, woodwork varnished and painted. New curtains, drapes and carpets were installed and the floor of the ballroom refinished. With the two-story center section and both lower wings open, the mansion contained ten bedrooms, six bathrooms, two drawing rooms, a dining room that would seat forty, a parlor, library, country kitchen and the ninety-foot ballroom with three giant crystal chandeliers. Already swamped with work on the farm, Libby hired two maids and a full-time cook. They lived in the east wing.

Inspired by the transformation and a bottle of champagne, Libby and Maripat named the sprawling white-columned mansion Windsong Manor. The doors were thrown open for the big party on Wednesday, May 1, three days before the Derby.

"Cuttin' in!" John Kershaw yelled, grabbing Maripat and whirling her away without missing a beat. The band had just switched from "Deep Purple" to a Benny Goodman favorite— "Sing, Sing, Sing"— and the adults had surrendered the floor to the younger set.

"Hi, John!" Maripat smiled, red hair flying as they jumped and jived to the swing tune. "Where you been?"

"Hanging on the old feed bag. You guys lay on a mean table!"

"Did you leave anything for the starving multitude?"

Long arms and legs going in all directions, John retrieved a hand to pat his stomach. "After all this exercise, I'll have to go back for more." He looked around. "Uh, oh, here comes short, blond and ordinary."

"He's at least six feet," Maripat said, waving at Bob Albright as he crossed the crowded floor. "Just because you look like Ichabod Crane doesn't mean everybody else is *short*."

"Like you," John grinned.

"Five-two, mister. And don't you forget it!"

"Yes, Ma'am! Greetings, Mr. Albright. She's all yours." Moving his lanky body to the frantic beat, John headed toward the dining room, grabbing startled girls and swinging them away from their equally startled partners as he passed.

Maripat gave Bob a tour of Windsong Manor. "I thought our place next door was big, but it doesn't hold a candle to this!" he said as they crossed the foyer and entered the west wing.

Maripat opened a door. "This is the library. Libby has one of the finest equine collections in the world."

Bob stared at the rows of books that covered two walls and reached to the ten-foot ceiling. "Those are all horse books?"

"No. There are the classics, right next to those encyclopedias and history books. Modern fiction, too. Libby and I read a lot."

Hands clasped behind his back, Bob studied a row of books. "Sometimes you scare me, Maripat."

Green eyes rounded. "Me?"

Bob turned. "Yes—you. You've got more smarts between those cute little ears than anyone I know."

"Is that bad?"

"A little frightening, but I like it. How about me taking you to dinner at the Idle Hour Country Club?"

"It sounds neat, but aren't you a little old for me?"

"Is that what you think?"

"Noooooo. Just thought I should mention it."

"Friday night?"

"Terrific! Should I bring Libby?"

"You're not *that* young! I promise to be good."

A wide grin. "And spoil the evening?"

23

The war in Europe brought an unexpected bonanza to Kentucky in the fall of 1940. The Aga Khan—who had sold Blenheim II to Arthur Hancock Sr. in 1936—escaped the Nazis in France and arrived in Switzerland short on cash. Choosing between disbanding his Irish stud farms or selling the famous English Derby Winner, Mahmoud, and British Triple Crown champion, Bahram, he sold the horses to American interests for a third of their value.

Another famous stallion, Princequillo—a descendant of the great St. Simon—arrived in America from Ireland. In five years, four of the world's finest stallions were exported to the United States. The quality of European bloodstock suffered accordingly...a fact borne out graphically in the spring of 1941 when Whirlaway, a son of Blenheim II, became the fifth American Triple Crown winner and launched the white and devil's red of Calumet Farm as the dominant racing colors of the decade.

The first Triple Crown winner—Sir Barton in 1919—didn't receive his "crown" until 1930 when "Triple Crown" was popularized in racing stories describing Gallant Fox's successful pursuit of the Kentucky Derby, Preakness and Belmont Stakes. Five years later, Omaha, a son of Gallant Fox, became the first Triple Crown winner to be sired by another. Two years after Omaha's sweep of the three classic races, Man o' War's most famous offspring, War Admiral, joined the illustrious trio in a "clean sweep" year when he won all eight of his races. By then, Triple Crown was firmly established in the lexicon of Thoroughbred horse racing.

Maripat's arrival in Lexington had coincided with War Admiral's first Triple Crown race. Now, four years later, she was enrolled at the University of Kentucky. She often thought about that first Saturday in May when War Admiral won the Kentucky Derby, and she had slept under a tree on the UK campus.

John Kershaw was attending Rutgers University in New Jersey, and they kept in touch by mail. Most of his letters were full of funny anecdotes and silly cartoons. Now and then he injected a serious note about Hitler's growing dominance in Europe. France had surrendered the previous June, and that fall all American men between twenty-one and thirty-five were required to register for the draft. Of the over sixteen million who complied on October 16, 1940, thousands were drafted thirteen days later.

Bob Albright hadn't been drafted yet, but Maripat knew it could happen anytime. She worried about her men. If America was drawn into the war, the age limit would drop to include John. She expressed her concerns one night as Bob drove her home.

Bob said. "Forget all that talk about 'America First' and the isolationists who want peace at any price. I'm joining up. I can go in as an officer. I was going to tell you tonight."

Maripat's breath caught. "Have you told your folks?"

"No. They're both old; it's going to hit them hard."

"You can't wait?"

Bob shook his head. "I'm twenty-three with a college degree. The army is hurting for officers. One of my classmates enlisted six months ago. He's smoothing my way in."

Maripat looked down at her hands. "I'm going to miss you."

"Same here. That's the toughest part—leaving you."

Eyes glistening, Maripat said, "I'll be here waiting."

Bob drew her close. "I hoped you'd say that."

He enlisted the following morning. Two months later, the Japanese bombed Pearl Harbor.

24

April 23, 1942

Dear Bob:

Everything is just fine here on the farm. Between UK and helping out with the horses, I have been busier than a tick on a dog's back!

...and isn't that something about them putting Jap civilians in horse stalls at Santa Anita? Sounds like there won't be much racing out west, with Santa Anita closed and North American Aviation taking over Hollywood Park. They are going to have the Saratoga meet this August, but if the war doesn't end soon, they will hold next year's races at Belmont Park.

We will run our horses at Keeneland and Churchill Downs this spring and fall but not much else until we know what is going to happen. With the restrictions on rail shipping, it might be best to spend our time on breeding...

John visited just before he was sent with his Marine unit to the West Coast. He said to tell you hello.

I think about you so much and hope I can see you before they ship you out. Can you let me know ahead of time? I'd like to fix something special just to prove I can cook!

"Write soon, and, yes, I promise to be good.

Yours,

Maripat.

June 8, 1942

Dear Maripat:

Greetings from the biggest lake in the world! It's called the Pacific, and I hope after the war I never see it again! Us Marines are supposed to be tough, but that sure doesn't apply to our stomachs. I've spent more time hanging over the ship's rail than we used to spend hanging out at the White Tavern. Just thinking about those hamburgers makes me drool (when I'm not hangin' over the rail)!

...picture you sent gets more whistles than Hedy Lamarr's! I inform one and all that you are pining away until I return.

They are going to pick up the mail in a few minutes, so I better finish this up. Write soon, and don't believe everything that Bob character tells you! He may be a lieutenant, but he's still a banker and a HARVARD graduate. A sorry combination if there ever was one!

Keep them cards and letters comin'!

Your TALL friend,
John.

November 21, 1942

Dearest Maripat:

Hi from "over there." It seems like a year since I saw you, but it's only been four months, three days and sixteen hours (and eleven seconds)! Remember how you yelled when we rode the roller coaster at Joyland Park? We'll do it again when I get back.

...and you made the dean's list again! Didn't I say you have lots of brains between those pretty pink ears? You are probably prouder about winning that tri-state jumping contest. I never though I'd be jealous of a horse, but it is hard knowing how much time you spend with Iron Man!

That's really sweet of you to drop in and see Mom and Dad. They appreciate it so much. Dad turned seventy-seven last month. I hope this war is over before he has another birthday...

Last night I was lying on my cot and imagining you walking across the campus at UK—wearing a green sweater to match your eyes and your pageboy haircut bouncing on your shoulders. White knee socks, too! Am I close? Send a picture with your new haircut.

They'll be having mail call pretty soon. If I'm lucky, I'll get a letter from you. Maybe two or three! Sometimes they come in bunches.

Love,
Bob.

25

Christmas, 1942, was a subdued affair at Elkhorn Farm. American and British forces with a small contingent of Free French were battling the Germans in North Africa. Leningrad and Stalingrad were under siege. In the Pacific, the Japanese Navy had recently suffered a major defeat trying to reinforce the battle for Guadalcanal.

Maripat had no idea where Bob and John were, although she suspected that Bob, now a captain, was in North Africa and John on one of the many islands with unpronounceable names that were referred to daily in newspapers and on the radio.

With three of the farmhands in the army, Christmas Day began with Maripat and Libby helping Shawn and the remaining men feed and clean stalls. After a breakfast for everyone in Windsong Manor's huge country kitchen, Maripat and Libby prepared Christmas dinner for Shawn and Travis and Helen Albright.

They were enjoying after-dinner drinks in the drawing room when Travis said, "I've had an excellent offer for the bank. If Bob agrees, the deal should close before spring. I posted a detailed letter to him last week."

"Won't that come as a shock?" Libby asked.

"Not at all," Travis said. "We've been corresponding back and forth about it since last summer. Discussed it when he came through last spring."

Maripat spoke up, "He mentioned something about it to me just before he left. I haven't heard anything since."

"Shows he can still keep some secrets," Travis chuckled. "There wasn't much to talk about until lately anyway. The negotiations have been going on for months."

Maripat clasped her hands in her lap. "Well, I never…"

Shawn grinned at her as he tossed a log on the fire. "Bet that gets your goat, not knowing everything that goes on."

She shot him a disgusted look.

"Don't feel bad, Dear," Helen Albright said. "Bob will write you as soon as he gets his father's letter."

Libby said, "Isn't Bob interested in running the bank?"

"If the war hadn't come along, it probably would have worked out," Travis said. "I'm not getting any younger, and the war looks like it might drag on for years. The offer is a very good one. Bob will have enough to buy into another bank if that's what he wants."

26

February 1, 1943

Hi Gorgeous!

We left Guadalcanal three days ago (now that it's over, I can say where I've been the last six months). I've never been so glad to leave a place in my whole life! And I thought life was tough in Mr. Gaylord's biology class!

…suppose it was a nice place before the war. The Lever Brothers soap company had coconut plantations along the beaches, and mountains grow right up out of the jungle. They call it a tropical forest, but it looked like a jungle to me. Sounded like a zoo, especially at night!

We had a lot of combat casualties, but a hell of a lot more from disease, mostly malaria. When they started handing out Atabrine pills to stop the malaria, the scuttlebutt was that they made you impotent (it's in the dictionary under "I"). A lot of guys wouldn't take the pills, so they made us take them every day in the chow line. A corpsman would stick it on your tongue, then look down your throat to make sure you swallowed it. It turned your skin yellow. Better limp and yellow than chattering your teeth off is all I can say!

...Were those your relatives who got caught with that 1,500 gallon moonshine still in the Cumberland Forest? If so, let's hook up with them after the war. I like people who think BIG!

I'm busy touring the islands hoping for my first sight of those girls in itty bitty grass skirts! Wonder if any of them have red hair?

Write soon,
John.

The Office of Defense Transportation banned the use of railroad transportation to the 1943 Kentucky Derby and with rubber for cars rationed, no out-of-state tickets were sold. Thousands rode the first "Street Car Derby" to reach Churchill Downs and watch Count Fleet win. He went on to triumph in the Preakness and Belmont Stakes and become the sixth Triple Crown winner.

Because it was rated by the government as a "suburban" track— meaning it could only be reached by car—racing at Keeneland ended with the fall, 1942, meeting. The restrictions on rail and automobile traffic brought about a huge bonus for the Keeneland Association, however. Because Kentucky yearlings couldn't be shipped to Saratoga, they were sold for the first time at Keeneland on August 9-11, 1943. The auction was conducted by Fasig-Tipton and held under a huge tent in the paddock area.

"Kentucky horsemen won't be selling their horses in Saratoga after what happened here," Libby said as Maripat drove their van onto Versailles Pike.

Maripat kept shooting worried glances at her mother. They were leaving early because Libby had suffered a dizzy spell.

"Stop looking at me like that!" Libby said sharply. She smiled and patted Maripat's knee. "The heat just got to me for a minute."

"It wasn't hot in May when you blacked out in the barn."

"It's just some kind of bug; you know how they hang on. Let's talk about something pleasant—like the three thousand average price...triple what Saratoga got last year! It never made sense to ship our horses from here to Saratoga, then have the majority of new owners bring them right back to Kentucky."

"Leslie Combs was sure wheeling and dealing," Maripat said.

"Wasn't he though! He sure has Elizabeth Arden's ear. She thinks he's the cat's meow when it comes to buying horses."

"Louis Mayer, too," Maripat said. "Combs strikes me more as a salesman than anything else. He started Spendthrift Farm six years ago, and he's already got better connections than people who've been here all their lives."

Libby rested her head back. "The buyers are still out there. That's what matters. Now all we need is for this terrible war to end."

27

June 21, 1944

My Darling Maripat:

I'm so sorry to learn about Libby's illness. She always struck me as so vital! Just being around her made me want to go out and tackle the impossible! I know how much you love her. Cancer is such a terrible disease...

You know now about the great Allied invasion of northern France. I don't see how Germany can hold out much longer. The Japs either. Now that our B-29's are bombing their cities, they can't keep telling their people they're winning the war.

...and that brings me to something very important. It doesn't seem like the time with Libby sick and all, but I can't wait another year or more to ask. Will you marry me, Maripat? I can't imagine spending my life with anyone else. And don't give me that baloney about you being younger. You're wise far beyond your years— mine, too!

I've been thinking a lot about what I'll do after the war. Would it surprise you that I might become a gentleman farmer? Horse farmer, that is! I don't know much about horses, but I know someone who does. Do you think I'm too old to learn? I'll have enough money to fix Albright Stud up. What do you think?

...so I better sign off. Give Libby my love. I'll be sitting on pins and needles waiting for your answer.

I love you,
Bob

August 4, 1944
Dear Snookums:

Here I am, basking on a sunny beach in Hawaii. Beautiful nurses, tall drinks and nubile maidens with things called leis hanging around their necks (big flower necklaces that hang over their mammary glands).

I picked up a little nick on my backside on Saipan, so rather than give me a medal, they decided to let me recuperate on this lovely island paradise. Beats a medal any day! I'm soaking up all the local culture I can before they send me back.

...then I got your letter about Libby after I started this. I know how torn up you must be. I'm going to wax poetic—just seeing you two together makes people smile. With all the terrible things I've seen the last two years, you guys have proved there's still something good in the world...

It's hard to believe this will be your last year at UK. How time do fly! You may be better educated, but I'm twenty-three days older!

Tell Bob hi next time you write. A major yet! I hope we don't meet while we're still in uniform. I hate to salute Harvard graduates!

Be seein' you soon,
John.

September 9, 1944
Dear Bob:

Maripat will blow a gasket when she hears I've written you, but it can't be helped. I've always admired her common sense until now. Forget what she said in that last letter. It doesn't mean diddley!

Of course, she'll marry you. It's all she talks about. Need I say I approve? I couldn't ask for a better man for my daughter! You work on your end, and I'll work on mine. She will come around to our way of thinking in no time.

She told me what you would like to do with Albright Stud. It's a wonderful idea. When I'm gone (one has to be practical at this point), why not combine the two farms under the Albright name? It's older than Elkhorn farm by nearly a hundred years! Let's compromise. Keep my red and white checked colors. How does that sound? I can't talk to Maripat this bluntly right now, but I will have to soon.

Don't give up. Maripat's worth fighting for. She is just suffering at the moment from a misguided sense of duty.

Love,
Libby

28

Standing between Travis and Helen Albright on the crowded platform at Lexington's Union Station, Maripat rose on her toes and looked down the maze of tracks.

Helen gripped her arm and smiled. "You won't have any energy left when he gets here."

Maripat grinned and returned her attention to the tracks. Bob had wired last week saying that he would arrive on the noon train. Germany had surrendered five months ago and Japan last month. It was October, and Bluegrass trees displayed the beautiful colors of autumn.

"Train's comin'!" The cry echoed up and down Water Street, relayed by dozens of excited voices. The ground began to shake, and the steel rails hummed. As the giant black locomotive rumbled into the station, Maripat thought her heart would burst from her chest. She hadn't seen Bob in three years.

"Goodness!" Helen cried. "He looks so much older!"

Maripat glanced in the direction of Helen's pointing finger. Bob was descending the stairs, carrying a large leather satchel and scanning the crowd. He was in full uniform and wearing the silver oak leaves of a Lieutenant Colonel.

"Here! Here!" Maripat yelled, red hair flying as she hopped up and down.

Bob grinned and pushed his way through the crowd. Maripat stepped aside at the last moment and let him greet his parents first. Travis was beginning to show his eighty years, and tears glinted behind his glasses as he clasped his son's hand. Helen stepped into Bob's arms and wept.

"Let's give the young people a chance," Travis said gently.

"Of course!" Helen said, wiping her eyes with a tissue. She smiled up at her son. "Maripat's been fit to be tied all morning. I don't think she's eaten since yesterday."

Time seemed to stand still for a moment, then Maripat ran into Bob's arms. "Ata boy, soldier!" a man yelled as they kissed long and hard, Maripat's arms around Bob's neck, feet dangling in the air. Whistles and shouts of encouragement followed. It was a common sight—couples meeting after years of separation—but the people couldn't get enough.

Maripat and Bob sat beside Libby's bed. He was appalled at the change in this once vibrant woman. Her mind was still sharp, but her body had wasted away until she weighed less than eighty pounds. Nurses tended her around the clock.

"Let's not have any long faces," Libby said. She patted Bob's hand. "I'm glad we got together and ganged up on Maripat. She can be stubborn as a mule sometimes."

"Maybe she was just playing hard to get," Bob said.

"Says you!" Maripat protested. She sat on the opposite side of the bed, holding Libby's other hand.

"I'm just glad you're together now," Libby said. She looked at Maripat. "When will John get home?"

"He hopes next month."

Libby gazed out the window. "December seems such a cold time of year for a wedding. It's so lovely here in the spring."

Maripat's said, "We think December is perfect." They all knew Libby had little chance of living much past the end of the year.

29

Saturday, December 1st, arrived, and Maripat and Bob were married in the Windsong Manor ballroom. Nearly four hundred family members and friends attended, and Libby watched from a bed near where the couple exchanged vows. Towering over the wedding party, John Kershaw acted as best man. He had promised Maripat and Libby that he wouldn't pull any pranks—during the ceremony.

Looking lovely in a flowing white gown and with her bright red hair tied with a white ribbon, Maripat led her husband to Libby's side before they walked up the aisle. The guests murmured approval as the young couple kissed Libby's cheeks and extended their love.

The reception lasted late into the night. Because of Libby's rapidly deteriorating condition, Maripat and Bob planned to spend their first two nights together at Lexington's Lafayette hotel. They would return to Windsong Manor on Monday.

They let John and his cronies decorate the Packard parked in the big circular driveway, then sneaked out a back door to the Chevrolet sedan Bob had hidden in one of the barns. Everything went fine until Bob tried to start the engine. A potato was wedged into the tailpipe and a string of cans tied to the rear bumper. When they were discarded and the car began to move, a cherry bomb went off under the hood. Laughing hysterically, the newlyweds took a back way out and headed to Lexington.

It was well past midnight when they finally snuggled under the covers. "Mmmm, you feel good," Maripat said.

"Do you know how many times I've dreamed about this moment?" Bob murmured as he nibbled on her ear.

"Three?

"Idiot! Hundreds—no, thousands!"

"Now that it's real, what do you think?"

"I think you have the most surprising body in the universe. Everything's so *compact*! Like here, and here."

Maripat giggled. "That tickles!"

"Quiet, Woman. It's supposed to be exciting."

"Now that you mention it, there is a little sensation when you touch me down there."

"How about here?"

"Oh, yes!"

Kisses became more heated, movements more anxious. Maripat slipped her silk nightgown over her head while Bob tossed his pajamas on the floor.

Touching, exploring, sharing a love that has survived lonely years, they came together in the middle of the big bed.

Murmured endearments. Cries of passion. Exhausted whispers. Locked in each other's arms, they went to sleep.

PART II

1955-1975

"I would rather win the Kentucky Derby than any other race in America because when you walk in a bar and tell someone you're a trainer, they go, 'You ever win the Derby?'"

John Veitch

1

Standing on the back porch of Windsong Manor, Maripat watched Shawn settle her youngest son on the western saddle. "Let her rip!" three-year-old Cay cried gleefully, yanking on the reins and coaxing the fat pony forward. The bright sun accentuated the soft red highlights in his blond hair as he looked across the sloping lawn. "Look at me, Mommy! Shawn doesn't have to use the rope anymore. I'm doing it all by myself!"

"You sure are!" Maripat grinned. "Don't run Tubby into that oak. Daddy won't be happy if you hurt his favorite tree."

"You're funnin' me," Cay laughed. "Tubby can't hurt no old tree." Flailing his short legs, he kicked the pony into a semblance of a gallop.

A trail of dust appeared in the distance. An hour ago, Bob had driven north toward Elkhorn Creek. Shading her eyes, Maripat watched a Ford pickup turn toward the barns. By the way it wobbled and over-corrected, she knew their other son, Travis, was driving. Recently turned eight, he could steer, but his legs were too short to reach the clutch, brake and gas pedals. Bob had been talking about strapping wood blocks to the pedals to remedy that.

Nine years had passed since Bob came home from the war. Nine full years that had brought both joy and sadness. The saddest moment had come three weeks after the wedding. Libby's death was expected, but it had left a great void in Maripat's life.

Travis was born in early March, 1947. Then after two miscarriages that nearly destroyed Maripat's hopes for another child, Cawood arrived on the first Saturday in May, beating Kentucky Derby winner, Hail Gail, to the finish wire by nineteen minutes. Maripat called Cawood her "Derby Boy" and nicknamed him Cay.

Travis Albright died two years after his namesake was born. Helen lived until the summer of 1952, long enough to hold the newborn Cay in her arms and revise the large trust she and her husband had set up for Travis. Adding another five hundred thousand, she split the money equally between the boys. The money would be held in trust until each turned twenty-one.

Shortly after Libby's death, Elkhorn Farm was integrated into Albright Stud. Totaling two thousand acres, the farm had become one of the leading nursery studs and racing stables in Kentucky. This was due in no small part to the outstanding success of Devil's Fire's offspring on the track.

Fifty years earlier, John Madden—the great trainer and breeder known universally as the "Wizard of the Turf" and owner of Lexington's famed Hamburg Place—said, "A stallion is seventy-five percent of a stud farm."

This was graphically illustrated shortly before and after the Civil War when Lexington stood at Robert Aitcheson Alexander's Woodburn Farm on Old Frankfurt Pike. For fourteen consecutive years and sixteen out of eighteen years, the "Blind Hero of Woodburn" was America's leading sire, producing such greats as Asteroid, Kentucky, Norfolk and Preakness.

Beginning in 1916, Hastings produced five Belmont Stakes winners in twelve years at August Belmont Jr.'s Nursery Stud north of Lexington. His most famous son was Fair Play, the sire of Man o' War.

In the Forties, Bull Lea established Calumet Farm as the

premier producer of champions, including Citation, the 1948 winner of the Triple Crown.

For eleven out of fourteen years, Devil's Fire ranked among the top ten sires in North America, leading the list three times. Two of his sons—one standing in the Bluegrass, the other in Maryland, were consistently producing winners.

The task of running Albright Stud was divided between Maripat, Bob, Shawn and a foreman, Ned Jenkins, who supervised the day-to-day farm operations. While Maripat handled horse sales and purchases and planned matings, Bob managed the office and financial affairs. Shawn conditioned the racing string.

Fourteen colts and seven fillies were slated to run next week at Keeneland's spring meeting. They would be shipped from there to Churchill Downs and the races that kicked off Derby Week.

2

Sitting astride Bob's shoulders, Cay watched the Kentucky Derby horses parade around the Churchill Downs walking ring. "Which one's Na-sa, Daddy?" he cried.

Bob pointed at a bay colt. "That one. And it's 'Nash-ooa', not 'Na-sa.'"

Cay drummed his boots against Bob's chest. "Will Na-sa win the Derby?"

Bob grabbed the flailing boots. "Yes, *Nash-ooa* will win, and I'm going to tan your hide if you don't stop kicking me."

Cay giggled and wrapped his arms around his father's forehead. "Mommy says my hide won't tan like yours or Travis's. That's 'cause I'm white like her."

Maripat looked at her two sons. Travis had inherited his paternal grandfather's darker coloring, dark hair and eyes and heavy frame. Cay had his mother's green eyes, but his hair was light blond with red highlights.

Taller than Travis had been at the same age, Cay showed signs of having Bob's slender build. Maripat grinned as Cay yelled and pulled at his father's hair. The boy had a mischievous streak that often tried Bob's patience. Bob was more comfortable with Travis, an intense, aggressive boy who was scholastically ahead of most children his age. He was also a natural athlete, extending his leadership qualities to the playing field.

Bob's voice brought her back to the present. "Here come the California cowboys."

Rex Ellsworth and "Mesh" Tenney walked out of the paddock beside their chestnut colt, Swaps. The men had received less than favorable attention all week from horsemen as well as the press. Even the more sympathetic western writers referred to Ellsworth's sagging v-mesh-wire-enclosed horse farm near Chino, California, as "the stockyard."

In a scene reminiscent of the old days when competitors would steal a racehorse's pet and throw the runner off stride by "getting its goat," Mesh Tenney slept in Swaps' stall during Derby Week to prevent possible shenanigans.

No one could deny that Swaps had potential. A son of Khaled— purchased by Ellsworth nine years earlier from the Aga Khan and imported to America from Ireland—Swaps had arrived in Kentucky with impressive wins in California's San Vicente Stakes and the Santa Anita Derby.

Swaps was the second betting favorite to Nashua who was sired by Nasrullah, another stallion purchased from the Aga Khan in the last decade. William "Billy" Woodward Jr.—son of one of the syndicate members headed by Arthur "Bull" Hancock, Jr. of Claiborne Farm that brought Nasrullah to Kentucky—was running Nashua in the Derby under the red polka-dot-on-white colors of Belair Stud.

Pandemonium broke loose in the clubhouse high above the grandstand as Swaps drew away from Nashua at the sixteenth pole. Stunned, Maripat and Bob watched Bill Shoemaker boot the chestnut colt under the wire, the first Kentucky Derby win for the young jockey. It was a shocking upset, almost as big as the Derby two years before when long-shot, Dark Star, nosed Alfred

Vanderbilt's Native Dancer out in the only defeat of the gray colt's brilliant career.

"Holy shit!" Travis exclaimed.

Maripat tapped his shoulder. "Watch your mouth, mister."

"Can't blame him," Bob moaned. "Can you believe it—a California bred beating Nashua?"

"Na-sa!" Cay yelled, stamping the narrow heels of his cowboy boots on the tabletop.

"That's tellin' him, pardner," Maripat laughed, swinging the bright-haired youngster up in her arms. "Let's get out of here before Daddy joins the rest of the mourners at the bar."

3

Albright Stud flourished in the post-war years that saw yearling prices double in 1945 alone. Averages continued to rise, reaching a milestone in July, 1961, at the Keeneland Selected Yearling Sale when a son of Swaps sold for a record $130,000, the first time a yearling was purchased for more than $100,000 in North America.

The Albright Stud racing string—though small compared to leading stables like Calumet, C.V. Whitney's and King Ranch—was making its mark on eastern tracks. But it had yet to fulfill Maripat's dream— producing a runner in the Kentucky Derby.

It was a dream shared by many. Of the approximately 12,000 registered Thoroughbreds foaled each year, over half never raced. Ninety percent that did lost money for their owners. The chances of winning the Derby were better than 3000 to 1.

Two years after their birth, the odds dropped as thousands of juveniles were culled while running on twenty-five tracks around the nation. The nomination deadline for the Derby was six weeks after the candidates reached three on the universal Thoroughbred birth date of January first. The fee was $100.

After twenty races in Florida, New York and California, the pick of the surviving nominees were shipped to Louisville. Of those that arrived at Churchill Downs, it was not unusual for some to be scratched for health or other reasons during Derby Week. Owners of the remaining horses had to pay $1,000 two days before the race to pass the entry box, another $1,000 to start.

The Derby field had been ponderous at times, twenty on several occasions, twenty-two in 1928. Although the track was capable of accommodating twenty-eight horses, there was talk about limiting the field to twenty, with preference going to the horses with the most earnings in important races.

The Derby wasn't on anyone's mind when the Albright family gathered in a horse stall on a cold March night in 1963. It was nearly midnight, and Bob was livid with anger.

"What the hell do you think you're doing?" he shouted at Cay who knelt in the straw beside a sick filly." You've already got a cold; you'll be lucky if you don't get pneumonia!"

"Milly's a lot sicker than me!" the eleven-year-old boy said. "If I don't take care of her, she might die by morning."

"You might, too! Ever think of that? The vet's done everything he can. Sam said he'll keep an eye on her." Sam was a groom who lived in an apartment over one of the barns.

"Every few hours, maybe not at all," Cay replied mulishly. "He watches TV and goes to sleep with the test pattern on."

Maripat hid a grin behind her gloved hand.

Travis looked down at the prostrate filly. "Dad's right, Cay. You ought to be in bed. She's insured, anyway."

"*Insured?*" Cay leaped to his feet and pointed an accusing finger. "Don't you ever think about anything but *money?* I want her to *live*, not die and get hauled off to some old glue factory!"

"Cay," Maripat said quietly.

Travis laid a hand on the boy's shoulder. "I didn't mean it that way. There's nothing more anybody can do."

Cay knelt beside the filly and rubbed her neck. "She needs to know I'm here."Eyes glistening, he looked up. "You understand, don't you, Mom?"

"Of course, Honey," Maripat said. "But you're sick, too."

Bob kicked a pile of straw and leaned against the wall. "Too sick to study but not too sick to come out here."

"Not now, Bob," Maripat said more sharply than she intended. It had been a running battle for years—trying to get Cay to show the same interest in school as he did in horses. It had often forced Maripat into a role she didn't want—playing mediator between Bob and their youngest son. Bob loved Cay, but he expected the boy to reach the same scholastic heights as his brother. That would have been difficult in any household. Travis had skipped a grade and was aiming for a scholarship from Harvard. Considering his grades and skill on the football field, acceptance was assured. He would graduate from high school next year.

"Let me stay with her a while longer—please!" Cay begged.

"Oh, hell, I'll wait with you," Travis said. "I'm ahead on my schoolwork, so I can stay home tomorrow and sleep in." He punched his brother's arm. "You're sick, so you can sleep in, too."

"Hey great!" A sheepish look. "About Travis staying."

"Yeah, we know what you mean," Bob said. "One hour, then you come in. Make sure he does, Travis."

"No problem, Dad. I'll carry the little jerk if I have to."

Putting an arm around Maripat, Bob led her out of the barn.

4

A clod of dirt barely missed Maripat's face. On her right, John Kershaw's horse cleared a stone fence with two feet to spare. The Walker hounds babbled in the distance. It was cold, damp and miserable. Maripat hadn't had so much fun since the last time she had ridden with the Iroquois Hunt Club.

An exuberant "Tallyho" drifted over the heavily wooded terrain. Kicking her gelding, Elmer, in the ribs, Maripat tore off in the direction of the call. She was joined by other exuberant members pursuing the hounds.

John's dark brown Thoroughbred burst out of the woods thirty yards ahead. Looking over his shoulder, he saw Maripat and pulled on the reins until they were running neck and neck. A big toothy grin flashed under his black velvet safety helmet. "That pesky fox is making a beeline for parts unknown! At the rate he's going, he'll make Cincinnati by nightfall!"

"No way!" Maripat shouted. "He's heading for Louisville!"

John's tall rawboned figure bent over his horse's neck as they leaped a fallen tree. Pounding around a corner and starting to cross a narrow road, they saw some hunt members pulled up at a country store. "About time!" John said as they reined their geldings in. "My stomach was thinking my throat was cut."

"You're *always* hungry," Maripat said. "You had a huge breakfast— and two hours later you're starving."

"Got a lot to feed," John laughed as he swung his 6'4" frame easily out of the English saddle. He adjusted the long red jacket over his white pants and flicked a spot of mud off the top of his knee-high black boots. "Come on, Little Bit. I heard your stomach growling when we cleared that last gully."

Shaking her head with amusement, Maripat led Elmer toward the group gathered outside the store. John's grandfather had joined the Iroquois Hunt when it was organized by Brigadier-General Roger D. Williams in 1880, and John had ridden with Maripat and Libby until he enlisted in the marines.

He had never married and didn't return to the Bluegrass permanently until six years ago. This after graduating from Rutgers and working five years for a Manhattan law firm…"to get city smarts," as he put it. He might have stayed longer if his father hadn't suffered a near-fatal stroke. Partially paralyzed, Stanton Kershaw was no longer able to manage White Oak Stud, the horse farm that had been in the family since before the Civil War.

Returning home, John hired a farm manager and set up practice in Lexington specializing in business and corporate law.

Small compared to the big horse farms, White Oak Stud had five hundred acres, twenty-five broodmares and three stallions. After his father died in 1959, John put two horses in training. He now had seven runners.

"Want to place a side bet on that nag of yours against our colt next Saturday?" Bob asked. John and Maripat had returned late that afternoon from the hunt, and they were eating dinner with the rest of the Albright family at Windsong Manor. Living just a few miles apart, John visited once or twice a week.

John's eyes gleamed. "How much?"

"Watch it, Bob," Maripat said from across the table. "He took us for five hundred the last time."

"That's because our horse threw a shoe," Cay piped up. "Uncle John probably loosened the nails himself."

John drew back in mock horror. "You'd accuse the man who helped you place your first bet?"

"Ah, ha!" Maripat cried. "You finally admit you corrupted my son at age seven!"

"Seven and a half," Cay said.

"Be quiet and eat your peas."

Travis said, "Our horse will beat yours by two lengths."

John raised an eyebrow and looked at Bob who looked at Maripat. "Half a length," she said. "One hundred bucks."

"My friend, the big spender," John grinned. "You won't be smiling this time next week."

"Want to place a side bet with me, Uncle John?" Cay asked. "I've got fifty cents!"

Seven days later, they sat in the stands at Latonia and watched Albright Stud's three-year-old colt come in second with John's entry five lengths behind. An elbow in John's ribs drew his attention to an upraised palm. Smiling glumly, he watched his hundred-dollar bill disappear into Maripat's purse. On the way to the betting windows, he slipped a dollar into Cay's eager hand.

5

Spring arrived, then summer and fall. Shortly after winter arrived, Maripat and Bob drove into Versailles to sign some papers at the bank. As they returned home on Old Frankfurt Pike, wisps of smoke appeared in the cold January air. "Looks like our place!" Bob shouted. Flooring the accelerator, he sent the Dodge pickup racing toward the farm entrance.

Maripat pointed as they entered the long tree-lined lane. "It's the stud barn!"

Farmhands were hooking up hoses while others ran into the long barn to release the horses. Skidding to a stop on the icy ground, Bob leaped out and ran toward the barn, Maripat right behind.

Shawn trotted out of the barn, dragging a snorting bay stallion. "Five more to go!" he yelled.

"What happened?" Maripat yelled back.

"Don't know! Started in the storeroom at the north end. It's gone. All we can do is save the horses and protect the other barns."

Maripat ran inside just as a man appeared out of the dense smoke. He was leading a chestnut stallion, and Bob was slapping it on the rump. The wild-eyed horse kicked a hind leg, then pranced sideways toward the exit.

Two more men emerged from the blackness, battling a bay stallion that was mad with fear. Flames licked at the stalls in their wake. Bob arrived at Maripat's side just as a voice shouted, "Look out! Horse comin' through!"

Bob shoved Maripat as she dove to the right. That left him directly in the path of the big stallion as it burst out of the billowing smoke. Flames singeing mane and tail, the screaming horse slammed into Bob, throwing him into a post ten feet away. Sprawled on her stomach, Maripat flinched as Bob's head struck the post with a force that made the barn shake. The stallion stumbled, then lunged through the wide doorway to safety.

"Bob!" Maripat screamed. She reached his crumpled body the

same time as Shawn. Bob's head was at an odd angle, thick blood matting the hair above one ear.

Grabbing Bob under the arms, Shawn dragged him toward the doorway. Maripat held Bob's head. Several farmhands rushed in and lifted him off the ground.

Moments after they reached safety, a man ran out with the last stallion. Sirens wailed in the distance as they carried Bob to the farm office and laid him on a couch.

Maripat knelt at her husband's side. His color was changing rapidly, skin turning waxy as blood cells clotted and lost oxygen. She didn't need a medical diagnosis to know he was dead.

6

Maripat looked out the window at the blowing snow. The storm had arrived the day after the funeral and hadn't let up for nine hours. Occasional glimpses of the burned-out stud barn could be seen in the distance. The other outbuildings had been saved, and the stallions were quartered in one of the barns on the old Albright Stud property.

"Come on, Little Bit," John said gently from the couch behind her. "Sit down and drink your coffee."

Maripat turned, tears sparkling in her green eyes, fists clinched at her side. "It makes me so damn *mad!* A mouse chews into a box of matches and my husband is gone! Damn, damn, *DAMN!* My sons don't have a father because of a damn *mouse!*"

"Speaking of sons, is there anything I can do to help Travis?"

Maripat shook her head and sat beside him. "He'll come out of it. Just like I will. And Cay. Travis had Bob to himself for five years before Cay was born. That established a special bond. And they shared a common interest in business and finance. Travis can rattle off stock market quotes like I trace bloodlines! At least that's one area where Cay excels. When it comes to horses, he's got Travis beat six ways to Sunday."

"Going to rebuild the stud barn?"

A sharp nod. "I'm going to upgrade all the buildings on both properties and put in the best damn water-pressure system on any horse farm in Kentucky! If another damn mouse starts a fire, we'll drown the little bastard before it singes its whiskers!"

"You're saying 'damn' a lot," John said mildly.

"Damn right!"

John smiled and patted her leg. "You'll do, Little Bit."

7

School took on new meaning for Cay on his first day as a senior at Woodford County High.

"Hi!" A toss of long black hair. "I'm Lynne Ross."

Cay looked down at the sexiest girl he had ever seen. She was about 5'5" with a body that filled her white T-shirt and jeans in all the right places.

"You got a name?" Head cocked to one side, she offered a teasing smile. A small fist rested lightly on an out-flung hip, white teeth flashing in her dark face.

"Cay Albright. What brings you to this educational wasteland?"

Lynne waved toward the north. "Luck, I guess. We moved here a few weeks ago."

Cay followed the direction of her arm. "I live that way, too. Albright Stud on Old Frankfurt Pike."

Lynne's eyes rounded. "I've heard about your farm all my life! You live in that big old mansion?"

"Yep. Windsong Manor. My mom named it before I was born."

"I saw her at Pimlico last year when her horse won the Preakness!" Lynne cried excitedly. "She's so pretty with all that red hair!" A finger pointed at the reddish highlights in Cay's light blond hair. "Guess that's where you got that. You must make a lot of girls jealous. I'd give anything to have hair like yours."

Cay kicked a clod of dirt. "You're kidding."

"Never knew any guys back home with hair that color."

"Where's that?"

"Maryland."

"Where in Maryland?"

"Boring."

A puzzled look. "What's boring—me or where you lived?"

"Boring, Maryland."

"What's it like?"

Lynne wrinkled her nose. "Boring."

They laughed together. Cay said, "That why you came here?"

"My father's the new manager at Elgen Farm."

"George Ross! I met him at Keeneland. So he's your dad."

"For sixteen years."

"Who was your dad before that? You've got to be at least eighteen."

Shoving her hands in the back pockets of her jeans, Lynne thrust her chest out. "Think so, huh?"

"Yeah," he said softly.

Lynne arched her back, improving his view. "That would make me about your age."

"I won't be eighteen until next May."

"Good, I wouldn't want to be too young for you."

"Got designs on my body?"

"No more than you have on mine."

Cay whispered into Lynne's ear, "We're in deep trouble."

She giggled. "At least it won't be boring."

"You riding the bus?"

Lynne made a face. "A real bummer! I'm supposed to get a car for Christmas, but until then it's yucksville."

"How about me driving you home? Seems the friendly thing to do, us being neighbors and all."

"Great!" Lynne said. She walked close to Cay as the bell summoned them to the first classes of the day.

Three nights later, Lynne's father stood at the window and watched his daughter get into Cay's Ford pickup. "Nice boy," George Ross said. He looked at his wife. "Seems to have his head on straight. Could be driving a fancy car with all his mother's money. He sure beats that nutcase Lynne was seeing back home."

"Let's face it, George," Christina Ross smiled, "our child's a bit of a nutcase herself. A sweet nutcase but too grown up for her own good. Girls these days seem to mature so *fast!*"

"Got me," George murmured, uncomfortable discussing the metamorphoses that had changed his bright-eyed sparkling young daughter into a mysterious woman. Although Lynne still toured the barns with him as she had all her life, she exuded a sensual vitality that couldn't be hidden by even the most ragged outfits. George had witnessed the worrisome results during the year before they left Maryland. Farmhands who had once greeted her with teasing remarks followed her with hungry eyes. She stirred the same emotions when they arrived at Elgen Farm a month ago.

"At least Cay doesn't fawn all over her like most of the boys," Christina said. "I'll bet he's hooked a lot of girls with that lazy grin and those green eyes! He's got that long lean look like James Coburn. Remember him in *Our Man Flint?*"

"You're making me jealous," George said, sitting on the couch and hugging his wife. He had been a lonely young soldier when he met the orphaned Christina in the ruins of an Italian village in 1943. She was sixteen, slender with ebony hair and big dark brown eyes set in a lovely face. Speaking only a few words of each other's language, they fell in love, and George promised to return for her when the war was over.

He kept that promise two years later and took his bride to Maryland and the little house that was part of his salary on a horse farm. Lynne was born shortly after he went to work as assistant manager at Cherry Tree Place, a Thoroughbred nursery stud twenty miles north of Baltimore. Five years later, he was promoted to manager, a position he held until this summer when the owner died and the farm was sold.

Lynne's mother wasn't the only female charmed by Cay. Before he could walk, women had fallen victim to the devastating combination of reddish-blond hair, emerald eyes and a laugh that invited everyone to join in. Fortunately—and due in part to his practical upbringing—he was unaware of this unique appeal. Even if he had been, he was more interested in working on the farm than seducing girls—something his brother was adept at before he was sixteen.

Darkly attractive with strong facial features and a muscular build that helped make him an all-state quarterback his junior and senior years at Woodford County High, Travis had had his pick of girls. And at Harvard, where he cut a wide swath through the surrounding female population and on the playing field. A knee injury his junior year forced him out of football and resulted in draft deferment, allowing him to return to Harvard after graduation to earn an MA degree in business administration. He would receive that next spring. Having already worked two summers for a stock brokerage firm on Wall Street, he was planning to continue with that company for a while before taking over the front office at Albright Stud.

For Maripat, it was a perfect arrangement—Travis running the business end of the farm and Cay the physical plant. Travis's dislike for working directly with horses matched Cay's feelings about keeping records and sitting behind a desk.

8

Although her mother-hen warning system set off alarms when she met Lynne, Maripat took an instant liking to the vivacious girl. Lynne's knowledge of pedigrees and racing history was impressive.

"The Nearco line has done more for American racing than any other," Lynne said. "Look at Nasrullah, Nashua and Bold Ruler! Daddy took me to see Northern Dancer the year he was retired to stud at Windfields Farm. He's so *little!* Did you know that they had to make a box for him so he can cover a mare?"

"Listen to her," Cay said, walking his fingers around the back of Lynne's neck with easy familiarity. "Talking about sex in mixed company."

Lynne pushed his hand away. "We're talking about horse sex, bonehead. That's a big difference."

"Big is right," Cay grinned.

Sinking down in the chair like a deflated balloon, Maripat looked mournfully at the ceiling. "Where did I go wrong?"

Lynne laughed. "You're funny, Mrs. Albright."

"Got to have a sense of humor to survive in this family."

The conversation returned to horses, and Maripat voiced her anger at the way an exhausted Majestic Prince—a son of Raise a Native and winner of the Kentucky Derby and Preakness—had been driven beyond his endurance in the Belmont three months earlier. "We haven't had a Triple Crown winner in twenty-one years, and everybody figured the Prince was the one to do it," Maripat said. "The Prince lost his only race and ended up with a leg injury that forced him into retirement!"

Lynne said, "You can bet that won't happen to any of mine."

Cay said, "*You're* going to race horses?"

"Why not? You think women haven't got the smarts!"

"Good for you!" Maripat said.

"Well…uh…it takes money to race horses."

"So? Maybe I'll get lucky. Or marry a rich guy who's already got a racing stable."

"Yikes!" Cay cried, slapping his hands over his face and sliding further down on the couch.

"Know something?" Maripat said to John Kershaw the next day. "I think she meant it." They were walking between a row of paddocks, and Maripat had just finished recapping Lynne's visit.

"About racing horses or marrying a rich man?"

"A little of both. She's not dumb. Sure knows horses! Add that to her looks, and you've got a pretty potent package. Too much for Cay to handle, if you ask me."

"Listen to the expert on male hormones!"

Hands in the back pockets of her jeans, Maripat glared up at her tall lanky friend. "As if you know so much about women!"

A big grin. "Sounds like the pot calling the kettle black."

Maripat stamped a booted foot. "John Kershaw, You can be

downright exasperating at times!"

"Takes one to know one," John said cheerfully.

Maripat's shoulders slumped under her University of Kentucky sweatshirt. "I should know better than to get in an argument with a lawyer."

"Good!" John said, taking her arm and aiming her back toward the house. "Let's talk about important things."

"Like what?"

"Horses, of course."

"Okay," Maripat laughed. "You first."

They walked between the paddocks, a tall rugged man and a slender diminutive redhead, enjoying each other's company as they had for over thirty years.

9

Christmas tree lights decorated the Blue Grass terminal as Cay watched Travis descend the steps of the Delta 727. "Hiya, Little Brother!" Travis yelled, crushing Cay in a bear hug. He stepped back, big square hands gripping Cay's upper arms. "I still can't get used to looking up at you!"

"No problem for me," Cay laughed

"Where's Mom? I thought she'd be here whooping and hollering and making a spectacle of herself."

"She wanted to, but I persuaded her to stay home and finish the berry pie she's making. You ought to see the food! She's cooking all your favorite stuff."

"There goes the old waistline," Travis groaned. "What is it with mothers? Go away from home, and they think you're starving to death!"

"It's the umbilical cord syndrome. She who feeds you the first nine months knows what's best for you the rest of your life."

Maripat flew into Travis's arms. "I've missed you! I've missed you!" she cried between kisses.

Lifting his tiny mother so her face was level with his, Travis grinned. "You've got flour on your face."

"Wanna kiss if off?"

"Naw. I'll lick it."

"Aaaaah!" Maripat kicked and rubbed her nose. "Put me down or I'll wallop you one!"

"Cay said, "Better do it or you'll have bloody shins."

Putting Maripat down, Travis aimed her toward the kitchen. "Let's see what you've got that smells so good."

Later that afternoon, the brothers walked beside a paddock. Travis pointed at several broodmares heavy with foal. "There doesn't seem to be any limit to the way the yearling market's going. That record quarter-million for Majestic Prince was topped the very next year! It's a seller's market. Mom's got to get her head out of the sand and syndicate new stallions like Combs is doing at Spendthrift. Devil's fire was a great sire, but we need new blood."

"You're talking a lot of money," Cay said.

"A smart man doesn't use his own. He packages the deal and gets others to put up the dough."

"You talked to Mom about this?"

Travis shook his head and kicked a pile of dried leaves. "You know Mom—she's satisfied with the way things are. Every time I bring up something new, she talks about how much the farm has grown the last twenty years."

"Can't argue with that."

"Whose side you on?"

"Nobody's. Some of what you say makes sense, but I kinda like things the way they are, too. Running an operation like Spendthrift sounds like a headache to me."

"Not to me." Travis slapped Cay on the back. "We'll be a team someday—me doing the heavy thinking and you the grunt work out back. Mom can be hard-headed, but I'll bring her around."

Travis had heard a lot about Lynne Ross, but nothing had prepared him for the impact of seeing her in person. "It's Sophia

Loren's little sister!" he exclaimed as Lynne jumped out of the pickup and walked beside Cay toward the house.

"There is sort of a resemblance," Maripat said. They were standing beside the Christmas tree and looking out the bay window.

"Same face, same eyes, same boobs—same everything!"

"What's that 'same everything' mean?" Maripat said. "You been dating Sophia Loren without me knowing?"

"Don't I wish!" Travis watched the young couple ascend the wide steps. "She's got a kind of Gypsy look. I can't believe she's only sixteen!"

"Well, she is, and you're six years older. *And* she's your brother's girlfriend."

"You don't have to rub it in."

Lynne had also heard a good deal about Travis, not just from Cay but from the many stories told about the local sports hero who had made it big on the national college scene. She had seen his pictures displayed among the trophies at Woodford County High and thought how dissimilar the two brothers were in looks—Cay slender and fair-haired, Travis heavily muscled and glaring at the camera from under thick dark eyebrows.

Travis quickly dispelled the menacing image. He smiled broadly and squeezed her hand. "What's a gorgeous creature like you doing running around with a ding-dong like my brother?"

Widening her almond-shaped eyes, Lynne pulled her hand free and hugged Cay's arm. "I'm partial to ding-dongs. 'Specially this one."

"No chance for a well-balanced college type?"

"Well," Lynne said in a low husky voice, "we'll have to wait and see about that, won't we?"

"Give him an inch, he'll take a mile," Cay warned.

A shiver crept up Lynne's spine as the awareness in Travis' eyes turned into a look of frank admiration. It had become a typical male reaction, and she reveled in each new experience.

Like most girls who developed early physically, she had received attention for which she was emotionally unprepared. She had adjusted quickly, however, displaying a self-control that surprised her father but not her mother. From the time Lynne was a toddler, Christina Ross had been the more objective parent, recognizing her daughter's strong will and desire to succeed.

It may have seemed like a fanciful wish to Maripat and Cay when Lynne expressed her ambition to race horses, but she was deadly serious. Raised on one of Maryland's leading nursery studs, she had set her goal early in life—to be the mistress of a Thoroughbred horse farm. She had grown up watching fancy cars and lavishly-dressed women arriving at the Cherry Tree Place mansion for the parties that made the society pages the next day. She vowed that someday she would be a part of that world, and newspapers would carry pictures of her entertaining and standing in the winner's circle.

Ambition was superseded by a more primitive emotion in January when Cay brought his pickup to a sliding halt at the far end of a dimly lit barn. "You sure?" he asked Lynne.

A quick nod.

"It's going to be cold up there."

Lynne grinned. "Not for long."

They dashed hand in hand across the frozen ground. Moonlight reflected off lingering patches of snow and created dancing shadows as they entered the barn. Horses stamped in the darkness as Cay led Lynne up the steep narrow staircase.

"I'll get a fire going," he said as they entered the small loft apartment. Lynne sat on the bed and rubbed her hands together while Cay lit the small butane heater.

"How come I get the feeling you've been planning this?" she said. "Place is swept and dusted. Bed made, too."

"I...uh...thought it might come in handy someday."

"Like now?"

"Yeah." Cay sat beside Lynne and drew her into his arms. "The room's warming up," she said as the long kiss ended.

Cay nuzzled her ear. "You nervous?"

"A little. You?"

"Some. A lot, I guess."

"Me, too." Lynne lifted her sweater and put Cay's hand over her bare breast. She had removed her bra during the hour of foreplay that had resulted in the mad dash to the loft apartment.

Moments later, she was sprawled on her back, and Cay was running his tongue over a swollen nipple. "Under the covers," she gasped, reaching for the top button of her jeans. Clothes flew in all directions as they came together in a tangle of arms and legs.

Clay slid his hands over her buttocks. "Your bottom's cold."

"Your front's warm. And hard!"

"Easy," Cay groaned. "I'm about to pop."

Lynne jerked her hand away. "I thought it would take longer after what happened in the truck."

"Quick recharge. Ready? I don't want to hurt you."

"Just take it easy at first," Lynne said as she rolled on her back. "I'll be okay."

It was a clumsy and less than satisfactory union—two virgins joining after months of experimentation. The initial pain of entry dulled Lynne's pleasure, and Cay finished before she could recover.

But they were young and anxious to try again. An hour later, they were locked together in an explosion of excitement that made the dismal first attempt a distant memory.

10

"Are we nuts or are we nuts?" Cay said as he stood outside the Iroquois Hunt clubhouse and slapped his gloved hands together. Central Kentucky was recovering from a late February storm.

Maripat grinned and poked his red-jacketed arm. "Of course we're nuts! Who but an idiot would come out on a freezing day like this to chase a silly fox?"

John Kershaw rapped the top of Maripat's black velvet-covered hard hat. "I've come because it's the manly thing to do."

"Then why are so many women here?"

"They like to do manly things."

"Ahhhh!"

Cay spoke into his horse's ear. "Aren't human relationships exciting and wonderful, JD?"

Dogs barked as the Master of Foxhounds gathered his charges for the hunt. The ivy-covered stone clubhouse provided a colorful backdrop. Built in 1808 by Irish masons and operated as Grimes Mill on the banks of Boone Creek for nearly a century, the machinery had been removed and the building converted into the Iroquois clubhouse in the late 1920's. The mill wheel was still in the basement under the kitchen.

Maripat swung lithely up into the saddle and settled the derby hat on her head. "You guys coming?"

John winked at Cay as he stuck his boot on the stirrup. "Not only bossy, she's impatient, too."

Cay was in the lead, Maripat close behind. As Cay's horse prepared to leap a stone wall, something caught on its left rear shoe. "Wire!" John yelled, but neither Cay nor Maripat heard.

As Cay's horse cleared the wall and continued on, Maripat's gelding ran right into the unearthed wire. Front feet tangled, it stumbled to its knees, throwing Maripat into the wall.

John hit the ground as his horse slid to a halt. Maripat's gelding snorted, leaped up and kicked its feet free of the wire. John knelt beside Maripat. Her hard hat had come off and blood was running down her forehead and into a closed eye. He tore off a glove and wiped the blood away.

"Maripat!" he cried. Laying her head in his lap, he patted her cheek. "Come on, Little Bit, say you're just foolin'!"

Breath fluttered through partially opened lips.

John felt her shoulders, arms. They seemed to be intact. The memory of Bob's death in much the same manner made John tremble. He held Maripat close and rocked her back and forth.

A voice sounded through the thick woods. "Mom? John?"

"Cay—here by the wall! Your mother's hurt!"

John continued to rock Maripat as Cay's horse crashed through the thick underbrush. Cay knelt and touched his mother's face. Eyes filled with anguish, he asked, "Has she moved at all?"

Equally stricken, John shook his head. "We've got to get her to a doctor. Hold her while I get on my horse." Transferring Maripat gently to Cay, John leaped into the saddle and reached down. Moments later, Maripat was cradled in his arms. Grabbing the reins of Maripat's gelding, Cay mounted and led the way back to the clubhouse.

John slipped into the hospital room and rested a hand on Cay's shoulder. "I got Travis; he'll be here tonight. Take a break. You've been sitting there for over an hour."

"How did Travis take it?" Cay asked.

"He calmed down after I told him it's just a concussion, and she should come out of it anytime."

"But it's been over three hours!"

"We have to trust the doctors, Cay."

"I know." Cay looked down at the bandage on his mother's forehead and the long lashes that rested softly on her cheeks. "I've never seen her look so helpless! She's always so strong!"

"She will be again," John said. "Walk around a while. I'll let you know the second she wakes up."

"I'll call Lynne; she likes Mom a lot."

"Shawn's on his way. I called him after I talked to Travis."

"Cay grasped the doorknob and looked at his mother, then John. "You'll let me know right away?"

"Get out of here. You're making me miserable, too."

Cay flashed a tired grin and left the room.

Pulling a chair close to the bed, John took Maripat's hand. "Wake up, Little Bit," he said softly. "Do it for me...okay? Do it because I've loved you ever since we were kids. I stayed away from Kentucky as long as I could. It hurt to stay away, and it hurt to come back. Understand?"

A movement in Maripat's fingers made him jump. Eyes still closed and a smile tugging at one corner of her mouth, she whispered, "Why did you take so long to tell me?"

Enclosing her hand in both of his, he leaned closer. "When we were young, I was too scared, then it was too late. The last few years, I haven't wanted to ruin what we have."

Maripat opened one eye. "All that kidding was just to cover up how you really felt?"

"That's me...laugh-a-minute Kershaw."

A finger circled one of his. "We'll talk about it later. Get Cay."

John bent and kissed her lips. "I always wondered what that would be like."

"Kinda nice, don't you think?"

"You bet! Back in a minute."

11

Shortly after Cay completed his second year at the University of Kentucky, Maripat paid two hundred thousand for a Raise a Native colt out of a Nashua mare. Having spent the last year arguing the need for new blood in the Albright Racing stable and stallion barn, Travis flew from New York to be at his mother's side during the two-day July Keeneland Selected Yearling sale. By the time the sale ended, Maripat spent an additional eight hundred thousand on four colts and seven fillies.

"Cut it out, Cay," Travis said the next day in the library that also served as their mother's private office. "We're not going to get anywhere if we don't take chances. Right, Mom?"

Before Maripat could answer, Cay shot back, "Maybe it's a game to you, but to me it's hard work." He pointed at the window that overlooked the paddocks and the barns. "It might help to get your hands dirty out there once in a while. You can talk circles around me about Wall Street but not about horses!"

Travis's eyes flickered angrily. "Just because you've got shit on your boots doesn't mean you know more about horses than me, Little Brother."

"I've got more than dirty boots," Cay snapped. He held his hands out, palms up. "When did you last get calluses on your fingers? Playing football?"

Maripat glared at Cay. "You've been on Travis's back ever since he got here. I don't remember putting you in charge of the farm!"

"Me? Travis is the one who's been the one making all the changes around here. You would have kicked me into the middle of next week if I'd suggested half the stuff he has! What the hell do you want me to go to UK for? Travis has all the answers!"

Maripat sighed and leaned back in the leather chair. "Let's calm down and look at this objectively. Travis is *not* making all the changes around here. I've been considering this for years. Your problem, Cay, is that you won't talk things out. You're too busy doing *practical* things. That's good…but you need to do some thinking, too. Raising horses is a business. A tough *unforgiving* business! Going to UK will help in that respect."

Cay threw up his hands. "It's a lot more than that, Mom. Travis wants to turn Albright Stud into another Spendthrift. You spent a million today—what about ten-twenty times that?"

"Other people's money!" Travis flared. "When will you get that through your thick head?"

"Cay," Maripat said quietly, "this is a family business. Nobody's going to run roughshod over you. We'll talk things over every step of the way."

"Like we did yesterday at Keeneland?" Cay snorted. "It was two to one, not that anybody gave me a chance to voice my opinion. Travis comes roaring in and sells you a load of bullshit about making millions."

"You're the one who's full of bullshit!" Travis shouted.

"Damnit, that's enough!" Maripat barked in the drill sergeant voice that never failed to get their attention. Two pairs of eyes blinked at the small rigid figure behind the desk. "We won't make any other major decisions until Travis is here full time. That's a year-and-a-half away. In the meantime, we can be civil and respect each other's opinions!"

The brothers looked at each other. "What the hell," Travis grinned. "It'll all work out, Little Brother. I'm sorry if I pushed too hard. I just want what's best for all of us. Come on, let's go look at those critters we bought."

Cay rose. "Coming, Mom?"

"You guys go ahead. I'll catch up later."

Maripat watched her sons leave the office. It had been happening more and more of late, these arguments over how to run the farm. When Travis started talking about modernizing, she was a reluctant but attentive audience. Although she would have preferred moving slower, she knew certain steps were necessary to keep up with the fast-changing Thoroughbred market.

While she looked forward to turning the farm operation over to Travis, Maripat worried about the brothers working together. Hopefully by then—Cay had two years to go at UK—her hot-headed younger son would be thinking more realistically.

Cay didn't raise the subject again until after Travis left for New York; then he voiced his anger to Shawn in the farm office. "Travis wants to be bigger than Claiborne and Spendthrift put together and consign the most horses at Keeneland. I wouldn't put it past him to get a cane and auction horses off on our front lawn! He'll probably have his name put on pocket knives and cigarette lighters and pass them out like Tom Gentry does!"

Shawn leaned back in the wooden swivel chair and rested his booted feet on the oak desk. "A little compromising wouldn't hurt," he said mildly. "Your Mom bought some pretty nice horses. That Raise a Native colt might be our ticket to the Derby."

"It's more than that, Shawn. I wouldn't mind if I thought I had some say in what happens. Sometimes I think Travis's Harvard education has gone to his head. He won't let me get in a word edgewise, and he's got Mom buffaloed."

"That's where your wrong, boy," Shawn said. "It takes more than a Harvard education to buffalo your mom."

Dark Indian eyes narrowing under the bill of his Cincinnati Reds baseball cap, Shawn thought about the years he had spent teaching Maripat the horse business, and now her son.

When his father was killed, Cay turned to Shawn to fill the void in his life. Besides a mutual affection and respect, they shared a love for horses that transcended financial rewards. It was in this area that the brothers differed most. Cay loved the magnificent animals with a passion that was understandable only to a true horseman. Travis's admiration was limited to the bottom line on a balance sheet.

Not long after Travis left, Maripat described the confrontation to John. They were in the upstairs bedroom at White Oak Stud and lying close together after making love.

"Cay feels ganged-up on," Maripat said as she rested her head on John's broad chest. "If I'd explained more before Travis arrived, maybe he wouldn't have taken it so personal."

"Don't blame yourself, Little Bit. Unless you think it's your fault Cay turned out a lot like you."

Maripat punched John's ribs. "So it *is* my fault!"

"Seems I remember a girl with a hot temper. Stubborn, too."

"You're a big help, John Kershaw."

"I aim to please." A moment of silence while he rubbed her back. "They're both right to some extent. If you want to stay ahead in this business, you've got to keep up with the times and take chances. If that's all there were to it, bankers could run the industry. Some financial types think they can. The best horse people are born into the business—like the Hancocks at Claiborne, Alice Chandler at Mill Ridge and the Bells at Jonabell. Travis was, too, but he chose to work on the outside. Besides having different personalities, the boys look at the business from opposite viewpoints."

"Like they look at us."

John raises his head off the pillow. "Oh?"

"Travis hasn't been around much the last year, but I think he suspects. Even after all these years, he would probably think I'm betraying his father."

"And Cay?"

"From the looks he gives us and the hints he drops, I'm sure he knows. I've come close to telling him several times. He'll be happy for both of us; I'm sure of that."

John stroked her hair. "I'm just thankful that we can be together as much as we are."

"Me, too." Maripat rose on one elbow and kissed his nose.

John pulled her close. "I think I'm in the mood again."

12

Fourteen months after Maripat purchased the Raise a Native colt, Albright Stud got back nearly half the $200,000 purchase price when Fast Track, the name given the two-year-old bay, won the Heritage Stakes at Keeneland. Travis couldn't resist gloating. Cay smiled and congratulated him on possessing superior intelligence. Travis responded by ruffling Cay's hair and saying his little brother had been showing a lot of smarts lately.

Travis may have said it jokingly, but Cay's grade average at UK had been rising steadily. When he was interested in something, he could assimilate facts with a speed that bordered on genius. Majoring in equine management, he had no problem staying in the top of his class.

Lynne also attended UK, a year behind Cay and having the time of her life. An honor student throughout high school, she breezed through her college courses. With a host of young men vying for her attention, she became a familiar sight at campus hangouts and Lexington nightclubs. If she hadn't been living at home and under some degree of supervision, she would have subsisted on four hours sleep a night.

Shortly after Lynne entered her sophomore year, Christina Ross asked her daughter if she had broken up with Cay.

"No, Mama," Lynne said as she dried a plate and stacked it in a kitchen shelf. "It's just...well...he doesn't like to go out much. He's not a real fun person, if you get what I mean."

Arms buried in suds as she scrubbed a pan, Christina shot Lynne a disapproving look. "If you ask me, that's a compliment."

"I guess so, but he's changed a lot. He was so happy and easy going when I met him. Things aren't going well between him and Travis, and it isn't Travis's fault. Used to be, Cay could care less what happened outside the barns. Now he's getting into *everything!* It's driving Travis nuts. Mrs. Albright, too."

Christina handed the pan to her daughter. "Driving his brother nuts? Are you sure about his mother? Who told you this?"

Lynne's eyes wavered under her mother's steady gaze. "I bumped into Travis downtown before he went back to New York. We had coffee and talked about stuff."

"You mean gossiped about Cay." Christina shoved another pan in the water and scoured it angrily.

"Mama, it's not like Cay and I are engaged or anything!"

"I'm talking about *loyalty*, Lynne. Even if your feelings have changed, don't you think you owe him something?"

"But I still love him! I'm not sneaking around talking behind his back. Not to hurt him! Travis loves him, too. We thought we could work together to help Cay out, that's all!"

Christina dried her hands on a towel. "What about all this chasing around? Is that to help Cay, too?"

"No," Lynne said defiantly, "that's to help *me!* Sometimes I'm so lonely I could scream! I love Cay and I think he loves me. In his own way—whatever that is! He may seem friendly and all smiles to you, but he's got another side that shuts people out." She tossed silverware into a drawer. "He's done it to me, and Travis says he's doing it to him, too."

"Don't give up on him too quick," Christina said. "Young men like Cay don't grow on trees."

Not long after Travis took over the business management of Albright Stud in late February, the farm's prize colt, Fast Track, made an auspicious debut as a three-year-old by placing second in the Flamingo Stakes at Hialeah.

The popular "Roads" to the Kentucky Derby were the New York, Florida and California circuits. New York drew the biggest stables in April, but milder weather made Florida the first choice in January through March. The California route—which produced four Derby winners in the fifties and two in the sixties—was gaining respectability, and the "East versus West" rivalry was heating up more every year.

Casting a shadow over hopes for Fast Track was a colt from Meadow Farm in Virginia, a flashy chestnut named Secretariat. Although his stablemate, Riva Ridge, had won the Derby the previous year, Secretariat had been crowned Champion two-year-old colt *and* Horse of the Year, the first juvenile to receive the unanimous double vote since the divisional championships were formed in 1936. Native Dancer received the same honor in 1952, but of the three organizations making the selections— the Thoroughbred Racing Association, *Daily Racing Form* and National Turf Writers Association— the *Racing Form* had chosen One Count over Native Dancer as Horse of the Year.

Those separate polls were eliminated in 1971 when the three organizations combined their votes and created the Eclipse Awards, named for the great Eighteenth Century racehorse and dominant sire of the modern Thoroughbred.

Whatever Secretariat's accomplishments as a three-year-old, he would not be raced beyond this season. Five months after the death of his father, A.B. "Bull" Hancock, Jr., and one month after the executors had given him control over Claiborne Farm, twenty-three-year-old Seth Hancock had syndicated Secretariat for a record value of $6,080,00. Twenty-eight shares sold for $190,000 each, while four were retained by the seller, Meadow Farm. The syndication agreement stipulated that Secretariat be retired to stud at the end of his three-year-old season.

While Secretariat was winning the Bayshore Stakes at Aqueduct in March, Fast Track came in first in the Hutcheson Stakes at Gulfstream. The following month, Secretariat established himself as the leading contender for the Derby by winning the Gotham Stakes by three lengths, six days after Fast Track won the Spiral Stakes.

Then the unbelievable happened. Secretariat came in third in the Wood Memorial, four lengths behind Angle Light who beat the California horse, Sham, by a head.

"I knew it! I knew it!" Travis shouted as he jumped up from the couch and pointed at the TV. "First time around two turns and he loses! That's the trouble with Bold Ruler's get—they aren't worth shit over a mile! They haven't won one Triple Crown race— not one!" He slapped Shawn on the back and kissed his mother on top of the head.

Maripat grinned at Cay. "What do you think of that?"

"Sounds like bourbon time to me."

"I'll second that," Shawn said, standing and hitching up his pants. "Stay put," he added to Maripat as she started to rise. "I know where it is."

The celebrating reached a fevered peak the following day when Fast Track won the Blue Grass Stakes at Keeneland, twelve days before the Kentucky Derby.

13

5:45 AM. Showing his badge to the guard, Cay drove Maripat through the 4th Street backside gate at Churchill Downs. Parking at one end of Barn 42, they found Shawn standing beside a fireplug, hands clutching a steaming mug of coffee.

"Bout time you got here," Shawn said. "I was giving serious thought to going to the kitchen and ordering dinner."

Maripat said, "We were on the road while you were still having your beauty sleep. Seen Travis?"

"He's here?"

"Drove up yesterday afternoon."

"Probably catting around. If that boy was a horse, he'd make a great stud."

Maripat muttered under her breath and headed for the barn.

They paused as grooms led a line of blanketed horses along the shedrow—the narrow covered area that fronts the stalls. Curious horses poked their heads over the barriers, some chewing on clumps of hay, others stamping the packed earth, anxious to join the parade.

"Fast Track ought to be coming by any minute," Shawn said.

Cay was pouring coffee when a tall blonde led the bay colt around a corner. "Morning, Joy," he called.

"Morning, Cay—Maripat," Joy Loren grinned. Fast Track's twenty-eight-year-old groom was rawboned with legs that seemed to go on forever. She had soft brown eyes and a face that was very pretty when she smiled. And she smiled a lot.

She was dressed in her usual morning garb—tight jeans, dark blue sweatshirt and worn tennis shoes. During the fourteen years she had worked for Albright Stud, she had graduated from high school, married a local boy at eighteen and divorced when she was twenty. She briefly went into a drinking tailspin, then steadied out to become one of the best hands on the farm. Although marriage was the last thing on her mind, she never lacked for male attention.

Cay scratched the colt's ear. "Want to kiss me or bite my head off?"

"Not to worry," Joy said. "He already got his jollies trying to bite *mine* off! Onery critter." She patted Fast Track's muscled neck to let him know he was forgiven.

While Maripat and Shawn headed for the track, Cay grabbed his coffee and joined Joy as she coaxed Fast Track into a walk.

A dark brown colt lunged against the webbed barrier of its stall, teeth bared as he tried to bite Fast Track's rump. Ears flattened, Fast Track kicked his hind legs in response.

"Somebody ought to geld that raunchy bastard," Joy said, glaring back at the brown colt as it turned its head in the opposite direction looking for another victim. "If he isn't taking potshots at the guys, he's slobbering over the girls."

It was a typical morning on the backside. Rope-enclosed balls of timothy hay known as "haynets" hung outside stalls. Makeshift clotheslines displayed a variety of horse laundry. Radios blared, and the smell of liniment added a bite to the crisp morning air. Cats raced across the grounds while pigeons swooped in and out of barns. A speaker crackled, "If you're missing a white goat, it's tied behind barn thirty-one."

Cay nudged Joy. "Lose a boyfriend?"

"Bite your tongue, sonny, or I'll pop you one."

They made several more trips around the shedrow, then it was time to saddle up and head for the track.

Head high and sniffing the air, Fast Track moved ahead of the Albright Stud crew, red protective leg-wraps flashing with each prancing step. Tony Rule, a fifty-year-old ex-jockey who had been the colt's exercise rider the past year and a half, kept a firm grip on the reins. Turf writers and photographers flanked the bay colt. As they neared the track, a television crew joined the procession. With his recent win in the Lexington Stakes, Fast Track was a Derby favorite.

"Figured Travis would show up about now," Cay said. "Leave it to him to hog all the publicity."

"Fine with me," Maripat said.

"Same here," Shawn added as Travis spoke into a reporter's microphone. "My throat's raw from answering the same damn questions over and over."

They quickened their pace as the colt moved through the wide chute-gap gate and onto the track. With his entourage and the black letters, "Fast Track" and "Kentucky Derby 99" displayed on his gold saddle cloth, he attracted the attention of trainers and railbirds alike.

Ears pricked, looking every inch the celebrity he was, Fast Track watched the dozens of horses walking and galloping around the track. Shutters clicked and television cameras whirred while he checked out the competition.

"Give him a slow gallop, then a sharp four furlongs," Shawn said to Tony Rule.

After adjusting the strap of his leather safety helmet and checking the crop in the back pocket of his jeans, Tony nudged Fast Track with his knees. "Come on, old son. Let's show 'em."

"Don't try to win any races," Shawn cautioned.

Tony's weathered face broke into a grin. "Tell that to numb-nuts here. He don't like to look at the rear end of a horse."

"Just make sure he knows where the finish line is. He's got to have that down pat on Saturday."

"No chance! Finish pole stands out like the Eiffel Tower!"

"Shoemaker did in Fifty-Seven," Shawn said drily, referring to Bill Shoemaker's famous loss by a nose to Iron Liege when he misjudged the sixteenth pole for the finish line and stood momentarily in the irons, breaking Gallant Man's stride.

Two horses galloped past, puffing in ragged rhythm. Shawn

moved back as Tony trotted Fast Track onto the main thoroughfare.

A rider shouted as he galloped behind Fast Track, "Comin' through on your left!" Tony kept a tight rein on his mount. A horse has a visual range of about 340 degrees leaving a twenty-degree blind spot behind. An object appearing suddenly can spook a horse and cause it to dislodge its rider.

Gathered below the clocker's stand at the 5 furlong pole, they watched Fast Track gallop past, Tony crouching in the stirrups. As the colt neared the half-mile pole, stopwatches appeared along the rail. Thumbs poised, the two *Daily Racing Form* clockers on the stand centered their attention on Fast Track as he entered the turn.

Approaching the 3/8 pole, Tony sat down and leaned over Fast Track's neck. Stopwatches clicked as the colt dropped his head and galloped toward the 5/16 pole.

"Movin' good," Shawn said as Fast Track breezed past the quarter pole and entered the homestretch. The grandstand and the famous twin spires towered above while the gold ball gleamed brightly on top of the eighteen-foot-tall finish line pole.

"Thirty-five on the button," Cay said as the colt flashed under the finish wire and headed for the clubhouse turn.

Exercise riders stopped their mounts and stood in the irons as Fast Track thundered through their ranks. Even to hardened backstretch personnel, it was a special treat to watch a leading Derby entry running full out.

"Got him at forty-seven and change," one of the *Racing Form* clockers said.

Tony Rule rose in the irons and pulled on the reins as he slowed his mount down. Recording footage for a local television station, a cameraman turned slowly as the colt passed.

Shawn looked over his shoulder. "Put on your best smiles everybody. The press is heading our way."

"Is Fast Track as healthy as he looks?" a man in a black raincoat and tennis shoes asked Shawn.

"Scares me, he's so solid. Not a bad bone in his body. Legs a Penthouse Pet would eat her heart out for. Never sick. Grows hair good, too. Wish I knew his secret." The reporters laughed. Shawn Phelps could always be depended on for a good interview. While some of his remarks were unprintable, they provided colorful anecdotes to tell later in the bars.

"What workouts do you plan over the next week?" a man asked.

"We'll walk him tomorrow, then gallop him the next three days. Blow him out over five furlongs on Wednesday, walk him on Thursday, gallop him on Friday."

"Mrs. Albright, what do you think Fast Track's chances are against Secretariat?"

Reporters and onlookers edged closer. Every owner was being asked the same question. Maripat looked at the short rotund reporter who had asked the question. "What do you expect me to say, Billy? That Fast Track can't win? He's Kentucky bred. That's a big point in his favor—right?" Amid laughter, Maripat added, "I'll leave the guessing to you guys. That's your job."

"And our necks if we goof!" someone yelled.

"Secretariat lost his first race around two turns," a voice called out. "Fast Track won going away in the Jim Beam. Doesn't that give him an edge?"

"Different tracks, different conditions, Rick," Maripat said. "If that's true, Angle Light should be the favorite."

"Say it ain't so!" a man yelled.

The laughter was followed by more questions. Then Maripat motioned to where Tony was walking a sweat-lathered Fast Track through the chute-gap. "Hate to break this up, but we've got a horse to look after."

As they followed the colt off the track, Cay said, "I can't believe the press. The Derby's a week away, and they're crawling all over the place!"

"Just the tip of the iceberg," Maripat said. "There'll be twelve hundred or more wandering around pretty soon. Some won't know the difference between a Thoroughbred and a milk cow, but they'll be having the time of their lives. That's what the Derby's all about."

"Boy, are you yucky!" Joy said. Fast Track snorted and splattered flecks of foam as Tony Rule dismounted and stripped the saddle off. After Shawn exchanged the bridle for a leather halter, Joy led the colt toward a plastic tub filled with steaming water.

Cay held Fast Track while Shawn and Maripat left with Tony to saddle a filly they had entered in a race the following week. Travis had stayed on the rail to watch the workouts.

Joy lathered fast Track's neck with a big sponge dipped in a solution of mild detergent and warm water. When she worked up to his face, he tried to bite the sponge. "Serve you right if you swallow it," Joy said, rubbing it over his muzzle. A big bluish-brown eye rolled back and followed her movements as she scrubbed the other side of his neck.

Tony rode by on a sleek filly. "You do good work, kid. Someday you might get an exercise job where the *real* money is!"

"Up yours," Joy said. "Keep eating like you do, you'll go overweight and I'll get your job."

"Hardy-har-har-har!" Tony crowed. He nudged the filly into a faster walk. Turning at the end of the barn, he began to sing, "Gwine to run all night! Guine to run all day..."

Joy was resting on her heels and cooling off Fast Track's ankles with water from a hose when Maripat returned. "What's Tony so happy about?" Maripat asked.

"The usual early morning garbage," Joy said as she stood and rinsed off the last residues of detergent and dirt. "You know Tony...loves to bug the female help."

Cay winked at Maripat as he threw a blanket over Fast Track's steaming back and buckled the surcingle under the colt's belly. Female stable hands were once rare on the backside of tracks. Then as blacks and other minorities began dropping out because of the low pay and long hours, trainers hired young women who had grown up with horses and would endure any hardship to work with their first and enduring love. And they showed up on time and didn't drink and gamble and waste money like their male counterparts—making them less likely to take their grievances out on their expensive charges.

As Maripat and Cay watched Joy lead Fast Track away on his "hot"—the forty-five minute walk horses brought off the track needed to cool them down—a commotion erupted at the other end of the barn. They turned just as a magnificent red colt came into view, a flock of photographers and TV cameramen walking backwards, catching every move of the fast stepping chestnut.

"No horse has a right to be that perfect and run good, too," Maripat breathed, awed by the flawless conformation and beauty of the flashy colt.

"Lucien Laurin said the same thing the first time he saw him," Cay said.

"But how will he do at a mile and a quarter?" Maripat mused, voicing the question on everyone's mind. The Kentucky Derby was the first real test for a three-year-old. Some horsemen still believed it was too long a distance for the rapidly developing young horses. Samuel D. Riddle felt so in 1920 when he kept Man o' War out of the race.

Fifty-three years later, another "Big Red" was prepared to take up the challenge. Maripat and Cay continued to stare after Secretariat disappeared from view.

14

Derby Eve parties in the Bluegrass are the highlight of the week-long celebrations that lead to the first Saturday in May. Until her death in 1966, cosmetics queen and racehorse owner, Elizabeth Arden, owned Friday Night. Other hostesses seeking the cream of Kentucky society and distinguished visitors had to schedule their parties on another night.

After Elizabeth Arden's death, two women became the reigning socialites on Derby Eve. One was Mary Lou Whitney, wife of millionaire horseman, Cornelius Vanderbilt Whitney. Whitney's grandfather, William Collins Whitney, entered the racing scene in the late 1890's and spearheaded the restoration of the Saratoga racetrack at the end of the century. He later joined August Belmont, Jr., J. Pierpont Morgan and others in the development and opening of Belmont Park in 1905.

Grandson C.V. Whitney—or "Sonny" as he was known to his friends—also raced horses, when he wasn't involved in such diverse projects as helping launch Pan American Airlines and investing with his cousin John Hay "Jock" Whitney in the formation of Selznick International Pictures, David O. Selznick's company that produced *Gone with the Wind.*

Mary Lou Whitney's Derby Eve parties were held at the brick mansion on the Paris Pike farm that had been in the family since 1915. They were dignified affairs with guest lists that included such names as Princess Margaret, President Richard Nixon, Governor Ronald Reagan and actor Gregory Peck.

When William Collins Whitney entered racing in 1896, he retained John E. Madden as turf consultant, two years before Madden established Hamburg Place just east of Lexington. In twelve years, Hamburg Place grew to two thousand acres and became the breeding home of five Kentucky Derby winners, including Sir Barton, the first Triple Crown winner.

In the mid-fifties, John Madden's grandson, Preston, married his college sweetheart and brought her from her home in Ashland, Kentucky, to Hamburg Place. A lovely blonde with a striking figure, Anita Madden became deeply involved in the Thoroughbred racing industry and earned a reputation for throwing parties that were as flamboyant as her outgoing personality. Each Derby Eve, her parties grew bigger, more spectacular and daring. The one before the 99th running of the Kentucky Derby set a standard that even Anita Madden would have difficulty topping.

Shawn stood at the edge of the big swimming pool, mouth hanging open. Cay grabbed the little man's arm. "Better look out or you'll step on your tongue."

"Can't blame him," Travis said. "Those are excellent marine specimens."

John Kershaw moved closer. "Downright disgusting. Is there a boat around here I can borrow?"

The objects of their attention languished on tiny islands in the middle of the tent-covered pool, long strands of false hair covering their bare breasts. Smiling and waving, the shapely models flapped their mermaid tails to the heavy beat of a rock band.

Anita Madden chose a different theme for every Derby Eve party. Tonight's was "Alexander the Great." Helmeted, spear-carrying soldiers and scantily-dressed dancing maidens complimented the lavish period decorations and the colorful gowns and dresses worn by the women. Among the tuxedo-clad men was a scattering of outlandish bow ties, wraparound dark glasses and artistic cummerbunds.

Maripat elbowed John in the ribs. "Stop staring; you're setting a bad example for the youngsters."

Lynne glanced over her shoulder. "I'm afraid it's too late for Cay, Mrs. Albright." She rolled her eyes. "Travis, too."

"Humpf." Maripat cast a jaundiced eye toward her oldest son and his tall blonde companion. Travis had met Debbie Norris a week ago at an electronics show in Louisville. She was working as a hostess-model in a California company's booth when he strolled down the aisle. His first view was of her back—shoulder-length straight blond hair, a red dress that outlined firm buttocks and a pair of long shapely legs, trim ankles and three-inch stiletto heels. When she turned to point something out to the four men in the booth, he wasn't disappointed. She was stunning—big blue eyes, high cheek bones above a wide generous mouth and creamy breasts that threatened to burst out of the low cut dress.

Canceling plans to return to Lexington that afternoon, he moved in with the assurance born of a hundred conquests. He took her to dinner that evening and to his hotel room for the night. They spent most of Derby Week together, a good deal of the time in bed.

Arms folded across her chest, Maripat watched the young couple disappear into the crowd.

"That's a lot of woman," John said. "I hope Travis knows what he's doing."

"If he doesn't, he's going to get an education mighty fast. One thing in his favor, he knows more about women than you did at his age."

John traced a finger up the back of Maripat's long slender neck and touched the upswept graying red hair. "What gives you the idea that I didn't know much about women? All those years we were apart, you think I was sitting around pining for you?"

"Yep."

"Maripat, sometimes you can be the damnedest, most egotistical little cuss…"

Lynne had been observing Debbie, too. "Better watch that one," she said to Cay as they walked hand in hand off the dance floor. "She'd like nothing more than to wiggle that fancy butt into Albright Stud."

"Takes one to know one," Cay grinned.

Whirling, the flowing white gown emphasizing her dark beauty, Lynne said, "You are lower than a rat, Cay Albright! A snake—no, a worm!"

"Speaking of worms, I've got one that hasn't been exercised much of late. Think you can do something about that?"

A sidelong glance. "I'll have to check my schedule."

"Gotta squeeze me in between dates?"

"You really don't care how much I go out, do you?" Lynne said in a hurt voice.

"I want you to have a good time. You know how busy I am between school and the farm. I wish I could get out more—"

"What's with you two?" Travis said, beaming happily with Debbie in tow. "You'd rather stand around and talk than dance?"

"Cay would," Lynne said. She moved close to Travis and clutched his arm. "What about you? Think you can spare me one?" Debbie's tight-lipped smile provided a thrill of satisfaction.

"Your wish is my command." Travis looked over his shoulder as he led Lynne away. "Take care of my girl!"

Burning over the way Lynne had moved in on Travis, Debbie widened her big blue eyes and pressed against Cay's side. "I'd love to dance with you," she said, sincerely meaning it. She found him terribly attractive. Too bad he was a few years younger and going steady with that black-haired witch!

Across the room, Maripat looked up at John. "Guess you want

to sit. I assume the music's a bit upbeat for you."

"You assume right," he said. "Maybe next year Anita will have a country theme with square dancers."

"Too tame," Maripat said, glancing at the mermaids. "Bare boobs and fake fish tails wouldn't fit in."

Anita Madden stopped by their table a little after midnight. The aquamarine gown clung to every curve and was the exact color of her sparkling eyes. "Where's John?" she asked.

"Where else?" Maripat said. "Talking horses in some dark corner. Sit and rest a spell."

"Just for a sec," Anita said, dropping into a chair. She leaned forward, golden hair tumbling over bare shoulders. "Enjoying yourself, Carol?" she asked the petite woman sitting next to Maripat.

"Your parties get better each year!" Carol Jarvis said. From New York and married to a Manhattan banker, this was her fifth Derby Eve party at Hamburg Place. She patted Maripat's hand. "We were just talking about my daughter Millie's marriage next month and Fast Track in the Derby. I don't know which to be the most excited about!"

"The Derby!" Anita laughed. She batted her long false eyelashes. "Even a Yankee must realize the importance of having a horse in the Derby."

"I do now! I can't believe the attention this table's been getting all night."

"If you think that's something, imagine what it will be like if Fast Track *wins* the Derby!"

Eyes wide under curling silver bangs, Carol said, "Do you really think he has a chance? I hear so much about Secretariat."

"Of course he has a chance," Anita said. She waved a slender arm. "Walk around and listen like I've been doing. Fast Track is definitely one of the favorites. Angle Light's been mentioned a lot, too. He beat Secretariat in the Wood by four lengths! The *Racing Form* thinks Sham will win. Secretariat may be the betting favorite, but less than forty percent of the Derby favorites win. And the upsets! Look what happened to Native Dancer and Nashua!"

Maripat said, "I'm just glad it's almost over. A few more days of this, I'll be half a bubble out of plumb!"

Midnight passed, and hundreds of guests continued to dance, table-hop and hold impromptu meetings. Of the many deals that were struck, not all were business in nature. With the music pounding and lights low, conversation flowed as easily as the bourbon, cocktails and champagne.

"Haven't we met before? I'd never forget a face as pretty as yours."
"I saw you with a pretty face a few minutes ago."
"She's gone to the powder room. Want to dance?"
"Love to! I adore men who live dangerously."

"...so he looks me right in the eye and says, 'This colt's granddaddy in the tail-male line won four stakes races. You can't lose!"
An angry growl. "Like a fool, I paid more attention to that and the colt's looks than what his pappy and full brother did. Put him in training and know what? *I* can run faster than that dog! He'll probably end up pulling a buggy for one of them Amish in Ohio."

"If that man's a director, I'm the reincarnation of Irving Thalberg! Thanks to him, I blew the last take twenty-one times. I told my agent I'll sell apples for a living before I'll work for that little dipshit again!"

"Four thousand an acre for one of the finest pieces of land in Fayette County and you say it's too much? Damnit, Jim, it's not unimproved property! It's got four houses, including a restored Greek Revival that was built in Eighteen Forty-Eight—plus six barns and fifteen miles of fence!"
"I know it's a prime piece of land, Horace, but I've only got so much to spend. Make it thirty-eight hundred an acre, and we've got a deal."
"Will you throw in a case of that fancy French champagne

you've got hid in your basement?"

"Shake on it! Let's see if we can scare up some Maker's Mark. This calls for a *real* drink."

"Gene, you can't kiss me. We're both married!"

"So's Becky, and I saw her kissing Jack a few minutes ago."

"That bastard! Come here. Mmmmm. It's been a long time since we did this."

"Want to take a walk? My car's parked behind a barn."

"Like being in high school again! Let's hurry before the sun comes up!"

Lynne clapped a hand over her mouth, eyes huge and staring. "Travis wasn't kidding!"

"And to think I used to hold that boy in my arms and sing him lullabies," Maripat said.

Cay rose. "Come on, John, this deserves a closer look."

"Don't you dare!" Lynne cried, but they were already on the way.

Dozens of revelers were gathered around the pool, shouting encouragement to the "mermaids" who were swimming ashore. The women had discarded their false hair and tails, and their bare breasts glistened as they were helped from the water.

Travis grabbed a pneumatic blonde's hand and led her toward the dance floor, water dripping from her nearly naked form. The band got into the act and swung into a wild version of "Night Train," drums providing the beat for the sensual swaying of the ex-mermaids and their partners.

Maripat, Lynne and Debbie joined John and Cay at the edge of the dance floor. Lynne shrieked with laughter and Debbie glared daggers at Travis as he threw his husky body about, dark hair flying as he stared google-eyed at his partner's bouncing breasts.

"Go, Travis, go!" Lynne cried, clapping her hands in rhythm.

"Hey, Travis, it's my turn!" Cay yelled.

Lynne snapped, "Want something valuable twisted off?"

"Too late," John said as Travis surrendered the blonde to another man.

Travis staggered off the floor, sweat running down his face. "Now this is what I call a *party!*"

"Better pull yourself together," Maripat said. "We have to be at the governor's breakfast in five hours."

"How does anybody have the strength left for the Derby?" Debbie asked.

"It's one of the miracles of Derby Week," John laughed.

"Not even one more dance?" Travis said, looking back longingly as Debbie led him off.

15

THE FIRST KENTUCKY DERBY, MONDAY, MAY 17, 1875.

They came to the inaugural Derby in mule-drawn streetcars and on special "Derby Day" trains. High-stepping horses pulled fringed buggies and grand carriages, weaving through the throngs that had elected to walk. Picnic baskets swung to the beat of marching feet, and children skipped alongside huge coal wagons packed with Negroes and pulled by mules decorated with jingle bells.

By the time the bell rang at the track for the Derby, the grandstand at the new Louisville Jockey Club course was filled, the special ladies section a kaleidoscope of colorful parasols, plumed hats and stylish dresses. In the free infield, thousands scurried about looking for the best vantage point while women repacked wicker baskets and herded children into some semblance of order. The more fortunate stood in the backs of wagons and shaded their eyes against the blazing sun.

On the lawn surrounding the new clubhouse, magnificently gowned women and elegantly attired men strolled about waiting for the race to begin, ladies sipping lemonade while their escorts drank sterner stuff. On the clubhouse porch, the less ambitious sat in wooden rocking chairs and kept time to the sweeping strains of a Strauss waltz played by Schneider's band.

Below the grandstand, Negro women in aproned dresses and bright bandannas left their stoves and the aroma of fried chicken and fish, cornbread and burgoo stew to watch the Derby horses parade past.

Negroes were more than cooks that day. Besides the hundreds in attendance, others were there as stablehands and grooms, some even as trainers. Of the fifteen riders in the first Kentucky Derby, only one, Billy Lakeland, was white. It had long been a tradition, especially in the southern states, for the jockeys to be black.

Some Negroes had become famous riding for their masters. Twenty-two years before the Civil War, the Tennessee jockey, Cato, won his freedom riding Wagner to victory over Grey Eagle.

The crowd buzzed with excitement. Thirty yards from the starting point midway on the backstretch, Colonel W.H. Johnson, President of the Nashville Blood Horse Association, drew a line in the dirt with the butt of his flag. The Derby distance was a mile and a half for three-year-olds, little more than a sprint compared to the three four-mile heats that until recently older horses often ran in a single day.

The murmur of ten thousand voices grew to a steady roar as Johnson handed the flag to his assistant and mounted a box carrying a drum. Glancing 125 yards down the track, he nodded toward a man holding a flag. It was the man's job to signal a recall if Johnson didn't like the break.

Watching the riders slow their mounts to a walk and approach the line in the dirt, Price McGrath muttered from his place at the head of the stretch. "All we need now are a couple of false starts."

"Cheer up, Price," the man on his right said. "You'll feel better in a few seconds.

Laughing and slapping the rail, McGrath roared, "Right you are! Let's get on with it!"

Johnson's assistant raised his red flag, and the excited shouts from the crowd increased as the riders fought to keep their mounts behind the crudely-drawn line. For a heart-stopping moment, time stood still, then Johnson tapped the drum.

The horses leaped forward, and Johnson's assistant dropped his flag as the horses passed, signaling the timers to start their stop watches. Down the track, the recall assistant ran for safety, dragging his flag in the dust.

A small horse with a golden-red coat burst into the lead, its rider wearing the Irish-green and orange sash of McGrathiana. "Aristides!" McGrath's companion shouted.

Two horses closed in, one a chestnut like Aristides, the other a bay. As they neared the first turn, the chestnut took the lead.

"Chesapeake was left flat-footed!" McGrath yelled. He had entered two horses in the race. The plan was for Aristides to be the "rabbit" and set the early pace for Chesapeake who was famous for his stretch drives.

The chestnut, McCreery, flashed by with Aristides and Volcano at his heels. The rest of the field was closely bunched with Chesapeake trailing.

As Chesapeake passed, McGrath leaned over the rail and waved his arms. "Move up! Move up!" he shouted, but Billy Henry was too busy whipping Chesapeake to notice.

The crowd cheered as the horses sprinted past the grandstand the first time, McCreery still in the lead. Suddenly, McCreery faltered, and Aristides swept by and around the clubhouse turn. Ten Broeck was close on his heels followed by Volcano and Verdigris.

The little red horse increased his lead, finishing the mile in 1:45. Sitting up straight in the riding fashion of the day, Aristides' jockey, Oliver Lewis, glanced around as Ten Broeck and Bob Wooley narrowed the gap.

On the final turn, Oliver Lewis pulled on Aristides' reins so Chesapeake could pass. When he looked back, he didn't see Chesapeake, but he saw McGrath. The big bearded man was waving and pointing toward the finish line. "Go ahead and win if you can!" he shouted.

Lewis used his crop, and Aristides responded. Volcano closed to two lengths, then one length behind.

The infield was a mass of running men, women and children as they raced to catch a glimpse of the winner. From the grandstand, a thundering roar crashed down over the lunging horses.

In the judge's stand. Lewis Clark, president and presiding

judge of the Louisville Jockey Club, calmly leaned forward, one eye closed as he sighted along the rope stretched over the finish line.

Nostrils flaring, neck stretched and white-stockinged pasterns flashing in the brilliant sunlight, Aristides streaked under the rope, winner by a length over Volcano. Verdigres was third, Bob Wooley fourth, Ten Broeck a distant fifth. Of the two fillies in the race, Ascension came in tenth, Gold Mine last.

The first Kentucky Derby was over.

16

THE NINETY-NINTH KENTUCKY DERBY, SATURDAY, MAY 5, 1973.

Louisville didn't awaken because it hadn't slept. On the narrow residential streets around Churchill Downs, thousands picked themselves up off lawns and staggered out of RV's, campers and cars. Many were young and bleary-eyed from a night of drinking, dancing in the streets and various unmentionable activities.

It was still dark as they gathered along three sides of the track fence, waiting for the gates to open at eight. They didn't hold tickets for the stands; their destination was the infield. Many had no idea what horses were running in the Derby. Even if they did, less than a third had any hope of catching a glimpse of the race. They would be competing with over seventy thousand in the infield for the privilege.

The biggest percentage were college students from every part of the nation. Being college students, they considered themselves very clever. To fool security, which didn't allow liquor in the infield, they hid bottles of booze in loaves of bread, hero sandwiches and large bowls of potato salad. Some taped bottles to their ankles while others pre-mixed soft drinks. Infield veterans and locals who knew the officers were up to those tricks, whipped up concoctions like 90-proof jello and bourbon-laced ice cream while young ladies slipped past the guards with foreign objects in their bras and panties.

On the grounds of Churchill Downs, the track print shop finished the last of 160,000 official 99th Kentucky Derby programs. Around the stands, a gardening crew tended the 60,000 plants that had been recently removed from the track greenhouses and set amongst the colorful array of imported tulips. On the opposite side of the track, horsemen and backstretch personnel gathered for breakfast at Thompson's Track Kitchen.

Downtown, women at Kingsley Walker Florists cut and sewed seven hundred red roses on a six-foot piece of green broadcloth. When completed, they would add a swath of silk on the back. The shop had been making the mantle since 1932, when Grace Walker designed a new Derby Winner's garland at the request of track officials who wanted an alternative to the traditional horseshoe of roses. At 1 PM, a police cruiser would escort the florist van carrying the garland and jockey's bouquet to Churchill Downs.

Forty-five miles to the east, an army of cooks prepared eggs, country ham, biscuits, red-eye gravy, grits and pastries for the thousands who would attend the Governor's Derby breakfast on the state capitol grounds at Frankfurt. Later, they would caravan— with a police escort—in cars, buses and limousines to the track.

At Churchill Downs, horses appeared on the track for their morning workouts. Dawn was breaking as they galloped past the grandstand where high above, the twin spires pierced the slender patches of sky they had occupied since 1895. Far below, concessionaire stands fired up their grills and ovens, while vendors inside and outside the gates checked their wares.

Eight o'clock arrived and tens of thousands streamed through the four underground tunnels that led to the infield, Blankets were laid out, coolers opened and volleyball nets erected. As soon as it warmed up, some would strip to their swimsuits and men would encourage women to take theirs off.

By the time the Albright party arrived above the stands in the

Skye Terrace, a record crowd of 134,476 packed Churchill Downs. Debbie Norris had never been to the Derby and was awed by the enormity of the scene. Pointing at the participants in the third race as they galloped past, she exclaimed, "Those poor horses won't get their hearing back for weeks!"

"Wait until the Derby," Cay laughed. "*You'll* be deaf!"

Travis had his binoculars trained on the infield. "A horse just went into the ladies' room."

"Where?" Lynne cried, scanning the area through her glasses.

"By the five-furlong pole. The cops are waiting for it to come out. No telling if it's girls or guys under that costume."

"There's a girl pulling her T-shirt up so the guys can take pictures," Lynne said.

Cay swept the infield with his binoculars.

"She's gone," Lynne giggled. "Saw a cop coming and split. Look at her go! They ought to enter her in the Derby."

"Talk about live entertainment," John said.

"I'd prefer being up here," Debbie said.

"Who wouldn't?" Lynne said, waving an arm to encompass the Skye Terrace, better known as "Millionaires' Row."

"Lots of those characters down in the infield would rather be in the stands," Cay said, "but they've got no choice. Not unless they want to wait in a lottery for years to get a ticket."

Debbie said, "When I moved here from Philadelphia last year, I thought all I had to do was come out on Derby morning and pay as I went through the gate."

"You're not alone," Maripat said. She nodded toward the infield. "Some of them are out there."

The temperature was nearly seventy, and many who couldn't buy seats to the race had brought folding chairs and encamped around the tulip gardens behind the grandstand. The dress was informal—jeans, T-shirts, shorts and tank tops competing with light summer dresses and sport coats. The noise was constant, interrupted periodically by a thunderous roar as the horses in the latest race rushed toward the finish line.

By the end of the day, eighty thousand mint juleps, seven

miles of hot dogs and one thousand sixteen-gallon kegs of beer would be consumed at the Downs, along with twelve hundred filet mignon luncheons, one thousand pounds of shrimp and two thousand slices of Derby pie.

The parking lots were filled, but residents around the track were still flagging motorists, hoping to pack a few more cars onto their already crowded lawns. Signs offered Derby T-shirts, genuine Thoroughbred manure and requesting autographs from famous people. It was a once-a-year opportunity for the moderate-income neighborhood to make a quick buck, and enthusiasm was high. They would worry tomorrow about damaged lawns and shrubs.

Until 1895, the grandstand at Churchill Downs stood on the opposite side of the track, forcing fans to squint into the afternoon sun. A year after the new plant was built, the Derby length was cut from a mile and a half to a mile and a quarter. That distance is still the supreme test for a budding three-year-old.

During the Derby, a horse changes its gallop, or "lead" twice and breathes as often as one hundred-forty times a minute, inhaling four gallons of air with each breath.

In anticipation of the race, its natural nervousness increases as it approaches the gate. When the doors open, it leaps out like a rabbit, increasing its pulse rate more than fourfold. By the time it comes down the long homestretch, its heart is beating two hundred-twenty times a minute. While it struggles, the jockey is urging it to sustain its pace. In most cases, the horses taking the lead at the end of the race aren't speeding up; the others are slowing down.

Because they are tired, this is the time the horses are most susceptible to injury. But the Thoroughbred is bred to compete. Runners have been known to fracture a leg in the final yards of a race and struggle to cross the finish line before collapsing.

In the Jockey's room, the riders for the Derby weighed in with their tack. On the track, groundskeepers carefully raked away any marks that might distract the horses. Near the paddock, the pony riders who would accompany the Derby horses to the post checked their mounts. For this special day, the sturdy animals had colorful flowers braided into their manes and tails and attached to their bridles.

The loudspeaker crackled and the paddock judge called, "Bring your horses to the paddock for the ninth race." A murmur rose from the huge crowd as the horses were led through the chute-gap gate and onto the opposite side of the track. The 99th Kentucky Derby was a little over a half-hour away.

The fourteen horses were beautiful, but one stood out. Red coat glistening in the bright sunlight, Secretariat was fully aware of the attention as spectators crowded the fence, pointing and taking pictures. Despite gloomy predictions by the *Racing Form* and other negative voices, he was the star, and he knew it.

Fast Track pranced sideways, rolling his eyes at the crowd. Joy Loren yanked the shank, and he settled down.

"I'm getting goose bumps all over," Lynne said. She was standing between Cay and Travis in the center of the walking ring. Maripat was with Shawn in the paddock.

"There's Sham," John said, pointing at the Claiborne-bred colt as it was led into the ring.

"He's the hero of the hour in California," Travis said.

Angle Light, the winner over Sham and Secretariat in the Wood Memorial, came next. Until his win in the Wood, he was known mostly for his early speed. Because he was conditioned by Secretariat's trainer, Lucien Laurin, he was coupled as a single betting entry with the big red colt.

"Mom looks fit to bust," Cay said as Joy led Fast Track out of the paddock. Maripat walked next to the horse's shoulder, Shawn at her side.

The noise around the paddock area rose when Secretariat appeared. The overwhelming betting favorite, his fans clapped and shouted his name. Chris Chenery had died in January, but his daughter, Penny Tweedy, was in the ring to watch Secretariat prepare for his attempt to win a second consecutive Derby for Meadow Farm and become only the second Virginia-bred winner in the race's history, the first being Reigh Count in 1928.

Many didn't notice the man mount the presentation stand behind the Winner's Circle—the rose-filled horseshoe that is used only for the Derby—but everyone was aware moments later when the red-coated bugler sounded "Boots and Saddles"—the U.S. Cavalry signal to mount—on a four-foot brass horn. The crowd welcomed the call to the post with a thunderous roar.

Behind the stands, the paddock judge called, "Riders up," and Maripat stepped back while Shawn boosted Roscoe Sands into the saddle. Sands had been Fast Track's jockey from the beginning. This was his first Kentucky Derby.

"Don't let him burn himself out chasing Angle Light or Shecky Green," Shawn said. "Rate him into the stretch, then pump and peddle hard."

"Gotcha," Sands said, saluting Shawn with his crop.

Tugging on Fast Track's shank, Joy said, "Come on, Hose Nose, time to earn your keep." She grinned at Cay as she joined the long procession toward the tunnel. Joy's red jacket, white jeans and the red bow in her hair matched the Albright Stud colors. Fast Track's jockey wore a white blouse with a white "A" in a large red circle on the front and back. The alternating quarters of his white cap were also red.

The spectators moved away from the walking ring as those fortunate enough to have a seat in the stands hurried to watch the post parade.

The crowd stirred, then mounted a swelling cheer as the amplified voice rolled over their heads, "Ladies and gentlemen, Churchill Downs proudly presents the Ninety-Ninth running of the Kentucky Derby. Please join the University of Louisville Cardinal marching band in singing, 'My Old Kentucky Home.'"

Rising in the stands and the infield, the giant chorus serenaded the horses as they emerged from the dark tunnel. This was the magic moment that had inspired Irwin S. Cobb, the homespun philosopher from Paducah, to write, "Until you go to Kentucky and with your own eyes behold the Derby, you ain't never been nowheres and you ain't never seen nothin'!"

Beautiful ladies in picturesque hats and low-cut dresses dabbed their eyes while they sang the haunting Stephen Foster ballad. Shirt-sleeved men sloshed beer and bellowed out the words at the top of their lungs. Inebriated youngsters in the infield got woozily to their feet and threw arms around strangers' shoulders, singing lustily as the long line of horses paraded onto the track. In the press box high above the finish line, cynical newsmen joined in— eyes glistening from too much free booze and sentimental tears.

Few at Churchill Downs witnessed the near-calamity in the starting gate, but the nineteen million watching on TV saw Twice a Prince rear in his steel cage, throwing his jockey and thrashing about, kicking at Our Native in the next stall. While Our Native was led out of the gate, Sham slammed his head against the cold metal, tearing out two teeth. Fast Track bounced and snorted with fright, but Roscoe Sands got him under control.

While Twice a Prince was walked about, Secretariat and Our Native were led into the gate. Then Twice a Prince was reloaded, and the starter, Jim Thomson, pressed the button. A loud bell rang the length of the gate, and the doors exploded open. The 99th Kentucky Derby was underway.

The speedster, Shecky Greene, was in front, Fast Track tenth as the horses entered the clubhouse turn. Secretariat was last.

"Fast Track is catching up!" Lynne screamed, holding the binoculars to her eyes and pointing.

"So is Secretariat," Shawn said. Shecky Greene was still leading, with Gold Bag two lengths back. Sham and Angle Light were fifth and sixth, Fast Track eighth, Secretariat eleventh.

"Mother Mary, holy smoke," Travis breathed as the horses pounded down the backstretch. Fast Track was moving up behind Sham who was in second place behind Shecky Greene on the far turn.

But Secretariat was also on the move. Passing horse after horse on the outside, he drew into third ahead of Fast Track at the 3/8 pole. Sham now had the lead, and Shecky Greene was fading on the rail.

"Come on, Fast Track!" Maripat yelled as she leaned over the balcony rail to watch the horses pass the quarter pole and enter the homestretch. Ron Turcotte applied the crop to Secretariat as the big red horse passed Shecky Greene and pounded after Sham toward the wire.

Debbie whooped and waved her arms as Fast Track put on a burst of speed and nearly caught up with Secretariat. It was a three-horse race at the eighth pole, with Sham falling back.

Bedlam reigned as Our Native and Forego closed on the leaders. Nearing the 16th pole, Fast Track made a last valiant effort as Secretariat drew away from Sham and flashed under the finish wire two and a half lengths ahead.

The chestnut son of Bold Ruler had done the unbelievable. He had run each quarter faster than the last, the final one the fastest in Kentucky Derby history. And he had broken the two-minute barrier, setting a new Derby record of 1:59 2/5.

Sham also broke the old record of 2:00 set by Northern Dancer in 1964, but unfortunately, he came in second. Fast Track— exhausted from the grueling stretch drive—was fifth.

17

Maripat remained in a state of euphoria for weeks after the Derby. Just *having* a horse in the Run for the Roses had fulfilled what had been a decades-old dream. And Fast Track had made a good showing, beating nine other fine horses.

But when the colt tired quickly and finished far back in the Preakness, it was decided to skip the Belmont. That mile and a half distance had exhausted many a three-year-old and forced some, like Majestic Prince, into early retirement.

While Maripat and other owners of Classic runners saw their hopes fade, Secretariat appeared on the covers of *Sports Illustrated*, *Newsweek*, *Time* and *National Observer*, providing an unprecedented boost to the public's interest in Thoroughbred racing. After beating Sham in the Preakness by the same two and a half lengths as the Derby, "Big Red" went on to win the Belmont by a mind-boggling thirty-one lengths and a world-record time of 2:24 flat. For the first time in twenty-five years, America had a new Triple Crown champion. In three awesome performances, Secretariat had forever laid to rest the belief that Bold Ruler's offspring were suspect beyond a mile.

Travis boiled with frustration throughout the hot summer months. Sure of himself in most areas but unwilling to test his mother's temper, he vented his feelings to Cay.

"Are you nuts?" Cay said, stopping in the middle of the foaling barn and glaring at his brother. "It's *Shawn's* fault?"

"Calm down, Little Brother," Travis said, glancing around to make sure they were alone. "I didn't say it was his fault; I said he's getting old and out of step with the times."

"He knows more about horses than you and me put together! Goddamnit, Travis, you piss me off!"

"Maybe you're out of step, too! You sure as hell are if you side with Shawn."

Cay gestured angrily. "You talked about this with Mom?"

"I thought I'd discuss it with you first. Lot of good it's done!"

"You know damn well what Mom would say. They've been together since Mom was a kid! Did you think I'd join with you to gang up against Shawn?"

Travis leaned against a stall. "Look Cay, I'm not talking about friendship or loyalty; I'm talking about making a *business* decision. Can you swear on a stack of Bibles that Shawn made the right decisions conditioning Fast Track? A more knowledgeable trainer might have designed a program that would have prepared Fast Track for that long stretch drive!"

"No way."

"Shawn has to go."

"It isn't your decision to make."

"Someday it will be, Little Brother."

Travis's words stuck in Cay's mind as he entered his final year at the University of Kentucky. The plan was for them to share responsibility on the farm. He knew now that Travis would never accept anything less than total control. Six months after taking over the front office, he was making judgement calls that—in Cay's opinion—were beyond his expertise. It boded ill for the future.

When Cay expressed his apprehensions to Lynne, she defended Travis. Hurt and angry, he shut her out, burying himself in schoolwork and duties on the farm.

"I don't know what's come over him," Lynne said to Travis one day after they had met on a sidewalk in Versailles and ended up eating lunch in a nearby restaurant. "He's like a stranger."

"You'd think going to college, he'd be more open-minded," Travis said.

Lynne shrugged. "When it comes to making tough decisions, Cay lets his emotions get in the way."

Travis stirred at the sight of Lynne's breasts pressing against the table. Having lusted after her for years, he sensed a wedge. "You talk like that isn't your problem."

"I believe in doing what makes the most sense. That means every horse is for sale if the price is right, and employees should do their jobs or be replaced."

"I didn't realize you were so cynical."

"Practical. I was raised in a horse farm. Cay's attitude isn't unique."

Admiring the agile mind behind that gorgeous face, Travis said, "I have some ideas. Got time to listen?"

"The rest of the day. Why don't we go somewhere and park?" She blushed furiously. "You know what I mean."

"I hope so."

Travis sat on the blanket they had spread beside Elkhorn Creek. "They syndicate stallions in thirty-two, thirty-six, maybe forty shares—right?"

"To supposedly coincide with the matings per year," Lynne said. "I've heard of stallions covering sixty, even ninety mares in a season."

"Some stallion managers get greedy." Travis drew a dollar sign in the dirt. "What about selling stock in a farm? Like syndicating a stallion, only you sell lots more shares."

Lynne frowned. "Why would anyone do that?"

"If you want to make it to the top in this business it takes money—*lots* of money. Albright Stud is one of the biggest, but I can make it bigger…and better."

"Wouldn't that give outsiders a say in what's going on?"

"Not if you retain control. That's an important lesson I learned on Wall Street. Control is everything."

"I can't imagine your mother letting you do that."

"Not right away. It'll take time to put it together. A lot can happen between now and then."

"What about Cay?"

"Does it matter? Just how serious is it between you two?"

Lynne glanced down at her hands. "It would have mattered a year ago. Now, I don't know. I really loved him. I still do! But…"

"But things haven't been going so well lately."

Lynne nodded. "He's not fun to be with anymore."

"You telling me! He used to be laid back—nothing seemed to bother him. Now he wants to get involved in everything."

"That's what he says about you."

"There's a difference," Travis said. "I love Cay and wouldn't hurt him for anything in the world, but he can't see the whole picture. You're right; his emotions get in the way. We could make a great team, damnit!"

"With you as boss."

"That's right. It takes vision and experience to make my plan work. Cay's short on both. He may catch up—even pass me someday. If that happens, we can make new arrangements."

"Why do I find that hard to believe?"

"About him passing me up or taking over?"

"Both. You don't come off as the humble type."

"I won't stand still. Should be easy to keep a jump ahead."

Lynne lay back on the blanket, hands laced behind her neck. Her shirt stretched over her breasts and pulled away from her belt, exposing a deeply inverted navel. Acting oblivious to Travis's stare, she said, "Tell me more about this plan. Suppose you get all the money. What would you do with it?"

"Expand the stallion roster. Build up the racing stable. Invest some in the stock market. Have fun."

"I like that fun part. Life can't be all work."

"Speaking of fun, how about doing the town tonight?"

"What about Debbie?"

"Who's she?"

"Not serious, huh?"

"It takes two to tango. And she's in Louisville."

"When out of sight…"

"Something like that."

The months passed swiftly. One February afternoon, Maripat entered the east wing of Windsong Manor, a pile of folded clothes in her arms. With the maid out sick for nearly a week, Maripat had been washing clothes since early morning.

Respecting the east wing as her sons' domain, she seldom ventured this far. As she entered Cay's room, the sound of voices came from across the hall. She recognized Travis's and a moment later his companion's. She froze as the murmurings became more urgent and turned into cries of ecstasy that needed no interpretation. Dropping Cay's laundry on his bed, she fled down the long hall and into the main house.

While coffee brewed in the kitchen, she got a mug out of the cabinet and opened a box of cookies. When she poured the coffee, she frowned, then added a healthy shot of bourbon. Carrying the mug and cookies into the drawing room, she piled several pillows on one end of the couch, kicked off her shoes and stretched out.

Flames danced in the stone fireplace as Maripat contemplated her toes. She sipped the bourbon-laced coffee and munched on a cookie. A deep sigh escaped her lips. Some days just weren't meant to go right.

Not that the incident in the east wing had come as a great surprise. Travis and Lynne had been going steady for months. It would have been naïve to expect less than a sexual relationship from such an explosive combination.

When Travis started dating Lynne, Maripat had feared a confrontation between the brothers. But Cay only smiled and wished Travis luck—a far cry from what his reaction would have been a year earlier when Lynne was still an important part of his life.

Reaching in the box for another cookie, Maripat thought about Lynne and the way she had practically become a member of the family. First Cay, now Travis.

Lynne had a quick mind, but it could also be calculating, spurred on by a streak of selfishness that was congruent with youth. Hopefully, she would become less self-centered as she matured and had to take on more responsibilities.

18

April blossoms produced a rainbow of colors on the hillsides as the rented motorboat moved slowly down the Kentucky River and past the gleaming white state capitol in Frankfurt. Guiding the wheel with his toes, Cay handed another can of beer to his companion and popped one open for himself.

"You Yanks have done rather well since we gave you your freedom," Tim Grayson said. While completing two years of postgraduate study at UK, he had become Cay's closest friend.

"Are you thinking about our horses or our women?"

"Your women, of course. Not that you haven't bred some successful animals after pirating the best stallions from our shores." Tim's father, Sir Reginald Grayson, owned Broadheim Stud, one of England's foremost breeding farms.

Evading Tim's lighthearted dig, Cay said, "I thought we were talking about women."

"Ah yes! It's going to be difficult leaving them behind when I go home. Especially luscious Lynne. How could you turn her over to your brother? She was madly in love with you. Still is, I'll wager."

"I didn't turn her over to Travis," Cay protested. "It was a case of mutual consent."

"In other words…you ran, she rebounded."

"She was rebounding long before I ran."

"I'll take your word for it, old boy." Tim looked up at the heavily-forested hills that rose steeply from the river's edge. "Interesting to think that just a couple of centuries ago red Indians shot arrows at Daniel Boone around here."

"Makes us sound downright backward, doesn't it? How long has your farm been in the family? Three hundred years?"

"A little over four. Used to be two thousand acres, but death duty taxes reduced it three-fifty. Still quite large by Newmarket standards. I'm expecting you to visit. We Grayson's don't extend invitations lightly."

"Sure your family will agree? One look at me and they might run screaming out the back door."

"Never fear. Since the arrival of my little sister, we can survive *anything*! We've got our own wild Indian, minus bow and arrows, thank god." He ran a hand over his light brown hair. "I feel lucky to still have my scalp."

"You couldn't live without her," Cay laughed.

Tim's gaunt aristocratic features lit up in a big smile. "She's a handful, but we love her. Four more weeks and I'll be on my way home. I've already gotten bloody hell for missing her fifth birthday."

"Always wondered what it would be like to have a sister," Cay said. "Sounds like fun."

"I was eighteen when Maudie was born, Keith fifteen. She isn't really a bratty kid, just wild. And ride! You ought to see her on a horse. She has absolutely no fear and is already challenging jumps that I didn't tackle until I was in my teens."

"Don't be surprised if I show up on your doorstep someday. You can give me the grand tour of Newmarket."

Tim rested the beer can on his stomach. "Come anytime. I'll show you what *real* horses look like."

19

May came to the Bluegrass, creating a rippling sea of green flooded with a unique variety of savanna-woodland trees. Birds sang while horses grazed under giant bur oaks that were a century old when John Finley arrived in 1767 to hunt and trade with the Indians.

Cannonade won the Kentucky Derby, and Cay graduated from UK. In July, a colt by Raise a Native set a record at Keeneland, selling for $625,000. The success of Majestic Prince on the track five years earlier had set a trend, and breeders were happily predicting a steady rise in yearling prices. It reinforced Travis's call for modernizing to keep pace with the market. Tensions grew between the brothers as summer progressed.

One day in late August, Cay rode his Thoroughbred gelding, JD, along Elkhorn Creek, the stream that meandered through Woodford County and formed the northern boundary of Albright Stud. It had become a habit for Cay in recent weeks…getting away for a while in the late afternoon to think and plan.

JD snorted and tossed his head. A horse stood in the middle of the creek, ears flicking back and forth. Its rider rose in the stirrups and waved.

"What the hell?" Cay murmured as he pulled JD up.

"Hi!" Lynne called gaily. Water splashed over bare legs as she urged her horse forward. She was barefooted and wearing cutoffs and a tiny pink halter top that sagged under the weight of heavy breasts. Her long black hair was tied in a ponytail.

"What brings you here?" Cay asked, annoyed at the interruption. Except for brief greetings when she appeared at the house with Travis and a few words when they met on campus, they hadn't really talked since Lynne had sided with Travis last September.

"It's been so hot," Lynne said, leaning forward to pat her horse's neck. "I got to thinking how nice it would be to soak my feet in the creek and saddled up."

Cay grunted and looked around. "Even the creek water's warm on a day like this."

"But it's wet." Lynne smiled. Swinging a slender leg over the western saddle, she dropped lightly to the ground and dug her toes in the damp earth. "Come on. It'll do you good."

Harboring a strong suspicion that this meeting wasn't accidental, Cay dismounted and led JD to the tree where Lynne was tying her horse. "It's been hot all summer. Why the sudden urge to come out now?"

"Why not?" Lynne said, avoiding his eyes as she sat down on the bank and stuck her feet in the water. "Wonderful!"

Rolling up his jeans and removing his tennis shoes and socks, Cay rested on his elbows and stretched out beside Lynne. "Now tell me why you really came."

"I can't just come out to cool off?"

"I know you, Lynne. As well as anyone. Maybe more. You've got that gleam in your eye."

Lynne heaved a deep sigh, a move that stretched her halter top to the limit. "I wanted to talk, that's all," she said.

Cay watched a frog hop along the opposite bank.

A pleading note. "I thought maybe we could talk about stuff… you…me." A whisper. "Us."

An incredulous look. "Us? You're practically engaged to Travis and you want to talk about *us*?"

"That's it," Lynne said, hugging her legs and resting her chin on her knees. "Travis is talking marriage. It scares me."

"You don't want to get married?"

"In some ways, but…" She looked down at Cay. "I guess I love him, but I'm not sure I love him enough. You know, like I loved you."

Cay stirred uneasily. "What are you getting at?"

"Us, damnit!" Lynne hovered over Cay, nipples brushing his chest. "We had something good, and I don't know if I'll ever find it again."

Cay dropped flat on the ground, trying to avoid those probing breasts and lovely face just inches from his. "Lynne, this is crazy talk!" he said lamely. "It's getting us nowhere. You can't jump back and forth between Travis and me."

Lynne's jaw fell, and she slapped him hard. "Bastard!" She sat back, appalled. Tears appeared in her eyes. "Oh, Cay, I'm sorry!" She sprawled across his chest, and buried her face in his neck. "I love you so much!"

Cay wrapped his arms around the sobbing young woman. He knew that many of their problems had been his fault, but he had been hurt, too. Particularly by the way Lynne had taken up so quickly with his brother. Although he had hidden it well, his heart had ached for months.

Lynne squirmed in his arms and kissed his ear, then followed his jaw line with a series of pecks. Reaching his lips, she thrust her tongue in his mouth.

Cay pushed her away. "Lynne we shouldn't—"

"Shouldn't what?" she hissed. "Kiss? Hug? Make love? Maybe we shouldn't even be talking! Is that what you think?"

"Stop playing with my head."

"I'm not playing with your head!" Lynne shouted, "I'm just trying to get mine on straight!"

Cay grinned in spite of himself. "You sure have a strange way of going about it."

She kissed him again. "All's fair in love and war."

Cay tried to sit up. "Can we get serious about this?"

"Later," Lynne said, pushing him back. "First I want you to make love to me."

"Lynne---"

"No deals," she said, placing a finger over his lips. "No promises. Give me what I want, then we'll talk." In one swift motion, she whipped off the pink halter top and bared her breasts. The nipples protruded like dark brown pennies.

It was a sight that could make a priest renounce his vows, and Cay was no priest. He rolled the nipples between thumbs and forefingers. Lynne threw her head back and moaned.

Tearing at his belt, she pulled his jeans and shorts down. She massaged him while he continued to knead her breasts.

"Take everything off," Cay gasped as he struggled to remove his shirt.

Lynne stripped, then pulled Cay's jeans below his knees. "I can't wait," she cried, lowering herself over his groin.

While Lynne rode Cay furiously, he fondled her breasts and flicked his thumbs over swollen nipples. Her face reddened, and she screamed in the midst of a shattering climax. He came moments later. She fell limply on his chest.

Lynne lay beside Cay, one leg thrown over his stomach. He said, "I thought you came out here to cool off."

"Something more interesting came up."

"Aaaagh."

"Well, it did."

"We better get dressed. Never know who might come along. A couple weeks ago, some kids floated by on inner tubes."

"Maybe they're hiding in the bushes right now."

"Move it. You're making me nervous."

They ended up in the creek, where Cay tried to duck Lynne's head under the surface. By the time he chased her along the wooded bank, their bodies were dry. Five minutes later, they were clothed and sitting side by side with their feet in the water.

Lynne looked at Cay. "Guess we should talk."

He nodded and threw a rock in the creek.

"I suppose you want to know about Travis and me."

A shrug. "Until today, I had stopped wondering."

"What about now?"

Cay looked at the ground, regretting his moment of weakness. He had enough troubles without this. "You say you love me and you're thinking about marrying Travis. It doesn't make sense."

Lynne put a hand on Cay's arm. "I've always loved you. We talked about marriage—lots of times. Then you started having fights with Travis, and things got all muddled up. It was like...like we didn't have any future."

"It's the farm, isn't it?" Cay said. "That's what you mean about things being muddled up. You don't see much future with me because of where I stand in the hierarchy."

"Oh Cay," Lynne said quietly, tears springing into her dark eyes, "there's lots more to it than that."

"But being mistress of Albright Stud is important, isn't it? You wouldn't want to be the wife of the number two man."

Lynne bit off an angry retort. Cay was right. She didn't want to be married to the junior partner. "You must think I'm terrible."

"You're smart. The way things are going, I may not be able to stay here."

"What else can you do? This farm is your *life!*"

"Might be my death if I stick around." Cay had ideas, but he wasn't ready to voice them, certainly not to Lynne. He believed she thought she loved him, but he mistrusted her motives.

"What about us?" Lynne asked in a barely audible voice.

"I think it best that we forget about today. I'm not saying I don't have feelings for you, but it won't work. Let's not do something that will make us hate each other."

Throwing her arms around Cay's neck, Lynne laid her head on his shoulder. "That's it? I should marry Travis?"

"Would it be so bad?"

"He's been good to me. He keeps telling me he loves me and wants us to get married."

"What have you been saying back?"

"That I love him but I want time to think."

"No reason to refuse."

Clutching Cay's neck, Lynne whispered, "But you're the one I really love! I'll never love anyone like I love you!"

Cay smoothed her hair.

"What am I going to do?" she wept. "Do you know how hard it will be married to Travis and seeing you everyday?"

"Maybe I can do something about that."

20

In an area where parties are a way of life, the engagement bash for Lynne and Travis was *the* October event. Hundreds crowded into Windsong Manor and spilled out onto the surrounding lawn.

George and Christina Ross sat with Maripat and John and watched their daughter dance with Cay. "They look nice together, don't they?" Christina said. "I got a crush on Cay the first time I saw him, didn't I George?"

"Ruined my day."

"It's that hair and those eyes and that sloppy grin," Maripat said. "Had me drooling before I got him home from the hospital."

John said, "What she means is no hair and the grin was gas."

Maripat said, "Listen to the big authority on kids!"

John stuck his thumbs under the black cummerbund that encircled his flat stomach. "I was a kid once. You oughta know. Remember when we let the air out of that tobacco farmer's tires when he yelled at us for crossing his field?"

"I'm talking about itty bitty kids!"

"Speaking of kids," George said, "here comes Cay."

Grabbing the back of his mother's chair, Cay said, "Your turn, Mom. How did you say it in your day——'Let's cut a rug?'"

"*My* day!" she cried, jumping up and seizing his hand. "Come on, youngun; I'll show you who's old!"

They squeezed their way onto the packed dance floor. "You sure couldn't do your kind of dancing in this crowd," Maripat said.

"More fun this way. I can feel your backbone and those little boobies."

Maripat giggled. "That's a disrespectful way to talk to your mother."

"It's a compliment. Bet you don't weigh any more than you did when you were my age. Look at Mag Ellis over there—lots younger than you and she looks like a broodmare about to foal. Got a rear on her that would make three of yours."

Maripat sighed and rested her cheek against his chest. "You always say the nicest things to me."

"Only to you, Mom."

"Not that I don't like hearing those sweet nothings but it seems a shame you don't have a steady girl to whisper them to."

"Why do I need a steady girl when I have you?"

Maripat looked up, green eyes the same color as Cay's, a smile twitching at one corner of her mouth. "If I have to explain that, you're in a peck of trouble. Maybe we should have a quiet talk and get your priorities straight."

"Why don't we do that?"

Two days later, Cay and Maripat walked along a tree-shaded lane that divided a series of paddocks.

"We should do this more often," Maripat said.

"Pretty this time of year with all the leaves changing."

"Sure is." A sidelong glance. "Is that what we're here to talk about?"

"Among other things. I guess you know I'm not happy with the way things are going on the farm."

"Yes."

Cay stopped and grasped Maripat's shoulders. "It won't work, Mom."

"I see problems," she acknowledged, "but where there's a will, there's a way."

"There's a way, but I don't think you'll like it."

Maripat searched his face. "Try me."

"I made up my mind two months ago—thought about it for a long time before that."

"Made up your mind?" Maripat said softly. "You couldn't talk it over with me first?"

"That's what I'm doing now. I couldn't come to you until I had thought it through. It was too complicated, and I didn't want to hurt you anymore than I have to."

"It's that bad?"

"I hope not." Cay's next words confirmed Maripat's worst fears. "I have to get my own place. Travis and I can't work together. You must know that by now."

Maripat took his hand and started off at a brisk pace. They walked in silence toward an area where picnic tables had been set up for the farmhands. Sitting on a table with her feet on the bench, she said, "I've seen this coming for a long time. It can't be worked out?"

"Do you think Travis will change?"

"He might, What about you?"

"Travis and I have completely different views on how to run the farm, Mom. I don't think small, but he's got ideas so big they scare me to death! This is a family operation and I want to keep it that way."

"Leaving brings that to an end, doesn't it?"

"It'll still be in the family. Unless Travis brings outsiders in."

"I'll never allow that."

"You sure? He can be pretty persuasive."

"I'll never give up ownership. Not as long as I'm part of Albright Stud. I love this farm as much as you do." Maripat touched his cheek. "I'll help you fight this through."

"What about the millions Travis wants to spend on horses? He's been butting in on everything from selecting matings to how to run the racing string! Has he ever talked to you about bringing in another trainer over Shawn?"

A surprised look. "Never! When did that come up?"

"After Fast Track lost the Derby."

"And?"

"I told him he was nuts. He didn't speak to me for a week."

Maripat's eyes snapped angrily. "Shawn's not just a good trainer—he's family. Have you talked to him about this?"

"He'd picked up on it already. Travis is easy to read."

"Oh, lordy." Shoulders drooping, Maripat picked at a thread on her plaid skirt.

Cay sat beside her and put an arm around her small shoulders. "I said I want to leave, not get out of your life!"

"What do you want to do?"

"I've got that money that my grandparents left. It was a little over a million-three the last statement."

"It's been drawing interest for twenty-two years. Your half, anyway. Travis claims he's doubled his on the stock market since he withdrew it four years ago."

"I want mine in land and horses."

Maripat laid a hand on his. "A million seems like a lot, but it won't go far in this business."

"I can live cheap and work hard. Travis may disagree, but I know how to run a horse farm."

"He may not agree with the way you go about it, but he knows you're one of the best horsemen around. He'll miss having you running things out back."

"Shawn, too?"

Maripat's eyes widened. "Shawn's leaving?"

"Do you think he'd let me go without him?"

"You've already talked it over with Shawn?" Maripat said, saddened that she wasn't the first to know.

"We've been talking about it for a long time. It happened bit by bit. I didn't want to bother you until it was definite."

Maripat blinked back tears. "Does this have anything to do with the engagement party?"

"Not a bit. That was over a long time ago."

"I hope so...for both your sakes. That's one reason why I decided to fix up the old Albright home for them. Not to mention that two women rarely get along under the same roof."

Cay hugged her tighter. "I'm not moving far away either."

Red eyebrows shot up. "You've already found a place?"

"Maybe. You know the Deeter Farm on Midway Road?"

"Where old man Jackson used to raise pigs?"

"Yep. Left it well fertilized. Ten years since anybody's lived there. Bill Goodwin's been leasing it as grazing land for his cattle. The outside fences are still good. That two-story Federal brick house was built in eighteen twenty-five. It could be fixed up real nice."

"Probably got weeds growing in the attic. How many acres?"

"A little over five hundred. When the original owner's great-grandson died seventeen years ago, he left no children and no will. The relatives have been squabbling over it ever since. They came to an agreement a month ago. Abe Crawling's got the listing. If I pay cash, I can get it for a thousand an acre."

"You'll spend that much again fixing it up and buying equipment."

"It'll be worth twice that when I'm finished."

"You can't have a horse farm without horses."

"I can borrow on the property; that'll give me a good start buying horses. I'm not in a hurry, but Shawn is. He doesn't want to be a hundred when I win the Derby."

"Oh, lordy."

"Think of it as a plus. Everyone will live happily ever after. Talk to John, He'll agree it's best."

A sharp look. "You don't mind?"

"John's family." Cay bent down and whispered in Maripat's ear, "In more ways than one."

Maripat's face turned as red as her hair. "You're being impertinent, youngun'!"

"Hey, you're my favorite mother, and John's been like an uncle to me all my life. You guys can tell the whole world as far as I'm concerned. If you decide to get married, I'll ride JD down the aisle and throw flowers."

Face still tingling, Maripat said, "We've never talked about marriage."

"Then live together! It's all the rage these days."

Maripat hopped off the table. "Come on. We've only got an hour of daylight left. Let's look at this farm of yours."

21

Maripat called John and arranged to meet him at the Idle Hour Country Club for dinner. He reacted to the news with a loud laugh and signaled the waitress for another round of drinks.

"You think it's funny?" Maripat fumed.

"Nope. I'm just surprised it didn't happen sooner."

"Don't tell me Cay's been talking to you, too!"

"Calm down, Little Bit. He hasn't said a word to me."

Maripat twisted her napkin. "I should have wrung that twerp's neck when he was still pint-sized."

"Admit it; you're proud of him."

A reluctant smile. "He *has* had access to that inheritance for a year and hasn't withdrawn a penny. Spending it on a farm sounds better than gambling it on the stock market. It's a reasonable solution considering the problems between the boys. He can't come back after he leaves. It would be too disruptive."

"So?"

"You're the lawyer. What would you do?"

"I'm hardly a disinterested observer."

"Cut the evasive maneuvering, John! I have my own ideas, but I want to hear yours first."

"Give Cay his share of the stud and send him on his way. That provides him with the needed working capital and ends the discord."

"And leaves me without Shawn and working exclusively with Travis," Maripat said.

"Now *that's* an interesting scenario," John grinned.

"Thanks a bunch!"

"You've heard my side. Agree with yours?"

"Essentially. Cay and Travis were close before all this fighting started over how to run the farm. With Cay on his own, they can be friends again."

"Good point."

"It will eliminate a volatile situation with Lynne around."

"*Very* good point."

"Looks like we're in agreement."

The talks continued for a week, first with Cay, then with Travis. Travis was delighted. Someday the farm would be his!

Cay gave up his share of Albright Stud for $3 million and twenty broodmares and yearlings. With that and his inheritance, he could buy the Midway property, refurbish the residence, fences and outbuildings and purchase additional stock. The capital left would carry him for years.

It hit Lynne hard. Had she shown more faith in Cay, she might be helping him build what could be one of the most beautiful farms in the Bluegrass! Black walnut, ash, hard maple, oak hickory and elm trees dotted the land, and Elkhorn Creek wound through the park-like meadows. After touring the farm with Travis and Cay, she fell into a blue funk that lasted a week.

By late April, the outbuildings and fences were nearly

completed. Cay lived with Shawn in one of the three farm residences while the main house was renovated.

On the second Saturday in June, Travis and Lynne were married, and Cay was best man.

The next morning after seeing the couple off on the first leg of a honeymoon to Hawaii, Cay returned home, put on his old jeans and boots and went back to work.

PART III

1979-1984

"A man who writes of the Kentucky Derby as he would about the running of the Belmont Stakes would have his license taken up and social security number canceled, and nobody would read him either."

Turf writer, Joe H. Palmer

1

Four years of hard work and over a million dollars brought about spectacular changes on the old Deeter property. A new name—Woodland Farm—was etched in bronze plaques on the tall limestone pillars that flanked the entrance, and a low slave-built mortarless rock wall bordered the property along Midway Road. Barely visible in the trees at the end of a long curving lane, the completely restored Federal brick house was surrounded by manicured lawns sweeping down over a gentle slope.

Five barns, three new and two rebuilt, gleamed with fresh paint, and miles of four-rail fencing separated verdant paddocks where horses grazed under the spreading branches of giant trees.

Joy Loren had joined Shawn in the move to Woodland Farm. An employee at Albright Stud since she was a freshman in high school—a job that had included being Fast Track's groom—Joy had worked her way up there to assistant trainer. At thirty-three, she couldn't imagine any career except one with horses.

The Albright Stud racing stable was now in the care of a public trainer. Yearlings were broken on the farm, then shipped to Lem McCarthy's stable in New York. McCarthy had done well with the string, producing five stakes winners in three years.

As predicted, the relationship between the brothers improved. With Cay no longer a threat and Shawn gone, Travis brought about many of the changes he had advocated for so long. Knowing his mother's attitude toward selling any interest in the farm, he kept silent and bided his time.

Making liberal use of the stock market profits made from investing his inheritance, Travis and Lynne threw elaborate parties and traveled extensively. They toured Europe, cruised the Mediterranean, gambled in Las Vegas and the Caribbean and became frequent visitors to Aspen, Palm Springs and New York City.

Maripat set her foot down when the young couple vacationed in Mexico at the height of the breeding and foaling season. Angry at being restricted but having no alternative as long as his mother retained control, Travis curtailed traveling during the busy times of the year.

Cay and Lynne seldom saw each other outside family or social gatherings. The strong sexual attraction had not diminished. If anything, it was heightened by the knowledge that Lynne was off limits— a tempting but forbidden fruit.

2

Cay's fourth spring at Woodland Farm was the busiest yet. The Kentucky Derby was just weeks away, and along with the breeding and foaling, several yearlings were being prepared for the Keeneland July Selected Yearling sale.

Soon guests from all over the world would descend on the Bluegrass for the festivities that surrounded Derby Week. Cay would be entertaining for the first time, and his guests were coming from England. Five years had passed since his friend,

Tim Grayson, had returned to the family estate in Newmarket, the principal center of British Thoroughbred racing. They had kept in touch by mail and telephone, and last Christmas Cay had invited the Graysons to visit. They would arrive in late April—Sir Reginald and his wife, Alicia, Tim and his younger brother, Keith, and their ten-year-old sister, Maudie.

Tim introduced Cay to his family near the Blue Grass Field check-in counter.

Reginald Grayson was six feet tall with the same light brown hair and lean aristocratic features as his eldest son. Alicia was nearly as tall as her husband, a lithe English beauty with a peach-blossom complexion, wide-set brown eyes and golden hair.

Keith was twenty-two, tow-headed, and the tallest in the family. Six-three and slender, he could have been mistaken for a guard on the Kentucky Wildcat basketball team.

Cay looked past Keith at an unruly mop of dark blond hair that kept appearing and disappearing. Raising an eyebrow, he asked Tim, "Is that timid creature the holy terror I've heard so much about?"

Grinning, Tim reached behind his father and produced a squirming protesting girl. She was all arms and legs and thin as a rail. A sprinkling of freckles decorated her nose. Blushing furiously, she glanced at Cay with huge saucer-like hazel eyes, then stared down at her feet.

Tim shook his head sadly. "Look at her...destroyed by the famous Cay Albright charm. A shame...and she's so young."

Still looking down, she kicked Tim's ankle. "Beast!"

Laughing, Cay held out his hand. "Anybody who kicks Tim is a friend of mine. Shake, Maudie. We're going to be buddies."

"Oh, that will be lovely!" she cried, flashing a sunshine smile and gripping his hand with long bony fingers.

Leaning on the check-out counter, Tim rubbed his ankle. "You're in for it now, old chap. Don't say I didn't warn you."

The next two weeks passed swiftly. Once word got out that Sir Reginald Grayson of Broadheim Stud was in the area, invitations poured in from all over the Bluegrass. It was impossible to visit every farm or attend all the parties, but the Graysons and Cay, sometimes with Maripat and John, made a valiant effort. In between, Cay conducted private tours of various horse farms.

Reginald—or "Reggie" as he insisted on being called—said as they passed the entrance to Elmendorf Farm, "Didn't this once belong to Daniel Swigert?"

Cay nodded. "He bought it from Milton Sanford back around Eighteen-Eighty. It was called Preakness Stud then. Swigert renamed it Elmendorf after his wife's Dutch grandmother."

"Ah, Preakness," Reggie said. "That's a story we're not proud of. When he was imported to England by the Duke of Hamilton, some questioned his bloodlines, but others were quite excited. The duke had a temper. So did Preakness, but that's not unusual for a stallion. A sad, sad tale."

"What happened?" Maudie asked from the back seat of the big Suburban.

Looking over his shoulder from his place beside Cay, Reggie said, "Not long after Preakness arrived, he chased the duke out of his stall. The duke got a gun and shot him."

"That's terrible!" Maudie exclaimed. She looked at the trees and rolling acres that formed the corner of Paris and Iron Works Pikes. "He traveled all the way from here to get killed! Too bad that dumb duke didn't shoot himself!"

"My thoughts exactly," Cay said.

Maudie smiled and wriggled with delight.

Cay said, "The horse park's just down the road."

"Yea!" Maudie yelled at the mention of the new thousand-acre Kentucky Horse Park. Offering a museum, exhibits and various breeds of horses, it hosted a wide variety of equestrian shows and competitions, including the World Three-Day Event Championship that had been held there the previous September as part of the opening celebrations.

Cay looked back at the smiling girl. "You're beginning to sound more like an American every day, Toothpick."

Maudie quivered with happiness. She loved her new nickname. She loved everything about Cay. She loved *Cay*! The fact that he was seventeen years older was a minor inconvenience. Someday he would be hers forever!

At the intersection of Iron Works Pike and Newtown Road, Reggie said, "One expects smoke from an iron works factory."

"There was one here once," Cay said. "It produced shot and cannon balls for the Battle of New Orleans." He glanced at Tim. "You might remember reading about that in your history books."

"I thought it was a song…about the Yanks firing on us with alligators loaded with cannon balls and powder."

"That's the one," Cay grinned.

"Too bad Maudie wasn't on our side then," Tim said. "Those alligators wouldn't have stopped until they got to Cuba."

"If you'd been there they would have laughed so hard they would have drowned!" Maudie shot back.

"Here! Here!" Keith said. "That's telling him, Sis."

Alicia Grayson laughed. "Sure we aren't wearing you down, Cay? This constant bickering can get on one's nerves."

Cay's forehead wrinkled above his aviator sunglasses. "Maybe we should drop the kid off somewhere. With her out of the way, it would be a lot quieter."

"You better not!" Maudie cried. Looking back, Cay received the full force of her crossed eyes and protruding tongue.

"*Maudie!*" Alicia exclaimed. "How many times have I told you not to do that! If you could just see yourself!"

"She does!" Keith crowed. "Practices in front of a mirror."

Tim grabbed Maudie before she could clobber Keith. Holding the struggling girl, he smiled at Cay. "Still think it would be fun to have a little sister?"

"Might be worth reconsidering," Cay laughed as he turned into the horse park.

3

Maudie stuck close to Cay throughout Derby Week. He enjoyed her bubbly personality and the long rides they took on the farm and the back roads.

Having grown up around horses, she had assisted in the birth of many—a point she proved dramatically one night when Cay stayed up with a favorite broodmare. It was past Maudie's bedtime, but Cay talked her parents into letting her help.

It was nearly eleven as Cay and Maudie hurried through a warm spring downpour toward the foaling barn. Eleven months and four days had passed since the mare was bred. The night watchman had reported she was restless, lying down, then standing up, pacing the stall and pawing the ground. This particular broodmare—one of the selections Cay had made from the Albright Stud herd when he left—had difficulty with her last foal, and he wanted to be there should it happen again.

"Does she mind having people around?" Maudie asked as they walked down the long dimly-lit aisle that separated the double row of stalls.

"Not Sally. I helped deliver her ten years ago. We've been close personal friends ever since."

Maudie giggled. "Close personal friends with a horse?"

"I thought you loved horses."

"I do, but they don't *talk* to me!"

"Must be because they're English horses."

"Silly goose!"

The watchman was peering through the bars of the big foaling stall. Twenty feet square and covered with a thick layer of straw, it provided ample room for the mare to move about.

"She's gettin' ready," the lean elderly black man said. "Broke her water a few minutes ago." He had retired from Albright Stud two years ago, but Cay had persuaded him to take the apartment above the barn and help during the foaling season.

"Thanks, Joe," Cay said. "We'll take it from here."

"Cute little helper you've got there," Joe grinned. "Ready to give Cay a a hand with the foal, Maudie?"

"Rarin'to go," she smiled, trying out some recently acquired American slang.

Joe went up the stairs that led to the loft.

The mare sniffed the straw, Not wanting to disturb her, Cay and Maudie stayed outside and watched her movements. "She traces back in the tail-female line to Devil's Fire," Cay said. While they monitored the mare, he told Maudie about the champion colt that had won the Hopeful at Saratoga forty years ago.

The mare raised her tail and rocked back and forth. "Let's check her," Cay said. They went inside, and Maudie held the mare's head while he donned an arm-length rubber glove and thrust his hand into the mare's vagina. Working carefully, he split the placenta, then withdrew his arm and stripped the glove off.

The mare made a grunting sound and lay down. "It won't be long now, sweetheart," Maudie cooed, petting the soft muzzle.

"It's been a good ten minutes since she broke her water," Cay said. "Contractions should start anytime."

Maudie knelt beside Cay in the straw. "Do you have a name for it if it's a filly?" Cay had said earlier that he was going to keep the foal if it was.

"How about Little Maudie?"

A big smile revealed a mouthful of braces. "I'd love to have it named for me!" She made a face. "Maudie, not Maud! It sounds like something smelly you step in. I love my grandmother, and it's nice being named after her, but I do wish she had been named something besides *Maud!*"

The mare's stomach contracted as she went into labor. Cay glanced at his watch. "Might arrive before the witching hour."

The rain increased and pounded against the window set high in the wall. "Its front legs are showing!" Maudie cried.

"Hold Sally's tail out of the way," Cay said as seized the foal's legs and assisted the mare with a gentle pull. The foal began to make feeble movements.

Peeling the placenta away, Cay exposed the nostrils and cleaned the mucus so the foal could breathe. Its head appeared, tucked against the legs. The mare pushed down hard, forcing the muscles in her abdomen to contract mightily.

Still holding the mare's tail, Maudie watched the foal slide wetly onto the straw. Peering under its rear leg, she smiled. "It's Little Maudie!"

After dousing the broken navel stump with iodine, Cay stuck his finger in the foal's mouth. It began to suck, and he smiled with satisfaction.

While the mare scrambled to her feet and bent over the foal, Cay gathered the remains of the placenta and amniotic sack from under the mare's tail and tied them in a big knot. It kept the mare from stepping on the strands and applied a downward pull to the afterbirth. Weighing between ten and twenty pounds, it had to detach itself within three hours to prevent infection.

"Isn't she beautiful?" Maudie said as the mare licked and nuzzled the long-legged foal.

Still half-blind, it rose shakily to its feet and staggered about, red lips curled back, sucking the air. "Give her a break, Sally," Cay said as the mare touched noses with its offspring. As if obeying the admonition, the mare presented her side to the foal that was now running in frantic circles.

Maudie laughed as the foal stuck its head between its mother's forelegs. "The other end!" she cried, making shooing motions with her hands.

The foal butted the mare's side until it reached the flank. Plunging its soft muzzle underneath, it seized a teat and began to suck. "About time," Cay said while Maudie clapped.

It was nearly two when they returned to the house. Maudie went to sleep dreaming that someday her namesake would race in England and win the Epsom Oaks.

4

Bluegrass hostesses knew that to have a good turnout at their Derby parties, they had to choose earlier days in the week. Thursday night and Derby Eve were owned by socialites like Marylou Whitney and Anita Madden. Working up to Wednesday often took years.

Knowing how much Lynne wanted the opportunity, Maripat yielded her Thursday night hostess duties to her daughter-in-law. The party was held as usual at Windsong Manor, and the majority of the three hundred guests were horse people. They came from as far away as Canada, New York, Florida and California, and all were anxious to meet the guests of honor, Sir Reginald Grayson and his family. The history of Sir Reginald's Broadheim Stud extended back over two hundred-fifty years, and an ancestor had entered a colt in the first English Derby in 1780.

Guests turning off Old Frankfurt Pike were greeted by the sight of the huge mansion at the end of the long tree-lined lane. Towering white columns glowed under a battery of lights. At the top of the circular driveway, teams of valets parked cars while men in tuxedos and white gloves assisted ladies to the ground. Once through the receiving line under the glittering chandelier, the guests moved into the main house where waiters with trays of drinks and hors d'oeuvres weaved through crowded rooms. Music from a twelve-piece orchestra drifted over manicured lawns while couples strolled under hanging lanterns and groups discussed horses and the upcoming Derby.

Maripat touched John's arm. "What do you think Cay and Travis are talking about?"

"If I know Travis, he's probably trying to sell Cay something. When it comes to making money, that boy never quits."

"Reminds me of a car salesman with that cigar."

"Part of his new image."

"Hmmmpf. Maybe it turns some people on, but it doesn't do anything for me."

John gave her a quick hug. "I know what turns me on."

"Hold that thought for a few more hours, and we'll see if you can do something about it."

One foot on the rail of the portable bar, Travis jabbed his cigar at Cay. "Take them up on it! If I had a lock like you do with the Graysons, I'd go to England every chance I got. The Brits are buying more from us every year."

"Haven't you ever heard of visiting just for the fun of it?"

"You can have fun, too," Travis grinned. "Why not make a little money to pay for the trip while you're at it? Tell you what... when you go, I'll tag along. I'll do a little business while you play. Might do some playing myself. Those English girls have legs up to here."

"Lynne might have something to say about that."

"Not if she doesn't go. She wouldn't mind a trip to a health spa while I chaperone my little brother."

"Why do I get the feeling I'd be better off without you? Cay laughed. Tossing down his drink, he slapped his brother on the back. "Come on, let's mingle."

Maudie saw Cay the moment he entered the ballroom. Taller than most, his reddish-blond hair shone like a beacon as he threaded his way through the crowd. She hugged herself tightly. With his tailored tuxedo and scarlet cummerbund showing off his slender frame and that handsome face and emerald eyes above the white ruffled shirt and black bow tie, he looked like a movie star. He was the most beautiful man in the world.

She started to move in his direction, then stopped, trembling with anger and despair. Two stunning women—one a brunette, the other a svelte blonde—grabbed his arms and led him to one side. Waylaying a passing waiter, the women lifted three glasses of champagne off the tray, the brunette pressing one into Cay's hand. He smiled and gestured as they talked, touching their bare arms and shoulders with a familiarity that pierced Maudie's very soul.

She wanted to turn away, but a streak of masochism kept her eyes glued to the trio across the room. After ten minutes of excruciating torture, Cay took his leave and headed her way. She was prepared to ignore him, but she melted the moment he put his arm around her thin shoulders and asked if she was enjoying the party. She murmured something about having the most wonderful time of her life, which at the moment she was.

Lynne had also watched Cay's exchange with the two women, and her feelings weren't much different from Maudie's. Unlike Maudie, she knew who the women were. The blonde was the daughter of a prominent Louisville surgeon, and the brunette owned a Lexington interior design shop. Nudging Travis, she asked, "Does Cay have anything going with those two?"

"If he doesn't, he should," Travis said, eyeing the women appreciatively. "Hard to tell about Cay. He doesn't talk much about his private life. Want me to ask?"

"Of course not!" Lynne snapped. She turned away as a rush of color swept over her cheeks.

"One thing's for sure," Travis said as he watched Cay cross the room and put his arm around Maudie, "he hasn't got anything going with *her*." A wicked grin. "Not unless he has a thing for skinny kids with buck teeth."

5

Standing on the Skye Terrace beside Cay, Tim Grayson swept the Churchill Downs track with his binoculars. "Not quite up to Epsom Derby standards. A few suits and ties and a lot of bare flesh." He lowered the glasses and looked at his brother. "Did I exaggerate about the infield on Kentucky Derby day?"

"Every word should be carved in stone," Keith said solemnly. "Did you and Cay really go out there?"

"My word as a gentleman."

"For about five minutes," Cay laughed. "Tim started to hyperventilate in the middle of the tunnel on the way back, and I had to drag him the rest of the way."

"*Really?*" Maudie cried, relishing the thought of her oldest brother succumbing to such a human phobia.

"Absolutely not!" Tim protested. "I kept a stiff upper lip, thought of England and forged ahead with Cay sniffling and stumbling behind."

"Don't believe a word they say," Maripat said, eyes twinkling under her green floppy hat. "They were in the infield so long I was ready to send out an armed escort to bring them back."

"That was my second Derby," Tim said. "It was the *first* one when Cay froze in the tunnel."

"I do remember a long time elapsing between your entry and exit," Maripat mused, "but didn't that have something to do with those girls you picked up in the infield?"

Alicia Grayson's brown eyes widened. "Do tell us about that, Tim! It sounds much more interesting that claustrophobia."

The winner of all five of his races as a three-year-old, Spectacular Bid, the gray son of Bold Bidder, was the overwhelming favorite to win the Kentucky Derby. Shawn liked General Assembly.

"I know you're thinking I'm sentimental because he's got the size and looks of his daddy," Shawn said to the group around the table, "but I think he'll give Bid a run for his money. They've both got the same granddaddy on the tail-male side in Bold Ruler, but General Assembly is by Secretariat. That gives him a boost in my book. This is the first time any of these horses have run a mile and a quarter, and a lot can happen at that distance."

"Cannonade was by Bold Bidder, and he won the Derby in Seventy-Four," John Kershaw said.

"I didn't say Bid won't win," Shawn grinned. "I just said I like General Assembly."

"Leave it to Shawn to hedge his bets," Maripat said, squeezing the little man's arm affectionately.

"Spectacular Bid looks like a good American Triple Crown prospect," Reggie Grayson said.

Cay said: "We didn't have a Triple Crown winner in twenty-five years, then Secretariat won it in Seventy-Three, Seattle Slew in Seventy-Seven and Affirmed last year. If Bid wins this year, that will be three Triple Crown winners in three years!"

"We went thirty-five years between our last two Triple Crown winners," Reggie said. "Bahram in Nineteen Thirty-Five and Nijinsky nine years ago." One of the highlights of the Grayson's trip had been a visit to Claiborne Farm where Nijinsky II and Secretariat were standing at stud.

Travis and Lynne and their houseguests—a young stockbroker and his wife from New York City—visited between the sixth and seventh races. Travis had purchased a table in the Skye Terrace two years ago when a Louisville car dealer died, and his heirs sold the choice location on "Millionaires' Row."

Signaling Maudie with a jerk of the head, Cay walked to the window that overlooked the track. When she arrived at his side, he pointed toward the backside. "One more race, Toothpick, then it's Derby time. Who do you want to put your money on?"

Maudie tugged at the bows on each side of her blue dress. "Spectacular Bid. Two dollars on the nose."

"Last of the big spenders," Cay grinned.

"It's your fault that I bet the lot on that filly!" Fiddling with the catch on her purse, she looked over her shoulder. "Mummy has eyes in the back of her head. Can I pay you later?" The last of the ten-dollar bill she had slipped into Cay's hand early that morning had been lost in the previous race.

"Call it a gift. Oh, I put two dollars for you on that gray colt you like in the seventh."

Standing on her toes, Maudie eagerly watched the horses parading to the post. "This is the big one—I just feel it!" she cried, clasping the purse to her flat chest.

Her faith in the longshot proved correct. It came in first, paying nearly forty dollars. "What's your secret?" Cay whispered as he passed the money to her under the table.

"I like grays," she hissed back. "I would have bet on Spectacular Bid even if he weren't the favorite."

"Some system."

"It worked, didn't it?"

As the small Derby field of ten horses was led toward the

paddock, they were halted for the playing of the national anthem. Spectacular Bid reared and pulled at his shank, threatening to yank his handlers off their feet. "Sure sign of a winner," Cay said. "General Assembly still looking good, Shawn?"

"This is my fifty-fifth Derby. I pick my own winners and never change a bet."

"Fifty-five! Mom! I think he's been lying about his age."

Skin crinkled around Shawn's dark eyes. "That's the nice thing about us Indians. We stop showing our age after forty."

When the horses broke out of the gate, Spectacular Bid ducked in slightly and settled back well off the pace. Brushing by Great Redeemer, Golden Act chased after the pack, which bunched tightly entering the clubhouse turn.

"Make him scrape paint!" Shawn chortled as General Assembly— red coat shining and looking very much like his sire, Secretariat— shook off Shamgo and fought Flying Paster for the lead as they passed the 7/8 pole.

"Bid's right behind them!" Maudie squealed, clutching Cay's arm and jumping up and down, then groaning loudly as Spectacular Bid failed to catch the leaders.

At the 5-furlong pole, King Celebrity, Shamgo, Screen King and Sir Ivor Again began to fall back. Lot o' Gold was in last place, fourteen lengths behind the leader, Flying Paster.

A roar went up as Spectacular Bid drew alongside Flying Paster near the quarter pole. Then General Assembly forced Flying Paster wide in the final turn, causing the leader to bump Spectacular Bid. "They should have dumped Ronnie Franklin after the Hutcheson!" Shawn shouted. "He's going to get Bid in trouble again!" Ronnie Franklin was Spectacular Bid's controversial young jockey. Counseled by the majority of the racing community to replace Franklin with a veteran rider, Bid's trainer, Bud Delp, had elected to stay with his inexperienced protégé.

As the horses entered the stretch, Franklin's right hand rose and fell as he whipped the gray colt. Putting on a burst of speed, Spectacular Bid took the lead at the eighth pole. Laffit Pincay, Jr. applied his crop to General Assembly, but the horse was tiring.

Golden Act thundered past Flying Paster. The crowd was on its feet as the horses neared the finish line. Cay lifted Maudie onto a chair.

Shifting the crop to his left hand, Franklin roused Spectacular Bid with five sharp blows. The colt flashed under the finish wire, going away. General Assembly finished second, Golden Act third.

"I'm rich! I'm rich!" Maudie cried, whirling around on the chair and waving her purse over her head.

"You probably didn't make three bucks," Cay said, looking up at her flushed face. "And not so loud. You're not supposed to be betting."

"Yeek!" Eyebrows flew up as she slapped a hand over her mouth.

Cay laughed as he grabbed her by the waist and lifted her down. "Entertain the troops while I collect the loot."

6

On Monday following the Derby, Cay and Reggie Grayson crossed one of the three stone bridges that spanned Elkhorn Creek on Cay's land. "I can't tell you how much we've enjoyed this visit," Reggie said. He looked out over the rolling green meadows, stately trees and dozens of grazing horses. "I didn't think anything could rival our part of England for beauty, but this certainly does." A smile spread across his lean aristocratic features. "Had we known, we might have fought harder to keep the colonies."

"Kentucky was nothing but Indians, buffalo and deer in those days," Cay said. "Even in the colonies, it was considered the wild west."

"It certainly isn't now," Reggie said. "I read somewhere that there are bluegrass areas in other states, but the vegetation doesn't thrive like it does here."

"The Kentucky Bluegrass covers roughly a thirty-five mile radius around Lexington," Cay said. "The soil is unique—a combination of minerals and decomposed limestone. It's perfect for vegetation and horses. The drainage is excellent, and the calcium in the soil produces strong bones. The climate is mild. Central Kentucky gets a few inches of snow while the surrounding areas are up to their necks. Guess that describes me—up to my neck with information about the Bluegrass and horses. I can go on all day."

"When you visit us, you'll find out we have the same problem. To an outsider, our interests must seem limited. Horsemen speak a common language."

"Looks like we have company," Cay said.

Alicia Grayson crossed the meadow with long lithe strides, a wide-brimmed white hat shading her exquisite features, hands stuffed in the deep pockets of her skirt. Walking beside her, Maudie waved her arms as she talked, her mop of tangled dark blond hair bouncing with each excited step.

"That ends our horse talk for now," Reggie said.

The day before the Graysons flew back to England, Cay took Maudie on a last ride around the farm. She may have been awkward and uncoordinated on the ground, but on a horse she was poetry in motion.

Cay peered under the cowboy hat he had given her soon after her arrival. "You have to promise me something, Toothpick."

"Anything!" she cried, huge hazel eyes searching his face.

"You have to write me at least once a month."

Standing in the stirrups, she looked like she was going to leap into his arms. "I'll write everyday!"

Laughing, Cay pulled the hat down over her nose. "Don't get carried away. Once a month will do." When he saw her smile fade as she pushed her hat up, he added hastily, "Twice a month?"

"If I feel like it," she said loftily. A suspicion of tears. "Will you write me?"

"Of course I will. You're my little sister, aren't you?"

Maudie's mouth flew open, and she stared at Cay for a long moment. A mysterious smile crept over her face, and Cay caught a glimpse of the woman she would become. "I'll look forward to your letters, dear brother," she said softly.

"And I'll look forward to yours, little sis—"

Clumps of grass flew as Maudie wheeled her horse and raced toward a low hill. Letting out a rebel yell, Cay took off in pursuit.

7

Six months later, Cay attended the fall sale at the Fasig-Tipton paddocks north of Lexington on Newtown Pike. He didn't buy the Nashua filly that had drawn him to the sale, but he found another that interested him more.

She was stunning. Five feet, six inches tall, with a willowy body, turquoise eyes and long straight hair the color of newly harvested wheat. He found her peering into a sales catalogue, then looking up with a perplexed look in those marvelous eyes.

"If you're lost, don't feel bad," Cay said. "Happens to the best of us."

"Oh!" she said, rising on her toes as if poised for flight. "I didn't see you there."

Hands in the back pockets of his jeans, Cay offered his most disarming smile. "Sorry about that. Want me to go away and make a lot of noise when I come back?"

"That's okay," she laughed. "You can stay if you'll tell me where the Spendthrift consignment is."

"I'll do better than that; I'll take you there."

"You don't have to bother."

"No bother. I'm going in that direction anyway."

"In that case..."

"Good!" Cay said as the started off toward the barns. "I'm Cay Albright. Are you in the horse business?"

"Arlene Olson, and I know absolutely nothing about racehorses. I had a pony once, but my parents sold our farm when I was ten and moved to central California. That was fourteen years ago. My uncle died and left his bakery to my father." A flash of white teeth. "I know a lot about making pastries."

"Want to trade information? I know a lot about horses."

"You also seem to know how to pick up stranded women."

"Oops!"

"You're forgiven. I don't think lechers get much satisfaction hanging around horse auctions. They like shopping malls."

"Don't be so sure. Lots of nice ladies show up at these sales. Take today for example, but I selected you."

"How nice! Now that I'm selected, what happens next?"

"I deliver you to the Spendthrift barn, then make myself available as your personal guide. And if you aren't engaged for the evening—or to some lucky guy—I'll take you to dinner."

"Well!" Arlene waggled the fingers on her left hand. "I assume you noticed the absence of rings?"

"Two seconds after we met."

"After you picked me up."

"Right."

Tapping the sales program against a long slender leg, she studied his face. "How do I know I can trust you?"

"Would it help if you met my mother?"

Laughing gaily, Arlene said, "You're impossible! Come on. I'll never get to that barn at this rate."

Falling in beside her, Cay said, "If you don't know anything about horses, what are you doing here?"

"My cousin is a groom at Spendthrift. I'm new in town, and she invited me out. She thinks I should know something about horses if I'm going to work in Lexington."

"Smart lady. What do you do? Besides making pastries."

"I'm the new public relations director at the Hyatt Regency. I was working at the downtown Hyatt in San Francisco when this job came up. It sounded great—a chance to get out of the city and breathe country air. I start next week."

"I've never known a public relations person."

"I've never known a horse person. You *are* a horse person, aren't you?"

"Every chance I get."

After meeting Arlene's cousin, Irene Broadquist, and saying he

would return in an hour to take Arlene to the sales pavilion, Cay
left the young women alone. As he walked away, Irene stared at
Arlene. "I'm gonna tag along and pick up your leftovers. Do you
know who that is?"

"Cay Albright," Arlene said, arching an eyebrow as she looked
down at her cousin. Irene was about the size and weight of a very
small jockey. "Is he an axe murderer or something?"

"That, dear cousin, is the youngest *unmarried* son of Maripat
Albright. She owns Albright Stud, which is about the same size as
Spendthrift. Cay has his own farm a few miles from his mother's
place over in Woodford County." Brushing a lock of dark hair out
of her eyes, Irene sat down on an upended bucket. "And to think I
was feeling sorry for you—all alone in a new town!"

Arlene watched Cay talking to a group of men, a distant figure
in jeans, rough out boots and tan suede jacket. "He invited me to
dinner."

"Go! *Go!*" Irene cried. "Take a doggie bag—an overnight bag,
a douc—" Arms flailing, she fell off the bucket.

Grinning, Arlene stepped back and dusted off her hands.
"Next time, I'll push you in a horse trough. Maybe if you got rid
of those rubber boots and that old shirt you'd feel more like a lady.
You sure don't talk like one."

"Yeah, but I can still beat you up," Irene groaned, getting to
her feet and wiping straw off the backside of her tight jeans.

"You may be older, but I'm bigger," Arlene said, eyes dancing
as she recalled the fights they had had as children on adjacent
Minnesota farms. "Now show me those horses you've been dressing
up for the sale."

Cay took Arlene to the Merrick Inn on Tates Creek Road.
Once the main residence of J. Cal Milam's Merrick Place farm
and named for the hardy gelding, Merrick, who started 205
races and died at age 38 in 1941, the inn was a favorite meeting
place for locals and politicians. Arlene was impressed with both
the atmosphere and the special treatment given to Cay. He was
obviously a favorite of the staff, and no one seemed to notice his
jeans and open-necked shirt.

"Cozy," she said as they sat near the giant stone fireplace that dominated one end of the lounge.

"Lots of business goes on in this room," Cay said. He nodded toward a group of men with their heads close together in a far corner. "If a guy could bug these tables, he'd make a fortune."

Arlene rested her chin on laced fingers. "I couldn't get over how casual everyone seemed to be today. Horses selling for a year's pay and nobody batting an eye!"

"I guess it's a shock to an outsider, but the fall and winter sales are our smaller ones. A yearling by Hoist the Flag sold at Keeneland last July for a million-six."

Arlene stared. "What makes a horse worth that much?"

"Pedigree, confirmation, the combination of a lot of things. Bidders get carried away and buy some duds. Yearlings have sold at Keeneland for hundreds of thousands and haven't won a dollar on the track—not that any sane buyer would expect to realize a profit from racing. The real return on investment is in standing a stallion at stud. The stud's performance on the track has a definite impact on breeding fees. One big win like the Derby or the Belmont can really increase a stallion's value and fees."

"Is that the Kentucky Derby?"

"Arlene," Cay said patiently, "when a horseman in America says, 'Derby,' he means the Kentucky Derby. That's especially true in this state. Keep that in mind at all times, especially in your position as a public relations person. Don't, and you'll be demoted and end up in Anchorage, Alaska or Bismark, North Dakota."

"That bad, huh?"

"Would I lie to you?"

"Why is the Derby so important?"

"The first Kentucky Derby was in Eighteen Seventy-Five, and it's the oldest *continuous* classic stakes race in America. The Travers is the oldest, and the Preakness and Belmont are older, but they all missed a year here and there. That's—"

Arlene held up a hand. "You're getting ahead of me. What's a classic stakes race?"

"Classic races are the most prestigious, toughest tests for three-year-olds and cover distances from a mile to a mile and a half. They used to put the money wagered in a purse and stick it on a stake at the end of a race. The winning rider grabbed the money as he went by. In today's stakes races, the owners put up the money and the track adds a certain amount. Because they offer more money, stakes races attract the best horses.

"I thought all races were the same."

"Nope. There are allowance races, handicaps, claiming races—"

"Help! I give up!"

"That's what you get for asking so many questions."

"You told me I have to learn about the business if I'm going to be a successful public relations person."

"I didn't say you have to know *everything!* A good handicapper has to study the horses in the race—pedigrees, past records, track conditions. They aren't dummies."

"I always visualized a seedy-looking guy with rundown heels and a cigarette stub dangling from his mouth. Or a gangster with a blonde bimbo hanging on his arm."

"Some of that's true. Gangsters in the Thirties and Forties were great race fans. They say Bugsy Siegel named his Las Vegas hotel after the flamingos at the Hileah racetrack in Florida. You see lots of characters at the track...professional football and basketball games, too. The big difference is that the racing fan has to *think*. If he does his homework, he increases the odds of winning. When the horses come down the homestretch, he's involved like no other sports fan in the world."

Arlene blinked. "Guess I asked for that, too. Now explain why the Kentucky Derby is so important."

"Call it the result of hype or what, it's *the* horse race, the best known in the world. Ask anybody in the business—owners, breeders, trainers, jockeys—and they'll all say they'd rather win the Derby than any other race in America. It wasn't always that way. It got so bad around the turn of the century that only four or five horses would show up. Three a couple of times! Then a guy named Matt Winn took over in Nineteen-Two. There's a man you should study; he was a public relations genius. A regular P.T. Barnum! He invited sports writers from all over the country, gave them freebies during Derby Week and built a press box on top of the grandstand right smack above the finish line. Harry Payne Whitney gave the Derby a big boost in Nineteen Fourteen when his filly, Regret, won the Derby, and he said she had won the greatest race in America. It's not a race; it's a happening."

Arlene touched a slender finger to her forehead. "I think I get the picture."

"Your eyes are glazing over; let's change the subject. Tell me about that bakery in California. What did your parents think about you moving so far away?"

"They would prefer having me closer, but I left home for UC Berkeley seven years ago and haven't been back except for visits. They live in Turlock; it's in the San Joaquin Valley southeast of San Francisco. The bakery's just six blocks from home. Dad walks to work. Turlock's a little farming town with about forty thousand people, but it's got a big claim to fame. Bet you can't guess."

"They have a sign on the edge of town—'Welcome to Turlock, the home of Arlene Olson.'"

"No, dummy. It's the biggest Swedish settlement west of Minnesota!"

"No kidding! Does everyone say, 'Yah' and stuff like that?"

"My dad still does," Arlene laughed. "Paul, my oldest brother, drove my parents nuts putting on his Swedish act. Dad came close to braining him a few times."

"How many brothers do you have?"

"Three. Two older, one younger. Being the only girl, I got beat up a lot."

"Somehow I picture it the other way around."

Arlene grinned and made a fist. "I got my licks in."

On the way to Arlene's apartment where they had left her car earlier, Cay invited her out to his farm on Friday. Having learned that he had horses in training, she asked if she could watch the morning workouts. When Cay said that would mean getting up before dawn, she laughed and said a former farm girl *and* bakery assistant would have no problem with that.

8

Friday arrived, and Arlene jumped out of her car at five AM. Cay whistled with appreciation as he took in her platinum pigtails, small perfect breasts under a blue cotton turtleneck and tight jeans hugging long slender legs.

"Hey, lookin' good!" he said as he met her at the foot of the stone steps that led to the house. "Welcome to Cay's Corner."

"Pretty big corner," Arlene grinned. She stared up at the two-story brick home. "You live in that monster alone?"

"Yup. When I bought this land, all the buildings were in bad shape—especially this house. It's over a hundred-fifty years old, and no one had lived in it for years. My mother said I'd probably find weeds in the attic, and I did! A window was broken, and birds must have brought in the seeds."

Cay enjoyed Arlene's wide-eyed curiosity as she prowled the house peering into closets and running her fingers over the ornate dark wood trim. "Where did you get all this period furniture?" she asked, turning slowly in the middle of the drawing room.

"Lots of it was still in the house. The attic was full of stuff. Beat up but valuable as antiques. I'm no decorator, so I turned the whole mess over to Mom. She got everything refinished and upholstered. Some pieces came from her place. You think this house is big, wait until you see Windsong Manor!"

"What a lovely name."

"I think Mom got inspired by some Harlan County moonshine."

A blank look. "Harlan County? Moonshine?"

Cay pulled gently on a silver pigtail. "Best to wait a while before we get into *that*. Follow your nose to the kitchen. We'll grab some coffee and head for the track."

Morning mists clung to the ground as the half-dozen horses

walked and jogged around the quarter-mile oval track. As Cay parked, Shawn wheeled his roan gelding away from the fence and trotted up to the pickup. He peered down at Cay, then caught sight of Arlene. Touching the bill of his baseball cap, he flashed a big grin. "I was going to give the boy here a piece of my mind for being late, but now that I see the reason, I don't blame him. My name's Shawn Phelps, Ma'am, and I run this place. If Cay told you different, it's a big fat lie. You need help handling him, let me know. I changed his diapers and put him on his first pony—know all the buttons to push and when to kick his butt."

Laughing with delight, Arlene scrambled out of the truck and introduced herself before Cay could get his door open.

"Hey Shawn," Cay said, "I brought her out here to watch the workouts, not hold your hand."

"Don't listen to him," Arlene said. "He's just jealous."

Another horse moved up beside Shawn's. "What's this—old home week?" Joy asked.

Cay said, "Arlene Olson, meet Joy Loren. Joy's been around forever. Almost as long as Shawn."

"Cay's full of it," Joy said as she shook Arlene's hand. She jerked a thumb toward Shawn. "Do I look that old? I went to work for Cay's mom right after I started high school. Cay was still looking up little girls' dresses, so he thinks I'm ancient."

"All right, break it up," Shawn said. "We've got work to do."

Arlene sat beside Cay on a fence rail. "You called that horse a gray. It looks brown to me."

"All grays are born dark with a few gray hairs around the muzzle, head and ears. The gray spreads with age, faster on some, slower on others. They get lighter with each shedding, eventually turn almost white."

"Well! How long have you been training these horses?"

"A couple of months. Galloping them up to two miles now. Walked and jogged them first, then graduated them up to half-mile gallops. There's a big difference between running alone in a pasture and on a hard track carrying the weight of a saddle and rider. These six are being conditioned together because they're the quickest learners. The precocious ones challenge each other and develop faster."

"Like kids in school!"

"Exactly. You don't want to put the less talented or immature yearlings with these because they'd get discouraged. Age is a factor. The universal birthdate for Thoroughbreds is January first. It was May first until England changed it in Eighteen Thirty-Four and New York eight years later. The southern states didn't switch until after the Civil War.

"So if a foal is born in June, it's actually six months old when January first comes around. With the breeding season running from mid-February through June, owners like to breed as early as possible. That way the yearling will be closer to its real age when it turns one. It wouldn't normally be fair to make a six-month old compete with a yearling months older."

Arlene pointed at a metal contraption mounted on wheels and hitched to a tractor. "What's that?"

"A training gate. Like a starting gate on the track, only smaller."

"You race horses here?"

Cay shook his head. "You have to get the yearlings used to going in and out of the gate. At first, the rider walks it right through. It takes a while before a horse learns to stay calm with the doors shut. Even after years of training and racing, some act up and have to be pushed in by the starter's assistants."

"I've never been to a big racetrack. Back home, the San Joaquin County fair in Stockton had horse racing. I went a few times but never paid attention to how the gate works."

"They have electro-magnetic catches. A horse is walked in with the front gate closed. Then the back one is shut. When all the horses are in, the starter pushes a button that cuts off the electricity and releases the magnets. The spring-loaded gates fly open simultaneously."

Joy jogged up on her chestnut filly. "Your butts are going to get creased on that fence."

"Tell me about it!" Arlene said. She smiled as the filly sniffed her knee. "Can I pet her?"

"Sure. She's just a big baby. Always wants attention."

"I forgot how soft their noses are," Arlene said, reaching out and touching the filly's muzzle. "I had a pony once, but we left the farm when I was just a little kid."

"Just the opposite with me," Joy said. "I grew up in Versailles and never got near a horse until I was in my teens. Rode my bicycle out to Cay's mother's farm and begged Shawn for a job. He started me cleaning stalls. I worked my way up to groom and exercise rider." She flipped the heavy blond braid. "Now I'm big time— assistant trainer to that sawed-off Indian over there."

Arlene looked at Shawn who was walking his gelding between two yearlings and talking to their riders. "Shawn's an Indian?"

"Half Cherokee and proud of it. Get him started, and he'll have you believing one of his ancestors greeted the Pilgrims with a pumpkin pie in one hand and a turkey under the other arm." Arlene gurgled with laughter as Joy rode off to join the others.

They all ate breakfast in the main house. Cay had a woman come in weekdays to cook and clean. "The downstairs bedrooms are used only when I have guests," he explained to Arlene,"but there's always something for Betty to do."

"Yeah, like baking his favorite pie or darning his socks," Betty Hahn said as she plunked a plate of biscuits down on the kitchen table. A big pleasant woman with three grown children, she lived with her husband in nearby Midway.

The talk revolved around horses. "That bay's still acting up," Joy said. "I'd like to take a whip to the bastard who got him that way."

"What happened?" Arlene asked.

"The colt was a summer purchase—has more bad habits than a kid from reform school. Probably had an abusive groom. It happens. One rotten apple can ruin a horse for life."

Arlene said, "I can't imagine anyone hitting a horse. They're such beautiful animals."

"Some have nasty tempers," Shawn said, "but beating them isn't the answer. A few colts are so unmanageable they have to be castrated. It straightens them out quick."

"Wouldn't be a bad idea for some men," Joy said.

"Easy, Joy," Shawn grinned. "You'll embarrass Arlene."

"With three brothers?" Arlene laughed. "Besides, I agree."

"Ouch!" Cay said.

Arlene patted his arm. "Only the mean ones."

"That's comforting…I think."

"Horses are real sensitive to a human's being's mood," Shawn said. "If the rider's nervous or unsure of himself, the horse reacts in kind. That's one reason why horses are so strung out before a race. Everyone's jumpy and excited. It's catching."

"Do the yearlings get any training before they go to the sales?" Arlene asked.

Shawn said, "A halter is put on right after a foal's born; that way it gets used to a lead rope before it develops ideas of its own. The same with rubbing it down, lifting its feet and checking its teeth. The handler has to walk a fine line between being kind and firm. 'Bout the same as raising kids."

"Cay said it's like teaching kids in school. How long have you been a trainer, Shawn?"

"Since the late Thirties—a few years after Cay's mom came to what's Albright Farm now. I trained there until I moved over here with Cay. I've never been a public trainer."

"What's the difference?"

"A public trainer usually has his headquarters on the backside of a racetrack, more than one if he moves around a lot. He handles several owners at once. A private trainer may work out of a track, too, but he works exclusively for one owner. I work for one owner, but so far, we haven't used any outside facilities. Haven't raced anything either. Next year will be our first."

"Sounds exciting," Arlene said.

"And expensive," Cay added.

Arlene said, "A week ago I would never have imagined spending a million dollars for a horse!"

"Horse racing and breeding is a gamble all the way," Shawn said. "Makes Vegas look like a backroom card game."

The day passed in a happy whirl. After driving Arlene around the farm, Cay took her on a Bluegrass tour. They ended up at

Albright Stud and had dinner with Maripat and John. The two women took an instant liking to each other, and John showed his approval by inviting Arlene to visit White Oak Stud.

Returning to his home just before midnight, Cay gathered Arlene into his arms and kissed her gently as she prepared to get into her car. She responded by throwing her arms around his neck and covering his mouth with hungry lips. Pressed close together, their tongues touched, then darted away. They broke apart, holding hands and staring into each other's eyes.

"I can't believe I did that," Arlene said shakily. "I'm acting like a high school girl on her first date!"

Cay squeezed her hands. "No way I'd mistake you for a high school girl. Something you should know about me, Arlene…I haven't had a steady girl in years. Haven't been looking for one either. This farm's been my whole life." He released one hand and touched her cheek. "I think we might have a chance at something special. Do you feel it too?"

Nodding, Arlene pressed his hand against her cheek. "I'm not a promiscuous person," she said softly. "The way I reacted just now shocked me." She smiled and kissed his wrist. "But it was a good kind of shock, if you know what I mean."

"Sure do." Cay slipped an arm around her slim waist and guided her toward the car. "I'd better get you on your way before I ask you to stay the night."

"Thank you," Arlene said in a small voice, wondering what she would have done had he extended the invitation.

9

The following week proved frustrating for both Cay and Arlene. While Cay flew to upstate New York on a previously arranged trip to look at horses, Arlene took over as public relations director at the Hyatt Regency hotel. It was doubly hard for her—having to learn a new job while distracted by thoughts of Cay and looking forward to his phone calls each night.

After eight days, Cay decided to cancel his Florida trip to visit several Ocala horse farms. "I didn't have any specific meetings set up," he told her on the phone. "I never thought the day would come, but I'm tired of looking at horses. All I want to do is come home and look at you."

"Maybe I should send you a picture," Arlene laughed. "That way, you won't have to cut your trip short."

"Bad idea. It would just make me want to come home sooner." A moment of silence. "Arlene?"

"Yes?"

"I miss you."

"I miss you, too." Another moment of silence. "Cay?"

"Yes?"

"Nothing like this has ever happened to me."

"Me neither. Do you believe in love at first sight?"

"I didn't ten days ago. Please hurry back!"

"Tomorrow night soon enough?"

"No! I mean yes! Ten minutes from now would be better!"

"Dinner! Pick you up around six?"

"Yes! Yes!"

They ended up ordering pizza because they never went out. Arlene met Cay at the door, freshly shampooed platinum hair shining and a new ice-blue dress highlighting her sparkling eyes. The roses Cay carried ended up on the floor as he crushed her to his chest. The long kiss left them gasping for breath.

Sweeping Arlene up in his arms, Cay carried her into the living room and set her on the couch. "You really missed me?" he whispered against her lips.

"I hardly slept last night."

"Better get you to bed early."

"How early?"

"Right after dinner."

Arlene buried her face in his neck. "How about before?"

"My sentiments exactly," Cay said, lifting her easily as he stood. "Which way?"

She pointed to the right. While he walked quickly toward the rear of the apartment, she laid a hand against his chest and felt the heavy beat of his heart.

"You won't run if I let you go?" he asked as they entered the bedroom.

"Only if I have to chase you."

"Funny girl." Laying Arlene on the bed, Cay sat on the edge and smoothed her hair. "You're beautiful."

"Hold me."

"Let me take my shoes off. I don't want to mess up this pretty white spread."

"I better take my dress off. I bought it special for tonight."

"You can wear it next time we go out."

Wearing only bra and panties, Arlene dived under the covers. Stripping to jockey shorts, Cay joined her. The hall light brought out the flecks of blue in Arlene's turquoise eyes.

"Comfy?" Cay asked as he drew her into his arms.

"Wonderful!"

"You didn't tell me you had such a great body."

"Really?"

"You put a swimsuit model to shame. Maybe I should take this bra off. It must hurt, pinching into your back like that."

"Terrible!"

"Better?"

"Oh yes! Thank you!"

"You're welcome. How about these panties? They seem...uh, confining."

"Well..."

"If you'd like to wait..."

"It isn't fair. Me with nothing on and you...still confined."

"Flip for who goes first?"

"How about together?"

"Excellent solution. Hey that's *lots* better."

"Oh, yes!"

"Come here."

Soft laughter was stilled by tender kisses. Bed covers fell unnoticed to the floor. Bodies joined, found release...parted.

Cay fitted himself to Arlene's back. She kissed his fingers, placed his hand over a small breast and drifted off to sleep.

Waking a half-hour later, they talked quietly in the semi-darkness. Arlene told about her three affairs, two short and one that lasted nearly a year. That one with a San Francisco attorney had ended fourteen months ago. "It was all right at first," she said. "We had our careers and didn't get in each other's way. Then he asked me to move in. I value my independence too much. He took that as a challenge and began to press for marriage. I broke it off, but he wouldn't accept that it was over. I had to get nasty, and I hated that." A small laugh. "It's amazing how fast he recovered! He married one of the secretaries a year ago. They're going to have a baby."

"Did you love him?"

"I thought I did, but I've learned there are many degrees of love. I've never..." Her voice trailed off.

Cay trapped her hand in his. "Never what?"

"Never felt like this with anyone," she whispered.

"Same here. I've only told one woman that I loved her, and that was mostly a teenage affair. What I felt for her couldn't compare to what I feel for you."

"And that is?" she murmured, snuggling closer.

"I love you, Arlene. I've never felt so...so *complete* with anyone, so damn *sure*! Should I have waited? Is it too quick?"

Arlene hugged him tightly. "You could have said it that day at your farm and I wouldn't have thought it too soon. My stomach was doing flip-flops an hour after we met. Maybe I didn't recognize it then, but I do now. I love you, Cay Albright."

10

The word soon got around the Bluegrass that Cay's bachelor days were numbered. Anyone seeing the young couple together knew this was no fleeting affair. They didn't have to touch or speak. Their eyes said it all.

Lynne got the unwelcome news at a Junior League luncheon. One of the women—recently divorced and angry at Cay for spurning her advances—downed the last of her third martini and said that it was just what he deserved, getting hooked by a goldbricking bitch.

"Who? What?" a striking redhead said. "Did you say Cay Albright?"

Fork poised in midair, Lynne asked, "What about Cay, Joyce?"

"Hey, that's right!" the martini drinker said. "You used to have a hot thing going with him. Well, kiss him goodbye. He's playing footsie with that anemic blonde over at the Hyatt."

"An anemic blonde?" another woman said. "Is she undertaker anemic, or just off her feed?"

Narrowing her eyes, Lynne said, "I don't know any anemic blonde at the Hyatt, Joyce. Why don't you enlighten us?"

"She's talking about the hotel's new public relations director," the woman sitting next to Joyce said. "If she's anemic, I hope it happens to me!"

Lynne felt a sinking sensation in the pit of her stomach. She pointed the fork at Joyce, who was starting on her fourth martini. "What makes you think it's serious?"

"I saw them at the Mansion the other night. Have any of you ever seen Cay hold a woman's hand all through dinner? They were billing and cooing and feeding each other stuff from their plates and guzzling champagne. Disgusting!"

"Sounds heavenly," the redhead sighed.

"Did you say anything to them?" a petite brunette asked.

"With the way they were carrying on? It would have been like bursting into someone's bedroom!" Joyce shot a malicious look at Lynne. "Think of it this way…you won't be losing an ex-lover; you'll be gaining a sister-in-law."

That evening during dinner, Lynne asked Travis if he had heard anything about Cay's new girlfriend. He nodded as he buttered a slice of bread. "Yeah, Mom said he brought a girlfriend out a few weeks ago. Name's Arlene something or other. Guess they get along pretty good. Why?"

"One of the girls was talking about her at lunch today."

"I bet," Travis grinned as the maid refilled their wine glasses. "Did she bare her teeth or just her claws?"

"She wasn't nice about it. It was Joyce Winston."

"*Joyce?* Her brains are between her legs. She'd lay a snake if it would stay put. I wouldn't trust anything she says."

"You should know. Some of the stories I've heard about you two are X-rated."

"That was before we met."

Lynne sipped her wine, wondering if Travis was telling the truth. They had both played around on occasion, but never in Lexington. The Bluegrass was a tightly-knit community, and intimate secrets had a way of leaking out.

Travis broke the silence. "What did Joyce say?"

"Something silly about Cay and this woman cuddling up at the Mansion. She's the new public relations director at the Hyatt."

"Too bad we're going away for Thanksgiving. Mom invited her out for the day."

"Oh?" Lynne murmured. Travis hadn't really wanted to go to Palm Springs for the holiday; he had a lot of work to clean up before they left after Christmas for two weeks in Aspen. "Would you mind if we canceled Palm Springs?"

"You were the one who was so gung-ho on going. All of a sudden staying home is more exciting. Wonder why?"

Coloring slightly, Lynne said, "Aren't you interested in meeting this woman?"

"I'll call Mom and give her the good news."

Arriving at Windsong Manor Thanksgiving afternoon, Travis

and Lynne followed the delicious aromas to the kitchen. The sight that greeted them confirmed Lynne's worst fears. Lovely face flushed and wearing a frilly blue-checkered apron over her white dress, Arlene was vigorously stirring something in a bowl while Maripat peered in the oven. They were chattering happily while Cay and John looked on from the counter. The blissful scene made Lynne feel like an intruder.

"Hey, it's about time you got here!" Cay called. "Come in and meet Arlene. She and Mom have been cooking up a storm."

"Maripat's been cooking up the storm," Arlene laughed. "All I've done is make a couple of pies."

"Don't believe a word," Maripat said, patting Arlene's shoulder. "I'd be two hours behind without her help."

Arlene smiled and clasped Lynne's hand. "I'm Arlene Olson; you must be Lynne. I've heard so much about you!"

"All good, I hope," Lynne smiled in return, unable to resist Arlene's infectious good humor. They stood close together for several moments, two beautiful young women about the same height but entirely different in looks. Lynne's hair and eyes were dark, unfettered breasts swaying under the low-necked peasant dress, every movement calculated to draw attention to her smoldering sensuality. Compared to Lynne, Arlene seemed fragile, a slender Nordic princess with platinum hair and unusual turquoise eyes.

She has such natural elegance, Maripat thought as Arlene brushed a lock of hair from her forehead and shifted her weight from one long leg to another.

Travis put an arm around Lynne and gripped Arlene's hand. "As Cay's big brother, all I can say is his judgment's improving with age. You two ought to make beautiful babies!"

"*Travis!*" Maripat shouted. "Apologize right now or I'll bend a frying pan over your head!"

"Oh, please don't do that," Arlene cried. "You might make it bigger—I mean flatter!"

"That'll teach you to get smart with my girl!" Cay said. He jumped up and hugged Arlene. "I should have warned you, Travis. She's got three brothers and a mean right hook."

Lynne froze under Travis's arm. She had never seen Cay show

such affection for another woman. The impact was devastating. For years she had secretly believed he had remained single because of her. It had soothed her longing and provided a confidence that now lay shattered at her feet. Suddenly she wanted him with a need that left her weak. How foolish she had been not to have reached out to him sooner! He must think she no longer cared.

That night, Travis wanted to make love, and Lynne gladly obliged. Imagining she was with Cay, she turned the bed into a battleground, draining Travis quickly, then waking him in the middle of the night for another round.

11

Five days after Thanksgiving, Cay received a call from England. "Dust off your fancy duds, old boy," Tim Grayson said. "Yours truly is getting married, and your presence is requested!"

"I can't believe it! Who's the unfortunate lady?"

"Miss Caroline Hutchinson. I had planned a long courtship but circumstances call for a hasty wedding."

"You didn't!"

"No, but her parents did. Her father's in the diplomatic corps, and he's being transferred to Singapore in March. Hence the hurry-up wedding. Just imagine a June wedding in Singapore with my bride sweating her way down the aisle. I'm going to sweat enough as it is. Say you'll come. If you won't, I'll call the whole bloody thing off!"

"When?"

"February Second."

"Right in the middle of breeding season!"

"It's the stallion that does the work, old chap. I'm sure you can cobble up some help to give him a hand. Did you catch the humor in that last line?"

"Can't you hear me laughing?"

"I expect you to come over at least a week before. Make it two weeks and I'll sing at *your* wedding!"

"A week's about it. Mind if I bring a friend?"

"Not at all! Our house will hold an army. Anyone I know?"

"No, and if you weren't getting married, I wouldn't allow you near her."

"Her? Good lord, did you say *her*?"

"Surprised?"

"Flabbergasted! Is it serious? What am I going to tell Maudie?"

"Maudie?"

"She has you pegged for the altar. Started working on her trousseau the moment we got home."

"I love her madly," Cay cried, "but I can't wait that long!"

"Ah well, I'll break it to her gently."

"Never mind. Arlene might not come. She's new on the job."

"A horsewoman no doubt."

"Public relations at the Hyatt Regency. She's from California, been here since October. I'll ask her and let you know."

"Jolly good! Hip, hip and all that! Hold on a minute. Someone's banging on my door."

Cay heard muffled voices, then the receiver clattered in his ear. "Hello, Cay!" Maudie said in a breathless voice. "Tim says I have two minutes. Are you coming to his wedding?"

"Wish I could but weddings make me sad."

"You don't mean that!"

"Just teasing. I'll be there with bells on."

"You will? Oh—oh! That's wonderful! What do you mean— bells on?"

"Old Southern saying. Comes from, 'I'll dance at your wedding with bells on.'"

Maudie giggled. "You would look terribly funny."

"That's me!"

"Did you get my last letter, the one about my winning a first at the horse show?"

"It arrived three days ago, I was just getting ready to write you. I'm proud of you, Toothpick."

"We'll go riding when you're here. Oh Cay, I'm so excited! Tim says I have to go now. He'll be waiting for your call. I can't wait to see you! Goodbye, Cay. I love you!"

Much to Cay's disappointment, Arlene couldn't make the trip. For one thing, she said, the hotel was hosting a big sales convention the first week of February, and she wouldn't even consider asking for time off with so much going on. Not only that, they would probably fire her for making such a request during her first months on the job! Furthermore, she lectured him sternly, she couldn't afford the expense and there was *no way* she would let him pay for it! She did let him talk her into spending the night at his place, a consolation prize they both enjoyed immensely.

12

Early Christmas morning after they exchanged gifts, Cay saw Arlene off on the first leg of the flight that would take her to Chicago, then to San Francisco where her younger brother, Ed, would be waiting. He would drive her to the San Joaquin Valley.

Cay, Shawn and Joy spent the day with Maripat and John at Windsong Manor. Travis and Lynne were there also, along with Lynne's parents, George and Christina Ross. Returning home that night, Cay spent a half-hour on the phone with Arlene, then went to bed feeling lonely.

Outside of feeding the horses and cleaning stalls, there was little activity on the farm the following day. After driving into Lexington that afternoon to purchase supplies, Cay picked up a pizza on the way home. A cold wind howled outside, and he was soon dozing in front of the television.

The door chimes brought him awake with a start. Walking in stocking feet to the front door, he opened it just as Lynne hit the button again. "I wasn't sure you were at home," she said brightly. "The house is so dark! Are you going to invite me in or do I stand out here and freeze?"

"What are you doing out on a night like this?" Cay asked as she stamped her boots on the rubber mat and stepped inside.

"I knew you were alone, so I thought I'd cheer you up." She whipped a magnum of champagne and a corkscrew from under her long leather coat. "Travis is working late; he has a lot to do before we leave for Aspen on Friday. We can console each other."

"I didn't know I needed consoling."

"Sure you do! All alone on a cold winter's night! Same as me. When Travis holes up in his office, he might as well be a thousand miles away. Where are the champagne glasses?"

"In the kitchen. Does Travis know you're here?"

Lynne shot him an indulgent look as she entered the kitchen and tossed her coat over a chair. "Do you think I'd leave on a stormy night without telling him? Hey, you've got this place well organized! That's right, you've got a housekeeper. You always were neat. Remember how nice you kept our apartment over the barn? Excuse me for rattling, but I'm kinda nervous all alone with you in this big bachelor pad."

"No problem," Cay said as he produced the glasses and an ice bucket. "I'm harmless."

"Have you got a fire going? I want to get these boots off and warm my feet."

"Won't take a minute." Dumping ice in the bucket, he twirled the champagne bottle around.

While Cay got the logs burning in the brick fireplace, Lynne opened the bottle of Perrier-Jouet. "I lifted it from our wine cellar," she explained as she twisted the cork.

By the time they were seated on the couch with their feet on the coffee table, the fire was crackling merrily. Twenty minutes later, the bottle was two-thirds empty.

"Have you and Arlene talked about marriage?" Lynne asked.

"Joking like. Ha, ha, and all that."

"She's really beautiful."

"She said the same about you."

"I'm just a fat old married lady!"

"Cut it out, Lynne. You haven't gained an ounce since you got out of high school."

"Do you still think I'm beautiful?"

"Drop-dead gorgeous."

"Why thank you! I don't know about you, but I'm burning up." As she yanked the sweater over her head, the cotton blouse underneath caught in the fabric and exposed her bare breasts. "Oops, sorry," she grinned. Pulling the blouse down and refilling their glasses, she settled down beside Cay.

They were silent for a time, slumped in horizontal positions as they watched the leaping flames. Lynne moved closer, pressing a heavy breast against Cay's arm. "How did you and Arlene meet?"

While Cay talked, she rested her head in his shoulder. A nipple hardened as she rubbed it lightly over his arm.

"I'm so glad you found someone," she said softly. "I don't want you to be lonely like me."

Cay almost spilled his wine. "You—lonely? How do you have *time* to be lonely? You're always off somewhere—parties, New York, the Bahamas, even Europe, for god's sake!"

"That means nothing." She laid a hand over her breast. "I'm lonely in *here*! Inside, I'm *empty*!"

"Is something wrong between you and Travis?"

"It's more like nothing's *right*! We never really loved each other, not like you and I did. It wasn't bad at first. Then he began to lose interest. We don't have sex much anymore. When we do, it's slam-bam and he's off. I hardly ever have a climax."

Cay stirred uncomfortably. "Have you talked about it?"

"Several times. Travis doesn't know how to satisfy a woman. He *thinks* he does. He made me come in the beginning. Even with a lousy lover, it's exciting at first. The only way I've made it the last few years is to fantasize."

"Jesus, Lynne. We shouldn't be talking like this."

"Why not? You know me better than anybody, and you're practically a married man."

"What's the point? I can't give you advice, and I'm sure not going to talk to Travis if that's what you want."

"Oh Cay, I wouldn't even *think* of asking you to talk to Travis that! All I want is a little understanding. I've bottled things up inside so long! Just telling you makes me feel better already. You can do that for me, can't you?"

"Guess so, but I feel funny talking about your sex life. What would Travis think? What would *Arlene* think?"

"We're not hurting them." Lynne moved closer and rested a knee on Cay's leg. "What's done is done, and I have to accept it. Maybe Travis will go with me to a marriage counselor. Until then…" She sighed deeply. "Hold me—please! Tighter! I know it's impossible, but I wish you *could* talk to him. He could learn so much from you about making love. You were always so considerate. Remember how you made me come before you did?"

"Stop it!" Cay said in a strangled voice. "This is wrong."

"I'm sorry." She trailed her fingers over his stomach and played with his belt. "I shouldn't be dredging up old memories. I have to tell you this…when I have a climax with Travis, it's because I'm imagining he's you. Do you mind?"

A bulge appeared over Cay's crotch. "Damnit, Lynne!"

"I know you love Arlene," Lynne said quickly, "but will you help me—just this once?"

"Help you? How?" The bulge was growing.

"Play with me. Use your finger to make me come. It won't take a minute. I'm already wet."

Cay tried to move away, but she pushed him down. "Please! I'll go right home afterward. I promise!"

He wanted to say no, but the champagne and his own arousal had weakened his resolve. "Just this once," he said thickly.

Jumping up, Lynne stripped off her jeans and panties. Her thick triangle was damp, black hairs sparkling in the firelight. Sitting down and placing her feet on the coffee table, she spread her legs wide.

Kneeling on the cushion beside her, Cay caressed the little button at the top of her cleft. She cried out and pulled her blouse up over her breasts. "Play with my nipples!"

While his fingers worked, her pungent aroma filled the air. When she felt his crotch, he didn't resist. She unbuttoned his jeans and pulled them down. Reaching into his shorts, she exposed his throbbing erection. "Put it in me!" she gasped. Lifting her feet off the coffee table, she stretched out on the couch. Cay knelt between her legs, and she placed the tip of his penis just inside the moist pink lips.

A popping log went off like a gunshot alongside Cay's head. He drew back, horrified at what he had almost done.

"Cay, don't!" Lynne cried as he leaped off the couch and stumbled about, pulling his shorts up over his fading erection.

"Crazy!" he shouted. "Sick crazy! I should have known better. We *both* should have! Did you plan this…the champagne, the sexy talk? I bet Travis doesn't even know you're here!"

"Cay, please!" Lynne begged. "I love you. I've never stopped loving you! It's not too late. We can still be happy—"

"That's it, isn't it?" Cay yelled. "You thought you could come here and everything would be hunky dory. One quick fuck and we'd live happily ever after! We may have had a teenage crush on each other, Lynne, but it wasn't love. We had good sex, but by itself that isn't worth shit in the long run."

Tears flowed over Lynne's cheeks. "You loved me," she sobbed. "You told me so—over and over!"

"I *thought* I loved you. That was kid stuff. I never really knew what love was until now."

Lynne's voice turned cold. "Until Arlene."

"That's right, and I almost ruined everything for us. Do you think I could have looked her in the eye after I'd made love to you? She *trusts* me!"

Lynne leaped to her feet. Legs spread, the blouse still hiked above her jutting breasts, she snatched up her panties and waved them under Cay's nose. "Smell that? That's *me*! Take a good whiff because it's the last time you'll ever smell my pussy!"

Her voice rose—shrill, cutting. "You think you're such a great lover! I lied about Travis. He makes me come *every* time we fuck! Not just him! I've had lots of lovers! So has Travis. You think you're so damn smart. You don't know *shit*! You're a goddamn hick! You'll never be anything else!"

White with shock, Cay said in a pleading voice, "I don't love you, Lynne, but I care. Please say you didn't mean what you said about you and Travis."

A fleeting look of remorse. "I came here thinking if we got

together, I could put it all behind. If you had wanted me years ago, we would have married, and none of that would have happened."

"What about before you started going with Travis? You had other lovers then, didn't you?"

"Yes, but I wouldn't have if you had paid any attention to me. You shut me out!"

"We were drifting apart," Cay said helplessly.

"*You* were doing the drifting!" Lynne snapped. "I tried to tell myself you still cared. Now you've shown me what a fool I was to love you all these years." She threw the damp panties in Cay's face. "Smell them! Think about me balling all those men!"

Cay exploded. "Get your clothes on or I'll throw you out naked. You ought to be horsewhipped—dragging my brother down into the cesspool you wallow around in!"

Lynne shrieked with laughter. "Who do you think got me started playing around? Travis had at least a dozen affairs before I decided to get even. And boy, have I!"

Cay grabbed Lynne's jeans and threw them at her feet. "Three minutes, then I throw you out!"

Lynne drew her jeans slowly up over her hips, careful not to catch the dark pubic hairs as she zipped the fly. She glared at Cay as she yanked the blouse down over her breasts and put her sweater on. Stamping her feet into her boots, she said, "Travis *is* working in his office, but I told him I was visiting a girlfriend." Hands on hips, she unleashed a parting shot. "They say love and hate are just a thread apart. You pushed me on the other side tonight. I hope you rot in hell—and that bitch with you!" Whirling, she got her coat from the kitchen and left the house, slamming the front door so hard it activated the chimes.

Cay dashed to the hall bathroom, spilling vomit on the toilet's edge as he fell to his knees and retched violently. When he washed his face and mouth, he avoided looking in the mirror.

Returning to the drawing room, he seized a poker and hooked the soiled panties into the fire. While they burned, he carried the ice bucket, corkscrew, champagne bottle and glasses to the back porch and dumped them in a garbage can. He didn't want anything left to remind him of this night.

Shaking two large garbage bags open in front of the fireplace, he removed the cushions from the couch and stuffed them inside. He would take them to the cleaners tomorrow.

Mixing ammonia and water, he cleaned the bathroom and everything Lynne had touched. On a final trip to the back porch, he stripped off his clothes and added them to the trash.

Cay was in the shower when the phone rang in his bedroom. Dripping his way across the carpet, he picked up the receiver.

Arlene's warm happy voice was like a knife in his gut. "I let the phone ring and ring! I was getting ready to hang up!"

"I was taking a shower," he said hoarsely.

"Darling, are you all right? You sound terrible!"

"Just catching my breath. How are you, Honey?"

"Missing you. Wishing I could be there. Isn't that awful? I haven't seen my family in months, and I can't wait to get back!"

Sitting on the bed, Cay clutched the receiver as if it were a lifeline. "You really love me?"

"More than anything. Bigger than a breadbox!"

"I love you, too—Arlene?"

"Yes?"

"I don't want to lose you. I don't know what I'd do if you went away."

"I'm not going anywhere, Darling. Not unless you make me."

"Never! Wish you could be here right now."

"Me, too. My internal clock is going to be messed up when I get back tomorrow. It's six o'clock here."

"Tomorrow seems like forever."

"I'm bringing you a nice Christmas present. Very special, very personal. Hard to wrap but fun to open."

"Will I need scissors?"

"Fingers will do; I'll help."

"Hurry back, Honey. I need you!"

A long silence. "Are you sure there's nothing wrong? You sound strange, not like yourself."

"Just lonely."

13

Cay slept little, drifting off, then jerking awake to relive the events of the previous evening. He was heartsick—not just over his betrayal of Arlene's love and trust but also about Lynne's revelations. Was she lying? Switching the blame to Travis? He recalled rumors and direct hints from Travis. It was probably true. It made him physically sick.

He thought about Arlene's call and the loving concern in her voice. He didn't deserve her. Certainly not after last night. But if she would have him, he was ready to make a commitment.

After an early morning tour of the barns, Cay returned to the house and impatiently paced the floor, checking his watch every few minutes. Shortly before ten, he was standing outside one of Lexington's exclusive Chevy Chase shops.

"Morning, Cay," Sam Brodin said as he stepped up on the curb. He was a jovial little man with a round stomach, white mustache and goatee. "What brings you to my neck of the woods?"

"You...and what you've got inside."

"A robbery, is it? Want some coffee first? I don't expect an avalanche of customers, this being a holiday week and all."

"Mind if we go in now? I'm sorta anxious. I've been thinking about this all night."

"Come in! Come in! Coffee can wait."

Five minutes later, Cay was examining the sparkling diamonds on a blue velvet cloth.

"They can be set in any band you choose," Brodin said.

Cay looked up. "By this afternoon?"

Laughing, Brodin slapped the top of the glass counter. "By noon! If you don't take all morning making up your mind."

"I haven't popped the question yet. Are you going to stick me with it if she says no?"

"Pay for setting the diamond and we'll forget the rest, but it won't happen. She'll say yes; I'll bet my store on it. There isn't a bookie around who would take odds against it. Only bets I've heard proposed are the ones guessing how long it would take you to ask her!"

"You know who she is?"

"The whole town knows! You two are an *item*, boy!"

Cay laughed. "Considering you know the lady, maybe you should show me what will look best on her finger."

Brodin studied the tray of diamonds. "For Miss Olson, I would say a pure white brilliant cut. Something to go with that beautiful hair. Two carets?"

"Sounds like a vegetable to me, Sam. Show me what one looks like."

Using a pair of tweezers, Brodin selected a diamond and placed it on a small square of velvet.

"Nice." Cay bent down and looked at it from all angles. "How about one a little bigger?"

Eyes twinkling, Sam Brodin said, "You're talking my language, Mr. Albright."

"That's pretty formal for a guy who used to let me play horsey on his back."

"You're way past that stage, my boy. *Way* past! I call my closest friends Mister when they go beyond two carats."

Returning to the jewelry store at noon, Cay collected the gift-wrapped four-and-a-half carat ring. Sam Brodin sent him off with an encouraging pat on the back and a solemn promise to keep his mouth shut.

On the way home, Cay purchased an ice bucket and picked up the sofa cushions from the cleaners, a rush job that cost an extra ten dollars. By late afternoon, the house was in order, and he was ready to pick up Arlene at the airport.

Arlene flew into his arms, murmuring, "I love you! I love you!" against his lips. Passengers in the crowded terminal smiled at the handsome couple, and men stopped to stare at Arlene. She was stunning in the thigh-length shearling coat Cay had given her for Christmas, the fawn-colored lambskin and white wool collar a perfect match for her long platinum hair.

Cay hugged her tightly, breathing in the fresh clean smell of her hair and the touch of Joy perfume behind her ear, another of his Christmas morning gifts.

Arlene slipped under the covers and pressed her nude body against his. While they nibbled and tasted each other's lips with long leisurely kisses, their fingers explored. When they came together, it was a quiet union of love that left them shaken.

Cay stroked Arlene's hair while she pressed her breasts against his chest. The perfume still lingered behind her ear, and her breath was warm against his neck. He shuddered as he recalled the sordid events of the night before.

"What's the matter, Darling?"

"Nothing." But he couldn't hold back the tears.

Arlene touched his cheek. "Cay?"

"I love you so much," he said in a choked voice. "You're the best, most wonderful thing that's ever happened to me."

Arlene smiled through her own tears. "That's what I was going to say to you!"

"I don't deserve you."

"Yes you do. You're a wonderful, kind, loving man, Cay Albright, and I love you. Now hold me, and let's not talk."

While Cay lit the logs in the marble fireplace, Arlene sat in the bed, hands folded in her lap and smiling. She wore the white night-gown he had given her after they had showered together, and her hair shone from an energetic brushing. A bottle of Dom Perignon champagne nestled in the new ice bucket.

"When I was a little girl, I used to dream about being pampered like this," she said as he sat beside her and poured the champagne. "You're spoiling me, you know."

"I hope so. A toast?"

"To us...to the best Christmas of my life. To happiness!"

"Amen," Cay said, touching his glass with hers. They held hands and sipped the vintage champagne.

Arlene lifted Cay's hand and kissed each knuckle. "What a

beautiful way to end a day. I'm going to sleep so good. Full of love and champagne and curled up next to you in my new nightgown. You will let me keep it on, won't you?"

"Long as you cooperate."

"My glass is empty."

"Mine, too. Fancy that."

Cay upended the empty bottle in the bucket. "Lights out," Arlene murmured sleepily as she slid under the covers. "Thank you for the loving and the nightgown and the champagne, Darling."

"You can't go to sleep yet. There's something else."

Arlene opened one eye. "Do I have to sit up?"

"You'll need both hands to open it."

"Another present?" she cried, scooting up against the headboard. "You shouldn't!"

"Okay. Go to sleep."

"Spoil sport! Where is it?"

Cay laid the small package in her hand.

A low cry escaped her lips as she fumbled with the tiny bow. The wrapping came off the blue velvet case. Fingers trembling, she lifted the lid and stared at the huge sparkling diamond. "Oh Cay," she whispered. "Oh, Cay!"

"Do you like it?"

Tears filled her eyes as she hugged the case to her breast.

"Hey, don't cry."

"I'm not crying," she blubbered.

Retrieving the case, Cay removed the ring and lifted her left hand. "Will you marry me, Arlene?"

Raising her other hand to her eyes, Arlene brushed the tears away, only to have a fresh outburst flow over her cheeks. She shook her head and bit her lip.

"I'm sorry," Cay said miserably. "I should have waited. I thought..." He dropped her hand.

"Oh, Cay, you crazy man! Did you think I was saying no? You overwhelmed me! I've dreamed about this but never expected it so soon. Yes! Yes! I'll marry you! Put it on quick! Kiss me!"

Cay slipped the ring on her slender finger. It was a perfect fit.

After the long kiss ended, Arlene raised her left hand behind his neck and smiled as the diamond sparkled in the firelight. Releasing her grip, she fell back against the pillows. "The telephone! It's only eight at home. Everybody will still be there. I've got to tell them. Do you mind?"

"Go ahead. Because it's a special occasion, you'll only have to pay half the charges."

"Meanie." She punched out the number. Sitting against the headboard and waggling her ring finger under the light, she listened intently. A big smile broke across her face. "Mother? Are you sitting down? I have the most wonderful news..."

By the time the long call was over—and Cay had talked to the entire family—Arlene was wide awake. She insisted on going to the kitchen for a cup of hot chocolate. The heat had been turned down, so she wore a pair of Cay's wool socks and the shearling coat over her nightgown. Making the chocolate took quite a while because she kept stopping to admire her ring.

The nightgown came off when they got in bed. "To make it official," she said as she moved into his arms. She went to sleep hugging the pillow, the diamond resting softly against her cheek.

14

When Maripat got the news the next morning, she hugged and kissed the smiling couple. "I told John just yesterday, Arlene, that if Cay didn't ask you, I was going to do it myself! Welcome to the crazy Albrights! Too bad Travis and Lynne left early this morning. They could have helped us celebrate!"

I bet! Cay thought. He had made sure they were on their way to Aspen before coming over.

Maripat cried: "We have to have an engagement party! How about New Years? All the regulars are coming. What do you think, Arlene? Will that do? They're mostly horse people—people I've know most of my life, friends of the family and so forth."

"Oh, no!" Arlene cried, slapping her forehead. "That's a big night at the Hyatt! I'm supposed to be there."

"Leave that to me," Maripat said. "I've got pull with the powers that be. Look at the publicity they'll get with their PR director on the front page of the society section!"

Cay grinned at Arlene. "If Mom says she can do it, she can. Better give in."

"How many will be there?" Arlene asked weakly.

"Two hundred or so," Maripat said. "Being a special occasion, we'll probably get more. Give me a sec. Gotta get something to write on." She flew out of the room.

"Oh, my," Arlene murmured. "Mind if I sit down?"

Cay guided her to a couch by the fire. "Put your feet up. If I know Mom, she's going to run you ragged—both of us!"

Maripat returned waving a yellow pad and pencil. "Let's see," she said, sitting beside Arlene. "We've only got four days, so invitations are out. I'll use the phone—can get help if I need it. Do you have a nice photo Arlene? Sure you do; the newspaper had one with that story about your new job. We'll need a glossy fast. I'll call the society editor and see that it gets in the Sunday paper. Cay, why don't you make some coffee? Fresh rolls are in the cabinet above the toaster, bottom shelf. Can your family make it, Arlene? You have that cousin over at Spendthrift, and you must have made lots of new friends. Hmmm. Where was I?"

Between phone calls and the featured four-column spread in the society section of the *Lexington Herald-Leader*, word got out all over the Bluegrass. Pulling off a last-minute coup, Maripat got Arlene's picture in the Louisville *Courier-Journal*.

Her greatest achievement, however, was getting Arlene's parents to Kentucky without Arlene's knowledge. Carl and Beth Olson were willing accomplices, telling Arlene they felt terrible, but they couldn't travel all the way to Kentucky for the engagement party. This while they were packing to leave. They arrived at Windsong Manor Sunday afternoon and were presented to their daughter when Cay brought her for supper. Wide-eyed with shock, Arlene stood frozen for a moment, then ran laughing and crying into their arms. While she showed off her ring, Maripat and John broke out the champagne. They celebrated late into the night.

Nearly three hundred attended the New Year's Eve gathering at Windsong Manor. Seasoned partygoers—and in the Bluegrass there are probably more per capita than anywhere—claimed it was one of the best parties ever.

As midnight drew near, the band's horn and drum sections sounded a loud flourish that brought instant silence to the huge ballroom. Wearing a pale green gown and with her long neck accentuated by fashionably-cut short hair, Maripat stepped up to the microphone. The crowd showed its appreciation with a thunderous cheer and enthusiastic wolf-whistles.

Maripat smiled and waved. This was her favorite party—welcoming in the new year with old friends and neighbors. "You know how I hate to make speeches," she began.

"Don't get modest on us, Maripat!" a voice called out.

"Watch it, Purdy, or I'll make you come up and handle this."

"Don't do it, Maripat!" another voice yelled. "Five minutes of Purdy and we'll all go home!" Accompanied by loud laughter, someone handed a grinning Purdy Simpson a glass of bourbon.

Maripat held her hands up for silence. "This is more than a New Years party—Albright Stud's twenty-sixth by the way." Cheers and applause made her pause. "I'm sure by now you've all met Arlene Olson and her parents, Carl and Beth. If you haven't, make sure you give them a big Kentucky welcome before you leave." Another round of applause.

Maripat smiled and extended a hand toward the left side of the platform. "Cay, bring Arlene up here."

Fingers entwined with Cay's, Arlene glided across the stage, long white-blonde hair falling softly over bare shoulders. Her delicate face was flushed with pleasure, and her smile invited everyone to share her happiness. Pale blue gown clinging to her slender body, she faced the crowd and executed a tiny bow. Amidst the applause, she pulled Cay close and kissed his cheek.

Taking Arlene's other hand, Maripat said, "I have a toast to make. Gentlemen, you may proceed." A murmur rippled through the room as an army of waiters passed out tulip glasses of champagne.

Maripat lifted her glass. "For a while there, I was afraid Cay was going to remain a bachelor, and I was going to have him nosing around my kitchen the rest of my life." Laughter drowned out her next words. "...it all worked out, and he's fallen in love with a young lady I'm proud to introduce as my future daughter-in-law. Here's to Arlene and Cay. They're planning on a June wedding. That's fine with me—as long as they don't schedule it during the Belmont!"

15

While Cay worked his way through London's Heathrow airport customs shed, he was entertained by the antics of Maudie, who was just outside the enclosure with Tim. "You were dancing around like you had to go the bathroom," Cay said as he gave her a big hug.

"I was getting ever so furious at those pompous little men!" she cried. "They were so bloody *slow!*"

Cay raised an eyebrow as he shook hands with Tim. "*Bloody?* Isn't that word a no-no here?"

"Definitely," Tim grinned. "She's been getting too big for her knickers of late. Or should I say britches?"

"I get the idea," Cay laughed. Lifting one of his suitcases while Tim took the other, he held Maudie's hand as she skipped beside him to the parking lot.

Tim's Jaguar was painted British racing green, and he drove accordingly. "Yikes!" Cay yelled as they roared around a blind curve in the left-hand lane. "I'm going to die of fright before I get used to driving on the wrong side."

"You've got that backwards, old boy," Tim said as he downshifted and whipped around a slow-moving truck. "We're the ones using the correct lane."

Maudie thrust her head between them from the back seat. "Don't listen to him, Cay. He almost crashed several times after he got back from Kentucky."

"How far is it to Newmarket?" Cay asked.

"Sixty-two miles from London," Tim said. "Our stud is near Chevelry village."

Cay looked out the window. "Sure is green."

"We've had a good deal of rain lately."

"Tim's lucky," Maudie said. "He's going to Bermuda for his honeymoon."

Cay punched Tim's arm. "Hey, great! You can hop over to Kentucky and meet Ar—" He pretended a coughing fit. "Meet our horses," he finished lamely.

"We'd love to meet your horses," Tim said, grinning at Cay over Maudie's tousled head. "And anyone else you'd like us to meet."

"Yeah," Cay said, avoiding Maudie's inquisitive look. He knew what it was like to have a crush at her age. For him, it had been a pretty grade school teacher, and he had thought he was going to die when she returned one fall wearing a wedding ring. That was why he had asked Tim to let him break the news.

He squeezed Maudie's arm. "You should see your namesake, Toothpick. I brought some pictures. Little Maudie's going to be a beauty— just like you."

Blushing, Maudie put a hand over her mouth. "I'm not a beauty. Especially with these ugly braces!" She rolled her big hazel eyes. Why does growing up take so *long*?"

The sight of Broadheim Stud took Cay's breath away. "Is that a castle or what?" he said, looking up at the towering white brick building that dominated the small valley. Eight chimneys protruded out of the tiled roof and at least thirty windows looked out over park-like pastures bordered by tall beech trees.

"Just a large manor house," Tim said.

"On cold nights I have to sleep with a hot water bottle on my feet," Maudie said, "but the view is lovely from upstairs."

Cay grinned at Tim. "Been suffering from cold feet lately?"

"Not the kind a hot water bottle will cure. But every time I consider backing out, I think how Caroline will keep me warm."

Maudie tapped Tim's shoulder as he parked the car in front of the house. "Tell Mummy I said bloody and I'll tell Caroline what you said about her keeping you warm."

"Can't have that, can we?" Tim looked at Cay. "Despite the threats, I'm going to miss having this little monster spying through my keyhole. Not that I won't be seeing her every day. Caroline and I will be living less than three miles away, and I'll be working at the stud as usual."

The following day, Cay rode with Maudie to a hilltop that over-looked the valley and several other studs surrounding Chevelry village. While Cay's bay mare and Maudie's huge seventeen-hand black gelding cropped the lush grass, he sat against a tree and talked about Arlene. By the time he finished describing the engagement party, Maudie's head was hanging from drooping shoulders, unruly locks of hair hiding everything but the tip of her nose.

Still looking down, she asked, "Is she pretty?"

"Want to see her picture?"

Maudie nodded and wiped the sleeve of her riding jacket across her face.

Cay handed her a copy of Arlene's engagement photo.

"Oh!" Maudie stared at the photo through tear-stained eyes. "She looks like an angel!"

"Must be the blond hair," Cay said, peering closer.

"How old is she?"

"Twenty-four. She'll be twenty-five in August."

"Isn't that terribly old for a woman not to be married?"

"Haven't you heard about the feminine revolution? Women don't want to rush into marriage anymore. They want to experience what it's like to be free and compete with men."

"I'm never going to get married!" Maudie burst out.

"Sure you will, Toothpick. You already live in a castle. Someday a knight in shining armor---"

"I don't want an old knight in shining armor! I—I want to grow up and be free like those women you talked about."

Cay put a hand on her back and wondered if she would push it away. She stiffened, then rested her head on his shoulder. "Don't ever give up your independence to *anyone*, Toothpick. You're a smart little cookie. Be yourself, and everything will work out. Hey, know something?"

"What?"

"Arlene doesn't know much about horses. When you visit us, you can be her teacher!"

Maudie's face brightened. "Really? Wouldn't she resent having a girl tell her things?"

"Arlene? She'll love you to death, just like I do."

"You'll still answer my letters?"

"I'm getting married, not going to jail! Nothing will change between us."

Tim's fiancée, Caroline Hutchinson, was a petite brunette with sparkling brown eyes, short curly black hair and a bubbly personality. The only child of a career diplomat, she had grown up in four countries, including the United States. She had graduated from USC while her father was stationed in Los Angeles. Tim met her at a London party a year ago.

"She's good for me," Tim said to Cay as they drove toward Newmarket after a two-day trip to London. "With her around, my life will be interesting, to say the least."

"And how!" Cay laughed, recalling their tour of London's discos the night before. "I can't believe she did the Charleston on top of that table. Makes me wonder how she'll come down the aisle on Saturday."

"Very dignified. She can put on quite an act when she wants."

With Tim and his father as guides, Cay visited many of the fifty stud farms around Newmarket, including the National Stud, the home of Kentucky-bred Mill Reef, England's leading sire the previous year. They also toured Stanley House and Woodlands Studs, owned by Lord Derby, the descendent of the 12th Earl of Derby, for whom the English and Kentucky Derbys had been named.

The National Stud bordered the straight July course where the summer race meetings were held. It ran almost parallel to the Rowley Mile Course, another straight run that was used in spring and autumn. "The Two Thousand Guineas is a tough test for a young three-year-old," Reggie Grayson said. "See how the Rowley Mile goes downhill at the seventh furlong, then back up the next? Unlike your flat American courses but mild compared to Epsom."

Cay recalled his reaction when he saw the Epsom course while with Tim in London. He had been amazed that the English Derby—the most important race in Great Britain—was run over such a demanding uphill, downhill course.

Standing on the Newmarket heath and looking out over the site of the 2000 Guineas Stakes, he experienced a special thrill. The was the first leg of the British Triple Crown, followed by the Epsom Derby in June and the St. Leger in September. The oldest, the St. Leger, held its meeting ninety-nine years before the first Kentucky Derby.

The sense of history was brought home even stronger when they visited the National Horseracing Museum and Library in Newmarket. The museum contained the bones of Eclipse, the great chestnut stallion that was never beaten in eighteen recorded races. Foaled in 1775 and the great-great grandson of the Darley Arabian, Eclipse was the progenitor of eighty percent of modern Thoroughbreds.

"Eleven King's Plates, contested over four miles and carrying a hundred sixty-eight pounds," Tim said as they stood in front of the glass-enclosed case. "Imagine asking a horse to do that today! Eclipse didn't race until he was five, but that's still an unbelievable amount of weight."

Later, when they exited the Jockey Club headquarters a few doors away, Reggie stopped and looked back at the imposing Georgian-style house. "Racing rules were a bit ragged before they set up this final court of appeal. Even at that, it took a while to iron everything out."

"Like a hundred and fifty years to outlaw doping," Tim said. He grinned at Cay. "Actually it was the Americans who brought it to a head—about the same time your jockey, Tod Sloan, was showing our riders how to stop sitting up straight and win with his 'monkey on a stick' forward seat. Your black jockey, Willie Simms, introduced the short-stirrup crouch here two years earlier but without much success. Sloan rode in an even more exaggerated fashion."

"Sloan was a wild one," Reggie said. "Making owners pay him big rewards and bribing jockeys to let him win. I don't know if he got into doping, but it was American trainers like Wishard who perfected the use of cocaine and introduced it on our racecourses. Using opium balls and putting heroin on the runner's tongue was quite common here and in Ireland—that's how heroin came to be called 'horse'—but cocaine stimulated horses to far exceed their natural abilities. It took another ten years after doping was outlawed before the saliva test was developed to detect abuse. Despite the saliva and urinalysis tests, cases still crop up around the world."

"Urinalysis found traces of bute in Dancer's Image's urine and cost him his Derby win," Cay said. "If he had won seven years earlier or five years later, it wouldn't have been illegal. Now it's allowed in every major racing state except New York and Arkansas. It's just an anti-inflammatory agent."

"Makes one long for the days when horses were given whiskey before a race," Tim said. "Riders, too!"

"Not a bad idea," Cay said. "Especially on a cold day like this."

"Brilliant thought," Tim said. "Shall we proceed to the nearest pub?"

At three the following afternoon, Cay called Arlene. It was 7 AM in Lexington, and she had just exited the shower. "Wish I could be with you," he said.

"Mmmmm. Me, too. I'm wearing nothing but a towel. A *small* one! It doesn't come together in front. Oh, look! A drop of water is running down over my stomach. It's...it's running into my..." Her voice trailed off.

"How can you do this to me?"

"I just wanted to give you something to think about when you look at those pretty English girls."

"I was at the Tattersalls sales paddock today. Made me think how we met."

"Wouldn't that make a great headline?" Arlene laughed. 'Man picks out bride at horse auction!'"

"And I got you for the price of a dinner."

"I love you."

"Love you, too. Wear a bigger towel next time, okay?"

Rain clouds threatened on the day of the wedding, but not a drop fell until Tim and his bride had departed for London. They were staying at the Claridge that night, then flying to the Bahamas the following morning. They planned to visit Cay in Kentucky near the end of the month.

When the rain began to fall the night after the wedding, it came down in torrents and didn't let up for twenty hours. By the time the Graysons drove Cay to Heathrow airport on Monday morning, he was secretly happy to be heading for a drier climate.

Alicia Grayson kissed his cheek. "You must come back again, Cay. And please stay longer. It seems that you've barely arrived and you're on your way home!"

"Come when the races are on," Reggie said. "I know the spring is a busy time for you, but what about September? Your bride will love it."

"Maybe next year. In the meantime, you're welcome to visit us anytime." Cay rested a hand on Maudie's shoulder. "Don't forget to bring my little buddy along."

When Cay's flight was announced, Maudie gripped his hand. "Promise to write?" she said, trying to hold back tears.

"Promise," Cay said. "I'll give Little Maudie a kiss for you."

Throwing her arms around Cay's neck, Maudie pressed her thin body against his chest. "I'm going to miss you so terribly, terribly much!"

"Same here, Toothpick. We'll see each again other before long."

"Oh, I hope so!" she cried, giving him another hug as he picked up his luggage. Standing on her toes, she waved wildly until he disappeared around a corner.

16

Four months after Cay left England, another marriage took place, this time in California's San Joaquin Valley, the home of vast flat farmlands that without irrigation would be a sea of moving sand and dust. It was a dramatic change from the rugged forested hills around Harlan that Cay and Arlene had recently visited with Maripat and John.

"Welcome to Turlock!" Arlene cried as she bounded down the steps of her parents' home and threw herself into Cay's arms. She had flown out from Lexington two weeks earlier to prepare for the wedding. "I meant to come to the airport, but they messed up on my wedding gown and had to take new measurements."

"Your measurements look pretty good to me," Cay grinned.

As Arlene broke away and hugged Maripat and John, Shawn said, "What about me? The only reason I took this best man job was to get a crack at you."

"You didn't need an excuse for that," Arlene said, hugging the little man and kissing his cheek.

Standing beside Arlene's father who had picked them up at the Stockton airport, Joy Loren said, "Better look out, Arlene. He'll be expecting it all the time."

"I'll take my chances," Arlene said, hugging Joy, then starting up the steps. "Come in and meet the rest of the tribe."

It wasn't an elaborate wedding, but Arlene's ethereal beauty added a touch of elegance that no amount of money could buy. The Covenant Church was packed with the bride's family and friends, including several carloads of Arlene's former coworkers from the Hyatt Regency in San Francisco.

When the ceremony ended and Cay bent to kiss his wife's lips, he experienced an overwhelming sense of happiness. With Arlene at his side, he could accomplish anything!

There was also a moment of sadness. As they walked up the aisle amid the waves and smiles of brightly-colored guests, an important face was missing. Five years ago, Cay had stood at his brother's side when his brother married Lynne. Now Travis was away on a holiday in the Mediterranean, purportedly on a cruise that was impossible to cancel.

Only Lynne and Cay knew what lay behind the rift that was widening between him and his brother, a growing discord that even threatened Travis's relationship with his mother. Lynne's bitter influence was back of it all.

Shaking himself free of those morbid thoughts, Cay went out into the sunlight with his radiant bride.

17

While Cay's Woodland Farm breeding program and racing stable grew steadily over the next year and a half, Travis became increasingly frustrated over his failure to get any of his ideas launched at Albright Stud. Lynne added to the pressure.

"Every year it's the same old story!" she yelled, arms waving as she paced back and forth in front of the desk in his office. "You say every year that the next one will be different. We're going backwards, damnit! It's been three years since we bought a good stallion prospect. All those plans you talked about before we were married—they aren't worth shit!"

Travis jumped up and leaned across his desk. "I've got a minority say in what goes on around here. It sure as hell hasn't helped the way you've turned into such a bitch! We don't even get together with the family anymore!"

"What for? So I can bow and scrape to your mother and kiss your sister-in-law's ass? The way things are going, we'll be the poor relations for the next twenty years! Maybe a whole lot more! Your mother will probably outlive us all!"

"What do you want me to do—pull up stakes and leave?"

"Anything's better than beating our brains out here. Cay left. Look how well he's doing!"

"That's different. He had that inheritance money and his share of the farm. My inheritance is gone, and who knows what might happen if I tried to get Mom to buy me out. She might sell the farm and give half the money to Cay! She's been really pissed at me lately."

Lynne slammed her hand down on the desk. "You're nothing but talk! You won't stand up to your mother because you're afraid she'll spank you!"

Travis hit Lynne, an open-handed slap that sent her sprawling on the carpet. White-faced with remorse, he rushed to her side.

"Don't touch me, you bastard!" she screamed, scrabbling back against the wall.

"I'm sorry!" Travis cried. "You know I didn't mean it."

"Real men don't hit women," Lynne hissed. She touched her cheek. It was rapidly turning red.

Kneeling beside her, Travis held out a shaking hand. "I'll never do it again—I promise!"

"You haven't kept your other promises," Lynne said in a tortured half-whisper. "How do I know you'll keep this one?"

"What other promises, Hon?"

"All the things you were going to do with this farm. I thought I would be involved, too!" She pointed at the computer on the desk. "I've spent hundreds of hours storing information and pedigrees on that. You're good at making money, but I know more about running a horse farm than you ever will! I'm sick of womens' lunches and playing hostess while the men talk horses." Dropping her head on her knees, she burst into tears. "I want to *do* something! I want to make things happen!"

Travis drew her into his arms. "I understand, Babe. It's driving me nuts, too. That's why I flew off the handle."

Lynne rested her forehead against his chest. "Will you talk to your mother? I can't go on like this. We can do so much together!"

"It may take a while, but I'll get it settled one way or the other as soon as I can— okay?"

"Okay," Lynne sniffed. She looked up, dark Gypsy eyes glistening. "I want us to make a new start—with everything! I'm tired of all this fooling around we've been doing. I could drop it in a minute. Wouldn't you like that?"

"You know I would," Travis said fervently. He regretted his affairs that had led to Lynne's. He had discovered that he really cared. As much as he could ever care for another person.

"Let's go to the bedroom, Lynne whispered. "We have some making up to do."

"Better believe it." Sweeping her up in his arms, he carried her out of the room.

Five days later, Travis walked into Maripat's office in the west wing of Windsong Manor. She eyed the bulging leather briefcase he set on the big walnut desk. "Looks like you've got some serious business to discuss."

Travis nodded as he pulled up a chair. "That's why I asked you to set some time aside for this meeting."

"My afternoon's free. What's up?"

Travis removed several manila files from the briefcase. "I've made some graphs. The first shows the profit and loss figures of our breeding program the last five years." He propped it against a lamp and pointed with a gold pen. "The red line shows the actual figures. The blue is my estimate of what would have happened if we had made *half* my suggested changes."

Maripat's eyes narrowed. "We're back to discussing some of your hot-shot ideas."

Travis flushed under his mother's scrutiny. "We haven't really talked about it in over a year."

Lacing her fingers behind her neck, Maripat leaned back in the swivel chair, closed her eyes and pursed her lips.

Travis nervously tapped the pen on a folder. His future, perhaps his marriage, depended on this meeting's outcome.

Maripat's eyes snapped open, and her feet hit the floor. "Okay," she said. "Let's hear it."

Sighing with relief, Travis explained the first chart. Producing another, he traced the blue line that ended at the top of the scale.

"These are my projections for the next five years if we raise outside capital and bring in new stallions."

Maripat rested her elbows on the desk. "You're talking a lot of money."

"Not ours', Mom. Other peoples'."

"We've gone over this before."

"I know, but look where we'd be now if we'd acted on my recommendations five years ago. At least two million ahead!"

Maripat's eyes flicked to the first chart, then back to Travis. "What if the yearling market had taken a plunge?"

"But it hasn't!" Travis enthused. "The average yearling price this year will be at least twenty thousand higher than it was in Seventy-Six!"

"All right. Let's see what else you've got."

Travis talked for an hour. Maripat asked questions but mostly listened and took notes. When he finished, she studied the figures. Travis's nervousness increased with each ticking moment.

Maripat looked up. "I'm not going to say anything now. Give me a couple of days. Okay?"

"Sure, Mom." As he gathered up his files, Travis couldn't resist asking, "How does it look so far?"

"Later, Travis. We'll talk later." She rose and walked to the window, a small slender figure in jeans and UK sweatshirt.

Stuffing the files in his briefcase, Travis left the office.

18

"At times like this, I feel like moving back to Harlan," Maripat huffed as she paced John's living room carpet. "I couldn't wait to leave when I was a kid. Now it seems downright peaceful compared to what's going on around here."

"Sounds great," John said. "Can I go, too?"

Maripat stopped in front of the roaring fireplace and pointed an accusing finger. "You're a smartass, John Kershaw."

"Come here."

She hesitated a moment, then sat on his lap. "I'm gettin' old," she murmured as she laid her head on his broad shoulder.

"That's funny," John said as he stroked her hair. "I'm twenty-three days older, and I feel younger than springtime."

"Me, too...most of the time. What am I going to do, John?"

"Hey, since when have you needed help making up your mind?"

Maripat sat up. "Suppose we forget this personal stuff and you act like my lawyer."

"Maripat..."

"I'm serious!"

"Okay."

Maripat held up a finger. "I'm fifty-eight. A long way from retiring but too old to fight Travis every day. He's taken the fun out of running the farm."

Three fingers joined the first. "I have four alternatives. One... go along with Travis. Two...buy him out and send him down the road. Three—and this is pretty far-fetched—bring Cay back after buying Travis out. Four...sell the farm to Travis and get out of the horse business."

"Number four is out," John snapped. "At least the last part. You'll dry up and blow away if you stop working with horses!"

"Is that the lawyer or my lover talking?"

"Both!"

"How about number one?"

"You'll go nuts if you stay around Travis. His ideas are pretty far out. You could lose everything."

"What about buying him out?"

"You'd have to fire most of Travis's hand-picked staff and run the whole operation. You want that?"

"I could divide the farm and let Travis have the old Albright Stud half. He's already living in the house."

"Most of the buildings are on the other property." A pat on her jean-clad bottom. "That doesn't sound like much of an option."

"What about bringing Cay in?"

"Cay's got all he can handle with his own farm. It would alienate the brothers, could ruin Travis. He's got a big ego."

"So I'm left with two alternatives," Maripat said. "Buy Travis out or sell the farm to him."

John smiled and rubbed her back.

"Aren't you going to give me any help?"

"Nope."

"Some lawyer!"

John continued to rub her back.

Maripat clasped her hands in her lap. "Running the farm is a big job. I'm capable, but I don't want it at this stage of my life. Not to mention what it would do to Travis."

"That leaves one alternative."

A nod.

"I'll make a suggestion—not as a lawyer but as a lover. Sell to him and live with me. We'll beef up the breeding stock and racing stable and have a high old time."

Maripat stared at John's grinning face. "People will talk."

"To hell with 'em! How about getting married?"

Maripat shook her head. "We've been over that before."

"How does living together sound?"

"Think you can put up with me day in and day out?"

"That's the dumbest question you've asked all night."

At the current rapidly rising prices for prime Bluegrass land, the farm was worth at least seven thousand an acre, closer to ten if it were sold on the open market. The total acreage of Albright Stud was just over two thousand, making the farm worth a low of $14 million. Adding the value of sixty-seven horses, the package was worth a conservative $25 million.

Considering Travis's share of the farm and all factors involved, Maripat offered Albright Stud to him for $11 million, a figure he gladly accepted. Anxious to cash in on the financial boom in the Thoroughbred industry and Bluegrass farmland, local banks competed to make the loan he needed to pay his mother off. Escrow was closed in mid-December.

Maripat retained one piece of land—ten acres extending from

Elkhorn Creek to a hundred yards past and on each side of the small family cemetery. Included in the deed was access via a private road belonging to Albright Stud.

The only personal items Maripat kept were paintings, furniture, and her valuable collection of rare equine pictures, books and manuscripts.

She moved in with John right after escrow closed, and they celebrated Christmas together in his home for the first time. Cay and Arlene joined them for dinner. Travis and Lynne stopped for a brief exchange of presents, but the atmosphere was strained. All seemed relieved when they left.

January 6, 1982

Dear Maudie,

I'm sorry I didn't write before, but things have been real hectic around here. I'm sure you've heard about Mom selling Albright Stud to Travis. It's been featured in several Thoroughbred magazines.

...so we won't be able to visit you this summer. I know you'll be disappointed, as we are, but this is going to be the busiest year yet on the farm.

Why don't you come here? Arlene really wants to meet you (how many close buddies do I have?), and we can do lots of things together. Mom would love to see you, too.

I'm enclosing newspaper clippings about Little Maudie's win at Belmont in November. Five wins and three of them stakes races at two! Unbelievable! Yeah, I know...you tried to tell me! Shawn and Joy both think her three-year-old season will be even better. They're taking her with twelve other horses to Florida next month.

Gotta run. Breeding season is coming up, and you know how busy that gets! Write soon, and we hope you can visit.

Love,

Cay, Arlene, Maripat and Little Maudie

19

When Travis took over Albright Stud, the Thoroughbred industry was in the midst of a boom that had begun in the Seventies, not just for horses but also for Bluegrass farmland.

Much was due to the invasion of foreign horsemen and investors. British, Europeans, Arab sheiks, Japanese and South Americans increased their purchases at Keeneland from less than $4 million in 1970 to $54 million in 1980.

They also bought choice Bluegrass farms, a move that was welcomed by sellers and those who wanted to save fertile farmland from urban expansion. Farmland around Lexington became so expensive that it was no longer attractive to residential developers.

Not all were happy with the influx of foreign money. In 1980, legislation to limit foreign ownership to ten acres was defeated in the Kentucky General Assembly.

Texas oilmen, real estate investors and manufacturing tycoons also got in on the Thoroughbred buying spree. They helped boost the average price of yearlings at the Keeneland July Selected Yearling Sale from $66,575 to $501,495 in eight years.

Stallion syndications and stud fees reached astronomical figures. Spectacular Bid was syndicated for $22 million, and the cost of breeding a mare to Northern Dancer reached $1 million.

"Next stop, the moon!" Travis chortled as he walked into the bedroom wearing a towel. "Who would have imagined that a colt would sell for over ten million at Keeneland today? Even *I* wasn't that optimistic! It's just the beginning. I feel in my bones! I feel it in my cock!" He tossed the towel on the bed. "See?"

Sitting nude at the dressing table, Lynne glanced in the mirror. "It looks a little shrunk to me."

"A temporary setback. Feel it."

"Down, Fido. This is our big night—remember?"

"Speaking of big..."

"Go away before it gets any bigger. Now ain't the time."

"Guess I'll get my rocks off selling investment units."

"Do that, and I'm yours the rest of the night. I'll be your slave."

"Talk about incentive! If traders on Wall Street got an offer like that, the Dow would go through the roof!"

Lynne said, "With limited partnerships in Thoroughbreds selling so well, shares in the farm should do even better." A nipple puckered as it brushed the dressing table. "Hey, I'm getting a hard-on, too!"

"Get dressed before I work you over with mine," Travis laughed as he wrapped the towel around his erection.

The party was at Millstream Farm, eight miles north of Lexington on Paris Pike. The owner was a rich Virginian who had married a model from New York. Both in their mid-thirties, they had taken the Bluegrass by storm.

"They've added lots of outdoor lighting," Lynne said as they drove up the lane that led to the two-story brick and frame house.

"Nice, but it isn't Windsong Manor."

A smug smile. Their home dwarfed this one. Recently featured in a national magazine, Windsong Manor was one of the finest examples of Greek Revival architecture in the U.S.

Uniformed attendants helped Lynne out and parked their new white Rolls-Royce. They had three cars now—the Rolls, Travis's gold Mercedes sedan and Lynne's red Jaguar convertible.

Taking Travis's arm, Lynne lifted her flowing black gown with the other hand as they walked up the steps.

Larry and Vicky Moore greeted them in the glittering foyer. "Lynne, you look wonderful!" Vicky cried, looking gorgeous herself in a gold beaded long-sleeved low back gown that revealed every line of her tall slender frame. The two women made a stunning pair, Lynne's dark sensual beauty contrasting sharply with Vicky's cool blond elegance.

The son of a wealthy investment banker, Larry Moore was shorter than his nearly six-foot-tall wife. He had the soft look of a man who had never done a day of manual labor in his life. Running a hand over his thinning brown hair, he said, "We've got a good showing of Keeneland buyers tonight. No Arabs, but what the hell, you can't have everything."

A few feet away, a famous horse trainer was talking to a California professional football team owner who was fast becoming one of the nation's leading Thoroughbred breeders. Almost all the two hundred guests were involved in the horse business. "I can imagine the main topic of conversation," Travis said.

Larry Moore laughed. "If it has something to do with ten million dollars, you've got it."

Vicky hugged her husband's arm. "Larry stopped when the bidding got to five million. I would have screamed if he had gone any higher. She looked at Lynne. "Just think of the *clothes* that would buy! We spent three million on five horses, but ten million for one! Horrors!"

Travis said, "I doubt if that's horrifying to the Doobie Brothers. How many buyers arrive in their own Seven-Forty-Seven?"

"The three Thoroughbred foundation sires were Arabians," Lynne said. "Seems right that the Arabs should get into racing."

"I loved watching them beat Sangster and his crowd today," Travis said. "Can't let the Brits have all the best ones."

The Maktoum brothers, three sons of Sheik Saeed ibn Rashid al-Maktoum, ruler of Dubai, one of the seven oil-rich city-states on the Persian Gulf that formed the United Arab Emirates, were buying Thoroughbreds all over the world. They had over seven hundred horses in training, mostly in England and Ireland. They also kept horses in Australia, the European continent and the Bluegrass. Earlier that day, they had purchased a Northern Dancer colt for $10.2 million. That record bid had beat out Robert Sangster, the British soccer-pool gambling king whose syndicate had been buying up the cream of Keeneland's Selected Yearling crop for years.

Vicky lifted her champagne glass. "God bless the Doobie Brothers! They may not come to our parties, but they're helping pay for them!"

Weaving her way beside Travis through the crowd, Lynne said: "I don't know which Vicky drips the most—money or venom! Did you catch the dig she made about Lila Matson? Do they think they can *buy* their way into Bluegrass society?"

"They may not be all the way in, but they've sure got a foot in the door," Travis said. "This bash must have cost at least thirty grand. They spent twice that on their Derby party."

"Cash, flash and trash," Lynne muttered.

"Speaking of venom…"

Lynne lifted a glass of champagne off a passing waiter's tray. "Not venom, Dear. Just calling it like it is."

"What about your parties? Seems I recall a story in the *Herald-Leader* about the 'Darling of the Bluegrass younger set.' When it comes to bucks…"

"That's part of running our business. How many deals have we closed at our parties? There's a difference between buying your way in and already being in." She stamped a spike heel into the expensive Oriental carpet. "This place is only ten years old, and the Moore's haven't been here a third of that. Neither one knows zilch about horses. *That's* the difference!

The party was still going strong when Lynne returned from the restroom well after midnight.

"Hey, pretty lady, where you been hidin'?"

Startled, she looked up at a tall leathery-faced man.

"Don't worry," he grinned. "I won't bite."

"Really? If you were a horse, I'd say you might have a mean streak."

Throwing his head back, the man laughed loudly. "Pretty *and* smart! Now that's a combination!"

"Who might you be?" Lynne asked, enjoying the exchange.

"Grant Alston of Midland, Texas. And you—are you single, married, available?"

"Which would you prefer?" Lynne laughed.

"The last. Get a yes there, the other two don't count."

"Sorry, the middle one is what you get. I'm Lynne Albright."

"Albright, Albright," Grant Alston said, snapping his fingers. "You horse people?"

"Albright Stud."

"By golly, I landed me a big one!" Alston said, long white teeth flashing in his dark face. "Drove by your place yesterday. Prettier than a picture. I sure love it around here. Trees everywhere! Where I come from, they're so scarce a dog has to grit its teeth gettin' from one to the next."

"Then we should have happy dogs," Lynne smiled. "Problem is, there aren't many on horse farms. Not undisciplined ones, anyway. It's bad for high-strung Thoroughbreds. Some horses have dogs for pets, but they're usually small ones."

"Don't say?" Alston scratched the back of his neck with big calloused fingers. "Sounds like I've got a lot to learn."

"I take it you're not into horses."

"No, but I want to." Bushy eyebrows waggled above intense brown eyes. "Horses have pets?"

"Sure…cats, dogs, chickens, goats. They really get attached to them. Their pets travel with them to the track. Leave the pet behind, you've got a messed up horse."

Alston followed Lynne toward a table laden with food. "You're a regular well of information, Mrs. Albright. Okay if I call you Lynne? Call me anything but Grant, I'll be lookin' over my shoulder to see who you're talking to."

Lynne handed a plate to Alston and took one for herself." You're getting into horses, Mr…uh, Grant?" She speared a slice of roast beef. "This looks really good."

"Everything looks good," Grant said, stealing a peek down her low-cut gown. "Especially you."

"Now, now," Lynne said, frowning over her next selection. She added a scoop of potato salad to her rapidly filling plate. A drop got on her finger, and she licked it off. "Yum."

"You know a lot about horses?" Grant asked. He had to move fast to keep up. Lynne was already halfway down the long table.

A sidelong glance. "I grew up on a horse farm. My father's worked with Thoroughbreds most of his life; he manages Elgen Farm down the road from us. I oversee all the sales and purchases at Albright Stud and plan the matings. Try this green jello stuff. It's great!"

"Does your husband lend you out?"

"I beg your pardon?"

"I'm a lamb among wolves when it comes to horses, Lynne. I need advice. I'd sure like to get it from you."

Lynne balanced a roll precariously on top of her heaped plate. "My husband's right over there. Let's ask him."

Travis had cornered Larry Moore earlier, and his enthusiastic sales pitch was bearing fruit. Larry mused, "Forty units. Like syndicating a stallion, only you're syndicating a farm."

"Not all of it," Travis said. "Forty percent. Seven hundred thousand a unit."

"You'll have it rolling in four months?"

"Or less."

"Put me down for two units."

Travis slapped Larry on the back. "You won't regret it. It's a sure thing if ever there was one!"

Lynne nudged Travis with an elbow; her hands were occupied holding her plate. "Travis, Larry, meet Grant Alston. He's from Texas, and he's interested in buying horses."

"Them's the magic words," Travis said, shaking Grant's hand. Both men had dark hair, but there the resemblance ended. Just over six feet, Travis was barrel-chested and taking on weight. Recently turned thirty-seven, he looked about five years younger than Grant. Two inches taller, Grant had a rawboned aggressive look, like a man who relished crushing opponents with his fists.

While Grant shook hands with Larry, Lynne sagged against Travis. "Let's sit down," she said. "This plate is heavy."

"I'll bet," Larry laughed. "I'd better tell the kitchen to have the table restocked."

"Can I help it if there are so many goodies to choose from?"

"You're forgiven," Larry said, putting an arm around her waist and guiding her toward a row of chairs.

Travis asked Grant why he was interested in Thoroughbreds.

"Quarter horse racing is big in my neck of the woods," Grant said, "but I believe we'll have pari-mutuel wagering before long. I'd like to get in on the action."

"What makes you think that?" Lynne said. "It's been banned in Texas for fifty years!"

"Since the oil boom started six years ago, population's grown by hundreds of thousands. Newcomers won't bend to pressure from religious groups. It won't happen overnight."

"You have a farm?" Travis asked.

"Nope." A smile split Grant's craggy face, almost closing eyes already squinted from long exposure to the elements. "All my land's in little pieces. Been wildcatting around West Texas for fifteen years, started working in the oil fields long before that. Left school after the tenth grade and don't know much else." His smile widened, and his audience got the distinct impression that under that rough country-boy exterior there was a very shrewd mind.

"Now you want to get into horse farming," Travis said.

"I want to get into *racing*. A farm sounds complicated. For a start, I'd like to buy some yearlings and put them in training. Might get some breeding stock later if I can find somebody to take care of 'em. I may buy a farm someday. Right now, I'm interested in a racing stable, pure and simple."

"Grant wants to borrow me," Lynne said. She pointed at the grinning Texan. "To advise him on buying horses and stuff."

"Sounds great!" Travis said, thinking of all the ways Albright Stud could benefit.

Grant said, "Maybe Lynne could show me around your place."

"Anytime," she said.

"Call you tomorrow?"

"Fine."

Travis took a card out of his pocket. "Give us a ring in the morning." A knowing look at his wife. "Not before eleven. Lynne probably won't get much sleep tonight."

As they drove toward home shortly after 2 AM, Lynne playfully pinched Travis's arm. "Did that remark about me not getting much sleep tonight mean what I think it does?"

"Consider yourself my slave tonight. I sold two units to Larry."

"You may rip my clothes off, tie me to the bed, violate my body! Oh, wow!"

"You didn't do too bad with Grant. Think he's for real?"

"I'll be surprised if he isn't. I'll check him out tomorrow

through the bank to make sure."

"Hope you're right. You can make some nice commissions, and we should swing a few private sales. Did you get that bit about him wanting to find a farm where he can keep his horses?"

Lynne tapped her forehead. "Got it filed right up here."

20

Arlene tiptoed into Cay's office. The drapes were drawn to block the late afternoon sun. "Surprise," she said, wrapping her arms around his neck from behind and resting her chin on his head

"You smell good," Cay said. "You *feel* good. Is that you or is that you?"

"I just got out of the shower. Haven't had time to dress except for these panties. You like?"

"I like." Cay turned and seized a small breast. "Perfect for munching." He drew a nipple into his mouth.

"I came to tell you dinner is almost ready," she gasped.

"Don't bother me; I'm busy," Cay mumbled.

"The food will get cold."

"Microwaves were made for moments like this."

"I feel like I'm in one now."

"Shall we retire to the bedroom?"

"The couch is closer. Maybe if we hurry we can make a baby."

"Sounds good," Cay said. He knew there was deep concern behind that teasing remark. Despite regular and very enjoyable attempts to procreate, she hadn't conceived.

Moments later, they were lying naked on the office couch. "I don't deserve this happiness," Arlene sighed as he pulled her into his arms.

Cay kissed her ear. "You're stealing my lines again."

"Do you think it will work this time?"

"It takes an average of one point seventy-five covers for a stallion to impregnate a mare. If we do it twice, it will greatly increase your chances to be in foal."

"Dinner in between?"

"My sperm count will need rest and revitalization."

"Shall we do the point-one first or the seventy-five?"

"How do I stop three-quarters of the way through? We'd better make it two whole ones."

"Goody."

The sound of their lovemaking was gentle at first, then louder as their movements became more frantic. Arlene cried out, gripping Cay's buttocks and drawing him deeper into her body. In the midst of a wrenching climax, she bucked and rolled her hips, smiling with satisfaction when Cay groaned and ejaculated violently. Cay withdrew and lay on his side, pulling her sweating body close.

They sat at the kitchen table, eating the warmed-up dinner. Wiggling her naked bottom on the vinyl-covered chair, Arlene said, "Something slipped out."

"Hope it wasn't anybody important."

Raising her T-shirt, she looked down. "Just a drop. Besides, we've got that second try coming up."

"I wonder if Travis and Lynne ever try."

"To have a baby? Would they want one—the way they live?"

"Doubt it. Probably best. The kid wouldn't get much attention."

"I talked to Maripat this morning. She saw Travis in town. He bragged about the success they're having. Said he's going to start selling investment units in the farm next month."

"Bet that went over well."

"She wasn't doing handsprings. He said something about how you should have listened to him. Does it bother you, Darling?"

"Not a bit. We're doing fine. Maybe not to Travis, but I can sleep nights. He hasn't got anything like Little Maudie."

"I feel so terrible that Maudie couldn't make it here and see her namesake win the Mother Goose."

"You can't feel near as bad as she does. Dumb kid, breaking her arm like that."

"Brave, if you ask me. I can't imagine riding over those big jumps. She was in first place until her horse fell."

"Well, she's out of competition for a while. Maybe we can visit her in Newmarket next year."

"If you hurry and get me pregnant. I don't want to have our baby in England. He's going to be foaled right here in the Bluegrass—a Kentucky-bred all the way."

"What's with this *he* business? You and Mom are in a rut. Nothing wrong with a girl."

"Nothing wrong with a boy, either. By the way, I'm helping her tomorrow. They're having a bunch of people over for dinner. We'll straighten the house up, and I'll bake some pies."

"Where does she get the time? Their breeding program is twice as big as it was when she moved there, and they've got sixteen horses in training!"

"Staying busy keeps one young," Arlene said in defense of her beloved mother-in-law.

"I know what keeps me young. Race you to the bedroom."

"I prefer the couch. Two complete covers in the same location should do it—don't you think?"

21

Three months after Travis proposed selling Albright Stud units to Larry Moore, an investment banking firm began soliciting wealthy businessmen and celebrities across the nation. Forty investment units, each representing fifty-six thousand shares at $12.50 a share, were offered at $700,000 each. As promised, Larry Moore purchased two.

Optimistic predictions that yearlings would reach record prices that year and a certified report that Albright Stud had posted an average eighteen percent profit over the last decade made the investment look rock solid.

There were added perks. Buying shares in Albright Stud offered a once-in-a-lifetime opportunity to not only receive a good return but to rub shoulders—even stand in the winner's circle on occasion—with glamorous and exciting people. The investor could also inform friends and associates that he was in the horse business and impress strangers at cocktail parties.

In six weeks, all the Albright Stud investment units were sold. Discounting the banking firm's commission and taxes, Travis and Lynne were $20 million richer.

Grant Alston visited Albright Stud that fall. "You guys are making me feel like a poor cousin," he said to Lynne as they inspected three yearlings he had recently purchased.

"I feel so sorry for you," Lynne said. "Did you miss hitting a well last week?"

Grant scratched behind the ear of a curious colt. "I've been a wildcatter too long to get rattled by a dry hole now and then. Taking a chance never bothered me."

Lynne arched an eyebrow. "If that's the case, why didn't you invest in this farm?"

"Figured you'd ask sooner or later. Come on, let's walk." As Lynne fell in beside him, he continued, "Whenever there's a boom, there's a bust. Yearling prices and stallion breeding fees can't keep going up at this pace. It's too damn volatile for me.

"Stallions are syndicating for ridiculous prices. Take that Texas syndicate that paid thirty-six million for Sunny's Halo! Conquistador Cielo went for four hundred thousand more, but that was for insurance. Thirty-six shares in Devil's Bag for a million each—and he hasn't even run as a three-year-old! Something's got to give."

"It'll level off," Lynne said. "Eventually Sangster and the Arabs will buy up all the Northern Dancer line they need and start breeding their own. If yearling prices drop, stud fees will, too. That will affect stallion prices."

"Having smarts is what attracted me to you," Grant said. He zipped Lynne's fleece-lined jacket up to her neck. "Suppose you weren't connected to this farm and were advising me. Would you tell me to fork over seven hundred thousand for one percent of Albright Stud?"

Lynne pulled the zipper down a couple of inches. "Considering the circumstances, I would advise caution."

"I'd be real disappointed if you'd said otherwise. No matter which way things go, we can do each other some good. Agreed?"

Lynne nodded, acknowledging that Grant was offering her a mutually-benefiting financial arrangement that went beyond building his racing stable.

22

Winter was still a few weeks away, but the chill in the air made Cay feel like it had already arrived. As he entered the house, the delicious aromas from the kitchen made his mouth water.

"I'm home!" he called.

"You're early!" Arlene cried. "Don't come in! I need a minute."

"Have you got a man in there?"

"Of course, Dear. How else can I cope with being alone so much? Go wash up. Don't come in until I say it's okay."

As Cay emerged from the bathroom, he heard the sound of high heels clicking across the kitchen floor. "How's it going?"

"One more minute."

"You said that five minutes ago."

"Perfection takes time. You may come in now."

Cay was greeted by two tall lighted candles on the table. The subdued lighting cast a flickering glow as Arlene twisted the cork off a bottle of Dom Perignon. Platinum hair fell softly over bare shoulders and teased the thin straps of her white gown.

"Wow," Cay breathed. "What have I done to deserve this?"

"Anything and everything," Arlene said, smiling radiantly as he kissed her cheek. "Here's your glass. Ready?"

"A toast?"

"To the top stallion at Woodland Farm. May he continue his fertile ways!"

A huge smile lit Cay's face. "Does this mean---"

"I'm in foal, six weeks gone. With luck we'll take our son to next year's Derby. He may only be a few days old, but he'll enjoy it."

Cay drew her into his arms. "I can't believe it!"

"I wonder if it had anything to do with moving our primary base of operations to the couch in your office? We've done it an awful lot there since last summer."

"Does Mom know?"

"I wanted to tell you first."

"Let's eat. We've got phone calls to make."

At a celebration dinner the following night, Shawn observed that it had been a banner year at Woodland Farm. "Best crop of yearlings we've ever had, and Little Maudie looks like a sure thing to win the Eclipse. Now Arlene's going to have a baby."

"Maybe you shouldn't push your luck, Shawn," Maripat said. "Might be a good time for you to retire."

"You kidding? This place would fall apart!"

Joy rolled her eyes toward the ceiling. "The man believes it. He really does!"

"Watch it, girl. I didn't take you out of mucking stalls to have you make fun of me."

Arlene said, "I wouldn't ever make fun of you."

" 'Course not. You're a fine sensible girl. Joy used to be, too. She's getting big-headed from all those trips to the winner's circle. Not to mention those men she's got in her little black book. Pulls it out the minute we hit a new town."

Joy whacked Shawn's head with a napkin. "Dirty old man!"

John looked at Cay. "Some training team you've got."

Arlene said, "I think it's sweet the way they get along."

"As long as they keep winning, you won't hear any complaints from me," Cay said.

Thanksgiving and Christmas came and went, and the new year brought Woodland Farm the honor of being both breeder and owner of the Champion Three Year Old Filly. Sired by Demon Racer—a great-grandson of Devil's Fire in the tail-male line and the daughter of a Raise a Native mare—Little Maudie won the coveted Eclipse Award by a wide voting margin. Retired from racing, she was sent to Claiborne Farm in early February for a mating with Spectacular Bid.

23

Parking the Lincoln Continental beside the barn, Arlene waved at the men standing inside. A mid-February storm had blown through central Kentucky the day before, and Cay's boots crunched in the snow as he walked toward the car.

"Leaving already?" he said.

"I'm going by the Fayette Mall before I go to the doctor's. There's a sale on maternity dresses."

"They ought to have a sale on them all the time. Think of the money they save putting holes in the skirts."

"I need one with a hole right now."

"A little one."

"I better get going."

"Take it easy," Cay said as he bent to kiss her lips.

"See you around three."

As she turned east on Old Frankfurt Pike, the sun broke through a bank of clouds. Lowering the visor, she took a pair of sunglasses out of her purse and put them on.

There was little traffic on the narrow rolling road. Snow blanketed the fields, and giant houses were surrounded by bare-limbed trees. In a little over two months, springtime foliage would hide many of the stately homes from view.

Nearing the outskirts of Lexington, Arlene turned right on New Circle Road, part of the wide thoroughfare that encircled the city. After driving a few miles on a route that took her south, then east again, she entered an off-ramp and slowed for the light on Nicholasville Road. Momentarily blinded by the sudden glare of the sun, she twisted the steering wheel too far to the right.

The car hit a patch of ice and went out of control. Surprised, she stamped on the brake. Realizing her mistake as the car began to slide, she switched her foot to the gas pedal. The heavy car hit a patch of dry pavement and shot through a red light, broadsiding a Toyota sedan. The small car was driven into the center divider as the Lincoln's grill buried itself in the passenger side.

Protected inside the big Lincoln, Arlene was dazed but unhurt, a situation that lasted only a few seconds. Head bent over the steering wheel, she didn't see the giant cement truck that plowed into her car. With a thunderous crash that was heard for blocks, the Lincoln was wrenched from the Toyota and knocked on its side, sparks flying as the truck pushed it relentlessly across the intersection and toward Fayette Mall. While the driver fought to control the huge vehicle, the Lincoln rolled on its back and broke free. When it came to a halt, the car was flattened to less than half its height.

Cay was outside the farm office talking to Joy when the phone rang. Moments later, Shawn stepped out on the porch, a stunned look on his face. "It's the Lexington police," he said in a trembling voice. "Arlene's been in an accident."

As Cay ran into the office, Shawn looked at Joy and shook his head. "It sounds bad."

Because he had known Cay since childhood, Officer Howard Jocklin had been chosen to make the call. When Cay demanded to know Arlene's condition, Jocklin took a deep breath and told him she had been pronounced dead at the scene. What he didn't say was the rescuers had been forced to cut one side of the car apart in order to extradite her body.

Cay sat at the battered oak desk. "Where is she, Howard?" he asked in a tortured half-whisper.

"St. Joseph's. God, Cay, I'm so sorry!"

"The baby...anything about the baby?"

A moment of silence. "It was a really bad accident, Cay."

"I see. I better hang up now, Howard. Got lots to do."

"I'll meet you at the hospital. Want me to call your mother?"

"I'll do it. Thanks." Cay dropped the receiver on the desk.

"Cay?" Shawn said from the doorway. He moved inside and stood beside Joy, unsure what to do.

"I've got to call Mom," he said, staring blankly at the wall. He picked up the receiver and listened. "No dial tone."

"I'll fix it," Joy said, stepping quickly to the phone and depressing the button. Tears leaked from the corners of her eyes as she watched Cay press the first two digits.

He looked up, confused. "I can't remember. Will you do it for me, please?"

"Sure." Crying openly now, Joy punched Maripat's number.

Shawn moved beside Joy. Arms around each other, they watched as Cay held the receiver tightly to his ear. He bit his lip, then said in a broken voice, "Mom? Arlene's been in an accident. Howard Jocklin called. It happened by Fayette Mall. She's…she's been hurt real bad, Mom. Awful bad. They took her to St. Joseph's." Clutching the receiver with whitened knuckles, he moaned, then cried out in a rush of words, "She's not alive! Howard said there was nothing they could do! Arlene, the baby—they're both gone!"

Maripat called John at his law office in Lexington. Within minutes, he was on his way to the hospital while Maripat drove to Woodland Farm and picked up Cay, Shawn and Joy for the trip into town.

Howard Jocklin informed John that Arlene was not the only one killed in the accident. A man, his wife and their twelve-year-old son had been in the Toyota. The woman was killed instantly. They were removing the boy's leg in emergency. He had also received severe head injuries.

"It's a tragedy on both sides, Mr. Kershaw," Jocklin said. "It looks like Arlene went through a red light and hit the Prentice car. Mr. Prentice was driving, and his wife was in the front seat. Their son was in the back and wasn't wearing a belt. He got thrown against the other side, and his head cracked the glass. Mrs. Prentice was crushed. Her husband got just a few scratches."

"You're sure Arlene went through a red light?"

"Witnesses said she skidded on ice, then accelerated right through the light. It wasn't like she was speeding or anything, just a case of hitting ice and panicking. We'll know more after all the reports come in the next day or so."

"The truck driver wasn't hurt?"

"The truck was carrying a full load of concrete—ten yards. That's a total weight of over thirty-three tons. The driver is real shook but okay physically."

There was little Cay could do at the hospital. Arlene's injuries were so severe that the doctor recommended he not see her until she was prepared for burial. Cay signed the papers releasing her body to a funeral parlor and went home with Maripat and John. After staying with Cay while Maripat phoned Arlene's parents, John left them alone.

Maripat poured two glasses of bourbon and gave one to Cay. Sitting beside him on the couch, she slipped a hand in his. They sat quietly for a time, nursing their drinks and finding comfort in each other's company.

Cay said, "What am I going to do, Mom? How can I go back into that house? She made every room special. No matter where I go, there'll be something to remind me of her. Our closet's full of her things. I'll smell her perfume. It'll still be on her pillow from last night!"

"Let's think about that later," Maripat said, heart aching for the beautiful young woman who had brought so much joy into their lives. "You can stay here until all this is over. Carl and Beth are flying out. They'll be here tomorrow morning."

"They must feel awful."

"Beth had to get off the phone. I wish we didn't have to talk about this now but we should before they get here. What if they want Arlene buried in Turlock?"

"She spent a good part of her life there. I won't fight it. Would the funeral be there? She had lots of friends in Turlock."

"We could have a memorial service here."

Cay looked at his mother with anguished eyes. "I don't know if I can handle going through it twice."

She pressed his hand. "Let's wait and see."

They were silent for a time, then Maripat released his hand

and rose. "I've got to call Travis."

Cay replied listlessly, "I wonder if he'll really care."

"Of course he will! He's your brother."

Lynne arrived home from shopping in Lexington to find Travis hunched in front of the television. "What gives?" she asked, dropping her packages on the couch and stripping off her gloves.

Travis pointed at the television screen. "Guess you haven't heard. They've already run the story twice. Arlene was killed in a car accident."

Lynne's eyes widened, and her fingers dropped from the zipper on her coat. "When did it happen?"

"Noon on Nicholasville Road. You should see her car. It—"

"My god! Was it by Fayette Mall?"

"Right at the off-ramp."

"I went by there not long afterwards! One lane was blocked, and a cop was pushing one of those things they use to measure distances. I had no idea!"

"Cay's over at White Oak. I went to see him a couple of hours ago. He's in bad shape."

"I'll bet. Jesus!"

"A woman was killed, too. Her son lost a leg, might have brain damage. Arlene went through a red light and smashed their car all to hell. A cement truck flattened the Lincoln."

"If Arlene was at fault, Cay's in big trouble."

"Better believe it. They'll go after everything he's got."

24

Because of Arlene's terrible injuries, the casket was sealed. Cay was relieved. He wanted to remember her alive, not dead.

After it was decided between Cay and Arlene's parents that their daughter would be interned in Turlock, a memorial service was held in Lexington's Episcopal Christ Church. Cay sat on Maripat's right in the front pew with John on her left. Travis and

Lynne sat beside John—a brief show of family unity.

The day after the memorial service, Cay, Maripat and John flew to California with Carl and Beth Olson. Arlene's body had been shipped ahead, and the following morning after the funeral, she was buried in the city cemetery.

By the time Cay arrived back in Lexington, he was physically and emotionally exhausted. He had little chance to rest, however, because a major lawsuit was underway.

"The ambulance-chasing bastards came down on the husband like a flock of vultures," John said to Cay and Maripat as they sat around the kitchen table at White Oak Stud. " He signed up with a firm in Louisville. They'll go for the jugular."

"What should I do?" Cay asked.

"Sit tight. We'll hear from them soon enough."

"What about my car insurance? Don't they have lawyers?"

"They do, but they haven't got any real grounds on which to fight. The police report lays the blame on Arlene. Besides, there's a cap of five hundred thousand on your policy. The plaintiff will ask for a lot more than that."

"How much is a lot?" Cay asked, struggling to cope with this additional disaster.

"They see you as a rich horse farmer. You've got a racing stable and have just won the Eclipse Award with Little Maudie. The plaintiff lost his wife, and his son will need therapy and treatment for a long time, maybe the rest of his life. They'll go for millions."

"I'll be ruined," Cay said.

"They don't care about that, but I do. I'll be in your corner every step of the way." John glanced at his yellow pad. "I need an appraisal of your farm, stock, everything. They can't get blood out of a turnip. You'll have to cut your operation back, sell a lot of stock. The farm's free and clear, so you can borrow on that. Hopefully, that will be the worst scenario."

"I don't give a damn if I lose it all," Cay said dully.

"That's today. I can't even imagine how you feel, but I know one thing— you'll get up and fight. You've got too much of your mother in you to quit. Try to keep your mind off what might happen and get those figures together like yesterday. I'll get you as much breathing room as I can."

25

While Cay worked with Shawn and appraisers ascertaining his net worth, Maripat and Joy packed Arlene's clothing and personal items and shipped them to her mother. It was Cay's decision. He would never part with many memorandums of their short time together, but the other things might be of use to someone else. Arlene's diamond engagement ring went to no one. It was buried with her.

Twenty-two days after the accident, Cay met with John and Maripat in at John's office. "They're asking for twenty million," John said. "They're blowing smoke, testing the wind, so to speak."

"Twenty million!" Cay exclaimed. "What do you think they can really get?"

"That's a tough one. If it goes through all the courts, they might end up with a fourth, maybe a third. Your various insurance companies will probably come up with a million. You'll have to come up with the rest."

"That leaves me between four and seven million short."

"Thereabouts," John agreed. But it may be a lot less if it goes to trial."

"Or more," Maripat said.

"A year or so from now, the sympathy factor won't be as strong. Permanent brain damage to the boy has already been downgraded to ten percent."

"I don't want to go through a long court battle," Cay said. "Let's settle up now, so I can get on with my life."

"It may cost you," John warned. "You're worth maybe eight-nine million, around half that if you sell under pressure."

"I don't give a damn. How soon can you do it?"

"We can't let them see our hand. If they know we're anxious to settle, they'll milk us dry."

"How long?"

"Weeks, months. Start cutting back on your stock. Don't make waves. This isn't a fire sale; you have plenty of time. Tell anybody who asks that you need to ease up a for a while, consolidate, take it easy, go on a vacation—okay?"

"Just get it over as quick as you can."

"That's it, then. Let's go to the Merrick Inn for dinner and drinks. Folks can see that things are getting back to normal, whatever that is."

26

The first thing Cay did was explain the situation to Shawn and Joy. "You're my friends, and I'm going to need help closing down. We'll let the farmhands go as we reduce stock. That includes selling the racing stable. Joy, you're a damn good trainer. I'll do everything I can to get you placed elsewhere. You—"

"You're kicking me out?" Joy cried. "Shawn and I've been a team for twenty-five years, and you're breaking us up?"

"Damnit, Joy, I'm not kicking you out. There won't be any work here when this is over. Shawn's fifteen years past retirement. We can sit on the porch in rockers and watch the weeds grow. You're just beginning a great career. Right, Shawn?"

"I don't know about that retirement shit, but you ought to listen to him, Joy."

Cay said, "I'm just trying to give you a head start, Joy."

"You're both nuts," Joy snapped. "I'm not going anywhere!"

"You want to watch the weeds grow, too?" Cay said.

"No! I want to help get this farm back on its feet!"

"There may not be any feet to put it back on when this is over."

"I'll take my chances." She glared at Cay. "If you go down, I'm going with you!"

Cay looked at Shawn. "Sounds like the captain of a ship,"

Shawn snorted. "Better believe it. If you don't keep her under a tight rein, she'll take over."

"Will you guys shut up? We've got work to do. We're keeping Little Maudie and those three brood mares. How many yearlings?"

Cay said. "What about that Grey Dawn colt? Let's hold him out for now. Where's that list? Now..."

27

No one had been more shocked and upset over the news of Arlene's death than Maudie Grayson. She, along with her family, wrote Cay, but the only response during the weeks immediately after the accident had been short notes of gratitude. Until one evening when Tim stuck his head in the doorway of Maudie's bedroom and said he had received a letter from Cay.

"He wrote you and not me?" she said in a hurt voice.

"Cay wanted me to break the news," Tim said. He sat on the edge of the bed. "Come here, Ducks."

"What news?" Maudie said, flopping down beside him. Barely fifteen and five foot, eleven, she was taller than most of the boys her age. She was still painfully thin with a mass of unruly dark blond hair and huge hazel eyes set wide apart on each side of a freckled nose.

Tim handed her the letter. "You can read this later. The accident left Cay with a really big problem. His wife ran a traffic light and hit another car. A woman was killed and her son lost a leg and has brain damage. The husband is suing Cay for twenty million dollars."

Maudie gasped. "Cay wasn't even there! Does he have that much money?"

"Of course not. It's the way solicitors work. They ask for much more then they expect to get."

"Poor Cay. Losing Arlene, now this."

"He's selling most of his horses—

"Not little Maudie!"

Tim put his arm around her shoulders. "Cay says if he ends up with just one horse, it will be Little Maudie. But he has to sell his racing stable and most of his breeding stock. Even with that, he may not have enough to settle the lawsuit."

A tear slipped over Maudie's cheek. "Should I call him?"

"Not yet. Give him time. He must be in a terrible stew—recovering from Arlene's death and facing the possibility of losing everything. Write, but be careful what you say. He's hanging on by a thread."

28

A tentative agreement was reached between the attorneys in mid-August. Cay met with John in his Lexington office.

"They'll settle for five and a half million," John said. They say this is their last offer, and there's the usual mumbo jumbo that if we don't get off the pot they'll go for the works."

"What do you think?"

"Frankly, I don't think we can do better. I've been butting heads with this bunch for months. They'll only give so much. And there's always the possibility that the boy's condition might worsen. That would raise the ante. It's good we didn't move too quick. Getting that two million for those three yearlings at Keeneland really helped."

John studied a row of figures. "Adding that and the sale of your other horses to the nine hundred fifty thousand from the insurance companies and deducting for taxes, you've got four million-three. You're a million-two short."

"I'll ask the bank to loan the balance. The farm and stock's worth four times that much."

"I won't respond until you get everything settled. Cash in hand is our best bargaining tool."

"I'll go first thing in the morning."

John rested a hand on Cay's shoulder. "See your mother

before you do anything. She couldn't make the meeting, but she's expecting you at the farm."

Maripat was in one of the barns, jeans stuffed in rubber boots, a lock of autumn-colored hair hanging over one eye. When Cay said he was going to the bank, she shook a small fist in his face.

"You're going to the bank when I've got all that money from the sale of the farm sitting around? Why do you think I insisted that Travis pay me all those millions—so I could buy a villa in France and spend my holidays in Monte Carlo? I wanted something left over for you! Travis has already doubled what he paid me. You need working capital. We'll go to the bank in the morning, and I'll transfer a couple million into your account.

" Damnit, Mom!"

"One more peep, and I'll make it three."

"May I kiss you?"

"If you toss in a hug."

By the time the lawsuit was settled and Cay had paid the legal fees, Woodland Farm was stripped to the bone. Of the original fifty-three horses—including fourteen in training—only twelve remained. Six weanlings, one stallion, four broodmares and Little Maudie, now in foal to Spectacular Bid. The farmhands were gone. Cay lived in the big Federal Brick house while Shawn and Joy shared one of the farm residences. The other two were rented.

From February through September, Travis and Lynne had watched the reversal of Cay's fortunes with morbid fascination. Having had little contact with Cay and Maripat since Arlene's funeral, they knew nothing about the settlement of the lawsuit until it was announced on a local television station.

"Where do you think he got the money to settle that suit?" Lynne asked.

"He sold a lot of horses, probably borrowed on the farm."

"Bet your mother forked over a lot. She always favored Cay."

"Personally, I don't give a shit," Travis said, irritated at Lynne's constant sniping at Cay and his mother. "It's over."

Lynne walked to the bar. While she poured another martini and Travis returned his attention to the television, she gloated over Cay's downfall. The fool could have had it all! If he had accepted her attention five years ago, she would have gladly left Travis. After things calmed down, she and Cay could have married, and they might now be running both farms.

She still burned with anger and humiliation whenever she recalled that night when she had done everything but grovel at his feet.

Now she was worth millions and shared ownership in one of the world's leading horse farms while he was teetering on the edge of bankruptcy. Sipping her martini, she watched with glee as the story of the settlement was repeated on the news.

Although Cay held up well in public, he often wept in the home that he had shared with Arlene. Her pictures hung on the walls, and one stood on the nightstand beside his bed. He thought about her every waking moment.

PART IV

1985-1993

"You can win all the other races you want, but there's only one Derby—and anybody who tells you different is full of manure."

Trainer Jack Van Berg the day after winning his 5,000th race and fourteen days after winning the Kentucky Derby with Alysheba.

1

In late July, two-and-a-half years after Arlene's death, Lynne lay on the floor of her parents' home, white shorts accenting her darkly tanned legs. Head propped on a pile of cushions, she described the day's sale price at Keeneland that had the horse world buzzing.

"If Klein had given Lukas the nod, he might have gone another million, but everyone thinks Sangster would have kept on topping him. It still beat the old world record by almost three million."

"Thirteen-million for a yearling!" Lynne's father said. "Far as I'm concerned, things are getting out of hand."

"They figure they'll make a profit through syndication and breeding fees," Lynne said. "That's the name of the game these days. With a British Triple Crown winner as sire and out of the dam of an American Triple Crown winner, they might eventually syndicate the colt for thirty-forty million."

"And he might not win a race and syndicate for a fraction of that," George Ross said.

"The Maktoums paid three million-three for Shareef Dancer and syndicated him for forty million after only five races. They haven't even raced Snaafi Dancer, and they paid ten million-two for him. God knows what they'll syndicate him for."

"I still say it's crazy. If yearling prices drop, the balloon's going to pop."

"You're turning into a real pessimist, Dad."

Christina Ross looked up from her knitting. "He's just being cautious, Dear. Like you should be. We both worry the way you and Travis spend money."

"We have lots to spend." Lynne lifted a bare foot in the air and examined her red-painted toes. "You think I'm bad, you should've heard this girl at Keeneland today. She couldn't have been over twenty. She came barging out of the sales pavilion behind this guy yelling, 'I wanted that horse!' The guy—I guess he was her husband—didn't look much older than her. He said, 'I'm sorry, Honey, but I just couldn't go any higher.' I looked inside and the board read a million-six!"

"Your first pony cost seventy-five dollars," Christina said, "and we had to scrape to raise that."

"Things are different now, Mom. We're just lucky to be in on the boom."

"Now you're talking about going public," George said. "Why do you need all that money? You've got a half-dozen cars and enough clothes to open your own store. That new swimming pool cost a fortune. You must be getting tired of traveling. How many times have you been to Europe—eight, ten?"

"A lot's going back into the farm," Lynne said. "I don't have to tell you how expensive it is to maintain a racing stable—around twenty-five thousand a year just to keep one horse in training. We've spent over fifteen million on yearlings the last two years and have built the stallion roster to eight. We'll add at least two more this fall."

George glanced at his watch. "Time for me to get back to work." He walked across the room and patted his daughter's knee. "I'll leave you two alone, so you can catch up on the gossip."

Noting her father's bent shoulders as he left the room, Lynne was glad he was retiring as manager of Elgen Farm in October. She asked, "Are you going to buy that place on Georgetown Pike?"

Christina said: "If the sellers accept our offer. I hope they do. Your father would feel cooped up on anything less than ten acres. It's just a short run into Lexington." A pause. "I saw Cay in Midway last week"

Lynne lifted an eyebrow. "Oh?"

"He has twenty-six horses now. I guess you know that."

"I heard he bought some broodmares and two-year-olds at the fall and winter sales."

"He looks so sad. You were close once. Don't you ever talk?"

"Not much, Mom. Let's not get into that again."

"All right." A disapproving look. "It just doesn't seem natural—living so close and hardly ever seeing each other."

During the Thoroughbred industry's phenomenal growth throughout the Seventies and into the Eighties, the most common way to invest was to buy limited partnership units that sold for $25,000 and up. The majority of the investors were professionals—doctors, lawyers and small businessmen. The profits and tax write-offs were very attractive. It looked like a good hedge against inflation.

But the average American had neither the money nor the means to buy into the glamorous industry. With this in mind and seeing a way to line his pockets with millions of untapped dollars, Travis took Albright Stud, Inc. public two months after the Nijinsky II yearling sold at Keeneland for $13.1 million. Brokers used that astounding price as a marketing tool.

Initially, 100,000 shares sold over the counter at $10.25 a share. Listed later on the American Stock Exchange, another 350,000 shares were sold, leaving 150,000 outstanding.

While Lynne supervised the expansion of their racing stable and the syndication of stallions, Travis instigated a number of improvements on the farm. This included a new one-mile training track and an indoor equine therapeutic swimming pool modeled after the one at Calumet Farm.

They also retained a New York advertising agency to place print and television ads in every major market. Albright Stud was fast becoming one of the best known names in the business.

2

Although the growth at Cay's Woodland Farm during that same period was miniscule in comparison, there was reason for encouragement. Cay christened a promising gray colt Little Bid. Foaled in early February the year before, he had been named after both his sire and his dam, Spectacular Bid and Little Maudie.

Little Bid was a big muscular colt with the promise of great speed. He was also aggressive and quick to take the lead of the small band of yearlings. "Look at that smartass," Joy said as Little Bid kicked up his heels and raced across the lush green paddock. "He thinks he owns the place."

"Probably could," Cay said, "considering what he'd bring at Keeneland if we wanted to sell him. That's one royally-bred smartass. We could buy a dozen yearlings for what he'd bring."

"Yeah," Shawn said, "and we can also slit our throats in unison after he wins the Derby."

"Pretty high hopes you've got there."

"As if you're not thinking it every minute. Probably sleeping with his picture under your pillow."

"He's going to be a lot more gray than his daddy was at three," Joy said. "His muzzle's already turned."

"Steel gray like Native Dancer," Cay said.

"I guess you'd like Little Bid to run like him, too," Shawn said.

"How about a combination of him and Spectacular Bid?"

"We're looking for a racehorse, not an express train!"

As if he knew they were talking about him, Little Bid trotted up to the fence, his entourage strung out behind. "Put it right there," Cay said, turning his face and pointing at his cheek.

"Better watch it," Joy warned. "He's not a weanling anymore. Those are *real* teeth."

"You wouldn't bite me, would you?" Cay said, scratching Little Bid under the chin. "See? He just wants to be friendly."

"Hope he still feels that way when it's time for me to crawl on his back," Joy said. She nudged Shawn. "You're closer to the right size than me. Sure you don't want the honor?"

A wolfish grin. "Ten-fifteen years ago, I would have jumped at the chance. Now that I'm past retirement age, I have to let you youngsters have all the fun."

A month later, Cay headed for his car in the tree-shaded parking lot at the Keeneland July Selected Yearling Sale. "Hiya, Little Brother!" Travis called from beside his Rolls. "Leaving?"

"Yeah, it's been a long day."

"How about stopping at the Piney Inn for a drink?"

"Sounds good. See you there."

They found a small table in one corner of the popular watering hole. "Just what I needed," Travis said after downing half his glass of beer. "It's hot enough out there to fry a man's balls. Buy anything today?"

"Even with prices down, it's too steep for me," Cay said. "I bought three nice yearlings at Fasig-Tipton last week for a third of what I'd have paid for one at Keeneland."

"Think you'll get back into racing?"

"Might next year. Depends. Costs mount up."

" I can help you there. Certain parties are interested in that Bid colt you've got. They'll go a million, maybe more."

Cay had wondered at the sudden friendliness after months of silence. "Little Bid isn't for sale. If I'd put him in the Selected sale, he'd have brought lots more than a million. Do I know any of these 'certain parties'?"

"Sorry, they approached me in confidence because I'm your brother and have acted as agent for them before. Sure you're not interested? They'll go top dollar."

Cay shook his head. "Little Bid's the best thing that's happened to me in a long time. I'm not giving him up."

The sudden anger in his brother's eyes told Cay what he wanted to know. "Another beer?" Travis said.

"I'll pass. Got a pile of work to catch up."

"Going to any of the sale parties?"

"I'm pretty much out of that scene."

Leaning across the small table, Travis seized Cay's wrist.

"You've got to get out more, Cay. Damnit, I really bled for you when Arlene was killed! Just because we don't see much of each other anymore doesn't mean I don't care. That's why I brought up selling that colt. With a couple million—I'm sure they'll go that high—you can—"

"Let it go, Travis," Cay said tiredly, pulling his arm free. "I've got to run."

Seething with anger, Travis watched Cay weave his way through the crowded room. Owning that Spectacular Bid yearling had become an obsession. Although he had never seen the colt, he had talked to others who had. Its pedigree was impeccable—sired by a Horse of the Year and out of a Champion Three-Year-Old-Filly. But the talk around the Bluegrass was also about the colt's flawless confirmation, graceful action and aggressiveness. All the ingredients that added up to a horseman's dream.

Following Cay's progress as he stopped at tables to answer greetings from the many who had dropped by the Piney Inn after the Keeneland sale, Travis also felt jealousy. No matter how hard he tried or how much money he spent, he would never experience the camaraderie Cay shared with his fellow Bluegrass horse farmers—a close-knit group made up of men and women who had grown up on the farms around Lexington and extended special favors to each other. Like breeding privileges unavailable to outsiders, something Cay had made good use of the past two years.

Travis shared the same heritage, but he had spent many years in New York. And his interest in horses had never gone beyond their financial potential. It was a well-known fact that without Lynne's help, he would have had little success running their huge breeding operation and racing stable.

3

The following morning, Cay described Travis's thinly veiled attempt to buy Little Bid. "You sure?" Shawn said. "He really might be representing a syndicate."

"No chance. Not with that gleam in his eye. It's possible he may be heading a group, but you can bet if he got Little Bid, he'd race him under Albright Stud colors. He really pissed me off, acting like he was doing me a favor!"

"You might take him up on it after this morning," Shawn said cheerfully as they approached the colt's stall.

Joy shot a sour look at the little man. "You wouldn't be so damn happy if it was you and not me sitting on his back."

Shawn held out the bridle. "Want to trade places?"

"You kidding? If you hit the ground, you wouldn't even bounce. Those brittle bones would turn to powder. We'd have to pick up what's left with a vacuum cleaner."

The big colt sniffed at the saddle in Cay's hands as they entered the stall. "Surprise time, boy," Cay said. "Joy's going to sit up in the irons today—all hundred-sixty pounds of her!"

"One hundred-twenty," Joy snapped. "And that's spread over a five-eight frame."

"Mad or nervous?" Cay grinned.

"A little of both, if you must know. This wall-eyed critter's too smart for his own good."

Little Bid watched over his shoulder while Cay tightened the girth. The colt was used to bridle and saddle now; they had been putting them on him for a week and walking him in slow figure 8's around the stall, the last three days with Joy lying on her stomach across the saddle.

"Guess this is it," Joy said, tightening the chin-strap on her green hard hat.

Cay steadied Joy as she draped herself over the saddle. Little Bid snorted and stamped a front foot.

"So far, so good," Shawn said.

"Tell that to my stomach," Joy groaned.

"I'll walk him a little," Shawn said.

"Do that," Joy grunted, hanging over Little Bid's back like a bank robber's body being returned to town by the sheriff.

Little Bid rolled his eyes to the rear.

"Lookin' good," Cay said. "Here, I'll help you up."

Sticking her left foot in the stirrup, Joy swung the other leg over the colt's back and sat in the saddle. "Piece of cake."

Little Bid erupted into a flurry of movement, fishtailing his rump and throwing Joy high in the air. She flew into a corner and landed face-down in a pile of straw.

"Lots of daylight between your ass and that saddle," Shawn chortled.

"Aaaagh!" Joy spit out a straw and held up a handful of mane. "At least I got something to show for my trouble."

Cay patted Little Bid's thick neck. "Willie Shoemaker said Spectacular Bid was a Cadillac. This ornery critter's more like a Mack truck."

Joy dusted off the seat of her jeans. "Thanks a heap."

"Save the mane," Cay said as she got back in the saddle.

Little Bid eventually accepted the weight of a rider, and throughout summer and into the fall, he and seven other yearlings were worked out on the farm's track and introduced to the training gate. After being jogged and galloped until late November or early December, they would be shipped to the milder climate in Florida where Shawn and Joy would condition them for the winter and spring races.

After an early snowstorm, the yearlings were sent to Florida the week before Thanksgiving. It proved a wise move. The weather remained unusually cold throughout December and into the new year.

4

A mid-January snowstorm swept across central Kentucky and coated the window of Grant Alston's Lexington hotel room as Lynne lifted her hips to meet his driving thrusts. They had been going at it all afternoon, attacking each other as if trying to see who would wear out first. It had been like that since their initial sexual encounter two years ago.

"Yeah, that's it," Grant gasped as Lynne tightened her legs around his waist. "That's it! That's *it!*"

Grant was on his way, and Lynne's orgasm built with his. The mattress sagged as he pounded her with jackhammer blows. He moved faster, growling deep in his throat. She clawed his back, moaning in the midst of her own powerful climax.

Grant rolled on his side and squeezed Lynne's firm buttocks. "You're the best, baby."

"You're not so bad yourself." She flicked a drop of semen off her leg. "Icky!"

"Yeah, but they're all blanks."

Laughing softly, Lynne recalled his words a few months after they started working together: "I knocked this girl up in high school when I was sixteen. Had a shotgun wedding and two kids. Got out before the oldest was four. Had a vasectomy right after. I enjoy the act but no more marriages or kids for me."

Grant stuck a pillow behind his head and lit a cigarette. "If I remember right, I flew out here to go over a few things."

"So you decided to go over me first," Lynne said as she ran a hand over the ribbed muscles of his stomach. She had never known a man with such lean wiry strength. It added to the cruel look she had noted the night they met at Larry and Vicky Moore's party. Grant Alston was not a man to cross.

"Everything set up for breeding my mares?" he asked. He was all business now, and that suited Lynne. She had the best of two worlds— a lucrative financial relationship with a man whose sex drive matched hers.

"I'll start sending them to the different farms next month," Lynne said. "Two to Jonabell for mating with Vigors, four to Claiborne—one for Secretariat, two for Mr. Prospector, the other for Danzig. That Caro mare's going to Walmac in March to be bred to Nureyev. Your wallet will be a lot lighter next year."

"Speaking of wallets, how's your husband's?"

"He's getting uptight. Looking back, we should have gone public sooner."

"Stashing the money you're making with me?"

"That and everything else I can get my hands on. I won't be able to touch Albright Stud funds much longer. Travis has taken complete charge of the books. I don't know if it's because he doesn't trust me or doesn't want me to know what's going on."

"Probably a little of both. He's got to be playing fast and loose to keep the bottom line looking good."

"He's playing the stock market, too. So far, it's more than made up for our losses on the farm."

"Sounds okay but watch your ass."

5

Three years and seven months after Arlene's death, Cay began to dream again. It happened at the Saratoga Springs racetrack on a hot August day when Little Bid broke his maiden in his second outing, winning the Sanford Stakes by two lengths. Ten days later, he won the Hopeful, repeating what his maternal great-great grandsire, Devil's Fire, had done nearly fifty years before.

"It brings back beautiful memories," Maripat said to Cay that night as they strolled along Broadway. "Libby and I walked this same street after Devil's Fire won the Hopeful."

"I wish I had known her."

"She saved my life after that awful trip up from Harlan. Even if she hadn't adopted me, I couldn't have loved her more. Your father was here, too. Those were happy times."

They walked in silence for a while.

Maripat said, "I got a card from Maudie the other day."

"Uh, oh, I forgot to answer her last letter."

"Which was four months ago. She would love to hear about Little Bid. After all, she's Little Maudie's godmother."

"Nutty kid," Cay said affectionately.

"Little Bid's given you new hope, Cay. Share it with those who stuck with you through the rough times."

Cay thought of Shawn and Joy. Thanks to Little Bid, they

would be training full time again.

Following in the steps of the mighty Secretariat, Little Bid went on to win the Futurity and Champagne Stakes at Belmont Park. After a disappointing third in the Laurel Stakes in Maryland, he closed out his two-year-old campaign by winning the Garden State Stakes by four lengths. This brilliant record of five wins out of six starts—four Grade I and one Grade II stakes races—earned him the Two-Year-Old-Colt championship.

By the time Cay accepted Little Bid's Eclipse Award in February, the precocious colt had triumphed in his first start as a three-year-old, winning the Grade I Flamingo Stakes at Hialeah and the Grade II Hutcheson Stakes at Gulfstream. He was the unanimous early favorite for the Kentucky Derby.

As Little Bid raced toward the first Saturday in May, he provided a silver lining to the dark cloud that was spreading over the Thoroughbred industry. The golden idol that had been created by the excesses of the late Seventies and early Eighties had developed feet of clay.

The yearling market was glutted. In ten years, the annual crop of registered Thoroughbred foals in the United States had increased from 30,000 to a peak of 51,293 in 1986. Caring only for the high price a yearling's pedigree would bring, many breeders ignored the poor physical characteristics of the mares and stallions they were matching. The result was inferior foals with no ability on the track or potential for the breeding shed.

Another factor in the tumbling yearling market was the decreased demand as Arab sheiks and major European buyers improved their own nursery studs and racing stables. They continued to buy at Keeneland but not at the frenzied pace of previous years.

Breeding fees plummeted—Northern Dancer from $950, 000 to $307,000, Seattle Slew from $750,000 to $400,000, Roberto from $200,000 to $69,000.

Bluegrass real estate was also affected. Prime farm land that had sold at thirteen to fifteen thousand an acre dropped to between eight and ten thousand. "For Sale" signs popped up all around Lexington. It was buyer's market with few takers.

6

Continuing his winning ways at Gulfstream Park, Little Bid won the Hutcheson Stakes by six lengths and the Fountain of Youth Stakes by four. His greatest triumph came in the $500,000 Florida Derby when he blew away the opposition and set a new Gulfstream track record.

In April, he was brought back to Kentucky to run in the Jim Beam Stakes at Turfway Park. He would have one more prep race—the Blue Grass Stakes at Keeneland—before being shipped to Churchill Downs for the Derby.

"Pull up! Pull up!" Shawn shouted as the horses raced toward the wire, but Little Bid's jockey had no chance of hearing.

Cay joined Shawn and Joy in the dash to the track. The gray colt limped to a halt in front of the grandstand, and the crowd went silent as Little Bid's jockey jumped out of the saddle and steadied the trembling colt.

Carefully loaded into a horse ambulance, Little Bid was rushed to the backstretch. The news that resulted from the x-rays and the veterinarian's examination was good and bad. There were no broken bones, but his left front ankle was badly swollen and inflamed. He would be out of racing for at least six weeks.

Looking every one of his eighty-four years, Shawn dropped into a chair outside Little Bid's stall. "For a minute there, I thought it was all over. Reminded me of when Devil's Fire pulled up lame, and we had to retire him early. We had no choice with the Devil but we do with Little Bid." He looked at Cay who was leaning against a post. "You're the boss; it's up to you."

"Don't give me that crap," Cay said. "I own Little Bid, but you guys are the trainers."

Joy said, "With his record, he's extremely valuable as a stud even if we quit now."

"Is that what you think should be done?"

"No matter what, he should be retired by the end of the year."

"We all agree on that. You're the old hand at this, Shawn. What's your opinion?"

"Why don't you take him home while Joy and I stay with the string? If he looks good enough by June, we can run him in the Belmont. If not, we'll wait until fall. At worst, we'll just officially retire him a little later. Go along with that, Joy?"

A nod.

"Okay," Cay said. He turned to Little Bid who was munching hay. "You're going home with me for some r and r, big guy. Maybe Shawn and Joy can win enough money to pay your vet bills."

Despite the terrible disappointment over missing the Derby, Cay's spirits remained high through April and into May as Little Bid showed rapid improvement. In late May after the veterinarian had given him a clean bill of health, the gray colt was shipped to Belmont Park. The press followed his workouts closely as the horse world waited to see if he could come back and finish his sophomore season as brilliantly as it had begun.

Little Bid electrified the racing scene by winning the Belmont Stakes by five lengths and the Arlington Invitational by eight, then the Whitney Stakes in August by six and a half. The day after the September Marlboro Cup—which he won by four lengths—a slight swelling was discovered in the same ankle. After consulting with the track veterinarian and another flown in from Lexington, the "Bid Bunch"—as they had been nicknamed around the circuit—made the decision to retire the colt immediately.

Cay flew home with Little Bid. The colt's reception by fans and the press at Blue Grass field was reminiscent of Secretariat's when he retired to stud at Claiborne Farm fifteen years earlier.

The following month, Cay began placing calls to a carefully prepared list of leading horsemen. He knew them all, and some had been friends of his mother's before he was born. In three days, he sold twenty shares in Little Bid at $450,000 each, an astounding price considering the depressed market. As with all syndications, each shareholder was entitled to one breeding a year, or the cash value of the breeding season should he decide to sell it privately or through one of the matchmaker auctions. After retaining twenty shares for himself, Cay realized $9 million from the syndication. He was back on his feet with a vengeance.

7

Despite his anger and disappointment over not being able to buy Little Bid, Travis might have been happy for his brother had it not been for his own misfortune. He was in trouble, and the news was threatening to leak out.

"Goddamnit, Lynne, do you think I did this on purpose!" Travis shouted. Bourbon sloshed from his glass and spotted the white bedroom carpet.

"Didn't you?" Lynne stormed. She unclasped a diamond bracelet and threw it on the dressing table. "We had all the money we would ever need, but oh, no, you had to have more!"

"I didn't hear you complaining! You sure didn't mind spending it. Your shopping trips to New York and Beverly Hills cost enough to maintain a small army!"

"What about the jets you charter instead of flying commercial like everybody else?" A disgusted look. He had gained fifty pounds. The tuxedo coat and cummerbund failed to hide his overflowing waist. He looked like the Pillsbury Doughboy.

They had just returned from a Christmas party at the Idle Hour Country Club. "Did you catch some of the looks we got tonight?" Lynne said. "I almost kicked that newspaper bitch's ass—beating around the bush to find out if we're in trouble!"

"That's all we need," Travis groaned. "You've got to cool it, Lynne. As long as the investors and the bank are happy, they'll stay off our backs. I can't have you spouting off while I'm doing everything I can to keep our heads above water."

Stepping out of her red gown, Lynne walked topless to the closet. "You can't rob Peter to pay Paul forever." Slipping on a robe, she whirled, yanking the knot tight. "Larry and Vicky Moore must have been doing that for a year at least. They even kept on throwing big parties! Now they're on the front page of the *Herald-Leader* and hiding out while the creditors count their losses! They owe more than ten million to local banks! God knows how much more to lenders and country clubs in five states, including jewelry stores in Dallas and Palm Beach! They didn't even pay the caterers and rental company for their last Derby party!"

"At least we're current on our bills."

"For how long? You're doctoring the statements for the banks and limited partners. What about the bondholders? They can get rough!"

"They're not going to find out," Travis said wearily. "Not unless you lose control and let the cat out of the bag. All I need is time. We'll come out of it—you'll see."

Two days later, the private phone rang in Travis's office.

"Travis?—it's me, Larry."

"Holy shit, where are you? No—the less I know, the better!"

"What's it like there?" Larry Moore asked. "Have I been tarred and feathered and burned in effigy?"

"Pretty damn close. Why in hell did you *run*?"

"I can give you about twenty million reasons."

"You're in that deep? Any chance of recovery?"

A harsh laugh. "With assets less than three million? We're holding off, but bankruptcy's the only way out."

"How's Vicky taking it?"

"Real hard. She loved Millstream Farm. It never meant as much to me as it did to her. You know how she liked to dress up and play hostess. Guess Lynne's really shocked."

"Not as much as you might think. She's pretty close to what goes on. Any plans for the future?"

"My father's willing to bankroll us after I clean the slate. I hate to ask this, Travis, but can you lend me a few thousand? I can't borrow on anything, including those two units in Albright Stud I bought for a million-four. They're not worth a fraction of that now."

Smarting from the subtle dig, Travis calculated quickly in his head. He could tell Larry to go to hell, but it might cause problems. They had been close once, and he had foolishly bragged to Larry about some questionable business practices.

Talking in low tones although there was no chance of being heard, Travis said, "I can let you have five grand. It—"

"Thanks, Travis! You saved my life!"

"It has to be in cash. My head will be on the block if it gets traced to me. The banks and bondholders are breathing down my neck. I don't have to tell you what that's like."

"God, no! When can I get it?"

"Anytime. I keep a reserve in my safe at home."

"I can drive down and meet you tonight. Name the place."

Hanging up, Travis stared at the stack of folders on the floor around the desk. It was a deadly game of chess, moving funds in the increasingly difficult task of warding off creditors. He was making interest-only payments to several banks and was behind on the last quarterly payment due the holders of fifteen million in bonds. He had been forced to raise that money after the stock market disaster several years ago.

Until that "Black Monday" on Wall Street when the Dow fell over five hundred points, he had recouped nearly all the losses Albright Stud had suffered since the sharp downturn in yearling prices. Then on that one unforgettable day that bankrupted thousands of investors and businesses, he had lost $19 million.

Unable to tell anyone, including Lynne, he had walked a tightrope ever since. With the pressures building and the juggling more frenetic, he had begun to drink in earnest.

8

As the years passed and Cay continued to prosper on and off the track, he made several improvements on his farm. The largest was the purchase of two hundred-fifty acres bordering the northern boundary of his property. With the addition of thirty broodmares and more horses in training, the extra land was a godsend. Woodland Farm now had fourteen employees, seven hundred fifty acres, sixteen miles of fence, five miles of roadway and six homes, plus the big Federal brick house in which Cay still lived alone.

Besides winning Horse of the Year honors and earning $2,326,000 on the track, Little Bid had three Grade I winners in his first crop of foals to reach racing age. His second crop produced a big leggy colt that promised to turn gray early like his sire. Named Harlan Ghost, he was out of a Nijinsky II mare Cay had purchased the year Little Bit was retired.

"Clumsy oaf," Shawn said to Maripat as Harlan Ghost galloped past. They were sitting on a platform that overlooked the Woodland Farm training track.

"He's running smoother than he did last month."

"He's about the same height as Longfellow; bet they were a lot alike at this age," Shawn said. A great racehorse and sire of the last century, Longfellow had been so ungainly that his owner, John Harper, hadn't raced him until he was three. The words, "King of racers and king of stallions," were etched on Longfellow's tombstone in a small cemetery a mile away.

"Still thinking about running the Ghost in the Champagne?"

"I want him to get at least one race under his belt at two, but the Champagne's only six weeks away. The Laurel Futurity will give him another two weeks to prepare."

Maripat frowned. "It's also a mile and a sixteenth." She had a special interest in this colt named after her birthplace.

"I would rather start him at six furlongs, but those races are past," Shawn said. "The experience will do him good if nothing else. There are only three good racing months left."

"What does Joy think?"

"We talked about it on the phone last night. She feels the same as me. With her following the circuit, she hasn't seen him run in weeks."

Pulling her straw hat down against the glare of the early morning sun, Maripat said, "How do you like staying home and working with the babies while Joy has all the fun?"

"Considering the advanced state of my body and the fact that I can still get out of the cold and do the Florida circuit, it ain't all bad."

Maripat watched Harlan Ghost trot down the backstretch. "What do you think of that Danzig colt of Travis's?"

"Lynne's Lad? He's got a lot of potential, already won two stakes. We'll know a lot more after he runs in the Del Mar Futurity next week. That'll be his first race at a mile. He's small but at two, a fifteen-three-hand colt runs a hell of a lot smoother than a seventeen plus hand colt like the Ghost. The big ones need more time to mature."

"Travis came to see me the other day," Maripat said.

"You don't say! Any particular reason?"

"Money." A deep sigh. "He hadn't visited in nearly a year. And all he wanted was to borrow money."

"Hell of a note. Give him any?"

"No. I told him I'd as soon pour it down a rat hole. He got red-faced and swore that he just needed a loan to tide him over until next summer. I think he hopes Lynne's Lad might be another Little Bid and bail him out."

"Could happen."

"Pigs might fly, too. He's really in deep: there are rumors that investors are about to sue."

"Could he lose the farm?" Shawn asked, sickened at the thought of Albright Stud ending up in a stranger's hands.

"It's possible. I told him if it happens, to come and see me. If I gave him every cent I've got, it wouldn't bail him out now."

"That bad?"

Maripat nodded. "Looking back, it would've been better if I'd sold the farm and given Travis his share. It would have hurt his feelings, but he would be in better shape today."

Shawn laid a thin hand over hers. "You did what you thought best. What we all thought was best at the time."

9

The fate of Albright Stud was very much on Lynne's mind six months later as she walked back and forth in one of the bungalows at the Beverly Hills Hotel. "Travis won't give up," she said. "Not as long as Lynne's Lad keeps winning."

"He won't have a choice much longer," Grant Alston said. He sat in a chair, a bottle of beer clutched in a big fist.

Lynne nodded. "It's like a house of cards. One puff, it all comes down."

"Calumet Farm covered up their troubles a long time."

"And look what happened. The creditors forced them into bankruptcy."

"About where Albright Stud is now."

Lynne sat on the arm of Grant's chair. "When should we make our move?"

Grant raised an eyebrow. "*Our* move?" He put an arm around her waist. "You're getting pretty uppity, little lady."

"You said you don't want the farm unless I run it." Lynne trailed her fingers over the weathered creases on the back of his neck. "And you need my help translating Travis's books. As for the actual negotiating, I'll gladly relinquish that task to you."

"Sure Travis doesn't have any idea about what's going on?"

"His ego's been punctured, but he's still got enough left to keep him from thinking I would side with you. Half the time he's too drunk to know which way is up."

Muscles rippling, Grant lifted Lynne onto his lap. "Got an interesting piece of news while you were seeing your husband off at LAX. His brother's got a takeover plan in the works."

Lynne's jaw dropped. "*Cay?*"

"That's the word. The man who told me is pretty high up in one of the Lexington banks."

"This can mean real trouble."

"Will Travis listen to him?"

"Travis won't listen to anybody until after the Derby. Cay's got the right connections. Local banks will back him quicker than an outsider."

"That part doesn't bother me," Grant said. "I've already got a commitment from my bank in Houston. This Cay a fighter?"

"Not in the physical sense, although I don't think many men would want to go up against him. He can be a real bastard."

Grant slipped a hand under Lynne's blouse and played with her bra strap. "The way you say his name, it sounds like you want to bite his head off. You used to get it on between the sheets. What happened? He stop licking your pussy?"

"Damn you!" Lynne raged, squirming to get off his lap. "I don't pry in your past. Stay out of mine!"

"Calm down," Grant grinned, holding her easily. "Just curious, that's all."

"Well, keep it to yourself," Lynne huffed, settling back in his arms. Grant's coarseness usually turned her on. Not now. Not after hearing that Cay was trying to buy Albright Stud.

Grant unsnapped the bra. "We better step up our schedule. I'll have my man keep a close eye on things. If your brother-in-law gets hot on the trail, I'll move in."

"Whatever it takes, we can't let him get the farm," Lynne said as Grant unbuttoned her blouse and slipped it off.

Tossing her bra on the floor, Grant said, "Turn this way a little. I want to suck on that left tit."

When Lynne awoke, the room was dark, and Grant was asleep. She was pleasantly sore from the fierceness of their lovemaking. Thinking back over their eight-year relationship, Lynne acknowledged that the separations—and the sexually explosive reunions—had much to do with the affair's success. That and a shared competitiveness that put winning above all else. Best of all, Grant was too busy with his oil fields and other business interests to spend much time in Kentucky. That made his takeover of Albright Stud especially attractive. She would be completely in charge. A perfect arrangement.

Had they not started discussing Grant seizing control shortly after the farm got in financial trouble, Lynne would have left Travis. The only feeling she felt for him was contempt.

Could Grant be wrong about Cay's interest in the farm? Not likely. Grant had sources even she knew nothing about.

She couldn't imagine a worse scenario—to have Cay come back from the brink of ruin to take away the deal that would set her up for life! It made her furious. She silently vowed that he would no more get Albright Stud than he would win the Derby eight weeks from now. She would make sure of the first and her namesake, Lynne's Lad, would see to the last.

Racing on opposite ends of the country, the two colts wouldn't meet until the Derby. While Lynne's Lad was listed among the top five candidates, Harlan Ghost was considered a long shot at best. Some thought he shouldn't even be entered in the Run for the Roses.

The big awkward colt had shown promise in his first race at two, but because he had bumped another horse in the stretch drive at the Laurel Futurity in Maryland, he was disqualified from second to last. In his only other juvenile race—the Garden State Stakes in New Jersey—he took the lead on the final turn only to run out of steam and finish fourth.

His three-year-old season started off well with a win in the Hutcheson Stakes at Florida's Gulfstream Park. Harlan Ghost didn't run again until the Lord Avie Stakes at the end of the month. A 25-1 longshot, he came in second, losing by a nose. Two weeks later, he missed winning the Florida Derby by half a length.

In sharp contrast, Lynne's Lad, the small colt that resembled his sire, Danzig, and grandsire, Northern Dancer in looks and running style, won the Hollywood Juvenile and the Balboa Stakes before placing third in the Del Mar Futurity. He completed his two-year-old season with a second-place finish in the Norfolk Stakes and a win in the Hollywood Futurity.

His sophomore debut in mid-January was a four-length victory in the El Camino Real Derby at Bay Meadows, then a heartbreaking photo-finish loss in the Santa Catalina Stakes at Santa Anita. Decisive wins followed in the San Rafael Stakes at Santa Anita and the Sausalito Stakes at Golden Gate Fields and a close second in the San Felipe Stakes at Santa Anita. The crown jewel of California's classic races— the Santa Anita Derby—was a week away.

Lying beside Grant Alston in the Beverly Hills Hotel bungalow, Lynne decided to check with her own spy network in Lexington. It would keep her up-to-date on any moves Cay might make toward taking over Albright Stud.

10

Two weeks before the Kentucky Derby, Cay met with John for lunch at the Merrick Inn. "The industry's gradually finding a middle ground," John said, picking up where he had left off when the waitress served their drinks. "It was a tough tumble for a while, but in the long run it's for the best. A lot of people got weeded out that didn't belong in this business. Real horse people look at the *whole* picture. They're not quick-buck artists."

"Like my brother," Cay said.

"Like your brother. He's not alone. They made the same mistake at Spendthrift pulling similar stunts with limited partnerships and public offerings. Spendthrift had a temporary recovery, and it took a Chapter Eleven reorganization and new ownership to accomplish that. Your brother has no chance for bankruptcy protection—not with the way he inflated the value of horses to produce an attractive prospectus. His ass is grass."

"Forced sale?"

"You're the only reason the banks are holding back. They were ready to land on Travis with all fours weeks ago. Nobody wants another repeat of the national attention we got when Calumet was auctioned off right down to the paintings and bandage boxes. They even sold a sheet metal spire off one of the buildings and a concrete jockey hitching post with a broken arm! Warren Wright must have turned over in his grave.

"Because of your interest in Albright Stud, the banks are willing to wait. I've got a tentative meeting set up with Nat Quinn for next Monday. His bank's carrying the most paper. The big problem is holding the others off. One little unsecured creditor panics and it's Katie-bar-the-door! They'll trample each other getting in the first claims."

Cay said, "Travis has all his hopes pinned on the Derby and Lynne's Lad. Can't blame him. After that victory in the Santa Anita Derby, his horse is an early favorite."

"Winning the Derby would help, but Lynne's Lad would have to sweep the Triple Crown and syndicate for fifty million to get Travis out of the mess he's in. The banks and bondholders won't wait that long. Consider mid-May a maximum deadline."

"When I fought with Travis over his big ideas years ago, I never dreamed it would come to this," Cay said. "For a while, it looked like he was right. Look at the Slew Crew—they paid seventeen thousand five hundred for Seattle Slew as a yearling and made so much money that they bought a Lexington bank and horse farms here and in Florida!"

"Lots of folks thought the boom would go on forever. After that ten million-two sale in Eighty-Three, Keeneland put an extra digit on the tote board! They got to use it once—in Eighty-Five when that Nijnisky yearling sold for thirteen million-one. You'll have to look long and hard to find somebody who thinks that eighth digit will ever light up again."

"Not in our lifetime, anyway," Cay said. "Maybe with inflation and all, it might happen in the next century."

"Yeah, with Captain Kirk and Mr. Spock looking on. Supply and demand, that's what it's all about! Ask any farmer— they go through it all the time. If beans sell good one year, *everybody* plants 'em the next year! *Splat.* The market's got beans up the bejesus. Supply exceeds demand, and prices go to hell.

"When yearling prices went through the roof, so did demand. That called for more stallions. Stallion managers said, 'Breeders should be makin' two-three times the stud fee, not four or five. Let's raise our prices so we can cash in on the bonanza, too!'

"So there was a big increase in stallions and their fees. Inferior horses syndicated for five-ten million! Then the demand for yearlings dropped and prices fell like an iron cloud. Stud managers had to cut their fees way back. Either that or have a bunch of stallions with nothing to do but piss through their expensive dicks. People got greedy and killed the golden goose."

Cay said, "Speaking of stallions, what do you think of that long-legged critter of mine?"

"Got me a nice winning ticket in the Blue Grass. Didn't do bad in the Jim Beam either—second place is better than a kick in the butt. You came out smelling like a rose after Perret opted to ride Rotsaruck instead of Harlan Ghost in the Derby. Chris McCarron's as good as they come."

"I was sweating bullets until Chris lost his Derby mount when it came up lame. Now I'm more optimistic than ever. The Ghost is developing fast."

"That's what makes the Derby so hard to handicap. It's tough to judge how much a three-year-old will mature in the spring. A few weeks can make a big difference. Hell of a note—you and Travis racing against each other in the Derby."

"Guess you saw that article in the *Courier-Journal* about Albright Stud being in trouble and the possibility that I might take over. How the hell did that get out?"

"We live in a small world. People talk."

11

Cay was thinking about the media's speculation two nights later as he sat in the lounge at a downtown hotel. Ten minutes earlier, a local turf writer had stopped him in the lobby and asked about the *Courier-Journal* story. Cay put him off with the promise of an interview at Churchill Downs during Derby Week.

Looking around the lounge, Cay wondered why his mother had asked to meet him here. She looked forward to her evenings at home with John and seldom went out at night alone.

A man entered the lounge, then a couple holding hands. Another couple appeared, and the man's companion caught Cay's eye. Not just his, considering the number of heads that turned her way.

She was gorgeous. Tall with a mass of thick wavy hair tumbling over bare shoulders. The man was a little shorter, but her legs were so long that her hips were inches above his. A simple white sheath dress clung to her slender body and outlined those spectacular legs. Cay could almost hear a collective sigh as she stepped into the room. Turning to her companion, the young woman said something and waggled her fingers. He smiled and headed for the bar. Clutching a small silver purse in both hands, she took a hesitant step forward and searched the lounge.

Her face lit up, and white teeth flashed in the subdued light. Cay jerked upright. She was looking at him! Now wending her way toward the booth with purposeful strides.

Cay almost drowned in those huge sparkling eyes. "Mr. Cay Albright, I presume?" she said in a lovely British accent.

Cay's jaw dropped. His mouth opened and closed, but nothing came out. He almost stuttered. It couldn't be! "Toothpick?" he gasped in a hesitant voice.

Laughing gaily, Maudie Grayson held out her arms, "Don't I get a hug?"

With a whoop that drew startled glances from around the room, Cay jumped up and pulled her close. Dark-blond hair teased his face. In high heels, she topped six feet.

Leaning back in his arms, Maudie shot Cay a wicked glance. "Did I surprise you?"

"No," he grinned, "I go around with this stupid look on my face all the time. Sit down and tell me how you pulled this off." An accusing finger as Maudie slid into the booth. "Mom! I wondered why she wanted to meet me here."

"She's such a dear," Maudie said. "We've been planning this for weeks."

A shocked look. "You've been here that long?"

"No, silly! The telephone—that clever instrument you Americans invented. I checked in an hour ago."

"Here?"

"The Hyatt Regency. I got lost in this hotel and had to ask that nice man for directions."

"I thought you were with him at first."

"He *was* very helpful," Maudie said, smiling sweetly. "I'm sure he would have kept me company if you hadn't turned up."

"Witch!"

A cocktail waitress hovered over the table. "Are you ready to order?"

Maudie said, "A Beefeater martini, very dry with a twist of lemon." She glanced at Cay. "And don't you *dare* say anything! I'm a big girl now. I suppose you'll want bourbon."

"Me? Refuse English gin? Make that two, please."

As the cocktail waitress walked off, Maudie grinned. "Cat got your tongue?"

"Proud of yourself, aren't you?" Cay shoved a fist under her nose. "I ought to poke you one."

Maudie kissed his knuckles. "You wouldn't dare."

"Seems I remember whacking you on your rear end a few times," Cay said, skin tingling from those cool lips.

Arching an eyebrow, Maudie said, "I was *much* younger then and *much* smaller...*everywhere!*"

Cay groaned. "I feel it in my bones...you've come to punish me for being such a lousy correspondent." He sketched an imaginary body in the air. "How did you get like this?"

Shrugging gracefully, Maudie said, "Oh, a little here, a little there." A wide-eyed innocent look, mouth hanging slightly open. "Did it turn out all right?"

"You know it did, you little wretch." Cay leaned closer and peered at her nose. "Aha! You've still got freckles!"

Crossing her eyes, Maudie stared at the offending member. "I don't see any."

Cay cracked up. "No change there! You're still nuts!"

The smiling waitress arrived with their drinks. "You guys seem to be enjoying yourselves."

"Family reunion," Cay said. "This is my little sister."

"Yeah, and I'm your long-lost aunt!" She walked off laughing.

"Toothpick—" Cay shook his head. "I've got to stop calling you that."

"Don't you dare! It's my special name you gave me."

"All right, but I'll suppress the urge in sophisticated company. Tell me…what brought you to our neck of the woods? And don't say it's my charming personality."

"Don't be so sure," Maudie said softly. She added hurriedly, "I'm here on assignment…working."

"Working? *You?*"

"Why not?" Maudie bristled. "I'm not a little kid anymore with braces on my teeth. Maybe you think women shouldn't work!"

"Sorry!" Cay cried, sitting back in mock terror. "That was just the male-chauvinist-pig side of me sounding off. Okay?"

Maudie touched his cheek. "You're forgiven. As long as you don't do it again."

"Tell me about this assignment."

"You know how I've done a lot of freelance writing for horse magazines the last three years."

"I have every article in a special binder."

"*Really?* Anyway, *Thoroughbred World*—I've been working almost exclusively for them the last twelve months—sent me here to cover your Derby Week. Notice I said Derby and not *Darby*. I won't risk upsetting the natives."

"Hey, that's great! How did you pull it off?"

"For one thing, I happen to be a very good writer. Having been here before with certain influential contacts helped." *And getting Daddy to take the publisher out to dinner and practically bulldoze him into giving me the assignment.*

"*Thoroughbred World*, huh?"

"Isn't that smashing? The upper crust is just *dying* to know how the Bluegrass elite dress and frolic during Derby Week."

"Pictures, too?"

"I have a great cameraman. Andrew Stiles. He'll be here Saturday."

"Tell me—"

"Not until we eat. My stomach's sending out distress signals." Maudie touched her purse. "I'm on an expense account. You can save your money to feed those lovely horses. How is Little Maudie, by the way? Wait! I have to eat something first. A bread stick will do."

"The Duck Club's in the hotel; it's one of the best restaurants in town. And *I'm* paying! With one stipulation. You have to tell me everything you've done the last thirteen years."

Maudie stared. "*Everything?*"

"Everything. No fibbing allowed."

Sighing, she rose and smoothed the dress over her hips. "The sacrifices one must make to avoid starvation."

Once Maudie got started, she talked non-stop. "Mummy was the one who insisted that I get 'finished' in Switzerland. It was boring—bloody boring! I hated every minute!"

"Some of it must have rubbed off," Cay said. "You certainly act like a lady. You're still saying bloody. Have English women added that to their vocabulary?"

"No—but they should," Maudie said as she polished off the last of her prime rib. "My parents believe I'm impossible. Tim thinks it's funny."

"How is Tim? Still producing children?"

"I think he's stopped with the last girl. They have two of each now." Maudie eyed Cay's barely touched steak hungrily. "Are you going to eat that or let it lie there and go to waste?"

Grinning, Cay cut off a generous portion. Dropping it on a small plate, he passed it under the table. It appeared miraculously in front of Maudie. Bubbling with laughter, she attacked it with knife and fork. "Remember how angry Mummy used to get at me when we did this in restaurants?"

"I remember lots of things," Cay said, finding it hard to associate this stunning young woman with the scrawny eleven-year-old tomboy he had last seen in England.

Spearing a piece of steak, Maudie waved it in the air. "When do I get to see Little Maudie? And Little Bid! Tell me about Harlan Ghost. I understand where the Harlan part came from. But the other…does he haunt you at night?"

"Gray Ghost was the name given the Confederate raider, John Singleton Mosby, during the Civil War. The Southerners wore gray; Harlan Ghost is a gray. And the town of Harlan is about twelve miles from the Virginia border—Mosby's home state."

Huge hazel eyes shining, Maudie said, "Now Harlan Ghost is running in the Kentucky Derby! Isn't that wonderful? You know how I love grays. Where is he?"

"Churchill Downs. Want to see him?"

"Silly goose! When can we go?"

"Anytime. Your schedule's probably tighter than mine."

"I don't have much to do until Sunday. I'm so excited! Imagine getting paid for having fun!"

"Going to any special parties?"

"Anita Madden's, of course. The Governor's Ball. A few others. Your mother's making arrangements. She's been working on it for weeks. I would be lost without her."

"I guess you two got a kick out of keeping me in the dark."

"It was so much fun! Your mother enjoyed herself immensely."

"I bet. Are you going to those parties unescorted?"

"Certainly not. I'm going with you!" A sorrowful look. "Unless you're too busy."

"How can I be?" Cay laughed. "Now I know why Mom insisted on handling all my social engagements."

Suddenly shy, Maudie touched his arm. "Is it all right?"

Stirred by feelings he hadn't experienced in a long time, Cay squeezed her hand. "I wouldn't have it any other way."

12

While the Bluegrass prepared to kick off Derby Week on Sunday with the High Hope Steeplechase, the Kentucky Derby Festival in Louisville was already underway. For ten days, seventy events—including parties, balls, parades, balloon and steamboat races and super-star concerts—would give the city on the banks of the Ohio River little rest. The original Festival, a Pegasus Parade in 1956, cost $640. This year's budget exceeded $2 million.

"You can wreck your feet tramping around with the tourists, but don't ask me to," Cay said as he drove Maudie through the small town of Midway. "My trips to Louisville during Derby Week are limited to the Trainers' Dinner and the backside at Churchill Downs."

"Party pooper," Maudie said. She wore a white crew-neck top, tight designer jeans and black leather boots with three-inch stacked heels. It had brought male traffic to a standstill when Cay had escorted her through the Hyatt Regency lobby earlier.

Cay patted her knee. "I know your story won't be complete without the Festival. I'm just a stuffy old guy."

"You're not old," Maudie protested.

"A lot older than you."

"What is that supposed to mean, Mr. Albright?"

"Well...uh...that I'm a lot older than you."

"An absolute scandal—being seen with a young bird like me!"

"I don't know that I would go that far."

"Good! Let's hear no more about age. Oh, we're here! It's just like I remembered."

"Bigger with the added acreage." Cay said as he drove between the stone pillars that marked the entrance to Woodland Farm.

Sitting on the edge of the seat, Maudie looked eagerly ahead. "I can't believe it—seeing Little Maudie after all these years!"

"She's not so little anymore. Producing eight foals is hard on the old back. Makes the stomach sag, too."

"Quiet! I won't have you talk about my namesake like that."

Cay parked behind a barn. "There's Little Bid. He stands there all day watching for vans bringing mares in. With the breeding season winding down, his nose is a little out of joint, He's mostly white now...a little gray left on his mane and tail."

"You should be more understanding," Maudie grinned. She jumped out of the Mercedes and hurried to the fence. Little Bid nipped at her arm, and she slapped him gently on the nose. "Stop that! Try it again and I'll give this carrot to your mother."

"How did you get that in your back pocket?" Cay asked. "There's barely enough room for you."

"It wasn't easy," Maudie laughed, patting a taut buttock. She extracted the carrot and held it up in front of the stallion's nose. "Are you ready to be nice?"

Pushing against the fence, Little Bid stretched his neck and whinnied enthusiastically.

"That's better." Sticking a third of the carrot between his teeth, she broke it off.

"You know the way to his heart," Cay said.

"That's an American saying, isn't it... 'The way to a man's heart is through his stomach?' Is that true with you?"

"I don't know. Is cooking among your talents?"

"It was part of my training in Switzerland. Perhaps we can give it a test one night after all the Derby excitement is over."

"You don't have to go right back?"

"Oh, I can stay for weeks. There will be facts to verify, research and other things. One can't be too thorough."

"It would be a shame to rush home and miss something important," Cay said.

"Wouldn't it though?" Humming softly, Maudie fed the last of the carrot to Little Bid.

After visiting Little Maudie, they stopped at the Federal brick house. While Cay went through the mail in his office, Maudie drifted about the lower floors, touching furniture and inspecting the equine paintings. When Cay appeared ten minutes later, he found a very different Maudie.

Absorbed with the picture on her lap, she didn't hear him until he was next to her chair. Startled, she looked up. Her cheeks were damp, eyes swimming in tears. "I'm sorry," she whispered. "It was here on the table. I shouldn't have…"

"Hey, it's all right," Cay said, sitting on the arm of the chair and taking Arlene's picture out of Maudie's trembling hands. He ran a finger around the edge of the frame. "She was beautiful, wasn't she?"

"Like a fairy tale princess," Maudie said in a choked voice. She took a tissue out of her shoulder bag and wiped her eyes. "Does it still hurt to talk about her?"

"It happened nine years ago. Time is a great healer. I have wonderful memories."

"I wanted to call you, but I didn't know what to say." Maudie rested a hand on his. "Even my cards sounded foolish."

"Not to me." Cay caressed her long slender fingers. "I'm sorry I cut you out, Toothpick . It wasn't right. I shouldn't have done that to my little buddy."

"No, you shouldn't have," she said, offering a teary smile. " It was terribly rude. Promise you won't ever do it again?"

He kissed her cheek. "Promise."

That night they went out on the town, Cay in a dark suit and Maudie in a raspberry-red satin and lace gown with spike heels to match. They ate at the exclusive Coach House on South Broadway, then took a ride around downtown Lexington in an open white carriage drawn by a white horse.

Maudie's mane of dark-blonde hair was in constant motion as she took in the sights of the brightly lit streets. Boys whistled at her from the curb, and she waved gaily back.

Moving closer, she searched out Cay's hand and held it tightly. For a while, he forgot everything except this beautiful young woman who was hanging on as if she would never let go.

More than teenage boys noticed the carriage and its striking passenger. "Jesus Christ on a crutch!" Travis exclaimed. "Where did Cay find *her*?"

"Got me," Lynne said, eyes narrowing as she watched the

carriage turn right on Main Street.

"Think she has a sister?" the man standing beside Travis said.

A petite blonde poked the man in the ribs. "Forget it, Tom. You have trouble servicing me!"

"That's telling him, Gwen," Lynne laughed.

"Might be worth a try," Tom said wishfully as the carriage passed out of view.

"This calls for a drink," Travis said.

"Since when have you needed an excuse for that?" Lynne said.

"I just love domestic scenes!" The blonde squealed. "Can Tom and I watch?"

Tom steered his wife in the direction of the padded door. "Here's the bar, Dear."

Following the couple inside, Travis shot Lynne an angry look. She answered it with a disdainful glare.

13

The following morning Maudie drove her rental car to Blue Grass Field and picked up the photographer, Andrew Stiles. After leaving him at the hotel to sleep and catch up on the hours lost during his long Atlantic flight, she had lunch with Maripat. After dessert was served, Maudie cautiously brought up the material she had read only hours before.

"My magazine retained a clipping service several months ago," she explained. "There was a large package of articles relating to Kentucky horse farming and the Derby waiting when I arrived. I was surprised to read about the troubles at Albright Stud and that Cay might purchase the farm." She added quickly, "I'm not asking as a reporter. I'm just interested in everything Cay does. I thought it best to ask you. He might take it wrong."

"You don't have to tiptoe around Cay," Maripat said.

"I guess you're right, but I'm so nervous! He must think I'm dreadful—bursting in on him like this!"

"If that's so, he's sure reacting funny. I haven't seen him so relaxed and happy in years."

Smiling radiantly, Maudie fluttered a hand in the air, then touched her throat. "That's ever so wonderful! I was so afraid he might think me forward."

"Cay can be very understanding." A wicked grin. "You've got him off balance. My advice is to keep him that way."

"How?"

"Be yourself. Everything will fall into place."

"I do hope so!"

Maripat took a bite of her cherry tart. "Getting back to that question about Albright Stud—yes, Cay is interested. If you were asking as a reporter, I wouldn't breathe a word. Things will be pretty touchy the next few weeks." She described the problems at Albright Stud and Cay's desire to keep the farm from falling into the hands of creditors.

"It was just a wishful thought at first," she concluded, "but the more we discussed it, the more feasible it seemed."

"Could Cay and Travis work together?"

Maripat shook her head. "They're not close anymore, and their lifestyles are so different. It would be even worse now than it was when Cay left to go on his own. And there's Travis's wife to contend with. She would never take orders from Cay."

"I remember how beautiful she was. That long black hair and those dark sultry eyes!"

"She still looks pretty good," Maripat conceded. "Some women improve with age. Lynne's one."

"How old is she?"

"Let's see…she's a year younger than Cay. That makes her forty."

"Oh." Maudie poked the chocolate mousse with her fork. "Would Cay combine the farms if he gets Albright Stud?"

"Impractical. They're several miles apart, and he needs only one. It will take a lot of money to settle Albright Stud's debts. Woodland Farm is prime land. Even with the depressed market, it should bring top dollar. Buying Albright Stud isn't necessarily a good business move. It will take lots of money and hard work to get it back on its feet. Cay loves Albright Stud the way I do; he's got his heart set on keeping it in the family. It will hit him hard if it falls into a stranger's hands. He'll be happy if his brother can manage to keep the farm."

"Cay hasn't said a thing to me about any of this." A sad look crept into Maudie's big hazel eyes. "I wouldn't have known if I hadn't read the stories."

"He's not as open as he used to be," Maripat acknowledged. "For a long time after Arlene was killed, he kept his feelings to himself, even around me." A bright smile. "I have a hunch he'll loosen up a lot the next week or so."

14

The annual High Hope Steeplechase on Sunday—a six-race event that donated all proceeds to the children's cancer fund at the University of Kentucky—was as much an excuse to eat and socialize as it was to watch the nation's premier jumping horses compete on the beautiful Kentucky Horse Park course.

Delicious aromas filled the air from scores of cooking fires at tailgate parties and hospitality tents set up by horse farms and local businesses. Thousands strolled about, pausing during each race to watch the horses thunder by. Because the course meandered over rolling terrain and was at times obscured by tall trees, it provided only a partial view of the running, leaping horses. No one cared. They were having the time of their lives.

Sitting with several men outside the Albright Stud tent, Travis took another beer out of the ice chest and popped it open. "Lynne's Lad is small," he said, "but so was Northern Dancer. He had the fastest Derby until Secretariat broke it by three fifths of a second. It's still the third best."

"Nobody's going to knock a Danzig colt," a man said. "Santa Anita Derby winners have won their share of Kentucky Derbys the last few years."

"That colt of your brother's looked real good in the Blue Grass," another man said. "Kinda reminds me of Phar Lap with that big rangy build."

"Did you see Phar Lap, George? That must have been fifty, sixty years ago."

"Longer than I care to remember. I missed that race when he set the track record at Aqua Caliente, but I saw him in Menlo Park just before he died. That was one big horse! Ran like blazes, too."

"I like Mighty Warrior," a lean man with a bushy mustache said. "Neil Drysdale says he's one of the best horses he's trained. Beat Lynne's Lad a couple of times."

"Not at Santa Anita," Travis said. "He was three lengths back and lucky to place."

Excited shouts drew their attention toward the nearby racecourse. "Here come the horses in the fourth race," one of the men said, rising for a better look. People crowded along the three-rail fence and cheered the eight contestants as they thundered by.

George watched the horses disappear around a bend. "Looked like mine was chasing the leader."

"Two miles over fences and timber takes a lot out of a horse," another man said. He stood as a roar came up from the finish line. "Gotta find Ern. Have a hundred riding on number six."

"I'll tag along," George said. "Ern's holding my money, too." The men walked off.

Moments later, Travis saw her. "Holy shit!" he burst out, sitting bolt upright and staring at the tall young woman who was talking to his mother.

A man whistled softly. "With legs like that, they ought to run her in the Oaks. Who is she?"

"That's what I'd like to know."

A recent arrival said: "She's a writer for that British magazine, *Thoroughbred World*. Cay introduced us a while ago. You should remember her, Travis. She visited with her parents the year Bid won the Derby. Her father is Reginald Grayson...owns Broadheim Stud. Her name's Maudie."

"Maudie *Grayson!* The last time I saw her she was a skinny little brat with freckles and buck teeth!"

"Not anymore," the man chuckled. "That is one gorgeous lady. Hangs onto your brother's arm and touches him every chance she gets. He doesn't seem to mind."

"Who would?" another man said in a hushed voice.

Travis watched as a small man with three cameras hanging around his neck joined the group. It was a happy scene, the women wearing big colorful hats and bright springtime dresses, smiling and gesturing gaily.

It brought home to Travis the misery of his existence. He should be there, loving and being loved by his mother and Cay.

It wasn't too late. If he could survive this crisis, he would turn over a new leaf and become part of his family again.

15

The following morning while Maudie went to Louisville with her photographer to cover the Kentucky Derby Festival, Cay met at White Oak Stud with Maripat and John and Nathan Quinn, president of Lexington's Commercial Bank.

Balancing a stack of papers on his knees, Nathan Quinn concluded, "There you have it...not a pretty picture."

Cay said, "Your loan and smaller ones by the other two banks are secured. Considering the value of Albright Stud land and stock, you'll get your money back no matter what."

"Eventually," Nathan Quinn agreed. He was a tall lanky man with rugged features and protruding ears that were accentuated by a nearly bald head.

Seated in a brocaded wing-back chair, Maripat said, "That leaves the bondholders next in line, followed by the limited partners, unsecured creditors and shareholders."

"All feudin' and fussin' and fightin'," John said from his slouched position on a couch. "If the bondholders force Albright Stud into bankruptcy, they won't get fifty cents on the dollar."

"Which leaves the rest with nothing," Cay said.

"Them's the breaks. It's tough on the unsecured creditors like feed stores and veterinarians, but the limited partners and shareholders went into it with their eyes wide open. If they wanted a sure thing, they should have stuck with government bonds or federally insured institutions like Nat's crystal palace downtown. Not that the banks and savings and loans are exactly solvent these days."

Betraying his roots with his eastern Kentucky accent, Nathan Quinn said, "Seems you've got a few bucks in my glass house, John. Proves you horse people aren't completely off your rockers."

"Look who's talking! Don't you have a couple nags in training?"

"All right, you two," Maripat scolded, "get back on the subject."

"Sorry, Miss Maripat, Ma'am," John said, sinking down with a sheepish grin. "I was just funnin' the good banker."

Maripat smiled. John had always been like that…cracking jokes and playing the clown while hiding a brilliant mind that could skin the unwary alive.

Cay said, "I don't want the farm to go into bankruptcy. It would be picked clean, not to mention the bad publicity."

"Nobody wants that," Nathan said. "The banks are in a relatively safe position, but they'll want the back payments cleared up. With accusations of fraud floating around, the bondholders are getting nervous. When everyone gets through filing suits and countersuits, the only winners will be lawyers. No offense, Counselor."

"I've heard worse," John smiled.

"I can pay the back interest and take over the bank loans," Cay said. "I'd like to pay on the principal as soon as possible. That will have to wait until I sell my farm and cull some stock." He looked at Nathan Quinn. "What about the bondholders?"

"I've talked to the ones that count. Catch up those quarterly payments, and they'll go along."

John said, "You can fight the limited partners and anybody else who wants to claim fraud. It'll take time and money, but you'll win in the end. Offer to buy them out for a quarter of what they paid. They'll grab it and run."

Cay punched his pocket calculator. "That's seven million."

John nodded. "Say another two million to buy out the shareholders and half that to the unsecured creditors. You'll settle a thirty-seven million-dollar debt with ten."

"They'll go along?"

"What choice have they got? If they force the farm into bankruptcy, they won't get a cent."

Nathan said, "If John's assumption is correct—and I'm inclined to agree—it would take about thirteen million-three to settle the back interest and pay off the unsecured creditors, limited partners and shareholders. Taking that and the thirty-one million you'll owe banks and bondholders, you'll pay forty-four million for the farm and stock…about half the market value."

"I can come up with most of that thirteen million-three," Cay said. "Nat, your bank will have to loan the rest. There's still Travis to think about."

John said, "Setting aside the personal relationship and speaking as your attorney, you can buy him off pretty cheap. He stands to get nothing if the bankruptcy court takes over. Plus being sued for fraud and facing possible jail time."

"I want him to come out with something," Cay said, "but I'll be taking on a pretty heavy debt until I can unload my farm." He looked at Maripat. "I was thinking a million right away and another four million spread over five years."

"That's more than fair," she said. "I'll help him, too."

"He pulled in around fifty million the last ten years," Nat said. "Where did it go?"

"High living," Maripat said. "A good deal into horses and improvements on the farm. Some of it's still solid equity. It'll take time to separate the *real* value of the horses from the prices Travis inflated to improve the financial reports. He lost a bundle in the stock market crash a few years back. Millions! I'm not supposed to know, and don't ask me how much."

"Getting him to listen won't be easy," Cay said. "Don't take too long," Nathan Quinn warned.

"Can you give me a week after the Derby for an answer?"

"May tenth?"

"Fine."

John stood. "Gotta run—have an appointment at the office. Keep on it, Cay. As my mother used to say, 'Time's a wastin'.'" A wide grin. "Or was that Mammy Yokum?"

16

Arriving at the Hyatt Regency late that afternoon to collect Maudie, Cay strolled around the lobby after phoning her room and receiving no answer. He was looking in a jeweler's case, when a red-tipped finger tapped his arm. "Cay Albright, as I live and breathe!" drawled a husky female voice. "It's been ages!"

"Hi Jennifer," Cay smiled, drawing the perfumed lovely redhead into his arms. "Here for Derby Week?"

"Where else would I be this time of year?" Kissing his cheek, she stepped back and eyed him critically. "You look better every time I see you. Do you ever think about that weekend in New Orleans?"

"What if I said I haven't thought about it once in three years?"

"I'd be terribly hurt," she pouted. "But I wouldn't believe you, either. I'm not insecure in that respect, darling."

"I guess you aren't," Cay laughed. He noted the large diamond on the third finger of her left hand. "Who's the lucky guy?"

"Henry Waterson. He owns part of downtown Atlanta." She looked at her watch. "His plane should be arriving anytime. We're meeting here."

"I'm waiting for someone, too. How about a drink?"

"Wonderful!" Jennifer clung to his arm as they went through the lobby. "I shouldn't have let you get away," she whispered in his ear. A soft laugh. "If you say the right words, I might tell Mr. Waterson to take downtown Atlanta and shove it."

The little man in the tweed coat and wrinkled slacks gazed up at Maudie from across the lobby. "Now that's a toothsome morsel.

I'd love to photograph her, but my camera might explode."

"You may keep your opinions to yourself, thank you," Maudie said, towering rigidly over her companion. Arms crossed, she tapped the toe of a high-heeled shoe rapidly.

"You said we would have a drink with him." Andrew Stiles understood what was going through Maudie's mind. They had worked on several assignments over the years, and he had heard a good deal about Mr. Cay Albright. Even more the past month as they prepared to travel to Kentucky. Well, there he goes into the lounge with that delicious redhead glued to his arm.

"Cay seems to be busy right now," Maudie said.

"We could go in the lounge for a drink."

"You could also drown yourself in a bathtub. A wonderful idea, actually, but I do need your photographs. Andrew, put that cigarette out before it burns your chin!"

"It is almost gone, isn't it?" he said, studying the drooping ash before crushing it in a tray. "Shall we go out into the night and seek a more friendly pub?"

"Brilliant idea, Mr. Stiles. I'll keep you after all." Maudie headed toward the exit with long-legged strides, Andrew Stiles trotting at her side to keep up.

Shortly after Jennifer's fiancée arrived, Cay rang Maudie's room with no result. He waited fifteen minutes, then tried again. This time she answered on the second ring. "Hey, remember me?" he said. "I'm the guy who's taking you to dinner. I've been calling your room the last hour."

"I'm sorry," Maudie said in a subdued voice. "I'm in a bit of a dither. It's been a hectic day."

"You sound a little down. Anything wrong?"

"Just a small headache."

"Maybe you should go to bed early. Derby Week can really wear you down. Want me to send some food up, bring aspirin?"

"Oh Cay, I don't want to cancel dinner. Really I don't!"

"Sure?"

"Positive. Give me thirty minutes?"

"I'll grab a newspaper and wait in the lobby."

"Thank you." A pause. "Cay?"

"Yeah?"

"You're sweet."

The phone clicked in his ear.

Falling backwards across the bed, Maudie angrily kicked off her high-heeled shoes. One caught on her big toe and flew over her head, barely missing her nose. "Just what you would have deserved!" she shouted, grabbing the shoe and throwing it across the room. Rolling on her stomach, she pounded a pillow with white-knuckled fists. "Oh bloody hell! Bloody, *bloody*, hell!"

At this rate, she *would* have headache! How could she let the sight of Cay with that sexy redheaded wench send her into such a tizzy! Resting her chin on laced fingers, she stared at the wall. What a ninny she was! What right did she have to expect Cay's exclusive attention? She had no prior claim, not unless loving him for fourteen years counted.

Tim had teased her unmercifully over those years—until just before she boarded the plane for America. Taking her aside, he hugged her tightly and whispered in her ear, "Get him if you can, old girl. Lord knows you've hung in there long enough. You know how welcome he'd be in the family."

Maudie gratefully hugged him back. "I'll do my best."

"Then Mr. Albright's single days are numbered."

"Oh, Tim, I do hope you're right!"

Sitting on the edge of the bed, Maudie recalled her youthful heartbreak when Cay married Arlene and the tears she had shed over Arlene's death. Then the years looking forward to occasional letters, fearful that one would announce he was marrying again.

She had taken a lover when she was twenty, but it was like loaning the use of her body. Her heart belonged to Cay, and she ended the relationship after a few months. There had been one affair since, and it only lasted three weeks. She had lived a lonely life the past two years, using Maripat shamelessly as she planned her assault.

Stripping of her clothes, she trudged into the bathroom and

turned on the shower. *You had better start paying attention, Mr. Albright. I'm not a little girl anymore!*

While Cay and Maudie enjoyed dinner at Amato's, Lynne and Grant Alston sat facing each other on the rumpled bed in his hotel room. Both were naked, and Lynne was sitting cross-legged between Grant's wide-spread legs. The view was distracting.

"Keep showing yourself like that and I'll jump your bones again," he said.

"Call this a test," Lynne grinned. "To see which is the most important—business or fucking."

"We've already made business wait once." Grant tossed a pillow in her lap. "Everything set for Wednesday?"

"I told Travis to hold one to three open, said we had an important prospective client coming in. At twelve-thirty, I'll tell him the guy can't make it and scoot."

"He won't tie you into the inside information I have?"

"We've never given him any reason to be suspicious."

"Heard anymore about what your brother-in-law's up to?"

"I don't think he'll make a pitch before next week."

"Be too late by then," Grant said.

17

On Tuesday, Cay, Maripat, Maudie and Andrew Stiles attended a Derby luncheon near Versailles, then drove to Louisville. Maripat had reserved rooms months before at the Hyatt Regency where the Kentucky Derby Trainers' Dinner would be held that night. John, Shawn and Joy joined them for cocktails at six.

"Jumpin' Jehosphat!" Shawn said when Cay presented Maudie. "I heard you were here, but nobody told me about how *much* of you had arrived! You could pass for one of them Rolex girls."

"Rolex girls?" Maudie said.

"You ought to punch him in the mouth," Joy laughed. "The

Rolex girls hit Louisville pretty hard a few years back. They were a bunch of good looking women who visited all the big sporting events across the country—the Derby, Indianapolis Five Hundred, fights in Las Vegas. They lured men wearing Rolex watches to their rooms, gave them knockout drops and stole their watches and everything else worth taking. One girl was over six feet tall."

"Well!" Maudie folded her arms across her chest and gazed down at Shawn. "Was it my height you were referring to?"

"Looks, too," he grinned. "You can lure me to my room anytime."

"And die of a heart attack in the elevator," Joy said.

Maudie hugged Shawn. "You don't need a Rolex watch for that."

"Better wait until after the Ghost wins the Derby," John said. "Shawn needs to conserve his strength. Can't have him passing out on the presentation stand."

"How's Harlan Ghost doing?" Maudie asked.

"Running with more confidence every day," Joy said. "Are you coming out tomorrow morning? It's his last big workout before the Derby."

"Oh, yes! I can't wait to see him."

"He'll make all of Harlan County proud on Saturday," Maripat said. "I feel it in my bones."

Joy said: "I'm praying you're right. I thought it was a big thrill leading Fast Track out of the paddock in Seventy-Three, but this tops that. It's like having my whole life aimed toward one day. But what a day!" Laughing, she felt her forehead. "I'm getting a bad case of Derby fever."

Andrew Stiles arrived, drink in hand. "What is Derby fever?"

Cay explained: "It's a disease that attacks the mind, rendering the victim incapable of making rational decisions—strikes owners, breeders and trainers without warning. The first signs develop during the juvenile season and become visible in November at the Breeders' Cup. The fever rises after the first of the year, and sleep is disturbed by visions of having a horse in the Derby. Race records are ignored. Owning or training a Derby entry is all that matters. The fever peaks on the first Saturday in May and miraculously disappears after the eighth race. Victims have been known to remain in a dazed condition for weeks afterward."

"Bloody marvelous!" Andrew Stiles said. "May I have your autograph?"

Maripat stared at her son in wide-eyed wonder. "For one suffering from the disease, that was very articulate."

"Don't ask him to repeat it on Friday," Joy said. "He's been deteriorating rapidly since the Ghost won the Blue Grass."

Sponsored by the Kentucky Thoroughbred Owners and Breeders, the Kentucky Derby Trainers' Dinner was a time for the presentation of awards and good-natured ribbing. To Maudie's surprise and delight, Maripat had arranged for English trainer, Charles Maxwell, and his wife, Adele, to sit at their table. Maxwell had conditioned horses at Newmarket for years and had visited Broadheim Stud many times. His Derby entry, Notorious, was owned by a neighboring stud near Chevelry village and had been Britain's leading two-year-old colt the previous year.

"The Kentucky Derby is becoming an international event." Maxwell said. "Two horses this year from England and one each from France and Japan."

"Does running on dirt bother you?" Shawn asked.

"I would prefer grass but having a horse in the Kentucky Derby has gained considerable worldwide prestige of late." A cheery smile. "Now that you Americans have invaded our island and won our Epsom Derby, we feel it only fair to reciprocate."

"Here! Here!" Andrew Stiles said.

"Will you be terribly put out if I root for Harlan Ghost?" Maudie said. "I'm godmother to his grandmother on the tail-male side. I helped deliver her! It wouldn't seem right to do otherwise."

"I'll keep that in mind when my horse comes under the wire first."

The evening ended with Cay and Maudie encountering Travis and Lynne in the hall. Weaving unsteadily, Travis grinned and put an arm around Maudie. "Look who's here!"

Smiling weakly, Maudie broke free and pressed against Cay.

Turning to his wife, Travis said, "You remember Maudie Grayson. She used to be little but not anymore!"

Maudie blushed and huddled closer to Cay when Lynne ignored her outstretched hand and tried to drag Travis away.

"Goddamnit, say hello to Maudie!" Travis snapped, yanking Lynne back to face the embarrassed girl.

"Damn you!" Lynne snapped at Travis. She freed her arm and glared at Cay. "Cut the pretending. We hate each other's guts."

"I don't hate you Lynne," Cay said quietly.

"Bullshit!"

Stepping between Lynne and his brother, Travis said, "I'm sorry, Cay. Things have been rough lately. Maybe after the Derby you and I can get together, have a drink—okay?"

"Anytime."

"Bring your girlfriend," Lynne sneered. "Travis would like to paw here some more, wouldn't you, dear?"

"I said shut up!"

Ignoring Travis, Lynne said, "Two brothers with the same problem—you can't get along with women your own age so you pick up young chicks!"

Cay took Maudie's arm. "Let's get out of here."

Lynne's laughter and Travis's angry shouts followed them down the long hall.

Maudie quivered in Cay's arms as they rode the elevator up to their rooms. "Travis was drunk," he said. "Probably won't remember anything in the morning. Lynne was just being herself." The doors opened, and he took Maudie's hand. "Your place or mine?"

"You choose."

"Mine, then."

As soon as they stepped inside, Maudie headed for the bathroom. Removing coat and tie, Cay opened the private bar and poured two brandies. Gratefully accepting hers when she returned, Maudie kicked off her shoes and sat beside him on the small couch.

"I don't care what Lynne said about you," Maudie said. "You can get along with women of any age." A sidelong glance as she gripped her brandy. "Even young chicks like me."

"*Especially* young chicks like you," Cay smiled. He slipped an arm around her shoulders. "I'm glad you didn't take that young chick business too seriously."

"You did."

"I did?"

"Not now—when I was ten! Remember how you called me your little sister and refused to look at me as a woman?"

"You *were* kinda young."

"You were, too. Three years older than I am now."

"Amazing deduction, Miss Grayson."

Sighing deeply, Maudie rested her head on his shoulder. "I'm glad we got that straightened out." She drained the last of her brandy and set the glass on a table.

"Feel better?" Cay asked.

"Much better, thank you. Give me your glass. There! Now our hands are free."

"I knew that."

"How clever of you." Maudie pressed her cheek against his and kissed his ear.

"Maudie..."

"Yes?"

"Should we be doing this?"

She kissed him lightly on the lips. "What?"

"That."

"You mean this?"

"Yeah, that."

"Are you afraid it's catching? Like Derby fever?"

"Not exactly. I feel sort of funny, like Tim might jump out of a closet with his Purdy shotgun."

"Tim? Never!"

"Well...your father."

"But he admires you ever so much!"

"What would he think if he caught me kissing his daughter?"

"He would be very upset if he thought you were playing with my feelings. Discounting that, he would offer congratulations and tell you to carry on. Would you play with my feelings?"

"Of course not! It's just hard getting used to you as a grownup. It's very confusing. All of a sudden my little buddy is stirring feelings that are definitely not brotherly."

"I'm so glad!" Maudie threw her arms around his neck. "Do you think you could manage an un-brotherly kiss?"

"Oh, hell," Cay muttered, pulling her close and tasting those lips that had been tempting him for days.

Making happy sounds deep in her throat, Maudie tightened her arms around his neck. When they finally drew apart, her eyes were closed, mouth curved in a satisfied smile.

Smoothing her hair over one ear, Cay felt a surge of tenderness that left him shaken.

Long lashes lifted, revealing eyes slightly out of focus. "Definitely unbrotherly, wouldn't you agree?"

"Definitely."

"Do you happen to own a white horse? Outside of Little Bid? Not a gray that's turned white. A real white horse?"

"No. You know how rare white Thoroughbreds are."

"How sad! You probably don't have any shining armor either."

"Sorry. Got a light charcoal suit, but it doesn't shine."

"Never mind. I think you should kiss me again."

Twenty minutes later, Cay accompanied Maudie to her room across the hall. After unlocking her door, she turned and melted into his arms. Several minutes passed. A noise down the hall made them step apart. Grinning at each other foolishly, they kissed once more, then Maudie slipped into her room.

18

Shortly before dawn the next morning, Cay drove through the backside gate at Churchill Downs. Sitting beside him, Maudie covered her mouth with a hand and yawned widely.

"Looks like you didn't get much sleep," Maripat said from the rear seat.

Maudie shot Cay a knowing look. "I kept waking up. Too much excitement, I guess."

Maripat and John exchanged smiles. The change in the couple's relationship was evident earlier when they arrived in the hotel coffee shop holding hands.

"There's Shawn," Cay said as he parked at one end of Barn 44.

"You look right chipper this morning," Maripat said to Shawn as she got out of the car.

"Ought to," he grinned. "Got me a horse in the Derby, coffee in my belly and the sun's comin' up on a beautiful Kentucky day. What more could a man ask for?"

"Guess that about says it. Harlan Ghost out yet?"

"Just went by on his fifth trip around the shedrow. Better watch him, Maudie. When he sees what's inside those tight jeans, he might try and bite a back pocket off."

"I'll keep that in mind," Maudie laughed. "Oh, is that him?"

"Sure is. Hey Joy, bring the big lug over here!"

Wearing a green blanket with white trim that matched the colors of Woodland Farm, Harlan Ghost blew air out of his nostrils and nudged Cay in the ribs. "Sorry," Cay said, patting the colt's shoulder. "You've got a heavy workout this morning. Carrots and other goodies come later."

"He's turning to gray so quickly!" Maudie said, moving closer and rubbing Harlan Ghost's neck. "And he's huge! Wouldn't he make a smashing hunter-jumper?"

"Now there's a thought," Cay said, stepping back and peering into one of the colt's bluish-brown eyes. "Screw up in the Derby and I'll ship you to England. Maudie can ride you in the show circuit and maybe a steeplechase or two."

Harlan Ghost nickered, and Maudie shot Cay a look that went unnoticed by everyone but Maripat. She smiled, thinking that Cay was in for a surprise or two before the week was out.

Joy pulled at Harlan Ghost's shank. "See you guys. A few more trips around the shedrow and it'll be time to hit the track."

Shawn headed for the barn. "Follow me. Coffee's on."

The big oval track was already full of walking, jogging, galloping horses when Harlan Ghost moved through the chute-gap gate and backed up against the rail to study the competition. It was a habit he had acquired when he went into training as a yearling. Press photographers snapped pictures while a TV cameraman recorded the scene for the evening news.

A horse galloped past. "That's Shedrow Hustler," Shawn said to Maudie. "Won the Wood Memorial. His trainer's John Veitch— John conditioned Alydar and Davona Dale and a lot of other good horses when he worked for Calumet." Shawn looked up at Harlan Ghost. "Have you seen enough?"

The colt snorted and stamped a front foot.

"I think that means yes," Joy said.

The exercise rider, Ross Slinger, nudged Harlan Ghost forward. Railbirds and the press came alert as the big gray broke into a canter and rounded the far turn.

"Look at that stride!" Maripat said, shading her eyes as galloped past the grandstand on the opposite side of the track.

"Native Dancer's measured twenty-nine feet," Cay said. "The Ghost's comes pretty close."

"He'll look even better when Ross turns him loose," Shawn said. "He's just passed the five-furlong pole. Won't be long."

Stopwatches appeared along the rail as the gray colt approached the half-mile pole. Thumb poised, Cay watched Ross Slinger sit down in the stirrups and lean forward. "Yeah!" Cay exclaimed softly as Harlan Ghost streaked toward the far turn.

Hands clasped in a prayerful attitude, Maripat followed the colt's progress as it breezed past the 3/8 pole.

"Twelve and three-fifths," Joy said. "Looking good."

"He runs beautifully!" Maudie cried. "Oh, Cay, I believe he's going to win the Derby! I really do!"

"Hope you're right," Cay smiled as Harlan Ghost reached the quarter pole in 24 2/5 seconds.

"I *know* I am!" Maudie said as the colt entered the home-stretch.

"Thirty-five and one-fifth," John said. Harlan Ghost had one furlong to go.

The gray colt was now running in front of the grandstand

and toward the finish pole, the famous twin spires gleaming in the morning sunshine high above. One eye on her stopwatch, the other on the colt, Joy murmured, "That's it, you big overgrown jerk! I love you! Forty-seven and change! Is that nice or what?"

As Harlan Ghost slowed down around the clubhouse turn, Cay noticed a small bay colt moving through the chute-gap gate and onto the track. "There's Lynne's Lad."

Maudie's head snapped around. "Is your brother here?" The memory of last night's encounter was still fresh in her mind.

"Don't see him." Cay pointed at a heavyset man on a paint horse. "That's Joe Ponds, Lynne's Lad's trainer."

"Here comes Harlan Ghost," Maripat said. She laughed as the gray passed Travis's colt. "Talk about Mutt and Jeff! Lynne's Lad looks like he could walk under the Ghost's neck with room to spare."

"But Lynne's Lad can run," Shawn said as the bay trotted by. "Remember how small Arazi was? He beat a lot of bigger horses in the Breeders' Cup Juvenile."

"And he was another Derby favorite that didn't even place," Joy said. "A record money-burner! If *not* being a favorite means anything, the Ghost should have a good chance. Poor guy, he don't get no respect."

19

Sixty miles to the southeast, Lynne lay awake in her bedroom at Windsong Manor. The drive from Louisville last night had been a silent one, with her at the wheel of the white Rolls Royce and Travis passed out in the back seat. *Hold on*, she had kept telling herself. *Another week and you'll be rid of him forever!*

She was furious—at Travis for forcing a confrontation with Cay and that English bitch and at herself for losing her temper. It would have made a juicy piece of gossip—just when Grant's negotiations for Albright Stud were at a critical stage.

Had that happened, Grant would have flown into one of his towering rages. She had witnessed several during their ten-year relationship but thankfully none had been aimed at her. From broad hints and snatches of overheard telephone conversations, she knew that Grant was not above taking violent measures to settle matters in his favor.

Lynne glanced at the digital clock beside the bed. Travis had to be wakened no later than eleven for the fictitious one o'clock meeting. After notifying Travis at twelve-thirty that the "meeting" was cancelled, she would leave immediately for a shopping trip to Lexington. Grant would be waiting off Old Frankfurt Pike and would proceed to the farm as soon as he saw her drive by.

Travis was at his desk when the maid announced over the intercom that Grant Alston had arrived and would like a few minutes of his time. Happy for a break in what had started out as a boring afternoon, he told her to send him down.

"Long time, no see!" Grant grinned, shaking Travis's hand. He jerked a thumb over his shoulder. "Quite a hike down that hall."

"Gives me lots of privacy from the rest of the house," Travis said. "Come on in. Drink?"

"Got any JD?"

"Sure do. Ice, no water?"

"Right." Grant sat down and gazed out the window that overlooked a vista of green paddocks and grazing horses. "Helluva view. Sure beats West Texas."

Travis handed Grant his drink. "What you been up to?"

"Trying to keep ahead of paperwork. Damn government regulations drive me nuts."

"Tell me about it! You just missed Lynne. She left about twenty minutes ago."

"Came out to see you, anyway. Got a proposition."

"Shoot."

Stretching his long jean-clad legs, Grant said, "It has to do with Albright Stud. You've got troubles. I've got the remedy."

Travis frowned. "I'm not really ready to talk about that, Grant. Next week, maybe, but—"

"You haven't got until next week. Not unless you woke up this morning and found fifteen million bucks under your bed."

Travis smiled weakly. "That's crazy. I'm not under any deadline. Saturday's three days away. If my horse wins the Derby—"

"It'll just give your creditors a little more to collect," Grant broke in. "You'll never see a dime of his added value."

Travis slashed his hand downward. "Let's get off the subject, okay? I apologize for being rude, but you can imagine the pressure I'm under."

"I said I have a remedy."

"I appreciate that, but it'll have to wait until next week."

Grant pulled a slip of paper out of his shirt pocket. "Guess I'll have to play hardball."

Rising out of his chair, Travis snapped, "I said later!"

Grant studied the paper in his hand. "You've sold eighty-four matings to four different stallions over the last five years. The income came to a million and a half. Funny thing, not one cent showed up on the books." He looked up. "That's fraud, pure and simple. The limited partners and shareholders will nail your hide to the barn door."

White-faced, Travis sank back in the chair. "That's a lie!"

"Oh? I suppose this is another one—misrepresenting assets by inflating livestock values. Hell, I wouldn't even call all your horses livestock. You carried six broodmares on the books for years after they died! The legal term for that is 'lack of full disclosure,' or something like that. It buys jail time, too."

"What's your point?" Travis asked in a barely audible voice.

"I intend to buy you out. Go along with me, it all gets swept under the carpet. Don't—I spill it to the press. I've got it all documented. Hell of an alternative, isn't it? It gets out, you lose everything and do time in prison."

"Bastard!"

"I've been called that and more. Ready to hear my terms?"

"Do I have a choice?"

"Nope. I'll pay off the banks and bondholders and get the limited partners, shareholders and unsecured creditors off your back. You walk out with a million in cash, the clothes on your back and debt free." Grant raised a hand as Travis started to speak. "Just to show I mean well, I'll toss in another million if Lynne's Lad wins the Derby."

Travis stared. "I give up all this for a million? Two if Lynne's Lad wins the Derby and becomes worth ten times that?"

"Better than the bankruptcy court taking everything and going to prison. With a million or two and that fine reputation intact, you can continue living the good life. On a smaller scale, but shoot, with your ability, you can be back on top in no time."

"I walk out the door with just the clothes on my back? What about personal things—furniture, paintings, cars?"

"The furniture seems to go with the place," Grant said. "Pictures, too. You can take odds and ends. Lynne can keep her Jag, and you can take your pick of what's left. Except the Rolls. I'll use that when I'm in town."

Travis stood and pointed at the slip of paper in Grant's hand. "You're bluffing. You haven't got any facts."

"That's where you're wrong. Want to hear 'em?"

Travis stepped forward, hand out. "Let me see."

"I told you—these are just notes."

"Where did you get your information? I've got a right to know."

Grant's voice hardened as he got to his feet. "That's where you're wrong. You gave up your rights when you started stealing from your partners and the public. You're just a common thief."

Travis thrust his hands out. "Get the hell out of here!" he shouted. "I'm through listening to your shit!"

With the speed of a striking rattlesnake, Grant seized Travis's upraised wrists. "In a minute I'm going to get real pissed and mop the floor with you, boy. That what you want?"

Travis struggled helplessly. "Let me go."

"When you promise to be a good boy. Come to think of it, a little lesson might be just what the doctor ordered." Muscles rippling, he forced Travis to his knees and slapped him several times. "Want more?" he asked, grabbing Travis's shirt and pulling him close. "Don't worry, I won't mess up your face or anything that'll show. But I'll work your body over and make you shit and piss blood for a week. It's that or let me have my say." He backhanded Travis across the face. "It's your choice, boy."

Eyes glistening with pain and humiliation, Travis looked down. "I'll listen," he whispered.

Smiling widely, Grant released Travis. "That's great! I knew you'd see the light. Sit down; I'll top off our drinks. No reason we can't talk this over like gentleman." Whistling a merry tune, Grant refilled their glasses. "Swallow that. It'll make you feel like a new man."

While Travis gulped down his bourbon, Grant lit a cigarette and returned the dented lighter to his shirt pocket. "I've put a lot of work into this, and I don't intend to come up with a dry hole. Don't get brave after I leave and try to put up a fight. I'll do whatever it takes to get what I want. I've got a file on you and your operation thick enough to choke an elephant. If I spill a tenth of what I have, you won't be able to show your face at Churchill Downs on Saturday. Understand?"

A dejected nod.

"Good! We'll meet tomorrow morning and sign a letter of intent. I'll give you ten grand and another ninety thousand on Monday when we sign the papers and put the deal into escrow. When it closes, you get nine hundred thousand and that extra million if your horse wins the Derby. That's damn fair. I could give you a thousand now and make you wait for the rest until escrow closes."

"Closing escrow will take a long time," Travis said dully.

"The banks and bondholders are easy—pay them off in full and they're out. It'll take a while to cut a deal with the limited partners and shareholders, but I'll get on that as soon as we sign the papers next week. Same with the unsecured creditors. I'm shooting for sixty days. Damn fast for a complicated escrow, but I know how to light fires."

"I have to talk to Lynne."

"Tell her everything; she'll go along. She knows which side her bread's buttered on."

"I have to decide today? You can't wait until tomorrow?"

Grant shook his head. "If the bad news doesn't come out on

Friday, it loses some of its punch."

Travis said, listlessly, "I'll talk to her when she gets back. Where can I reach you?"

"I'll be at the Lexington-Green Hilton. Call me by seven tonight. How's your time in the morning?"

"Whenever you want."

"Let's make it ten. You and Lynne will both have to sign. You can come to the hotel or I'll meet you here." Rising, Grant slapped Travis on the shoulder. "Look on the bright side. The way you were headed, you would have ended up with nothing and a long stretch in prison."

He paused at the door, hand on the knob. "I've heard that your brother wants the farm. Don't get cute and go to him for help. I'll run over you both like a steamroller. You'll know there are worse things than jail time. Be a shame to see your brother worked over, him being innocent and all."

20

Unbelievable, Travis thought as he drove along Capitol Avenue in Frankfurt, *Six hours ago I was being slapped around and threatened with prison. Now I'm on my way to the Governor's Ball!*

"We can't skip the ball!" Lynne had shouted after returning from Lexington and being told about Grant's visit. "We have to put up a good front until the Derby's over—there's enough speculation going around as it is! I suppose you'd like to stay home and cancel our party tomorrow night! The way it looks to me, Grant's giving us a break. He's right—you could go to prison. *I* could go to prison! You're only forty-six. It's not the end of the world."

"You don't really give a damn about me getting kicked around, do you!" Travis said.

"Of course, I care," Lynne said tiredly. "But you brought it on yourself. You should be glad it isn't turning out worse. I'm going to take a shower. We've got to leave in two hours."

Inside the Governor's Mansion, Maripat balanced a plate of hors d'oeuvres on her knees and observed the milling crowd. "There goes the mayor of Hazard—the guy with the long cigar." She grinned at Maudie. "It's hard to pick the men out with them all wearing tuxedos. Looks like a penguin convention."

Laughing gaily, Maudie said, "You put such a different perspective on things!"

"Speaking of penguins, there's Cay."

"A very handsome one," Maudie sighed as she watched Cay and John join several other men at the bar.

"How's the campaign going?" Maripat asked. "From the looks of things, I'd say you've made considerable progress."

"I worry so!" Maudie burst out. "Do you think he understands? It seems so sudden to him, but I've been thinking about this over half my life! I love him so! Am I being too forward? Do you think he'll send me home with a kiss on the cheek and a promise to write? I'm so afraid he won't take me seriously!"

Maripat smiled. "That's a lot of questions. I can't speak for Cay— lord knows he's got a mind of his own—but you've gotten closer to him than any woman since Arlene. Don't sell yourself short, Maudie. You're a beautiful young woman, and you two have a lot in common. If you want my opinion, I'd say the odds are definitely in your favor. Here he comes. That orchestra is playing some pretty nice music. Why don't you drag him out there and practice a little witchcraft?"

It was nearing midnight when Cay met Travis exiting the men's restroom. Intent on straightening his cummerbund, Travis didn't see Cay until he felt his brother's hand on his arm.

"Oh, hi," Travis said weakly, offering a lopsided smile.

"Hi yourself," Cay said. "Hang on a minute. I'll be right out. We can have a drink."

Travis hesitated, and Cay noted the strange look in his eyes. "Sure," Travis said, "I wanted to apologize for last night anyway."

"Forget it. I've already forgotten it. Be right back."

Panic seized Travis. What if Grant should learn he was talking to Cay? The man must have spies everywhere.

Cay returned and they walked toward the large tent set up outside the mansion. "Watched that colt of yours work out this morning," Cay said. "Looks like he's right on schedule."

"I've lost track of what's going on the last day or so."

"Hey, this is the *Derby*! You should be doing cartwheels!"

"Just tired. Derby Week and having a horse in the race really takes it out of a guy."

They ordered drinks at the bar. "Seen Mom?" Cay asked.

"Saw her a while ago. She was having a high old time with a bunch of her buddies. Where does she get all that energy?"

"Maybe she keeps some Harlan moonshine in the cellar."

"I miss talking to her." Travis's voice broke, and he turned away to hide the tears that suddenly glistened in his eyes.

"You can talk to her anytime," Cay said quietly. "Me, too. I know you've heard talk about me wanting the farm if you can't keep it together. That's true. But I'm your brother. I'll help any way I can. Yell and I'll come running—okay?"

Too choked up to speak, Travis could only nod.

"Pretty soon the orchestra is going to start playing *Good Night, Ladies* and hope we'll leave," Cay said as he held Maudie close on the dance floor.

"Would they be that cruel?" she murmured, resting her cheek against his. "It's only two in the morning, and there must be at least twenty other couples still dancing."

Cay kissed a bare shoulder. "You have beautiful bones."

"What a remarkable statement! You really like my bones?"

"These little ears, too. I'd nibble on one, but I might swallow an earring."

"Not much of me is little," Maudie mourned. "Tim says I've been around horses so long, I'm trying to be big like one."

"I hope he means like a select yearling—long legs and a great body. If not, next time I see him I'll punch his lights out."

"You would do that for me?"

"Anything. Your smallest wish is my greatest command."
"I'd love to be kissed."
"Try for something more difficult next time."

21

The next day while Maudie attended a Derby Week luncheon and conducted interviews on several Bluegrass farms, Cay drove to Louisville.

This was Thursday, the day the entry box for the Derby was closed and the drawings held for post positions.

The $10,000 fee for entering a horse in the Derby had to be paid before the drawing. Another $10,000 was due on Saturday to start in the race. Two owners who had failed to nominate their horses to all three Triple Crown races by January 16 at a cost of $600, had paid late fees of $4,500 each to meet the March 27 closing deadline. One owner—the Frenchman who's colt, Clovis Rules, had won the Prix Omnium II a week after the March 27 deadline—had paid a supplementary fee of $ 150,000.

"His horse will have to place at least second and even then the owner won't get all his costs back," Shawn said as he stood beside Cay in the crowded Kentucky Derby Museum where the drawing would take place. "With only three career wins and all of them on grass, I'd say he hasn't got the horse for the course."

"Here we go," Joy said as Jerry Botts, the Churchill Downs racing secretary and three men mounted the platform. The room quieted as Botts' assistants took their stations, one at the box that contained the names of the horses, another behind the glass bottle that held the numbered pills indicating the post positions and a third in front of a large board where the names of the horses would be displayed.

"I'll pass on number one," Shawn muttered. Right next to the fence, it put the emerging horse in danger of being slammed into the rail. Ferdinand, ridden by Bill Shoemaker in 1986, was the first Derby winner to break from the number 1 spot in twenty-two years. And that was accomplished after being nearly forced over the fence and into the infield before reaching the clubhouse turn.

"At least we got rid of the auxiliary gate," Cay said.

"Thank God for that," Joy said. "If Jazzercise hadn't been scratched, they would have had to put it in. I'd have died if the Ghost had been stuck way out there."

The auxiliary gate, used if the Derby field exceeded fourteen, was dreaded even more than the number 1 spot. Few horses had won from those extreme outside post positions.

Reaching into the box, the man on Jerry Botts' left drew the first name and handed it to the racing secretary. "Sensational Bob!" Botts called. Shaking the jar, the man on his right removed a pill and gave it to Botts. "Number six!" The man at the display board inserted a card with Sensational Bob's name into the number six slot.

Bald head shining under the lights, aging trainer Charlie Whittingham smiled his appreciation for the favorable position.

Freedom Prince, trained by Shug McGaughey, drew the number 3 spot, followed by Knight's Ferry, a California-bred colt, with number 12. Its youthful trainer, Phil Hauswald, shrugged and tried not to show his disappointment.

With eight positions selected and six to go, Shawn was getting nervous. Numbers 1, 4, 7, 13 and 14 were still open. "Come on! Come on!" he urged as the assistant drew another name and passed it to Botts.

"Lynne's Lad!" Botts accepted the pill from the man on his left. "Number seven!"

Cay had noticed earlier that neither Travis nor Lynne was in attendance, but their trainer, Joe Ponds, was. Ponds grinned and punched a fist in the air.

The number 1 spot went to D. Wayne Lukas's TV Starlet, the only filly in the race. The handsome gray-haired trainer of 1988 Derby winner, Winning Colors—only the third filly to win the race—smiled and shook his head.

Shawn's body went rigid and Joy chewed on her knuckles when the racing secretary called, "Harlan Ghost!"

Cay silently urged, *Number four, number four.*

"Number thirteen!"

Joy tore at her hair while Shawn groaned aloud. Faces in the crowd expressed sympathy as Cay rolled his eyes skyward. The next to the last outside post position and number thirteen to boot! He remained in a daze while the final three positions were handed out—number 11 to the French horse, Clovis Rules, 4 to the Japanese entry, Mighty Warrior, and 14 to Rotsaruck, a chestnut colt trained by Ron McAnally.

Travis didn't get word of Lynne's Lad drawing the welcome number 7 position until early afternoon. "Your brother didn't get a good number," Larry Ponds said over the phone. "He drew thirteen."

At least he owns a horse running in the Derby, Travis thought. *I just signed mine away, including the farm and just about everything I own!* Travis hung up and buried his face in his hands. He had just returned with Lynne from Grant's hotel where they had signed the letter of intent. The $10,000 check was in his wallet. He would bank it after the final papers were signed on Monday.

He listened to the sounds of activity that came from the main house and the lawn out back where workmen were setting up a huge tent. After over forty years hosting Derby Week parties, tonight's would be the last for the Albrights at Windsong Manor.

Travis rubbed his eyes and blinked away the tears. As had happened many times in the last twenty-four hours, he felt a compelling need to cry.

22

That night, Cay and Maudie attended a party at a horse farm on Paris Pike, the narrow highway north of Lexington that boasts some of the most famous nursery studs in the world and had been dubbed the "Park Avenue of the Bluegrass."

After two hours of circulating among the scores of guests and dancing to the music of a local band, Cay led Maudie outside. Fireflies danced in the warm spring air, and hanging lanterns lighted the way for strolling couples.

"So peaceful and lovely," Maudie said, looking up at the star-sprinkled sky, then out over the rolling paddocks and the scores of horses grazing in the moonlight.

"You're lovely," Cay said. He pulled her into his arms and kissed her hungrily.

"Oh, Cay," she cried softly, "I want to be alone with you. We've had so little of that the last few days."

"My sentiments exactly." Minutes later, they were hurrying out the front door and waiting anxiously while an attendant brought Cay's Mercedes around.

Driving away from the stately home and still a quarter-mile from where the private lane met Paris Pike, Cay parked under a spreading elm. "Come here," he said.

With a joyful cry, she threw her arms around his neck and covered his mouth with hers.

Cay murmured against her lips, "Do you have any idea what you've done to me?"

"I do hope it's something terribly wicked!"

"That among other things. I was reasonably happy with my life before you arrived. Now you've turned everything upside down and left me unwilling to continue on as before."

"What are you going to do about it?" she asked in a small voice.

"I have very few options. Only one, actually. I love you, Maudie. I don't want you to go back to England—not permanently. Would you consider living here...being my wife?"

"Consider!" she cried, hugging him even tighter. "I've been considering it for fourteen years! Oh, Cay, Darling, I love you so terribly, terribly much!"

The kiss would have lasted much longer if a pair of approaching headlights hadn't lighted the interior of the car. "Caught in the act," Cay grinned as they broke apart. He started the engine. "Let's go somewhere more private."

As he turned onto Paris Pike, Maudie rested her head on his shoulder. "I don't want to spend the night alone," she said. "Not this special night."

"Same here. I was getting up the nerve to ask."

"Silly goose! Don't you know how much I want you?"

"Well...it's just that I'm so much older and---"

"Stop that right now!" Maudie ordered, jerking upright and placing long fingers over Cay's mouth. "I don't ever want to hear anything about age differences again! Not one word! Understand?

"Yumph."

Maudie smiled and returned her head to his shoulder. They rode in silence for a while, then she said, "Cay?"

"Ummm?"

"My hotel room is so impersonal. Would you mind if we stayed at your house?" Her voice wavered. "I know you shared it with Arlene, and you might—"

"I've already considered that...ever since I started thinking seriously about us. At first I felt guilty, like I was betraying her. I haven't shared our bed with anyone since she died. Then I remembered how caring she was. She would never condemn me for finding happiness again. She's probably cheering for us now. You're coming home with me."

Lying under the covers, Cay waited for Maudie to emerge from the bathroom. They had stopped briefly at the hotel for her to pack a few things, then posted record time to the farm.

The bathroom light went out. Wearing a clinging nightgown, Maudie glided across the carpet, eyes shining in the soft rays from the window.

"Am I dreaming or what?" Cay said as she slipped under the covers and into his arms.

Maudie nuzzled his neck. "You terrible beast! Think of all the years I've loved you and all I got was an occasional letter!"

"*Stupid* beast." He ran his hand over the swell of her hip. "You were so far away and all I could remember was that skinny little kid who used to pester me all the time."

"You *are* a beast!" Maudie cried, sitting up and pounding his chest. "I never pestered you. You *loved* having me around."

"I did! I do!" Cay laughed, pulling her across his body. "Know something? You're a lot more interesting now that you've grown up."

"You like me this way?" She spread her legs so her soft mound rested against the bulge in his shorts.

"Definitely. Hey, you have an outstanding s-curve back."

"Is that bad?"

"Just the opposite. It sinks in here like this, goes back out further down, then in again. Very sexy."

"Scratch me where the top of the s goes out. Oh, heavenly! A little higher." Maudie squirmed on top of Cay, groaning with pleasure.

Arching her back, she slipped the straps off her shoulders and pushed the nightgown down to her waist. Crushing her surprisingly large breasts against Cay's bare chest, she devoured his mouth with hers. Their tongues touched, then intertwined.

Hooking his thumbs under Maudie's nightgown, Cay slipped it over her hips and down to her knees. While he used his toes to push it the rest of the way off, he removed his shorts. Their kisses and movements became more frantic as Maudie rubbed her naked body on top of his.

Cay kicked the covers to one side and rolled Maudie on her back. Her slender body was revealed briefly as they joined, and Cay was locked in the grip of those impossibly long legs.

They tumbled about, muffled cries growing louder as years of pent up emotions were released in a few precious moments. When Cay exploded inside Maudie, she was already screaming in the midst of a shattering climax. Still joined together, they kissed and talked quietly until they drifted off to sleep.

Sometime during the night, Cay awoke to find Maudie's nude body pressed against his side, a slim leg thrown across his stomach. Long eyelashes caressed her cheeks as she slept, and her breath stirred the fine hairs on his chest.

Looking at the nightstand on his right, he studied the picture of Arlene that was barely discernible in the muted light. As Maudie stirred beside him and murmured in her sleep, he said a silent goodbye to the lovely woman who had owned his heart for so many years.

23

When Cay and Maudie arrived at White Oak Stud the next morning to take Maripat and John to the Kentucky Oaks, Maripat knew instantly that something momentous had happened. "You've got that sloppy grin on your face, Cay," she said as she met them at the door. "You look right pleased with yourself, too, Maudie. Are you going to let me in on what's going on or do I have to guess?"

Cay grinned at Maudie. "You tell her."

Smiling radiantly, Maudie seized Maripat's hands. "We're going to be married!"

"That's wonderful!" Maripat cried, standing on her toes and kissing Maudie's cheek. "John! Come quick! The children have arrived bearing fantastic news!"

After John had hugged and kissed Maudie and congratulated Cay, Maripat asked, "Have you told your parents, Maudie?"

"Oh, my!" Eyes wide, she slapped a hand over her mouth.

"What if they say no?" Cay asked.

"No way," Maudie laughed. "They think the world of you. Considering how I've been going on about you for so long, they'll be vastly relieved." Her smile widened. "We can call them after the party tonight! That's the best time to catch them. They have breakfast at seven. Tim will probably be there, too."

Pleading an upset stomach, Travis skipped the Kentucky Oaks for the first time in his adult life. The premier race for three-year-old fillies at Churchill Downs, the inaugural Oaks was held on May 19, 1875, two days after the running of the first Kentucky Derby. Now held the Friday before the Derby, it was a special day for locals to get together and socialize. Next to the Derby, the

Oaks was the race Kentucky breeders wanted most to win.

Lynne attended with several friends she had invited to watch the races from Albright Stud's table in the Skye Terrace. This choice spot on "Millionaire's Row" would remain with the farm. Grant Alston had listed it as one of the assets in the letter of intent.

He had also invited himself to the Oaks, as well as the Derby the following day. Lynne was relieved that Travis had pleaded illness and stayed home. Having him around was depressing.

She had no chance to be alone with Grant at Churchill Downs, but they met that evening after returning to Lexington. With separate Derby Eve parties to attend, they had less than an hour.

"Three more days!" Lynne cried, dropping into a chair in Grant's hotel room and kicking off her shoes. "If I live that long! This has been the most exhausting week of my life."

"Getting any static from Travis?" Grant asked.

"Nothing. He just sits around with a drink in his hand and stares at the wall. Damnit, I shouldn't feel sorry for him, but I do. Go easy on him—okay?"

"He's an asshole! I'm surprised he lasted so long."

"Are you forgetting who's been propping him up all these years? And coordinating the entire operation?"

"Makes you sound indispensable."

"Well?"

"Don't get carried away, little lady. I might sell all the horses and raise sheep on the land."

"You'd still need me," Lynne laughed. "For a roll in the hay if nothing else."

"You think you're the only woman who can get my rocks off?"

"No, I just do it better."

Lighting a cigarette, Grant studied Lynne and the breasts half-exposed by the low-cut dress. Flaunting her dark Gypsy looks at every opportunity, she had turned a lot of male heads at Churchill Downs today. He wondered how many lovers she had besides him. She said he was the only one, but he found it hard to believe she could repress that smoldering sexuality during the weeks and months they were apart. It didn't matter. He had women stashed all over Texas and other parts of the country. One even claimed she had a child by him---despite the paper he produced to prove he had had a vasectomy. Even if there had been a slip-up, he wasn't worried about being sued for child support. The woman's husband thought the boy was his, and she wasn't about to tell him different.

"When do you think we'll be able to take over?" Lynne asked.

"I told Travis sixty days. Could take less, maybe more."

"I can't wait!" Lynne enthused. "Running Albright Stud without interference! Makes me want to pee."

Grant raised an eyebrow. "Forgetting about me?"

"Hardly. But you're too busy with other stuff to lean over my shoulder like Travis does."

Minutes after Lynne left, Grant thought about that last remark. He would have to rein her in but not until her help unraveling the legal entanglements at Albright Stud was no longer needed. If she thought he was going to let her run the farm without close supervision, she was in for a big surprise. Should she get too pushy, he would put her out on the street with her husband.

The frown on his forehead deepened, adding to the wrinkles made by the sun.

The hours slipped by as partygoers in the Bluegrass and Louisville celebrated Derby Eve. From elegant mansions to neighborhood watering holes, the names of the Derby horses rolled off tongues lubricated with fine bourbon and drinks mixed by sweating bartenders. Couples arrived at parties in fashionable dress, and some left with different partners. By the time most went home, the first Saturday in May was several hours old.

Leaving Anita Madden's party shortly after 1 AM, Cay and Maudie arrived at Woodland Farm in time to call England at 2:00. As expected, Tim and his parents had just finished breakfast.

Alicia and Reggie Grayson were delighted to hear about the upcoming marriage. With distance and the busy spring schedule at Woodland Farm important factors, it was agreed that Cay would give Maudie a ring before she returned home, then fly to England in mid-June for an engagement party at Newmarket. The wedding was tentatively set for late October.

Tim made a few humorous remarks, but his tone turned affectionate when he congratulated Cay on his good judgement and Maudie for her tenacity. She hung up shedding happy tears.

24

As if the gods in charge of the big tote board in the sky had bestowed a special blessing on this year's Kentucky Derby, Churchill Downs awoke to brilliant sunshine and the weatherman's prediction that afternoon temperatures would be in the mid-seventies. It had rained only once during the week, and the track was rated fast.

Hordes of media descended on Barn 44, conducting interviews and filming the Derby entrants as they were led about and washed and groomed in preparation for the big day ahead

On the clubhouse roof, television crews checked equipment while the infield began to fill below. To cover the activity on the backside and in the paddock leading to the Derby, the race itself and the presentation in the winner's circle, ABC-TV had brought twenty-two cameras and seventy-six crew members, including over fifty engineers. One camera would be mounted on the gate to catch the horses as they broke, while seventeen others filmed the race. Three of those cameras would isolate individual horses.

As participation of foreign horses in the Kentucky Derby increased over the years, so had the audience. The race would be televised to nineteen countries, including Russia, where sixty million were expected to stay up past midnight to watch.

Britain, Argentina, the Dominican Republic and the Arab city-state of Dubai in the Persian Gulf would also receive the ninety-minute program, culminating with the race that was recognized worldwide as "The most exciting two minutes in sports."

The Japanese—among the most avid horse race fans in the world— would be watching and cheering for Mighty Warrior, bred and raced by Tomonori Tsurumaki, the real estate developer who had campaigned A.P. Indy so successfully in the United States.

Each May, the Tokyo racecourse—where the size of the crowd rivaled and often exceeded that at the Kentucky Derby—would host the Japan Derby. Millions more were wagered on-track on that *one* race than on the entire Kentucky Derby card of *ten* races. The on and off-course betting there was triple the total handle in the U.S.

Standing on the roof with the twin spires in the background, Chris Lincoln wrapped up ESPN's Derby television coverage before turning things over to the sport network's parent company, ABC-TV.

"Who do you like for the Derby?" Lincoln asked commentator and Belmont Park track announcer, Tom Durkin.

"Sensational Bob looks very good. He's the betting favorite at seven to four, but I lean toward Shedrow Hustler. Having been raced on opposite sides of the country—Sensational Bob in California and Shedrow Hustler in New York—and with Shedrow Hustler missing last year's Breeders' Cup Juvenile due to an injury, this will be the first time they'll meet. Sensational Bob is a speedster, but I look for Shedrow Hustler to outlast his West-Coast rival on that long stretch drive. Shedrow Hustler was very impressive winning the mile-and-an-eighth Wood Memorial by four lengths. I think he'll handle the mile and a quarter Kentucky Derby very well."

"And he has a terrific trainer in John Veitch."

"Right. This is John's best Derby shot since Seventy-Eight when Alydar lost to Affirmed by a length and a half."

"Affirmed went on to win the Triple Crown," Lincoln said, "but Alydar proved to be the ultimate winner in the breeding shed."

Durkin nodded. "Having a royal pedigree and winning the Triple Crown doesn't guarantee a great stud career."

Chris Lincoln looked into the camera. "Before we go to the back-stretch for one last look at the Derby contenders, I'll ask Tom to tell you about our ESPN Longshot."

"Listen up folks," Durkin smiled. "Put some money on Harlan

Ghost, the homebred giant from Cay Albright's Woodland Farm right here in Kentucky. The Ghost looked like he was coming into his own when he won the Blue Grass; he was really gathering steam when he went under the wire. He's being ridden today by Hall of Fame jockey Chris McCarron. That's a plus for any horse. Harlan Ghost just might run away from the pack. If he does, you can say you heard it here first!"

Maudie leaned on the "Millionaire's Row" balcony rail and watched the horses for the fifth race being led out of the chute-gap gate on the opposite side of the track. "Shawn and Joy must be having fits," she said, eyes dancing under her wide-brimmed red hat. "Three more races to go!"

"I'm not exactly falling asleep," Cay said.

"How do you think I feel?" Maripat said, glancing toward the other end of the balcony where Travis had appeared briefly after the third race with some of Albright Stud's guests. "The way the press is carrying on, you'd think I should be spending half my time over there. My heart and money's with Harlan Ghost, but that doesn't mean I won't root for Lynne's Lad if the Ghost is out of it and Travis' horse has a chance to win."

Recalling how depressed his brother had been at the Governor's ball, Cay said, "I'll be rooting with you. He needs a break."

John said, "Call him sentimental favorite or what, but the Ghost's odds have dropped to sixteen to one. That's four points in the last couple hours."

"Still a longshot," Maudie sighed.

"Lynne's Lad's odds have dropped to seven to two," Andrew Stiles said. "That makes him the third betting favorite."

Welcoming twenty million Americans and many times that the world over to Churchill Downs, perennial ABC Derby host, Jim McKay, opened the program with a visually stunning display of springtime beauty in the Bluegrass and its world-famous horse farms. After showing playful foals that might one day compete for the roses, a live camera provided a panoramic view of the track.

"They've come from every corner of America and the planet

to see with their own eyes this greatest of all horse races," McKay said. "Women in a colorful array of hats and dresses that put a rainbow to shame. Youngsters in the infield wearing T-shirts and rundown sneakers. Giants of industry and blue-collar workers. Over a hundred fifty thousand gathered to witness the crowning of this year's Kentucky Derby champion.

"The press is here, too. Nineteen hundred credentials have been handed out, a hundred of those to foreign journalists from nine countries. It's seventy-six degrees, and the twin spires that have stood above the grandstand since Eighteen Ninety-Five are etched against a cloudless sky. Welcome to the First Saturday in May."

Travis shifted his gaze from the Skye Terrace television to the crowded tables and happy faces that only added to his misery. Resplendent in a tailored Western suit, black cowboy hat and boots, Grant Alston entertained several women. The Texan's hands roamed while he talked, and none of the ladies seemed to mind.

From his station overlooking the paddock, ABC commentator, Jack Whitaker, spoke to the television audience, "Here on this very ground that Secretariat trod the day he made Kentucky Derby history and began his ascent to Triple Crown greatness, we wonder if another super horse might be among those that will soon walk this hallowed ring. Will there ever again be a horse like 'Big Red,' whose flawless confirmation, relentless drive and charisma beat out pro football star, O.J. Simpson, for *Sport* magazine's Twenty-Seventh 'Man of the Year in Sports' award?

"Will this racetrack that echoes with the hoofbeats of mighty legends experience the making of another today? We can only wait and hope. For the sake of the industry and for the sake of racing fans everywhere, we pray it does."

Long lines formed at the pari-mutuel windows as the Derby drew near. Lynne's Lad and Shedrow Hustler had drawn even at 7-2, placing them second to Sensational Bob as betting favorites. Harlan Ghost held steady at 16-1.

Facing the television cameras, Derby race-caller, Dave Johnson, and commentator, Al Michaels, wrapped up their pre-race observations. "It's hard to pick a winner this year," Johnson said. "The top four have nearly identical records, and all except Sensational Bob have won their last races. Sensational Bob's half-length loss to Lynne's Lad in the Santa Anita Derby hasn't hurt him at the betting window, however. He's still favored to win. Who do you like for the Derby, Al?"

"I'm going with Freedom Prince, Dave," Michaels said. "His odds are twelve to one, but Shug McGaughey is one of the best trainers in the business. When the horses come down Heartbreak Alley, I look for Freedom Prince to take the lead."

"I'll take Lynne's Lad," Johnson said. "He has the classic running style of his sire, Danzig, and grandsire, Northern Dancer. He's mentally sharp. More than enough to go the distance."

Michaels smiled into the camera. "Better hurry and get those bets down, folks. The Derby horses are in the paddock."

Standing between Andrew Stiles and John in the center of the walking ring, Maudie watched Cay talking earnestly to Shawn and Joy as they followed the perky little blonde groom, Gussy Fowler, who was proudly leading Harlan Ghost around the oval path. The big gray kicked his heels, and onlookers cheered.

"I'm so nervous," Maudie said. "I'm beginning to wish I'd stayed upstairs with Maripat."

"She didn't stay there because of nerves," John said.

"I know. It must be terrible for her, having two sons with horses in the Derby and not wanting to be seen favoring one over the other. How can Travis *not* love a mother like Maripat? I don't think it's him. It's that bloody wife of his! She seems intent on keeping him away from his family."

Fifty feet away, Lynne had noted the possessive way Cay held the tall young English woman's hand when they entered the paddock area. And Lynne didn't miss the smiles that were exchanged as Cay walked around the ring beside Harlan Ghost.

You won't have that smile on your face for long, Lynne thought as Cay boosted Chris McCarron into the saddle. *Lynne's Lad will beat your horse today, and next week you'll find out that Albright Stud belongs to somebody else!*

The time arrived for the singing of "My Old Kentucky Home," that poignant moment that sets the Kentucky Derby apart from all other sporting events in the world. As the University of Louisville Cardinal marching band struck the first chord, the huge standing crowd joined in. Many knew the song by heart. For those who didn't, the words were printed in their programs. Some were shared as friends and strangers formed impromptu singing groups.

The sun shines bright in the old Kentucky home, Tis summer, the people are gay;

Led by their grooms, the first of the fourteen Derby horses moved out of the tunnel and into the brilliant sunshine. Lining the homestretch from the sixteenth pole to the finish line and forming a protective ring around the winner's circle, National Guardsmen in white hats, shirts and puttees faced the track and stood at ease with hands clasped behind their backs.

The corn-top's ripe and the meadow's in the bloom While the birds make music all the day.

In the 3rd floor box section—which provided a better view for Derby horse owners and the easiest access to the winner's circle—tears flowed over Maudie's cheeks as she sang the beautiful ballad. Kentucky was going to be her home now. Her impossible dream had come true. Hugging Cay's arm, she wished for another miracle as Harlan Ghost emerged from the long tunnel.

The young folks roll on the little cabin floor. All merry, all happy and bright;

With over seventy thousand voices in the infield joining those inthe grandstand, the long line of horses was enclosed in a giant wall of sound. Still youngsters by any standard, they danced about nervously as the leaders made the long turn that would take them to the backstretch and the starting gate.

By'n by hard times comes a-knocking at the door, Then my old Kentucky home, Good-night!

Travis had heard and sung it a hundred times, but he had never really paid attention to the words until today. Hard times had indeed come knocking at his door. As thousands of voices broke into the stirring chorus, he choked back an anguished sob.

Weep no more my lady, Oh! Weep no more today!

Eyes glistening beneath her green floppy hat, Maripat recalled the many times she had shared this magic moment with Libby, then Bob. Now John stood beside her, a comforting arm around her shoulders. Brushing a tear from her cheek, she joined in the final stanza.

We will sing one song for my old Kentucky home, For the old Kentucky home, far away.

"Well, it got me again," ABC"s Jim McKay said as cheers and excited shouts rose from the stands. "It's an emotional experience unlike any other." He turned to analyst Charlsie Canty, "Post time is ten minutes away. How do you see the race?"

"As always," Canty said, "the Derby is difficult to call. None of the thirteen colts and one filly have ever raced beyond a mile and an eighth. It will also be the first experience on dirt for the two British colts and the one from France. And they have been lightly raced compared to their counterparts here in America. The track is very fast. I have a feeling we might have an upset in the making."

"Do you have a particular horse in mind that might pull off the upset?" McKay asked.

"Harlan Ghost. He's a big growthy colt much like Risen Star was when he lost in the Derby but went on to win the Preakness and Belmont. The Ghost is by Little Bid and out of a Nijinsky mare. That combination of speed, toughness and determination might come together and produce a win today."

"Who do you pick for the Derby?" McKay asked.

"My heart's with Harlan Ghost, but my better judgement tells me Mighty Warrior has the best chance of winning."

"Mighty Warrior. That will certainly make our friends in Japan happy. I'll take Sensational Bob. The horses are arriving at the gate. It's time to go upstairs to Dave Johnson."

Shawn and Joy watched as the horses were loaded in the gate. Harlan Ghost—distinctive because of his size and steel-gray color—was held back by Chris McCarron as the horses with lower post positions were led in.

Wedged between Cay and Maripat, Maudie gripped the railing and chewed on her lower lip. Unnoticed, Andrew Stiles lifted a camera to his eye and recorded the tense balcony scene for posterity.

High atop the clubhouse roof, Dave Johnson watched through binoculars as the starter's assistants moved Shedrow Hustler into the gate. "The French horse, Clovis Rules, ridden by Laffit Pincay, Jr. is going into hole number eleven," Johnson said. "There's Knight's Landing, trained by Phil Hauswald and ridden by Pat Day, the winningest jockey in Churchill Downs history. Here is the big gray, Harlan Ghost, ridden by Chris McCarron and a sentimental favorite with many Kentucky fans. He's trained by the team of Shawn Phelps and Joy Loren and owned by Cay Albright, brother to Travis Albright who has Lynne's Lad in number seven."

Johnson paused while the handlers wrestled with the stubborn fourteenth and last horse. "Rotsaruck is the California speedball trained by Ron McAnally. Craig Perret will probably call on that early speed to get the flashy chestnut into early contention from its extreme outside position. Rotsaruck is going in now."

The television cameras zoomed back to show a front view of the gate. Time seemed to stand still, then the doors flew open.

"*They're off in the Kentucky Derby!*" Johnson shouted above the roar of the crowd.

"Lynne's Lad broke sharply and is in the lead as the horses pass the stands for the first time. Storm Warning is half a length behind with Notorious, the English horse up close in third. Cominhomebaby is fourth off the rail, Knights Ferry fifth off the rail. Here comes Shedrow Hustler from between horses to take the lead as they enter the clubhouse turn."

Eyes glued on Lynne's Lad as the horses swept around the clubhouse turn, Lynne groaned loudly as the little horse dropped back into sixth place. "Don't worry," trainer Joe Ponds said. "He's running just the way we planned."

"Look at Harlan Ghost!" she cried gleefully as her binoculars swept the field. "He's dead last!"

Dave Johnson took note of that as the horses straightened on the backstretch. Sensational Bob was now in the lead with the Japanese horse, Mighty Warrior, a length behind. As they passed the half-mile pole, the horses began to bunch up.

Johnson called: "Sensational Bob leads as they enter the far turn, but Mighty Warrior is coming up fast. Lynne's Lad is third, then the filly, TV Starlet, on the rail. *Here comes Harlan Ghost!* He's flying! Passing horses with every stride. And what a stride! He's a giant among pygmies!"

"Come on! Come on!" Maudie screamed, gripping the rail with her right hand while she dug long fingernails into Cay's arm with the other. Maripat hopped up and down, holding onto her hat and pounding John's shoulder. Shawn and Joy stood like statues while Cay stared open-mouthed.

"They're moving to the top of the stretch, and Harlan Ghost is pouring it on!" Dave Johnson shouted. "He's battling it out with Sensational Bob for fourth as they pass the eighth pole. *And down the stretch they come!*

"Mighty Warrior leads by a length over Shedrow Hustler with Lynne's Lad coming up between horses. Chris McCarron whips Harlan Ghost right and left, and the big horse responds. He's passing Lynne's Lad, now Shedrow Hustler. It's a two-horse race with Harlan Ghost gaining ground on Mighty Warrior with every stride. *Harlan Ghost has taken the lead!* It's Harlan Ghost by a length, now a length and a half! Harlan Ghost wins the Derby by two with Chris McCarron aboard! Mighty Warrior is second. Three lengths back is Shedrow Hustler. Then Lynne's lad!"

Surrounded by a phalanx of security guards and facing a continuous battery of news cameras, Cay led his triumphant party across the track to the winner's circle that was used only for the Derby. As they moved inside the big horseshoe of red roses, Joy cried, "Here comes Chris!"

Riding Harlan Ghost through the narrow aisle formed by the media and track officials, Chris McCarron beamed happily for the cameras. This was the greatest moment in an American jockey's career— winning the Kentucky Derby.

Displaying a grin that rivaled McCarron's, Harlan Ghost's blond groom, Gussy Fowler, stepped forward and led the big gray into the winner's circle. Laughter accompanied the clicking and whirring of cameras as she impulsively kissed the colt's nose.

"Oh, it's lovely!" Maudie cried as a man passed the six-foot mantel of roses up to Chris McCarron. After adjusting the red garland over Harlan Ghost's shoulders, McCarron laid the jockey's bouquet on his lap and leaned forward to pat the colt's neck.

Lining up for the cameras with Harlan Ghost in the background, Cay placed Maudie on his right and Maripat on his left. "Joy, stand beside Mom; John, you better prop Mom up; she looks like she's going to collapse. Better hang on to Shawn, too."

For many Kentucky Derbys, the relatives and friends of the winning owner filled the winner's circle. Not today. Because of the tense situation fueled by the media's speculation about the troubles at Albright Stud, Cay and Maripat had elected not to have Derby guests.

Chris McCarron's wife, Judy, was included in the winner's circle photo. No one had to say, "Cheese," to prompt smiles from the participants. The wide grins and laughter were as natural as the red roses from the Derby mantle that Cay presented to each of the ladies after the picture-taking session was over.

Television cameras zoomed in on the towering white presentation stand behind the winner's circle as Cay and his party mounted the steps. ABC's John McKay was there to greet them and host the ceremony that would be heard over the track's loudspeaker system and beamed around the world.

"The history of the Kentucky Derby lists many Cinderella stories," McKay's amplified voice echoed over the giant racing plant," and we've seen another today. What seemed like only a wishful dream yesterday has become reality today."

"First of all, the president of Churchill Downs, Mr. Tom Meeker, will say a few words."

"It's another great day for racing, and another great day for the Kentucky Derby," Meeker said. "The Derby has proven once again that it's full of surprises."

"Now, it gives me great pleasure to introduce our horseman governor, Mr. Brereton C. Jones."

One hand resting on the tall 14-K gold cup that glittered on the rail, Governor Jones smiled at Cay. "On behalf of the people of Kentucky, I want to present the Kentucky Derby trophy." The governor's smile widened as he turned toward the grandstand. "What you've seen today is the result of a one-hundred-percent Kentucky operation. Cay Albright is a Bluegrass native, and Harlan Ghost is a homebred colt named for Harlan County down near southeastern corner of our state. His trainers are Shawn Phelps, who came to Kentucky from North Carolina eighteen years before I was born and Joy Loren, who was born and raised in Woodford County. Don't look so worried, Joy; I won't reveal your age."

Amid laughter and the shaking of hands, Governor Jones relinquished the microphone to Jim McKay.

McKay thrust the mike toward Cay, who was holding the Derby trophy. "How does that feel?" McKay asked.

"Wonderful! I just hope I don't drop it on my foot and wake up to find I've been dreaming."

"I understand this lovely young lady is Maudie Grayson,

the daughter of Sir Reginald Grayson of Broadheim Stud in Newmarket, England," McKay said.

"And soon to be my wife," Cay added, putting an arm around Maudie.

Caught by surprise but recovering rapidly, McKay said, "Congratulations! What better way to announce an engagement then in the winner's circle on Kentucky Derby Day!"

McKay looked toward the grandstand. "Now, I want to introduce Cay's mother, a woman I've known and respected for many years. Maripat Albright's name has long been associated with winning Kentucky Thoroughbreds. Maripat, what do you think of your son's accomplishments—here today and with this smiling young lady standing at his side?"

"I'm so proud, I could bust," Maripat said, green eyes shining brightly in the late afternoon sunlight. "Proud of Cay, proud to know that Maudie will soon be a part of my family and proud for the place of my birth, Harlan County! The Ghost ran for all of you down there today!" She paused for a moment and touched a tissue to her eyes. "I've dreamed about winning the Derby all my life. Now my son has done it for me!"

25

In the Skye Terrace, Lynne stared at the huge television screen. "He's marrying her?" she exclaimed, looking at Grant with disbelieving eyes.

"Why not?" Grant said, watching the television as McKay talked with Shawn and Joy about Harlan Ghosts' performance. "For a face and body like that, *I* might consider marriage! What about you, Travis—wouldn't you like to pork your brother's intended?"

"Shut up, you filthy-mouthed son of a bitch"

"What's this?" Grant grinned. "Is the mouse getting brave with all these people around?"

"Let it go, Grant," Lynne said.

"What I ought to do is kick your husband's ass into the middle of next week!" Grant whirled and shoved a big fist inches from Travis' face. "Call me a name like that again, I don't give a damn whether we're in public or not, I'll put you in the hospital!"

Shrinking inside the new suit he had hoped to wear in the winner's circle, Travis looked at Lynne. "I'm going home. Coming?"

"And leave our guests?"

Nodding slowly, Travis walked away.

The post-Derby party was well underway in the Kentucky Derby Museum when a note was handed to Cay. He read it, then said to Maudie, "Got to leave for a few minutes, Honey. Try to be good."

"Only if you promise to come right back," she smiled.

Outside, Cay grasped Travis' hand. "What's this about not telling anyone?"

"I don't want to face Mom right now." Smiling crookedly, Travis clasped Cay's shoulder. "Congratulations, Little Brother. On the Derby win and your engagement. Maudie's a wonderful girl!"

"Tell her yourself. She'll be happy to see you. Mom, too."

"Can't." Travis' voice broke, and he looked away.

Cay put an arm around his shoulders. "What's wrong?"

"Nothing." Travis said in a broken whisper.

"Nothing, hell! We've got to talk. You can't go on like this!"

Travis took a deep breath. "You're right." He glanced around. "We can't talk here. You better go back inside. Somebody might come looking for you and see us together."

"Not until we set a definite time and place," Cay said, truly worried now. "How about tomorrow morning at eleven at my place? Maudie has to work with her photographer; they've got to send some material off to the magazine."

Eyes darting about, Travis said, "Eleven's fine. I'll say I'm going to the Kentucky Colonel's barbecue. Probably won't get a chance to tell Lynne, but I'll leave a note. I'm going home now. She'll be up half the night partying and will sleep until noon. The barbeque starts in Bardstown at twelve, so leaving around eleven won't seem suspicious."

"Suspicious? What the hell's going on, Travis?

"I'll tell you tomorrow." Travis seized Cay's arms. "Don't tell anyone. Not Mom, not Maudie. No one! Okay?"

"All right, but I don't like it."

Travis gripped Cay's arms, then hurried off.

26

When Maudie awoke alone the next morning, she padded barefoot to the kitchen. Cay sat at the table poring over the special Kentucky Derby supplements in the *Lexington Herald-Leader* and the Louisville *Courier-Journal.* They read the papers together, whooping with delight at every mention of Harlan Ghost and his spectacular triumph.

Travis arrived a half-hour after Maudie left. "Why all this sneaking around?" Cay asked as they sat in the drawing room. "Something wrong between you and Lynne?"

"Not Lynne. Grant Alston."

"*Alston?!* What the hell's he got to do with you?"

"Plenty," Travis said. "He bought Albright Stud. It's not official—just a letter of intent, but I'm locked in."

Stunned, Cay asked, "How?"

"I wasn't given any choice. He came into my office on Wednesday and threatened me with exposure to the press." Voice trembling, Travis avoided Cay's eyes. "He slapped me around, said it would get a lot worse if I didn't sign the papers. He threatened you, too."

Cay leaped up. "Who does that son-of-a-bitch think he is? Threatening you and me and making you sign bogus papers—"

"They're not bogus, Cay. I signed them in front of a notary.

Lynne, too. And I accepted a ten thousand dollar check."

"Did you cash it?"

"No. It's right here in my wallet."

"Even if you had, we can get the whole thing tossed out in court. The bastard *threatened* you, damnit! What kind of deal did he make?"

"He'll settle my debts and give me a million. I would have gotten another million if Lynne's Lad had won the Derby."

"Nice guy," Cay said as he paced the floor. "I was going to offer you a million up front and four more spread over five years. Mom was going to help, too. She still will, regardless of what happens. First, we've got to get you out of Alston's clutches. We'll worry about the rest later."

"You don't know this guy, Cay! He's capable of anything! I don't know which is worse—the physical threats or the verbal ones. If I don't go along, he'll get me thrown in prison!"

"How?"

Travis said dully, "Exposing things like inflating values of livestock, carrying horses on the books after they died, holding back income from partners."

"That's just a scare tactic. Spilling the story to the press would have ruined his chances for a sweet deal. Bad as it sounds, it can be taken care of out of court. John and Nat Quinn concurred when we met last week."

"Last week? Before Alston showed up?"

"Monday. Would it have mattered if I'd talked to you then?"

Travis shook his head. "You're right. I would have insisted on waiting until after the Derby." A short laugh that ended in a sob. "I tried to get Alston to wait. He pushed me down on my knees and slapped me silly."

Cay hurried to his brother's side and placed a hand on his shoulder. "We'll lick this bastard, Travis. You and me—together like in the old days."

Travis's shoulders shook, then an anguished howl emerged from deep in his chest. Slipping out of the chair to the floor, he buried his face in his arms and wept uncontrollably. Cay knelt beside him, a hand on his back for comfort.

Between broken sobs, Travis poured out all the guilt and hurt and anger that had been locked up inside for years.

After describing the unethical practices and fraudulent dealings, he stumbled into the bathroom and washed his face. When he returned, Cay was waiting with two glasses of bourbon. "I figure we both need this," he said.

"I've got to cut down on the booze, but not right now," Travis said, accepting his gratefully. "Cay. I'm worried. Alston isn't an ordinary guy. If you'd seen his face when he slapped me around, you'd know what I mean. He had that same look yesterday in the Skye Terrace." Clutching his drink, he repeated Alston's remarks about Maudie and the confrontation that followed.

Cay's face darkened with anger. "That does it! I don't care what it takes, we're going to stop him."

"How? He's got money and contacts everywhere—probably on both sides of the law. Look at all the stuff he dug up about me. He knows as much as I do!"

"I'll lay it all out to John tomorrow morning. Alston may have some smart lawyers, but they'll get an education when they come up against John. Don't worry about stories leaking out. If they do, they do. You may have to live with some embarrassment, but it'll work out. No one really wants to sue you for fraud, Travis. Cash is more valuable than getting revenge any day. They know they won't get a dime on the dollar if they drag you in court."

Cay sat down. "Where did Alston get all that information?"

"I've been going nuts thinking about it," Travis said. "Some of it could have been taken off the computers; mine and Lynne's are linked to the farm office. The real critical stuff is on discs and locked in my safe or in files I've been keeping for years. They're in the safe, too."

"Who has the combination besides you?"

"Lynne. Doesn't mean much. Alston's probably got sources that could crack it with their eyes closed. Could've been done in the middle of the night without anybody knowing. I never put in a burglar alarm, and my office is way to hell and gone in the west wing. A man could come down that back path and never be seen."

"Can you bring those discs and files here today? You can

brief me, and I'll take them when I see John. You have to get that material out of the house anyway. Alston might waltz in and grab it."

Travis looked at his watch. "It's a little after eleven. If I drive in the back way, I can park behind the equipment shed and walk in."

"What about Lynne?"

"She's probably still in bed. She sleeps in that big corner bed-room upstairs that used to belong to Mom and Dad." An embarrassed look. "I sleep downstairs. Lynne uses that bedroom next to hers for an office. The maid and the cook are taking the day off, so the house will be empty."

"What if she's up?"

"Won't matter. She doesn't come into my office much. I could die there, and nobody would find my body for a week."

"Let's keep her out of this," Cay said.

"God, yes! She'd scream so loud they'd hear her in Frankfurt! She's scared spitless about getting dragged into court."

Cay turned the bourbon glass slowly around in his hands. "How long will it take to get everything together?"

"An hour or so. I have to go through the file cabinets, too. There are some records there we'll need, too.

"Why don't I drive you over? You're supposed to be in Bardstown. Anybody sees your car, that alibi's shot to hell. I'll let you out behind the stud barn and pick you up later."

"I don't like it. If that bastard finds out you're involved, no telling what he might do."

"Let's worry about that when it happens."

A fearful look. "Bringing you into this really worries me, Cay. You should be out celebrating. You've won the Derby, man! You're getting married. Alston plays hardball. You can get hurt. I couldn't stand it if anything happened because of me."

Cay stood and placed a hand on Travis's shoulder. "We can play hardball, too. Let's go. I'm supposed to pick Maudie up at two."

27

Travis glanced at the clock on his office desk. Cay would be returning in half an hour. He pulled another file out of the cabinet.

He was making a final check of his desk when the sound of voices entered the long hall. Dashing to the open doorway, he listened for a moment, then stiffened with fear. It was Grant Alston! What happened next was inconceivable. The other voice was Lynne's. And she was *laughing*!

Confused and shaking with fright, Travis ran to the desk and picked up the box that bulged with incriminating records. There was only one place to hide—the bathroom. Slipping inside and shutting the door, he stepped into the shower enclosure, closed that door and sat down. The obscure glass offered only partial concealment, but it would pass casual inspection. Clutching the box on his lap, he listened as they entered the office.

"...making some changes here, too," Grant was saying. "That paneling goes. I'll keep the desk and the chairs. Carpet's okay."

Lynne's voice grew louder. "We can move some of the files from the farm office and put them against the wall."

"Why not put them in your office upstairs?"

"It's crammed already. Now that I'm taking over everything, I'll need more room, not less."

Travis gripped the file box. *Taking over everything?* What was going on? Grant's next words provided the answer, "Think that's a good idea getting rid of the office manager? You'll be busy enough without taking on his job, too."

"Only for a while," Lynne answered. "You said yourself that we have to start with a clean slate. Soon as I get the old stuff out of the way and things organized, we can hire a new manager."

Hugging the file box to his chest, Travis fought back the nausea that churned in his stomach. Lynne and Grant were in this together! He had been played the fool all along! No one had to break into the safe to get that information. Lynne had only to dial the combination and copy the material at her leisure!

The bathroom door opened, and the light flicked on. Grant's voice thundered off the tiled walls and crashed down on Travis's cringing head. "Not bad. A shower, too. We can fuck, then clean up. Too bad that couch doesn't make into a bed."

"I can get one." Lynne added in a deep throaty voice, "Speaking of beds, mine's upstairs."

"We'll check that out after we finish the tour," Alston said as he snapped the bathroom light off and closed the door. His muffled voice barely reached the man in the shower. "How many bedrooms in this wing? I'm going to..." His voice faded.

Travis staggered to his feet and leaned against the shower wall, legs straddling the file box. The pain he had thought was unbearable before was magnified a thousand times. He had been betrayed by his wife and beaten up and stripped of everything by her lover!

How long had it been going on? He must have been blind! No wonder Lynne had put him out of their bedroom years ago. She was getting all she wanted from Grant Alston!

The implications drove him to his knees. What protection could John Kershaw give him if Lynne was working hand in glove with Alston? And what terrible vengeance might be inflicted on Cay? Travis had already considered Grant capable of anything. He realized now that Lynne was, too.

Cay would be arriving at the back of the stud barn any moment. Rising to his feet, Travis stepped out of the shower. After months of indecision, he knew what he had to do.

28

After touring the opposite wing of the house, Lynne and Grant mounted the wide curving staircase. After inspecting her office, they went into the adjoining bedroom.

"Pretty slick," Grant said. "A little frilly, but I won't be sleeping here. You want to spend the night with me, you'll have to come downstairs to my place." He had decided to tear out several rooms at the end of the east wing and replace them with an apartment.

Lynne bounced on the mattress. "Like the bed?"

"I like what's sitting on it. Keeping it warm for me?"

"And wet." Lynne pulled her skirt up to her waist and leaned back on her elbows. "I took my panties off downstairs. In case you got tired tramping around and wanted to slip into something more comfortable."

Grant stared at the thick black triangle of hair that curled up toward her deeply inverted navel. "Get out of those clothes, woman," he said thickly. He reached for the buttons on his jeans. "Either that or I'll have to rip 'em off."

Lynne smiled and sat up. "Might be fun, but I just bought this outfit." Grant kicked his shorts aside and headed for the bed, huge erection swaying. Tossing her bra on the floor, Lynne laid down and opened her legs. Grant plunged his face between her thighs.

A sound made him look up. Travis stood in the doorway, a pump-action shotgun cradled in his arms. Leaping off the bed, Grant sank into a half-crouch, one hand dropping instinctively to protect the rapidly shrinking penis that protruded obscenely from his hairy crotch.

Lynne screamed and rose to her knees. Travis's eyes were bloodshot. Although his lips trembled, the barrel of the shotgun was steady. "Who wants to be first?" he asked in a hollow voice.

"No, Travis!" Lynne screamed. "Please don't!"

"Shut up, bitch!" Travis looked at Grant. "You know I mean it, don't you?"

"Guess so," Grant said, eyeing Travis warily. "Doesn't mean you can't change your mind."

Travis glanced at his sobbing wife, then back at Grant. "I was downstairs in my office bathroom and heard you talking. You—"

"In the *bathroom*?" Grant exclaimed. "It was empty!"

"Should have looked in the shower." Travis's reddened eyes flicked back and forth between the two nude figures. "I ducked in there when I heard you coming. Know something, Grant? I was scared to death! So scared I almost pissed my pants! That's what you've done to me. You weren't satisfied with just beating me down; you had to keep stepping on me every chance you got." A contemptuous look at Lynne. "You even fucked my wife."

Lynne whimpered and hugged the skirt to her chest.

Travis returned his attention to Grant. "You're a dead man, Alston. You threatened my brother, too. That was a big mistake. I'll ask once more. Who wants to be first?"

"I'm not going without a fight," Grant said, legs tensing as he prepared to leap.

"Suit yourself." Travis pulled the trigger as Grant pounced.

The roar of the 12-gauge sounded like a cannon in the confines of the room. Caught in mid-air, Grant flew back against the wall. Blood flowed out of his chest as he slid into a sitting position.

Jacking another shell into the chamber, Travis whirled on Lynne. Screaming hysterically, she scrambled off the bed, the skirt still clutched in her hands and urine spurting on her legs. As the barrel of the shotgun steadied, she held the skirt in front of her face. The blast blew it into shreds, mixing fabric with brains and gore.

A sound drew Travis's attention back to Grant. He was dragging himself across the floor. Taking three quick steps, Travis touched the shotgun to the back of Grant's head and pulled the trigger. The big Texan collapsed on what remained of his face.

After reloading and leaning the shotgun against the door frame, Travis went out to the staircase and sat on the landing.

When Cay heard the first shot, he thought it was distant thunder. He glanced around, but the sky was clear. Moving away from his car, he looked past the stud barn toward the house. When the second blast came moments later, he knew with a chill of certainty what it was. The shotgun roared again as he dashed to the car.

The farmhands had already finished the afternoon feeding and gone home, and the narrow paved road was deserted as Cay drove furiously toward the house. Skidding to a stop, he ran up the broad steps and pushed the door open. The house was silent, but the smell of cordite hung heavily in the air. A sound from above made him look up. Travis sat at the top of the curving staircase, face buried in his arms.

"Travis?" Cay walked toward the stairway.

Travis raised his head. "Hello, Little Brother. Have a seat, and we'll talk." He raised a hand as Cay continued to mount the steps. "That's far enough— okay?"

Easing down on a step ten feet below his brother, Cay asked quietly, "What happened?"

Travis nodded over his shoulder. "Know what those two were doing— my bitch wife and that bastard Alston? They were working together on this! I heard them talking. Lynne was going to run the farm. The inside information came from her! She was fucking him, too. His face was between her legs when I went in the bedroom."

Cay closed his eyes for a moment, then looked up at the forlorn figure on the landing. "Those shots I heard....that was you?"

Travis nodded. "I killed them, Cay. Had to. After hearing them talk, I knew Alston would win. Lynne would have fought right beside him in court. If he lost, Grant wouldn't have stopped until he got even with you. He might have had you killed! They both had to go. There was no other way."

"I'll get you the best criminal defense lawyer in the country," Cay said. "When the whole story comes out, you might get off clean. I'll help you get started again. So will Mom."

Travis shook his head sadly. "It won't work—too much water under the bridge." He stood. "Tell Mom I love her. Maudie, too. Have a good life, hear?"

Cay bounded to his feet, but by the time he reached the landing, Travis was entering Lynne's bedroom. Cay's shout of anguish was drowned by the blast that rattled the crystal chandelier and echoed throughout the great house.

Tears running down his face, he walked slowly toward the open doorway and the carnage he knew awaited on the other side.

AFTERWORD

1994

*"This Kentucky Derby—whatever it is—a race,
an emotion, a turbulence, an explosion—is one
of the most beautiful and violent and satisfying
things I have ever experienced."*

John Steinbeck

Maripat sat on the steep hillside, bare toes digging into the rain-softened earth. Blossoms and wildflowers of every variety turned the surrounding mountains into splashes of brilliant color. It was springtime in Harlan County, nearly a year after the tragic events at Windsong Manor. The first Saturday in May and the Derby were two weeks away.

Adjusting the wide-brimmed straw hat over her eyes, she studied the tiny cemetery in the narrow valley below. The weeds were gone, and fresh flowers had been planted around each grave.

Travis was buried beside his father in the Albright Stud cemetery. It was restful there, and she visited often. Her troubled son had at last found peace.

The shootings and suicide at Albright Stud had shaken the Bluegrass and made headlines around the world. The struggle to save the farm had lasted into the new year. It was not until early January that Cay was able to buy out the last of the limited partners and free the farm of all encumbrances except the large loan at Nathan Quinn's bank. Woodland Farm was sold, and escrow was closing in early June. The house had been empty since February when Cay and Maudie had moved into Windsong Manor.

They didn't sleep in the bedroom where the deaths had occurred; it no longer existed. The north end of the upstairs had been completely gutted, and a new master bedroom now occupied the opposite corner.

Cay and Maudie were married in Newmarket last December, two months later than originally planned. Because of the tragedy, there was a subdued tone to the wedding, but nothing could mar the happiness on Maudie's face and the love shining in Cay's eyes.

Three months after Shawn attended the wedding with Maripat, John and Joy, he died peacefully in his sleep. There was a smile on his lips when Joy found him in his bedroom in the house they shared. She liked to think he passed away dreaming about Harlan Ghost winning the Kentucky Derby.

Harlan Ghost's quest for the Triple Crown ended abruptly at Pimlico when he placed third in the Preakness. He recovered impressively, however, posting a four-length victory in the Belmont.

After a heartbreaking loss by a nose in the Breeder's Cup Classic in November, it was decided to continue racing him at four. Because of his great size, he was just beginning to mature. The decision was paying off. He had already won two Grade I races, and Joy was conditioning him for the $1 million Hollywood Gold Cup.

Maripat smiled as a Ford Explorer bumped its way up the dry creek bed and stopped below the little family cemetery. It's all working out, she thought as Cay, Maudie and John began the steep climb.

Maudie slipped on a patch of grass and grabbed Cay's arm, a sudden movement that nearly tumbled them back down the hill. After pulling Maudie to her feet, Cay got behind and pushed on her jean-clad bottom. Laughing, she tried to escape his busy hands.

Maripat noticed the edge of the zipper on Maudie's jeans was beginning to show. She wouldn't be wearing those denims much longer, not with the baby less than six months away.

Green eyes sparkling, Maripat looked out over the rugged hills. *I'm going to be a grandmother! We'll come up here, and I'll teach the child how to dream.*

ABOUT THE TYPEFACES

The Front Matter and Headings of this book were created digitally in Goudy Old Style and the Main Text in Adobe Garamond Pro.

www.ingramcontent.com/pod-product-compliance
Lightning Source LLC
Chambersburg PA
CBHW070205260626
47160CB00002B/457